THE CRITICS RAVE ABOUT SEAN FLANNERY'S THRILLERS

Gulag

"Flannery as usual offers a whip-like story full of fascinating local color, clever—even deadly—political maneuverings and characters whose fate the reader cares about."

—*Publishers Weekly*

False Prophets

"An elaborate . . . exciting spy novel!"

—*Publishers Weekly*

"A staple of that genre."

—John D. MacDonald

Broken Idols

"A cracking good thriller!"

—Alfred Coppel,
author of *The Apocalypse Brigade*

"An engaging jigsaw."

—*Publishers Weekly*

"Tightly drawn intrigue . . . non-stop suspense!"

—*Denver Post*

SEAN FLANNERY

MOSCOW CROSSING

BERKLEY BOOKS, NEW YORK

Grateful acknowledgment is made to Pantheon Books, Inc.,
to reprint portions of the poems of Yurii Zhivago,
from *Doctor Zhivago*, by Boris Pasternak,
copyright © 1958 in authorized revisions to the
English translation by Pantheon Books, Inc., New York, N.Y.
Used by permission. The poems of Yurii Zhivago. Translated
from the Russian by Bernard Gullbert Guerney.
All rights reserved.

MOSCOW CROSSING

A Berkley Book/published by arrangement with
the author

PRINTING HISTORY
Berkley edition/February 1988

ISBN: 0-425-10625-X

This book is for Inger Poulsen,
a special lady,
and for Laurie,
as always.

If I leave all for thee, wilt thou exchange
And be all to me? Shall I never miss
Home-talk and blessing, the common kiss
That comes to each in turns nor count it strange,
When I look up, to drop on a new range
Of walls and flowers . . . another home than this?

From *Sonnets from the Portuguese*
by Elizabeth Barrett Browning

PART ONE

1

The defection of Anna Feodorovna Chalkin had its beginnings on an extremely cold late afternoon in January. She emerged from the Bolshoi Theater a few minutes before four and hurried, head bent, eyes lowered, across Moscow's busy Sverdlov Square to the Metro station. In stature she was short and thin, but her movements were those of a dancer. Her stride was smooth, graceful, perhaps even powerful. Here was agility, one would rightly suspect from watching her. Here was art brought to the simplest of movements. Here was a Giselle or a Juliet, roles she had danced as prima ballerina. But those days were gone. At thirty-six she was on the program simply as an assistant artistic director. If one cannot travel with the company, one cannot dance with it. Simple. Final. The state has its rights too. Nonetheless it was tragic. Over her dancer's uniform of tights, a loose cotton top, and woolen leg warmers, she wore a matching rabbit fur hat and coat, and lined boots. She carried a soft leather bag over a thin, sloping shoulder, and as she walked, the tails of her coat flapped behind her. A sharp wind blew across the square, bringing with it hints of snow. At the Metro entrance she stopped for just a moment and looked back as if she were seeing the theater for the very last time. Tall, ornate, with its four bronze horses on top, it had been home . . . more than home for her since she was four. Now she was leaving it. The square was alive with soldiers getting an early start on the evening, with old babushkas waddling off to Detsky Mir, the

3

children's store, with Kremlin employees out early, imperiously shoving their way through the crowds as if theirs was the holiest of missions, and with lovers, hand in hand.

"Anna," someone called out of the crowd. "Anna Feodorovna."

Anna turned in time to see a plain, almost shabby woman hurrying toward her, a Bolshoi program in her hand. Her face was red from the cold and from exertion, her hair spilling out from beneath an old woolen headscarf.

"Hello," Anna said pleasantly.

The woman simply stared for a few seconds. Her cloth coat was threadbare. "I saw you in *Swan Lake*. Three years ago it was. My God, and here you are." The woman was gushing, out of breath. She held out her program. It was an old one, and it contained other signatures. "Could you please sign it?"

The square suddenly seemed colder and more distant to Anna. If there was an artistic region of Moscow, this was it, with the Maly Theater next door to the Bolshoi, the Children's Musical Theater on the other side, and just down Pushkin Street, the Operetta Theater, and Nemirovich-Danchenko's Musical Theater. Home. But distant now, to her. Finished.

Anna had to dig for her own pencil, but the woman was too flustered to notice. She signed the program and handed it back. There were stars in the woman's eyes. But something else too? Cunning? Anna wondered.

"Thank you," Anna said.

"Will you dance again? Will you . . . ?"

Anna looked sharply at the woman to see if it was a joke. She choked back a reply, then turned and fled down into the bowels of the Metro, plugging the turnstile with a five-kopeck piece and hurrying across the platform just in time to catch the Kakhovskaya-Rechnoi Vokzal line. As the train pulled out, Anna watched from the window. The woman came down the stairs and began to search the platform. She didn't seem so eager now. She seemed frantic. Then the brightly decorated station with its crystal chandeliers was gone as the train plunged into the tunnel south, and Anna sat back in her seat. Imagination, she told herself. She was jumping at shadows.

"Listen, my little chou-chou," her Uncle Stepan had told her. "You must accept this thing. It is a great honor, you know. First you have been trained from childhood by the finest masters in the world. Even Yuri Grigorovich himself. Next you have had nearly eighteen good years of dancing, prima ballerina for the last eight. *Giselle, Swan Lake, Sleeping Beauty, Nutcracker*—all of them, Anna. Are you listening? And now you are assistant artistic director." Uncle Stepan's hands were pudgy. He waved them in the air. "I should have Andropov's old chair, rising as fast as you."

Inside the subway car it was very hot and smoky. The man next to her was drinking vodka. He passed the bottle across the aisle to two others who kept looking surreptitiously over at Anna. She looked at them and smiled, then closed her eyes so tightly she could see bright spots and shapes and colors. A world of light and beauty. How many years ago had she heard those words? She screwed her eyes even more tightly, gritting her teeth to make the muscles contract further.

She remembered now naïve she had been as a young woman. The state trained, but it also protected. It was 1970, she was just nineteen, and the entire company had been invited to Brezhnev's dacha on the Istra River outside of Moscow. It was winter. They were between productions, recovering from *Don Quixote*, getting ready for their annual *Swan Lake*. A lot of other people had also been invited out, including generals and Politburo members and others. Uncle Stepan had driven some of them up the frozen river in a two-horse sleigh, the bells crisp in the clear, bright, cold air. It was nearing midnight and the stars had never seemed so close, so magical. They were bundled up beneath fur blankets.

They'd gone barely a couple of kilometers when Uncle Stepan slowed down and began to make a wide turn back the way they had come. Anna sat forward. She never wanted the moment to end. "No, not yet! Let's never go back, Uncle!"

Uncle Stepan smiled. "We must."

"Why?"

"Otherwise our sleigh will turn into a pumpkin and our horses into mice at midnight."

It was Prokofiev's ballet. Anna had first done it when she was fourteen. "It is a fairy tale, Uncle."

The other girls giggled. Uncle Stepan pulled up to a halt and turned to his niece. He had been drinking heavily, and his face was puffy and flushed. "But it is a fairy tale that was based on a true incident, chou-chou," he said in all seriousness.

The girls giggled again, and Anna looked at them, uncertain what sort of game they were playing with her. "It is nothing but a pretty story. A pretty ballet."

"No . . . no, believe me, it happened in France and then again in Germany and in Holland. It's a common story. It happens even today."

"It's impossible."

"No, Anna, nothing is impossible if only you believe."

They were playing with her. She knew it. She sat back, her arms crossed over her chest. "Then we'll stay a little longer and see."

"Not me," Uncle Stepan said, raising his whip. "You can return here if you'd like, though I wouldn't recommend it."

They started to move. Anna reached out for her uncle's whip hand. "No. Please, Uncle, I want to stay."

Her uncle laughed, evading her grasp, and cracked the whip over the horses' heads. They started forward with a burst of speed.

"No!" Anna cried.

Ekaterina, one of the other dancers, leaned forward. "He's teasing you, Anna. That's all."

Anna looked back at her, then at her uncle who had a huge grin on his face.

"We must get back, Anna, believe me. In the morning you shall receive your fur slipper."

Anna closed her eyes and sat back in her seat, sparks like dancing flames in her vision as a hot flush spread from her neck to her face. It had been cruel, and the others had shared in the fun.

"I don't want to turn into a rat, Anna. And all your fine clothes would turn into rags. Our handsome footmen would become lizards."

"That is enough, please, Comrade Major Patrenko," Ekaterina said softly.

Her uncle said something that Anna did not quite catch. A few moments later he laid his hand on her knee beneath the blanket. "I am just a cruel, thoughtless uncle, my little chouchou," he said gently. "Can you ever forgive me?"

The sleigh was swaying, just like the subway train now, Anna thought. She looked up into her uncle's contrite face and tears welled up in her eyes. She went into the protection of his arm, his odors of vodka and cigarettes and old wool overcoat familial and comforting to her.

"We bachelors don't understand little girls, I think," he said soothingly. "But we don't love you any the less."

Her naïveté had not changed, but she had become aware of it after that night.

She had to transfer to another Metro at the Novokuznetskaya station. But the wait wasn't very long. By four-thirty she had gotten off at the Oktyabrskaya station near the Warsaw Hotel, and had walked the six or seven blocks to the City Clinical Hospital. Gorki Park was just across a snow-covered sward down the hill from the pile of gray stone. The hospital looked more like a prison to her than a place of healing. A fortress of torture and death and pain where sentences were handed out by some totally arbitrary system with absolutely no rights of appeal.

Snow was beginning to fall in earnest. The wind was cutting, but Anna was content to wait on Leninsky Prospekt for a break in the traffic. She didn't feel the cold. In fact small beads of sweat had formed on her upper lip. She kept taking deep breaths, holding them, then letting them out with a big sigh in order to clear the tightness in her chest. The doctor's nurse had telephoned her at the theater. Her test results were ready. If she would care to stop by at four-thirty, the doctor would see her. Yes, it was important. Perhaps she could bring someone with her. A friend, a relative. She had thought about Uncle Stepan, or Uncle Aleksandr, or Uncle Georgi, or Ekaterina or one of the other girls from the company, but she'd decided against it and had in fact told no one, just as she had told no one she had come here in the first place seven days earlier.

She looked back toward the Metro station. Now she wished she had brought someone along. Her breath was white in the cold as were the exhausts of the cars and trucks and taxis. She suddenly wished her mother were here from Leningrad, or even her father from Vladivostok. Both cities could have been at the ends of the earth, however. And for her, just then, they were.

Anna crossed the broad avenue after a bus rumbled by, then she hurried into the park and entered the hospital. Inside, past a main reception area, a white-painted corridor led back to the outpatient clinic. An old woman wrapped in sheets lay moaning on a tall table outside X-Ray. Beyond her, a young boy, his left arm held immobile in a wooden splint, sat in a wheelchair, his head lowered, tears streaming down his cheeks. He was obviously in a great deal of pain. Nurses and doctors and attendants scurried indifferently back and forth while a nearly steady stream of announcements came over the public address system. The atmosphere reeked of cooking cabbage, antiseptic, urine, and feces. The outpatient clinic was adjacent to the emergency room. A narrow nurses station with a counter and a small glass window separated them. The only one inside was a broad-hipped receptionist in a white coat, her hair in a bun.

Anna went up to the window and tapped. The receptionist glared at her.

"I have an appointment. Anna Chalkin."

The receptionist got to her feet and opened the window. She seemed angry. "You are late. We have been paging you for more than ten minutes."

"I'm sorry. The Metro—"

"Who are you to think you can keep an important doctor waiting? You have no special privileges here."

Anna didn't know what to say. She was truly sorry she had ever come here. She wanted her uncle with her.

"I'll call for you now," the woman said, brusquely. She picked up a telephone, said something into it, and moments later the doctor's nurse appeared at a door across the room, beckoning for Anna. Several other patients in the waiting room looked up curiously as she passed.

"You are late," the nurse said severely.

"I'm very sorry."

"Under the circumstances I would have thought you'd be here on time. The doctor does wish to see you personally. She wants to spend some time."

Anna followed the nurse into the examination room area. The woman could have been the twin to the receptionist. Sour. Bitter. Broad-hipped. They stopped at the door to the doctor's office.

"What is it?" Anna asked. "Can you tell me the results of my tests?"

The nurse just looked at her.

"Do you know? Won't you tell me?"

The nurse knocked on the door, opened it, then stepped aside. "The doctor will see you now."

Anna sagged, and went inside. Dr. Galina Mazayeva looked

up from her desk, then got to her feet. The nurse softly closed the door.

"I'm sorry I'm late, Doctor."

"It's all right, Anna. I had some things to catch up with. Healing sometimes takes a back seat to paperwork." Dr. Mazayeva was athletically built, with a strong-jawed square face that nonetheless was sympathetic. Her fingers were short and blunt, but they had been surprisingly light and gentle during her examination last week. She came around her desk and held a chair for Anna. "Is it snowing yet?"

"It's just begun," Anna said, sitting. She looked up into the doctor's eyes. There was something there. Something not good. It made her breath catch in her throat.

The doctor went back behind her desk and opened a file in front of her. She read for a moment, then looked up. She nodded slightly, as if she had just come to recognize, once and for all, a very sad but nevertheless true fact.

"Tell me about this past week, Anna," she began. "The bleeding from your gums has gotten worse?"

Anna nodded, not daring to speak.

"Bruising?"

"Some."

"Soreness still in your armpits, at your neck beneath your chin, a little in the area of your groin?"

Anna nodded again.

"Fever?"

"The aspirin helps some. None of it is more than irritating."

"Yes," the doctor said, closing the file and sitting back. Her mood was heavy, her eyes downcast. Again she seemed to be on the verge of some decision that she kept trying to put off. "Many years ago I saw you as Giselle," she said, smiling.

Then Anna knew it was going to be very bad. Even worse than she had imagined, and she had a vivid imagination.

On weekends her mother used to come from Leningrad to visit. Anna boarded with a family of the dance company in those days, which in later years she found odd since her three uncles, two of whom were married with five children between them, lived in Moscow. She should have been allowed to live with them. Sometimes they came to visit, of course, but only on weekends. And once in a great while she was allowed to visit them, though she did not get to make a trip to Leningrad to see her mother until she was fifteen. By then her mother and she were nearly strangers, the separation so long and so utterly complete. But in the early days, when she was just a little girl of four and five and six, she learned the trick of saving her fears until the weekends. It was a little mental game for her of let's pretend in which she would talk herself into believing that absolutely nothing could hurt her except on a weekend, and then she would be safely with her mother or one of her uncles. In those days it was usually with Uncle Georgi and his wife Larissa. Only later when she became a young woman did she begin to spend more time with Uncle Stepan. Of course, after a while, the notion struck her that if she could pretend her fears were groundless, that nothing could hurt her on weekends, then what difference did a weekend make? It was the very first real step in her development. Much later, though, when her fears became based more on fact that on little-girl fantasy, she was driven in the opposite direction. Then she began to understand that there were indeed things and people and circumstances in the world that could do her real and lasting harm. Now she wished for her little-girl game of let's pretend.

"I was just a young medical student then. You and I are the same age, but while I was struggling you were already an accomplished ballerina. I was so jealous for a while. I loved you and hated you at the same time. What a performance."

"Now you pity me," Anna said, looking up.

Dr. Mazayeva was startled; then embarrassed because of the truth of it. She opened the file again and did something with the papers. "I think it would be wise for you to come into the hospital for a few days."

"For what reason, Comrade Doctor?"

Dr. Mazayeva was startled by Anna's sudden change of tone, her coolness. "Observation."

"Then you do not know what is wrong with me?"

"I know."

"Then why should I come to the hospital? Is there a cure? Do I need an operation?"

Dr. Mazayeva shook her head. "I wish there were, Anna. I . . . You have acute lymphocytic leukemia."

Anna closed her eyes.

"The low-grade fever, bleeding gums, bruising, soreness of the areas around your lymph nodes, your general anemia, all symptoms, along with a white cell count of thirty-five thousand. There is no doubt, Anna. Further testing . . . is not needed.''

"I have cancer."

"Yes."

Anna was surprised at her own sudden calmness. The office was cold. "Is it. . . . Am I going to die?" she whispered.

Dr. Mazayeva said nothing. Anna opened her eyes.

"Am I going to die, Comrade Doctor? Is my cancer fatal?"

"Yes, I'm afraid it is. We will start you on a course of treatments, naturally. Six-mercaptopurine, and then the antifolic acids if it becomes necessary. Much later perhaps hormones. We will see."

"There is no cure?"

Dr. Mazayeva averted her eyes. "There has been talk of bone marrow transplants. But, no, there is no cure for you, Anna. There will be no real discomfort, though. You will simply . . . weaken."

"What if I refuse the treatment?"

"You cannot, Anna," the doctor said sharply. "One minute of life is not to be wasted, let alone nine months."

The mention of a specific amount of time was shocking. Anna had somehow managed to hold herself intact to this point. Now she felt as if she were on the verge of a complete breakdown. Somehow, though, she could not allow herself to do that in front of the doctor. Of course it would not matter to the progress of her. . . . She skirted around the word. Lurking in her dark closets were cancers and diseases and illnesses, all with very specific names and symptoms. But she wasn't ready for the labels yet.

"When do I begin?"

The doctor was clearly relieved. "Today. But please tell me why you did not go to your own clinic. The facilities are very good there. You would have been referred to a hospital, of course. Not here."

"I didn't want them to know."

"But they must. You can see that."

"Not yet, Dr. Mazayeva. I beg you to give me just a little time before you make your report. If I have only months in any event, my condition will soon become evident. But first there is something I must do. Please."

The doctor sighed deeply. She closed the file and got to her feet. "Eventually you will have to check into a hospital. You will not be able to care for yourself. You must understand

that, Anna. By then I will have to make my report. There will
be questions asked at that time as well. Why, for instance,
did you not inform your company, after all it has done for
you? That is a question you will have to answer, Anna. Not
me. I will hold your reports. You will have to come here on
Mondays and Thursdays for chemotherapy, at least initially. I
will prescribe some capsules for your anemia. They will help
for only a short while, perhaps a month, perhaps six weeks.
By then the course of your cancer will be far enough advanced that we will be fighting other symptomology. You
understand all of this, Anna?''

Anna nodded. She was still holding on to herself inside,
but it was becoming increasingly difficult.

"There won't be any noticeable side effects of the treatments. Not at first. Perhaps some nausea . . .'' Dr. Mazayeva
stopped herself. She came around the desk and helped Anna
to her feet. "How do you feel?''

"I don't know,'' Anna said, looking into the doctor's
concerned eyes.

"Is there someone I can telephone for you? Someone to
come fetch you?''

"No. I think I'd rather be alone for a little while. There is
a lot to assimilate. It's strange. I don't think I believe it, and
yet I know it's true.''

The doctor nodded knowingly. "We'll begin with an
injection.''

Anna lived alone in an apartment six blocks north of the
Bolshoi Theater on the second of three *pereuloks*, or side
streets, named Neglin. It was a pleasant place. She had three
rooms all to herself plus a private bathroom. It was even
nicer than the apartment she'd been assigned as prima
ballerina, though not nearly as nice as Grigorovich's, or
Maya Plisetskaya's. But then Yuri was the director and Maya
was the Soviet Union's only prima ballerina assoluta. They
deserved something special. During her ride on the Metro
from the Clinical Hospital, and on the long walk from Sverdlov
Square, she went over and over in her mind what the doctor
had told her. It still could not be real; such things happened to
other people, though already her initial disbelief was turning
to anger, in the classic pattern. Catastrophic news had a way
of first totally overloading the system, much like a gunshot
wound first numbs the region of the projectile's penetration.

The victim feels no pain, only disbelief, and perhaps surprise that it has happened to her. By degrees, then, as the initial shock begins to wear off, the pain comes; turns to anger. Why me? I've so much left to accomplish. I've so many friends, so much family, so many dances to direct, restaurants to go to, summer nights to enjoy, symphonies to hear, plays to see, books to read—my God, so much. Retirement perhaps to a dacha to write memoirs. So much yet. Oh, the pain would come, she knew. Not the physical variety—Dr. Mazayeva had promised her there would be little of that—but the pain of lost years would, she suspected, become an even greater burden to bear than mere agony. It was a pain she knew all too well. She did not know if she would have the strength to endure both. At least this would last months, and not years like the other.

Mounting the stairs to her apartment a few minutes past six-thirty, it occurred to her that she was going to have to become an actress, lest someone in the company find her out. They were snoopy, all of them, curious like little children. Their lives had been so structured since early childhood that they were gossipmongers who loved nothing more than a juicy story. In many ways it was as if they were inbred. Most weren't malicious, but all of them were tattletales. She would have to be very careful, or at least she would have to be for the first few weeks. After that it wouldn't matter one way or the other.

Someone was in the kitchen when she let herself in the front door. She immediately smelled cigarette smoke and heard the rattle of a pan on the burner. Her first insane thought was that Dr. Mazayeva had somehow beaten her home and had come to apologize for making a dreadful mistake. They were someone else's files, Anna. You see, somehow it happened that your files were put in the wrong folder by mistake. That wasn't so bad, but the files of the poor person who is dying of leukemia were put into your folder. It is simple. You have a minor infection, nothing more. Some antibiotics, and within a week or two you will be fine.

"Anna, is that you?" Uncle Stepan called. He appeared in the doorway, his KGB uniform tunic unbuttoned, his belly rolling over his belt.

She didn't want anyone here tonight. Especially not Uncle Stepan, although she loved him. He had the ability to look right through her. His KGB training, he used to kid her. We're all psychologists over there at the Center. Nobody holds anything back from us. Uncle Aleksandr's children believed he was a psychic. He had the habit of showing up just when you didn't want him there. Snatch a *ponchiki*, hot and fresh with sprinkled sugar, and Uncle Stepan would be lurking around the corner to catch you. Call your teacher a bad name, and he was just outside to overhear. Think a bad thought, even, and he might wash your mouth out with soap. But need a friend and he was there as well. Kiss a bruise, bandage a cut, provide a couple of kopecks to jingle in a purse or a pocket, he was there.

"I didn't expect you, Uncle," she said, affecting as best she could a carefree tone.

"I'm making some tea for us, but I wasn't sure what time you'd be back. Anton said you'd left around four." He was a very tall man by Russian standards, more than six feet. His shoulders were powerful, his face broad and shaggy with thick eyebrows and big curving mustaches beneath a full head of jet-black hair with not so much as a hint of gray despite his fifty-four years. In many ways he was a bear: solid, shambling, patches of hair on his shoulder blades, the small of his back, and the backs of his hands. An American cigarette hung from the corner of his mouth.

"Anton is an old woman," Anna said, closing the door. He was the stage manager and everyone's mother.

Uncle Stepan went back into the kitchen. "I thought I would take you out for dinner tonight," he called. "How does the Aragvi sound? *Lobio, kharcho, osetrina na vertelye?* A little wine maybe?"

Anna took off her coat and hat and hung them on the hall stand. The injection was making her slightly sick to her stomach. The mention of the Aragvi's Georgian specialties of butter beans, meat soup—both highly spiced—and sturgeon didn't help.

"I think you've been working entirely too hard lately, Anna," Uncle Stepan continued from the kitchen. She could hear him laying out the glasses and saucers. "You're taking your new position too seriously. I prescribe a weekend in the country. Dominic's dacha is available. Perhaps Ekaterina, Natalia, Rimma, and some of the other girls would like to join us. Mother Anton could come along and do the cooking.

There are horses out there, finally. And a surprise which I have been saving."

Anna kicked off her boots and went into the kitchen. Uncle Stepan had laid out the tea things on the tiny table. "Well, what do you say?" he asked.

She sat down, took one of his cigarettes from the pack on the table, and lit it, drawing the smoke deeply into her lungs. It was a luxury she had never indulged in as a dancer. Now as assistant artistic director her wind no longer mattered. And as to thoughts about lung cancer. . . .

"Are you feeling well, chou-chou?" Uncle Stepan asked.

Anna looked up at the same moment he laid a cool hand on her forehead to test her temperature.

"You look peaked," he said. "Are you eating enough? Your mother asked about you on Tuesday."

Anna could feel his deep concern. He bent down and looked deeply into her eyes, his eyebrows knitting together, his lips pursed.

"Anna?" he said.

The ache in her stomach sharpened, a thickness came into her throat, and tears began to well up. "Oh, Uncle Stepan," she sobbed, dropping the cigarette into the ashtray.

He fairly lifted her out of the chair in alarm and enfolded her gently in his thick arms, her head against his massive chest, her tears, unhindered now by convention, spilling down her cheeks onto his shirt.

"Who has hurt you, child?" Uncle Stepan rumbled. "What has happened? Tell me. I am your uncle. I will fix it. I promise."

In the past he had fixed nearly everything, only this was impossible even for him. Not this. And she cried all the harder for the realization. Everything she had been holding back all week, and especially since she had seen the doctor that afternoon, came out in her tears. In many ways it was almost a catharsis, a cleaning, a washing away not of her fears, but of the veil of ignorance over her anxieties.

"Anna?" Uncle Stepan asked softly.

"It's too late," she sobbed.

"What's too late, chou-chou?" he cooed.

"Everything."

"Tell me one thing."

Anna looked up. "My dancing. I'll never dance again. Never, Uncle."

He smiled gently. "Is that it?" He held her shoulders. "Is that it, then? You are feeling a bit sorry for yourself? If that is so, then shame on you. Think of all you have had, all you have been, and seen and done. Shame on you."

Anna hung her head. She wanted to tell him. He would move mountains for her if he knew. She would be sent to the very best doctors at the very best clinics, probably down in Yalta. She would be poked and prodded, measured and tested, isolated in luxury—after all, she was an artistic director of the Bolshoi Ballet, and her uncle, General Stepan Patrenko, was a very important man in Moscow. But it was the isolation she feared most of all.

"What is it, Anna?" he asked. He felt her forehead again. "You are a little warm. Have you been feeling ill lately? Perhaps you should see the company doctor. I'll speak with Yuri. Perhaps you need a few days off. Get some rest. You're pale."

Anna shivered. Someone had just walked over her grave. She reached up and kissed her uncle on the cheek, then sighed deeply. "I'm fine, Uncle. Mostly tired." She went into the bathroom where she splashed cold water on her face. Her eyes were bloodshot, her complexion pale except for a flush high on her delicate cheeks and a little on her forehead. It was from the low fever.

He followed her. "I'm serious, Anna. I will speak to Yuri for you. He must understand the strain you've been under."

She blotted her face with a towel. "It's not necessary, Uncle, believe me."

"Then promise me one thing: you will see the doctor. Maybe you're anemic. Maybe you're not eating right."

"Maybe it's that time of the month. Did you ever consider that?" Anna said, and it instantly embarrassed him. He'd never married. It was one of the reasons they had such a good, understanding relationship: the old bachelor and the old maid. But menstruation, ovulation, and all the subtle and not so subtle changes that went hand in hand with a woman's monthly cycle were not in his lexicon of understandable phenomena.

"Then find that out too," he said bravely. "You're thirty-six, you have never had a child, perhaps there is a . . . hormonal imbalance." He threw up his hands. It had been hard for him. "I don't know, chou-chou, but I am worried for you. Lately you have not been yourself. And you are losing weight, too, I think.''

"Since I no longer dance, I no longer eat like a horse. Of course I'm losing weight.'' Her nausea had finally subsided and she didn't feel so bad now, although she did want to be alone.

"Will you listen to me, Anna?''

"I think our tea is getting cold," she said, brushing past him. "And I have a cigarette burning.''

"And since when have you started smoking? I just want to know that much," her uncle said, following her back into the kitchen.

"Are you becoming another Anton?'' she asked, sitting down.

Uncle Stepan finally laughed. "Are we going to have dinner tonight?''

She took a deep drag of her cigarette, then stubbed it out in the ashtray. It didn't taste very good now. "Not tonight, Uncle. I am tired, and just a little sick to my stomach.''

"There, you see . . . ?''

She held him off. "There you see nothing! I'm tired. It has been a trying day.''

"What about the weekend?''

"We'll see, Uncle. But I just don't know if I could take two days of Dominic *and* Mother Anton." She forced a smile. It was becoming increasingly difficult for her to hold on.

"The surprise out there is a new sauna bath. Dominic got it from Helsinki just last week. It is finally installed and ready. I thought some of the girls . . .''

"We'll see, Uncle, we'll see. Now, come drink your tea before it gets cold. You talked with my mother?''

Her uncle was getting old. It struck her at that moment that he had aged in the past year or so. She could see it in his eyes, and in the way he held himself. Like most older men he was careful of his back. Her life, she thought, would have been impossible without him.

That night she began her letter to Jason: "My dearest love, I am writing to you after all these years with the single hope that somehow it will be possible for me to look on your face one last time before I die." It was as far as she got on the first evening. Sitting propped up in her bed, listening to a

London recording of Puccini's *Madama Butterfly*, with Renata Tebaldi and Carlo Bergonzi, she found it impossible to decide which words to use, where to begin. The light was soft, the bed warm and snug, the wind outside harsh and cold, and she let the music drift over and around her.

"Non son più quella!" Madama Butterfly sang sadly, as she waited for her love to return.

> I am not the same anymore!
> Too many sighs have passed these lips,
> And these eyes have gazed too long into the distance.

The music rose and Anna began to cry softly, this time not only for herself, but for the poor, sad Butterfly who waited years for her lover to return from across the sea, only to learn when he does return that he is married, and now it is far too late for her. "He will come, he will come, you'll see," Butterfly laments at the last.

In the morning when Anna awoke, the first page of the letter lying on the bed beside her, the memory of the music fresh in her mind, she knew she would have to go through with it, no matter what the letter would cost her in pain, sorrow, or even in suffering. She would write to him. It had been so many years. *So long*, Madama Butterfly sang. She was not the same anymore. Nor would he be. But she would get a letter to Jason. She would.

During the following week, Anna was more her old self at the theater, bright, alive, even vivacious, though the effort it cost her was nearly superhuman. On Friday she joined her uncle, along with a number of others from the theater, for a weekend in the country with Dominic Shevchenko's new sauna bath from Helsinki. On Mondays and Thursdays she went to the City Clinical Hospital for her chemotherapy and to renew her supply of tablets for her anemia. Each evening, however, in the warmth of her own bed, she listened to *Madama Butterfly* over and over as she composed her letter, word by word, sentence by painful sentence, her task made all the more frustrating by the fact that she did not know his real name, only the code name Jason, and that it had been nearly eleven years since she had last seen or heard from him.

He had, however, given her two bits of information before he left that made her efforts worthwhile. The first was an address in Paris where he could be reached, though he wasn't French. And the second was the name of a man in Moscow, with instructions on how to contact him, who was able to get messages in and out. "Dangerous knowledge, Anna," he had told her the last time they'd been together, "but I want you to have it. If anything, anything at all ever happens to you, please write to me." His words. She remembered them clearly; she'd heard them in her mind thousands of times over the years, and they were no less clear now than on the night he had uttered them. She did not even have to close her eyes to see his face, to see the lines radiating from the corners of his eyes— laugh lines, he called them—or see the strong line of his jaw, his bright blue eyes, his sensuous lips. Nor did it take much for her to imagine his sure but gentle touch when they were nude in each other's arms on the fur rug in front of a blazing fireplace in their dacha, or in bed making love. Then, with him inside her, she would study his face, which for her had become like the seasons: new and alive as in the spring; warm and animated with passion as in the summer; deeply thoughtful, even a little sad as in the fall; and cold and aloof, as only an American could be when he thought their secret relationship was in jeopardy; as in the winter. Thinking about him like that made her nipples hard, and made it nearly impossible to go to sleep. There'd only been one boy before him, and no one since.

In those days she danced only for him. The critics called it her season. "A certain glow has come to our little Anna," one wrote. "We can only wonder at her recent surge of development. Though her technique still needs polishing, her line is lovely. Bravo! Bravo, Anna Feodorovna!"

Performing onstage was the only time she was able to profess her love for him in public. She was a Bolshoi dancer and he was an American. But it was worse than that: she was the niece of a KGB colonel, and he was a diplomat in the consular section of the American embassy. He used the name Jason and she was his Medea. A nest of spies, *Pravda* called the yellow brick building on Tchaikovsky Street. At least once a week she contrived to take a taxi past the embassy. She never saw him, of course, but she would often fantasize that she had caught a glimpse of him in some third-floor window, or just the back of his head through the gate, or his car parked at the side. She never told him of her taxi rides, but she did tell him that while she was onstage, there was no one with her, nor was there anyone in the audience except for him. He'd been touched, stirred, and deeply honored, he told her. She loved him all the more for his sensitivity, for his kindness, and above all for his understanding of her dancer's spirit. She had her love to give him, of course. She had her body. She had her hours. But in reality all those were secondary to her dancing, and he understood.

She wrote to him about those first years after he had gone, about her initial loneliness and fear that gradually mellowed into a deep longing and even despair. These things too, she said, came into her dancing, giving her—according to the critics who were now totally in love with her—a new depth, a maturity, a ripeness that quickly led to her elevation from soloist to prima ballerina. If there was any disappointment in those years among her fans, she explained, it was because she did not marry a premier danseur. It was expected. The husband-and-wife teams were ongoing legends. Nina Sorokina and Yuri Vladimirov for one. Ludmilla Semenyaka and Mikhail Lavrovsky, another. Even her friend Ekaterina Maximova married her dancer-lover Vladimir Vasiliev. "But Jason," she wrote, "foolish or not, I always held the hope that somehow we would be together again, someday we would meet. Even when I was denied an external passport, making foreign travel impossible, I dreamed you would return. That it would be the same as the old days. Only now it may be too late."

In the end, as dispassionately and as clinically detached as was possible for her, she told Jason about her illness, about her pains, her aches, about her weight loss and bleeding that had led her to the hospital for tests. She reported, as accurately as she could remember, Dr. Mazayeva's exact words: her diagnosis, her prescriptions, and her prognosis of death. Less than nine months, she wrote. A letter, a photograph, a visit. She could accept anything except silence.

> I am come to the portals of love . . .
> Where is gathered the happiness of
> Those who live and those who die.

Anna hid the letter in her apartment, and for the next five days went about her work and life as if nothing had happened, or was about to happen. She was making excuses, and she knew it. The letter was written; it was now out of her system. If she never sent it, she would eliminate the possibility of receiving a negative answer. She would never be rejected if she never ventured forth. In any event it had been more than ten years; the courier could no longer be active, or he could have moved to another city, or he could be in jail. He could even be dead. And even if he agreed to take out her letter, the Paris address could no longer be valid. With simply a code name—Jason—there would be little hope of finding him. He too could be dead.

In the end it was this last thought, this possibility that Jason could be dead and unless she acted she would never know, that drove her to act. You will need a courier, he told her. His name is Boyko, and he can be reached at the Arbat on Kalinina. He is very young and not trustworthy, Anna, but he is greedy and will do what he is told for fear that his supply of Western currency could be cut off. He works for the government, but in reality he works for himself. Whoever is the highest bidder, whoever pays the most, whoever gives him the greatest advantage without complications—for he is a coward, too—will receive his aid. But be careful, Anna. Boyko surrounds himself with important people for whom he also does favors. And they are not stupid people. They see and hear things. Be careful for yourself.

Anna approached the Arbat on the sixth day following the completion of her letter in much the same way she had approached everything else in the nearly two weeks since she had found out she was dying: with a forced gaiety that for all intents and purposes, at least for the people around her, was genuine. She was happy at last, they said of her, in her new role as artistic director. She had accepted her fate. She would grow old gracefully, perhaps even someday taking over from Grigorovich himself. She continued to surround herself with people: her uncle one evening for dinner; Ekaterina and her husband Vladimir on another evening at their apartment; Dmitri Naydenkov, their newest acquisition from Leningrad—so new he still had stars in his eyes for the big city—and a half-dozen swans from the corps de ballet for a night of dinner and entertainment of the lesser artistic variety that the Arbat provided. Located at 29 Kalinina Prospekt, the restaurant-nightclub was reputed to be the most expensive in all of Moscow. Reservations were required and the maître d's seating list was said to read as if it were a *Who's Who* of the

Kremlin. It was Boyko's hangout, Jason had told her. Or at least it had been ten years ago. Anna was afraid that too much had changed in the interim. She knew it was foolish to think that any such information could remain valid over such a terribly long period of time. Moscow was a volatile city in a volatile world, and Boyko's occupation was dangerous at best. But she had nothing else to go on, no other options other than the one of destroying the letter and getting on with her dying.

She made the reservations herself, and they were assigned a table for eight in an honored position very near the stage so that they could see the show, but also so that the other patrons could see that the Arbat attracted not only the Moscow bureaucrat and soldier, but also drew important people from the arts. Culture. Refinement. Polish. They were treated with respect and deference, the first bottle of champagne coming with the compliments of the house. The next was from Sergei Yevlampev, an important Politburo member, and the third from General Pavlovich Chetvertukhin, commander of the Moscow Defense Squadron.

In the first hour no less than a dozen important personages had come to their table to say hello, to chat for just a moment, to make certain that they were seen *appreciating* the arts. "After *The Nutcracker* I would have thought you poor children would have been absolutely exhausted. It is so good to see you out like this." Or: "The early pas de deux in *Don Quixote* this season I think was never done quite so well as by Maximova and her husband. Give them our regards." Even a certain adulation seemed to emanate from the people surrounding them. All eyes were turned their way. Here are the finest dancers in the world, here among *us*, not onstage, but *here*.

Throughout all of this, Anna kept relatively aloof, or at least as detached as possible under the circumstances. A certain shyness seemed to have come over her that was charming. She'd had a brilliant career in front of audiences; now that she was behind the scenes she had become gracious enough to allow the current stars their day in the spotlight.

It was the letter in her purse that frightened her the most, that made her reticent. It was that and the possibility, which seemed to grow into a certainty now that she was actually there, that Boyko could not be found or would no longer be active. But each time she came up against that wall of fear, she reminded herself that she had no other choice. One did not simply pen a letter, seal it in an envelope, and drop it with sufficient postage at the nearest post office. Perhaps with some letters, perhaps elsewhere in the world, but not with *her* letter and certainly not in Moscow. Also, she was frightened that she had not been sufficiently clear in her letter as to exactly what it was she wanted. She had been an ambiguous fool. What was he supposed to think if and when he received it? Were these the ramblings of a distraught woman? It had been eleven years; what in heaven's name could she possibly want? If her own doctor could not recommend a cure, what could he do? Was he a miracle worker?

Suddenly the man was there, at the end of the table, introducing himself to Rimma and Dmitri.

"I am Boyko. Vitali Ivanovich, at your service," he said expansively. He bent low and kissed Rimma's hand.

Anna stared at him as if he were an apparition. But it was he. The man indeed still existed. All these years she had hoarded his name, along with the Paris address, at the back of her mind, sure that she would never have to use it. Either she would go to Jason, or Jason would come to her. She would never have need of Boyko's services.

Now she was disappointed. He wasn't what she had expected. He was less somehow, though she had never really given a face to her expectation. Boyko was of medium height and very solidly built except for a large, old-man's stomach, though she didn't think he looked much older than thirty-five or forty. In Moscow, though, a belly on a man was considered a status symbol. It was meant to show unlimited access to calories and a soft office job. His head was bullet-shaped, his thick dark hair cropped short, his pig eyes narrow and close set, his chin weak and his lips too red. He wore a garishly striped suit that was a bit too small for him and a dark green bow tie that didn't match.

Rimma said something and smiled. Boyko straightened up and laughed out loud, throwing his head back and holding his sides. Dmitri, who was sitting next to her, looked up at him and shrugged. Boyko was doing it for attention, and he was succeeding. A lot of people were looking at him.

Anna could not imagine Jason and this man together. Each was the complete opposite of the other. Boyko was loud, coarse, and cheap, everything Jason was not.

Their eyes met, and Boyko came around the table to her.

"You must be Anna Feodorovna," he said respectfully. He took her hand and pressed his moist lips to it. She suppressed a shudder.

The others around the table were looking to see how she handled him.

"I didn't quite catch your name . . ."

"Vitali Boyko. Foreign Trade Ministry. And may I say I have long admired your dancing, madame."

"Thank you," Anna said demurely. Her heart was beginning to thump against her ribs. He started to pull away, but she held tight. "I believe we have had a mutual friend," she said softly.

"Oh . . . ?" he started, but then he stopped himself.

"It has been a long time," Anna said, forcing herself to hold his hand. Forcing herself to continue. "I was young then."

"We were all young once upon a time, madame, though much younger and you would have been a child."

The compliment was hollow, but it didn't matter. "His name was Jason."

Boyko's eyes narrowed. "An unusual name." He too had lowered his voice.

"I have lost track of him, though I do have an address."

Anna could feel the sudden tenseness, the wariness coming from him. It was like being next to a high-tension wire. The others around the table had lost interest in them. An older woman with a sable stole around her shoulders had approached the group for autographs.

"Then you should write. Always keep in touch, that's my motto."

"It's difficult," Anna said softly, drawing him closer. "It is a Paris address."

Boyko grinned. "Not so difficult. In fact I will be leaving soon for Helsinki, Athens, Hamburg . . . even Paris. Perhaps . . ."

"You would take a letter for me?"

"Of course." Boyko glanced toward the end of the table. "General Kedrov's wife. A first class lady." He looked back. "Give it to me now."

"What? Here?" Anna asked, alarmed.

"The very best place to hide a snowflake is in a blizzard. Yes, now."

Anna fumbled in her purse, took out the letter, hesitated for just a moment, then handed it up to him.

He smiled broadly, and produced a gold ballpoint pen. "First your autograph, please," he said loudly. "If you don't mind."

Anna signed the back of the envelope, handed back his pen, and then he was gone, and with him her letter, her hopes, her final dreams. Frighteningly simple, she thought, for a document so potentially explosive. And he had asked for no payment.

For the remainder of that evening Anna found she had a little trouble focusing on reality. And for the first time since her illness had been diagnosed, she was violently sick to her stomach in the ladies' room and Dmitri had to take her home. She'd had too much champagne, she told him. And the excitement of a new production. Alone in bed she dreamed about Jason coming for her. They were running, but somehow they didn't seem able to reach one another, until finally he began to fade into nothingness.

2

Unlike Anna, there was no grace in the character of Vitali Boyko, not in his lumpy body and certainly not in his dark little opportunistic mind. Despite the cold he was sweating as he hurried through Helsinki's night streets, his thoughts firmly planted on the deal he had cooked up, the golden opportunity that after all these years was his. But it was dangerous. The deceit, the lies after all these years was stunning. Even he had balked at first, coming to the obvious conclusion. But this would make headlines, wouldn't it? They would pay a lot to keep it secret, he had figured, and he had figured right. In a way he and Anna did share one similarity: in a way both of them were orphans—Anna practically a ward of the state because of her dancing, and Boyko a definite ward of the state because his mother had died giving birth to him, and no one knew his father. Anna had been trained for the ballet, but Boyko had been trained for an administrative job within the government once it was determined that he was too slow for science, engineering, or medicine. It was a few minutes before one in the morning, and the sky was so clear it seemed as if the stars had ripened and were about to fall to the earth. Lights from the President's Palace and the City Hall swirled blue and green in a thin ice fog that hung low over South Harbor. Traffic was still steady despite the hour. Somewhere a red light blinked on and off, warning perhaps of some danger.

"My darling, my darling, I love you. I miss you, I'm

dying," he whispered sotto voce to himself. Christ on a cross, the letter had made him want to puke. But Paris had been interested, all right, and so had Washington, despite what Sheshkin and his wife had to say about it.

Ten days it had been. He'd done more thinking, covered more mental ground, and made more intuitive leaps of imagination during the past week and a half than he had in his entire thirty-seven miserable years of existence. This was the big score, he kept telling himself. The one thing he'd waited for all of his life. The juicy bit that would put him over the top so he would never have to work another day in his life. If it had been nothing more than a letter from some lovesick dancer, he wouldn't have bothered with it. He was all but out of that kind of business now. All of his contacts at the American embassy had dried up. No one was left in the old network, at least no one active. And besides, his job with the Foreign Trade Ministry did have its perquisites, among them foreign travel. But it was the promise of bigger and better things that made him take it. Seeing her there like that at the Arbat, sitting all prim and prissy on the edge of her chair, her little heart obviously all aflutter with conspiracy, had brought back a flood of memories for him. But even then he'd taken the letter only as a lark. See what the lovesick little bitch had to say. And it was sickening, all right, wasn't it? But you can't go back, can you? Marx said we were destined to go forward, for better or for worse. It was party dialectic: it was up to us, up to our collective spirit to go forth boldly with strong arms and even stronger hearts to a new socialism despite the pain it would cause, despite—or almost because of—the upheavals and injustices.

The first night had been a dream. After the Arbat he had gone straight home to his apartment where he had steamed open Anna's letter, and sipping vodka until the early hours of the morning, he had read it slowly, word by word, and then had reread it, this time looking between the lines. If Boyko was nothing else, his years in the state orphanage and his fifteen years with the Foreign Trade Ministry had brought him an understanding—even a working knowledge—of a certain darker side of the human condition. Where emotions were rubbed raw, where courage flagged, where fears rose, where avarice dominated, where grievances or aches or yens were the driving force of a life, he was there with an understanding smile, a glad hand, and a suggestion for a simple solution.

Boyko the magician. Get a Western whiskey, procure a whore, mail a letter—let Boyko do it. Hiding the letter in the false bottom of his toilet tank, he had hurried over to Yevgenni Sheshkin's apartment on Zhitnaya. Sheshkin was one of the few from the old network with whom he still had any contact, though if it were up to Sheshkin's wife, their relationship would not survive.

"It's four o'clock in the morning!" she screamed down the stairs at the top of her lungs. Her hair was up in curlers and Boyko swore he saw sparks shooting out of her mouth.

Yevgenni came to the door in nothing more than his pajama bottoms. He wasn't too happy either, but he was holding his temper. "What is it, Vitali? Are you in trouble?"

"We have to talk," Boyko called up from the other side of the iron gate. He didn't want to raise his voice. This was no one else's business.

"Later, Vitali. Later. After work. It is going to be a very long day unless you let me get back to sleep." Sheshkin worked as a buyer for GUM, the state-run department store downtown.

"Go away, you bastard," Tatiana Sheshkin spat. "There is nothing here for you anymore. You are a weasel. A sewer rat."

Yevgenni turned to her and said something that Boyko couldn't make out. She waved her arms around, then slapped her husband's chest with the flat of her hand. "You might as well sleep with him too—you do everything else," she said in disgust. She turned on her heel and stormed back into their apartment.

"Yevgenni?" Boyko called up, but Sheshkin just stood there for several seconds staring into the apartment.

Boyko was a little frightened now. The others were gone. Sheshkin had been one of the last to hold out in the network, but he too had fallen by the wayside. And when he fell he had gone all the way: married on one day, and the very next he had become a model Communist. Maybe it had been an error coming here.

Sheshkin turned at last and padded down the stairs. It was very cold in the corridor. They could see their breath, but it didn't seem to bother Sheshkin.

"Now, what is it, Vitali? Have you gotten yourself into some kind of trouble?"

"No. But something has come up, Yevgenni. Now, open up." Boyko rattled the gate a little.

Sheshkin glanced back up the stairs. "I'd better not. You heard how she is. It's bad enough." Sheshkin was tall and very well built. In the old days he had been an outstanding soccer player. He'd aged a lot over the past few years. Gone to seed, as they say. It was the home life, steady meals, regular hours, and a job that required very little in the way of physical exercise and almost no mental drill. Once a year he got to travel. Two years ago he'd gone to New York.

Boyko leaned in closer. "Listen, I was just handed a letter from someone very important. A woman. Very big. She wants me to take it out."

"I didn't think you were still doing that. How much is she paying?"

"Nothing. But this was handed to me on a silver platter, you know what I mean?" Boyko glanced up the stairs to make sure Sheshkin's wife was not listening. "It was Anna Chalkin. Do you remember her?"

Sheshkin's thick eyebrows knit together. The name obviously rang a bell for him, but it was just as obvious he was having trouble recalling exactly who she was. He shook his head. "So you're taking out her letter for humanitarian reasons. Who is it addressed to?"

"Someone named Jason. But she is dying. She's got less than a year to live."

Sheshkin recoiled as if he'd just been shown a snake. "What are you talking about, Vitali? Did you open this letter? Did you read it?"

"Of course I did," Boyko said defensively. "What do you think I am, stupid?"

"Throw it away, Vitali. Believe me. Or give it back to her, or reseal it and mail it for her. But don't stand here at four in the morning and tell me about a letter from a dying woman. I don't want to hear about it. Even you should know better."

"I need the old Paris telephone number," Boyko blurted. "It's why I came."

Sheshkin was incredulous now. "What?"

"This is my big one, Yevgenni. Believe me . . ."

Sheshkin held him off. "I don't want to hear about it. Just get away from here. It's sick."

"Sick, is it?" Boyko puffed up indignantly. "Let me tell you about this little piece. She was fucking someone from the

American embassy, if I read her right. And I think I do. But she didn't even know the bastard's name. Still doesn't. Our little Russian whore spreads her legs for some foreign prick and she doesn't even bother asking his name. But I know him.''

"Get out of here, Vitali," Sheshkin said. "And don't come back." He turned and started tiredly up the stairs, a man who had already gone too many miles.

"I'll stay here all morning if need be," Boyko said, raising his voice. "Wake up the whole building."

Sheshkin continued up without bothering to turn around.

"You're not so clean yourself, you know," Boyko practically shouted. "You worked in the network. Spy!"

Sheshkin stopped halfway up. He held onto the banister with one hand. His shoulders sagged. Slowly he turned and looked down at Boyko standing in the cold, dimly lit vestibule and shook his head. He came back down.

"You would sell out your own mother, wouldn't you," he said softly.

Boyko grinned. "She's dead."

"Lucky her," Sheshkin said. He sighed deeply. "Is that all you want, Vitali? Just the old telephone number? Nothing more? Promise you'll never come back?"

"I promise."

Still Sheshkin hesitated.

"Don't be a peasant," Boyko said.

"You're going to sell them her letter, is that it?"

Boyko shrugged. "I'm going to tell them about it. Then the decision will be theirs."

"When are you leaving?"

"Next week. A buying trip for the Ministry's foreign exchange stores."

"Paris?"

"Probably not. They can meet me somewhere." Boyko smiled. "Listen, my friend, it's not as bad as it sounds, you know. If her letter is harmless they will deliver it for her and I will be out a few rubles. But who knows? Maybe something will come of it. Maybe I'm doing my own country a service . . .." Boyko was stopped in mid-sentence by the expression on Sheshkin's face. "I only just—"

"It's on the Avenue Gabriel. Do you know this street?"

Boyko shook his head.

"The number is 723-86-21."

"Who do I ask for?"

Sheshkin turned and started up the stairs.

"Who do I ask for at that number? What do I say?"

At the head of the stairs Sheshkin entered his apartment and closed the door. Boyko heard the lock snap shut. He suspected it was the very last he would ever see or hear of his old friend. But then, he told himself as he left the building, who needed him? Who needed anyone?

He crossed the Norra Esplanaden and stepped into the shadows at the east side of the City Tourist Office. From here he had a clear field of vision across South Harbor as well as up the busy street toward the square.

They said they would be sending a gray Mercedes with a big DK for Denmark on its trunk lid. One o'clock in the morning, they said. They would park half a block east of the Swedish Theater. Precisely one minute after its headlights were extinguished, Boyko was to approach alone on foot with the letter. If it was safe for the drop, the rear window on the passenger side would be lowered and the exchange would be made. No words, no conversation, no further contact would be possible. The switch would take one or two seconds at the most. Afterward Boyko was to continue walking to the Old Church without looking back. At that point he would be released from any further obligation. They would have the letter, and he would have his money. Ten thousand American. Less then he'd wanted, but more then he'd expected. There would be fallbacks, though. If the switch did not take place as agreed, someone would contact him before he returned to the Soviet Union.

"We're on your side, Mr. Boyko. Believe us when we tell you that there is nothing we wish more than to receive this letter." The speaker was French, which had surprised Boyko; he'd expected an American.

He was dressed in an expensively cut sheepskin-lined coat and hat. In his left pocket was the letter from Anna, in his right a Makarov automatic. It hadn't been easy getting the weapon out of the country despite his Ministry passport and status. He'd done it before, of course, but it had been long ago enough now that he was out of practice. (Once he'd even used the gun, though to this day he wasn't sure if he had hit anything, despite the stories he used to tell around.) He had sweated heavily on the flight out and right up until the moment he had actually cleared Finnish customs.

A gray Mercedes came around the corner and Boyko stiffened in anticipation, his mouth going dry. He watched through narrowed eyes as the car cruised slowly up the block, a big oval DK on its trunk lid. Instead of pulling over to the curb it continued across the square until it disappeared left toward the Old Church at the center of the town. He looked down the street in disbelief. It had taken him seven days to get out of Moscow and another two to set up this meet through the old Paris network number. Now they weren't going to stop? What was wrong with them? he asked himself. At that same moment, however, he realized that someone might be following them. He spun around, his right hand in his pocket, his fingers curling around the Makarov's grip. His skin was jumping all over the place, especially under his left eye and behind his left ear.

A taxi hurried around the corner and passed. No one was in the back seat. It turned right at the theater, its taillights winking in the distance.

If they thought someone was following them, they would not stop. The Frenchman had been quite specific about that point. The switch would be off. But then what? How long was he supposed to hang around outside in the cold? No one had told him. They hadn't said a word on that score, only that he would be contacted sometime before he returned to Moscow. That could be anytime, anyplace. What was he supposed to be doing in the meantime?

The same gray Mercedes came around the corner again, but this time it passed very slowly and pulled up half a block this side of the Swedish Theater. Boyko's heart was really hammering now. He had been too excited to take a good look inside the car as it passed, although he was almost certain he had seen at least one dark, shadowy figure in the back. The Mercedes's lights went out. Boyko stared stupidly down the block, his right hand still on the Makarov's grip. A shiver ran up his spine. He was cold and his feet hurt in his cowboy boots. He thought about Sheshkin's disdain. That had truly hurt him; they had been friends for too many years for it to end that way. It was his wife. . . .

All of a sudden Boyko remembered the Frenchman's instructions, and he nearly jumped out of his skin. One minute. But how long had it been? He jerked his gun hand out of his pocket and frantically clawed at his left sleeve so that he could get at his watch, but then he stopped himself. There was no way of telling when a minute had passed unless you knew when it had started. Of all the fools on earth, he felt like their king.

A big truck rumbled by and somewhere on the other side of the harbor a horn tooted twice. The red light was still flashing down the block. Actually he was doing nothing illegal here according to Finnish law, he told himself. Aside from carrying the gun, that is. But who would care that he was passing a simple letter over to some friends? No harm in that. Not under Finnish law.

Boyko stepped out of the shadows, glanced the opposite way up the street, then started toward the Mercedes. He reached in his left pocket and took out Anna's letter. Ten thousand dollars, he kept reminding himself. He had dreamed a long time about that kind of money, and now that it was practically in his wallet he was having a little trouble deciding exactly what to do with it. He could have a good time in Moscow. Or he could keep going. The French were understanding of a man with money. They would grant him asylum. It would have to be on his terms, of course. But an apartment in Paris or perhaps a little house in the country wouldn't be so hard to take.

Someone in the Mercedes's back seat turned and looked out the rear window. Boyko could suddenly see a white round face beneath a dark hat. For just a moment he thought he was seeing a death's head, and it gave him such a start that he nearly stopped in his tracks. But then the figure turned away and the illusion was broken.

Reaching the rear of the big German car, Boyko held up Anna's letter. The back window on the passenger side came down. Boyko stepped over to it. The inside of the car was dark. He could only see a vague outline of the figure. He handed the letter through the window, and a gloved hand accepted it. Boyko opened his hand to receive the package of money, when an incredibly massive blow smashed into his chest, driving him backward off his feet onto the sidewalk. A thunderclap exploded in his ears, and he was having trouble catching his breath. His head bounced off the concrete, and as the Mercedes pulled away, two more jackhammer blows hit him in the chest and stomach. Only then did Boyko fully realize that he had been shot.

The bastards, he kept thinking as he fumbled in his coat pocket for his gun, but he couldn't seem to make anything work. He could feel that his left leg was twitching, but he could not still it.

A whistle blew somewhere very close. Perhaps he could hear a siren, too, but everything was so far away now, so unreal. Boyko realized he was dying. The bastards. It wasn't fair.

A wide, kindly face loomed over him. Something silver on the man's uniform epaulets caught a gleam of streetlight. He was saying something in Finnish.

Boyko reached up with bloody fingers and grasped a handful of the policeman's tunic. "The letter," he breathed in Russian. "The letter from Anna."

The cop said something in Russian, but Boyko did not hear him. A moment later his heart stopped.

The tall Frenchman dismissed his driver and strode purposefully across the lobby of the luxurious Hesperia Hotel just a few blocks from where Boyko lay dead. He took the elevator up to his fifth-floor room.

It was time now to return home to Marseille, and he was glad of it. Helsinki was far too cold for his liking.

He let himself in, and with a practiced eye scanned the room for any sign that his security precautions had been breached. But no one had been there. Before he took off his coat he withdrew a small electronic device from his pocket and quickly and efficiently swept the room for bugs. Satisfied at last that he was still clean, he opened Anna's letter, read enough of it to make certain it was the genuine article, and then took it into the bathroom where he turned on the exhaust fan. He burned each page over the toilet and flushed the ashes.

"Poor little Anna," he thought. It hadn't been her fault. But the timing had been off, had been terribly wrong. Though he himself did not know all the details, he had been impressed enough to do what was asked without hesitation or question. But he did not expect it would end so easily.

Back in the bedroom he picked up the telephone and had the operator place an overseas call for him. The connection was made in less than two minutes.

"Yes," the long-familiar voice answered.

"It is done."

"The letter has been destroyed?"

"Of course."

"There may be others. Someone coming to investigate. Someone from Moscow. I may need you again."

"If it is containment you wish, monsieur, you will have our complete cooperation as usual. There is too much at stake. Too much to lose."

"For all of us, Emile."

Afterward the Frenchman was slightly bothered by the fact that he hadn't been asked about Anna's letter. It seemed . . . cold, even to him.

3

Ten hours later outside Innsbruck, Austria, Jack Horn sat on the terrace of his hotel reading the newspapers while his children skied. The sun shone brilliantly on the mountains, but the wind was getting up; long ragged plumes moved off the snow-covered peaks in the distance like an old woman's white hair in a gale. A storm was forecasted.

"Marc and Marney absolutely refuse to come in, so I've confined them to the bunny hill behind the equipment shop," Christine Horn said, sitting beside her husband.

Horn looked up and accepted a kiss on the cheek. This was the third morning of their seven-day vacation, and already Christine had picked up his unsettled mood. Once a fieldman, always a fieldman—that was the catechism, wasn't it? Though he hadn't exactly languished as assistant chief of Berlin Station for the Central Intelligence Agency, the job wasn't as fulfilling as he had hoped it would be.

"Talk to them, would you?" she asked.

"Sure."

Their white-coated waiter came and she ordered more coffee. When he was gone, Horn reached out and covered his wife's hand with one of his. "Are you having a good time so far?"

She smiled. "A riot. Too bad you couldn't have come along. We're missing you." She was dressed in ski clothes, her yellow jacket open, a band around her hair.

"That bad?"

"That bad, Jack," she said earnestly. He looked out

toward the mountains and she followed his gaze. "Something is coming, isn't it. Something is in the wind. You can feel it, can't you. I'm picking it up from you."

Horn shrugged and looked deeply into his wife's eyes. She was beautiful. Two children had done little more than soften the bony edges of her once girlish figure, and now she was a woman with a special glow that he had come to not only love but deeply respect as well. They were well suited for each other, a handsome couple. Christine's height and long, silken blond hair, her nearly flawless complexion and innate sense of style perfectly complemented Horn's rugged good looks and six-foot, two-hundred-pound frame kept hard by a daily regimen of exercise in the station's gym. There was no finer sight alive, according to Christine, than Jack in a tuxedo. She would admit to a weakness for his advances when they were getting dressed to go out. As a result they were often fashionably late for parties, but they always arrived happy, if breathless. The Horns have that special something that is so rare among Americans these days, it was said of them. A perfect marriage. He was proud of her and of their marriage. It was a badge of honor he wore.

"Berlin has been getting on my nerves, I guess," he said vaguely.

"Maybe we should have gone home for a couple of weeks. See your mother, my father, Dan and Viv, the old crowd."

She always mixed her tenses when she wanted something from him. She was trying to be helpful, but he *was* feeling vague, indistinct, as if his vision had become blurred by his two-year posting. Time to move on? he wondered. But that was the easy way out, wasn't it? At a deeper level he was beginning to fear he was losing sight of why he had become a spy instead of a priest. It had only been in the last few years that his mother had finally accepted Christine as anything but the great destroyer, the devil's handmaiden, for turning Jack away from a life within the Church. A poor choice, a tiny voice in the darkest recesses of his brain had begun to nag. He'd probably develop a complex worrying about it. His own dissatisfaction would be his ruination; it got to all spies sooner or later. Self-doubt. The questions. The night sweats. The constant over-the-shoulder feeling that you were being followed. But what wife could hold up to such a comparison? What marriage? What children? The list was endless when this mood came on him. A Catholic nun wore a gold band on the third finger of her left hand to signify that she was married to Christ. Priests were out there alone, however, just like spies, with nothing but their faith and each other. A gigantic boy's club, his mentor, Doxy, was fond of saying— but then he'd always been in love with Christine, and he was an outrageously outspoken atheist. He was Jack's only real friend.

"Maybe for Easter," he said, but out of the corner of his eye he caught the arrival of Sam Morrison from Berlin Station. The terrace was long and narrow. Everyone was dressed in ski clothes except for the waiters and now Morrison. He carried an attaché case and stood out like a sore thumb.

Christine turned. "Oh, damn," she said, spotting him about the same time he spotted them and headed their way.

"I didn't know a thing about this," Horn replied to his wife's accusing glare. "I swear it."

"Something always comes up, doesn't it," she said harshly, not bothering to lower her voice. "Oh, Jack . . ."

Morrison was out of breath by the time he reached them. "They said you might be out on the slopes," he said with a touch of ironic envy. He was tall and thin and very pale. He absolutely despised the outdoors. He was posted to the station's consular section. His real job was as an analyst, an East Berlin watcher. In effect he was the odd lot; Mark Ryan, the Berlin COS, had the habit of using him for the out-of-place bits and pieces.

Christine got to her feet. "He's all yours, Sam," she said, and she stormed off without saying good-bye.

Morrison looked after her, and then sat down. He had the face of a hound dog, heavily lined and perpetually sad. He had a good sense of humor, though. If you lose that in this business, you're as good as dead, he was fond of saying.

"You're not exactly the most welcome sight around these parts," Horn said, curious nevertheless despite his own morose mood of introspection.

"As long as you don't shoot the messenger who brings the bad tidings, we'll get along just fine," Morrison said. "Is Christine okay? The kids?" He was married, but his only daughter was away at a boarding school in the States. He and his wife missed her.

"We were just discussing the possibility of going home. Maybe a little rejuve stateside."

"Later," Morrison said tersely. "In the meanwhile something has come up."

"I gathered as much," Horn said dryly.

"Mark sent me down with a brief. You'll have to familiarize yourself with the situation on the run, I'm afraid. I'm to get you to the Munich airport in time for the four o'clock to Helsinki." He looked at his wristwatch. "Gives us plenty of time if we don't dawdle."

"It's not one of my East Berlin madmen, is it?" Horn asked. Almost from the beginning of his career, Horn had been an agent runner. His specialty was getting himself into a hostile country, constructing a network of agents, then getting himself back out where he could collect the product in relative safety. It was a matter of recruitment and communication. He'd worked most of the Eastern bloc countries, and for the past two years he'd been running networks in East Berlin out of the station in West Berlin.

"This goes back a lot further than that," Morrison said. He glanced at the other diners to make sure he would not be overheard, then leaned in a little closer. "I mean way back, Jack. It was one of your Russian people. He's gotten himself killed in Helsinki."

Horn's training had prepared him extremely well for his particular specialty. He'd gotten his master's degree in languages and linguistics from Georgetown University. From there he was supposed to have gone on to the seminary, but Vietnam reared its ugly head, he'd met Christine, and the lure of doing something real and worthwhile with his training was too strong to deny. He admitted to himself later that a big factor in his decision was the plain and simple fact that he was tired of school. Vietnam had passed in a blur of intelligence work, often at the front lines as they constantly shifted and were redefined, and suddenly he was married, his training at the CIA's Farm outside Williamsburg was completed, and at the tender age of twenty-nine he found himself in Moscow. His assignment was to set up a network of agents at as many levels of government as he possibly could, with a mechanism that would allow for easy communications. But that had been a million years ago. Or, as Morrison put it, way back.

"I'll just get my things, then," Horn said, and went up.

Christine's mood was brittle. They agreed that she would remain in Innsbruck with the children for the remainder of their vacation. If Jack hadn't finished by then, she was to return to Berlin where Mark Ryan would take care of things for her. But she was a capable woman: intelligent, resourceful, and only just a little bitchy when things did not go her way. She usually got over those kinds of moods in a big hurry, however. It was another of her plus points.

"Where are you off to, Jack?" she asked as he set his bags by the door.

"Helsinki," he said. "But that's not for public broadcast, Christine."

"That's awfully close to Russia."

"Far enough."

She came across the room to him. She was still dressed in her ski clothes, whereas he had already changed. "No chance you'll be going in?"

"Not likely," he said. He took her into his arms and they looked into each other's eyes.

"But you don't know how long you'll be?"

"No."

She sighed a little, then shook her head ever so slightly. "Have I ever told you just how much I actually hate your job?"

Horn smiled softly. "Never."

"Well, I do," she said. They kissed deeply. "Come back to me," she said when they parted.

"I'll say good-bye to the kids. If I can find them."

Sam Morrison had waited patiently outside in his rental car so as not to attract any more attention then he already had. Snow was beginning to blow and the temperature had dropped, so he had the car running to keep warm. The children were understanding; they'd always been flexible. Before Horn got in the car he looked up at the fifth floor and thought he might have seen Christine at their window, but he wasn't sure. They were all the way out of Innsbruck before he thought to open Morrison's attaché case to read his brief, and then it felt as if he were coming home.

Once a fieldman, always a fieldman.

"Can you tell me why your government is so interested in a Soviet citizen?" Helsinki Detective Investigator Jean Paasiviki asked gruffly, his voice echoing off the stark white-tiled corridor walls.

It was past eight in the evening. Horn had come directly from the airport, sending his bags along to the Klaus Kurski Hotel. He hadn't expected to be welcomed to Helsinki with open arms, but the investigator's hostility was mildly surprising. Horn figured him either for a Communist or an astute observer who rightly guessed that more was going on here than met the eye, or both. In any event, holding the body without announcement for twenty-four hours had been a request from the U.S. embassy directly to his federal government. The investigator would follow his orders.

"We're not even certain it is the correct man," Horn said respectfully. "Sears Roebuck in Germany asked someone to look into it, from what I was told. This man was supposed to meet one of their representatives. This was a buying trip."

"So I was told," the investigator said with a certain sardonic amusement in his voice. "That doesn't explain how your embassy was notified of Comrade Boyko's untimely demise."

"I couldn't say," Horn said. "But we certainly appreciate your cooperation."

They reached the end of the basement corridor where they pushed through the set of swinging steel doors marked PATHOLOGY. An autopsy had already been performed, though the Soviet embassy still had not been informed that one of their citizens had been killed. The request for a hold had been initiated at the behest of the CIA (though Horn saw nothing in Morrison's brief that explained how they had found out about the murder in the first place), but it had been passed on by the U.S. embassy ostensibly at the request of Interpol. Under no circumstances, the brief specified, was this operation to be announced to be anything other than a civil police investigation. Horn had been supplied with a City of New York Police Department gold shield, which had further confused the investigator. The actual details had apparently been worked out at a much higher level within the Finnish government, and were none of the investigator's business.

They came into the operating theater. The room was very cold and smelled strongly of disinfectant. The investigator opened a body drawer in a broad cabinet along the back wall. The figure of a human being was shrouded in plastic.

"Had he been to New York?" the investigator asked. They spoke in English, though Horn's command of the Finnish language would have been adequate.

"Twice," Horn said. "My department was investigating possible illegal activities."

The investigator's eyebrows rose. "So?"

"He may have been purchasing drugs. Heroin. Cocaine."

"For importation to the Soviet Union?"

"We think it's possible."

"And the German Sears Roebuck people?"

"A coincidence, I think."

The investigator shook his head, either in amusement or disgust, it was hard for Horn to determine which. He wasn't buying the story, but he had his orders. He carefully undid the plastic and pulled it aside. Horn was instantly brought back to the old days. He involuntarily sucked in his breath.

"Vitali Boyko, according to the man's papers."

"It's him," Horn said. He'd been hit three times, once quite high in the chest, once a little lower, the angle more oblique—he'd probably been hit on the way down—and a third time in the stomach. A very large hole had been cut into his chest and stomach by the pathologist and then the gross flap of skin and tissue had been sewn loosely back into place. Boyko looked as if he had died as hard as he had lived. An opportunist. Definitely not a man to be trusted, but as long as he was given a little money and a job to do every now and then, he was fine. Like so many other traitors to their country, though, it wasn't so much the money that motivated them as it was a feeling of importance, a feeling that what they were doing was making a real difference in the world. It was all a delusion, of course. And there wasn't one of them among the successful doubles who didn't know it, yet the self-deception was their way of dealing with the aberrations in their personalities that made them what they were. A sociopath killed people without a twinge of conscience. A traitor had nearly the same relationship with his country, all his frequent protestations to the contrary notwithstanding.

"Have you seen enough, Mr. Horn?" the investigator asked.

Horn looked up and nodded. "What did he have with him? In his pockets, that is, and in his hotel room. It was searched?"

The investigator tucked the plastic back in place. "Besides the usual—his papers, of course, money, hairbrush, wallet, tissues—he was carrying an automatic pistol in his right coat pocket. Makarov, nine millimeter. Unfired. The officer first on the scene fancied he was trying to reach for it. Luggage in his room. Clothes. Nothing else."

Horn held himself in check. "Was he still alive, then?" he asked calmly.

The investigator closed the drawer. "He died in my officer's arms."

"Did he say anything? Last words, anything like that?"

"Six words. In Russian. 'The letter,' he said. And then a pause. His lungs were probably filling with blood. And finally, 'The letter from Anna.' Then he died."

"Could I have a look at this letter?" Horn asked. "Is that possible?"

"He had no letter on him, Mr. Horn. Possibly it was something he wanted to accomplish before he died. Perhaps he was telling my man that he wanted his Anna to be notified."

Or, Horn thought, whoever had killed him at one o'clock in the morning within sight of the President's Palace, the City Hall, and the Swedish Theater had taken the letter. But who was Anna? Where was Anna? What did she have to do with the old network? And why, after all these years, had someone suddenly decided that Boyko was a threat to anyone?

"Did you know this Anna?"

"I'm afraid not, Investigator. But you say your patrolman was near enough to reach Boyko before he died. Might he have witnessed the actual shooting?"

"He was around the block, Mr. Horn. On foot. He heard the shots and came running. By the time he reached the scene the killer or killers had fled."

"On foot? By car?"

"Possibly by car. My officer reported seeing a large automobile, possibly a Mercedes, though he could not be certain, turning the corner toward the Aleksanterinkatu."

"I see," Horn said. They had moved across the room and were once again out in the corridor. They shook hands. "Thank you for your kind help, Investigator."

"Just one question, Mr. Horn. When we turn his body over to his embassy, would you like us to pass along any messages?"

Horn smiled and shook his head. "Not necessary. In fact I'd say it would *not* be advisable under the circumstances. This is an undercover investigation." He looked into the investigator's eyes. "And we can never be quite sure exactly whom to trust, can we."

The statement so startled the investigator, he found himself speechless. Horn gave a final nod, then turned and left, his footfalls on the tiled floor like pistol shots down a very long, dark tunnel, dangerous but thankfully receding.

4

Stockholm was busy. Alive. Bustling. Clean. It was, except for its climate, one of Jack Horn's favorite cities. It was also a frequently used preliminary debriefing area for agents leaving the Soviet Union and a staging area for agents about to enter the country. Riding into the city from Arlanda Airport with the taciturn driver they'd sent for him, Horn had mixed feelings. He'd be getting his brief here, and he suspected he'd be asked to go back into the Soviet Union. It bothered him to be going back into the fray on the heels of the death of one of his old madmen, and yet it somehow felt right. Chefs should cook, he once read. Poets should write. And operatives should spy. He'd once tried to explain his feelings to Christine, but she had strong notions of nesting and security. "Let someone else do it, Jack," was her standard theme. "You've done your bit for God and country. For heaven's sake, you spent nearly four years in Vietnam getting shot at. What more do they expect?" She believed in her country, she believed in the right of self-defense, and even in the much abused domino theory that said once a country—Nicaragua, for instance—fell to the Communists, then the rest of the region might go as well. Horn suspected, however, that she paid only lip service to that belief simply because she was married to him. If she were married to someone else, she'd gladly abandon that opinion for a more popular view such as, What the hell are we doing there? Yet for all her bravado about America's right to defend herself, Horn knew that when the time came for her Marc to join the military—a time not so terribly far off—Christine would be first in line with her stop-the-war-now banners. Joan Baez would be there, singing protest songs, and doves would fly overhead in perfect formation. The day was coming when she would become a zealot, strongly opposed to any fighting anywhere. His explanations that his job was meant to prevent global confrontations from happening fell on deaf ears so long as there was a possibility of him going back into the field. "For God's sake, Jack," she had said a few weeks before they'd gone on their Innsbruck vacation, "you're forty-three years old. Time to come in from the cold. Hitch your wagon to a nice, safe, comfortable desk. Virginia is lovely any time of the year."

The house just off Old Town's Stortorget was tall and white and very Scandinavian with a steep roof line, neat trim, and pretty flowers painted beneath all the windows. The entrance was behind a tall stone wall, but the narrow cobble-stoned driveway swung around to the back, affording absolute privacy for anyone coming or going. His driver took care of his bags as Horn went into the house. He'd been there before several times. It was like coming home all over again, strange and exciting and frightening all at once. Dropping his coat over a pine deacon's bench in the entry hall, he passed the living room and went back to the study.

"Ah, Jack, we didn't hear you come in," Farley Carlisle, assistant deputy director of Operations out of Langley, said, rising. He was a short, dark little ferret of a man whom no one liked but everyone respected.

Two other men were seated in the big, book-lined room. They rose as Horn entered.

"Didn't expect to see you here, Farley," Horn said, crossing the room to his old supervisor. They'd worked together in Moscow in the early days.

They shook hands. Carlisle made the introductions. "I don't think you know either Bill Oestmann, COS Helsinki, or Dewey Nobels, most recently our number two man out of Moscow Station."

They shook hands and exchanged pleasantries. Oestmann was an Austrian, Horn suspected from the man's accent, which made Helsinki an odd posting, though the Finns had been collaborators with the Germans during much of the war. Sympathies tended to run for a long time before they died out, if indeed they ever did. Nobels was a tall, academic-looking man with dark, penetrating eyes and longish hair that seemed to fly out in all directions at once. He'd smoked a pipe for a lot of years. His yellowed teeth were crooked where he'd clamped down on the stem. In Horn's mind now, the death of one of his old network men had taken on a new significance because of Carlisle's presence. He'd expected someone from Moscow Station, of course, and perhaps someone from the European Operations office in Paris, but Carlisle was a heavy hitter.

"Sit, sit," Carlisle blurted. "Can I get you something, Jack. Coffee? Something a little stronger? Your flight out was pleasant under the circumstances, I hope?"

"A little brandy, thanks, Farley. And the flight was fine, but my reception in Helsinki was something less than cordial." He glanced at Oestmann.

"We wanted to avoid any direct contact with you, Mr. Horn," Oestmann said distantly, crossing his legs. "Created enough of a stir as it was."

"A big mess, if you ask me," Carlisle said from the sideboard where he was pouring the brandy. "It has the undivided attention of the seventh floor, if you know what I mean. Undivided." He came back with the drink, handed it to Horn, and took his place on the couch. "We have a lot of ground to cover, but in the meantime, how is Christine, and those lovely children of yours . . . Marc and Marney?"

He should have been on the final run for the job of deputy director of the Company, but it was said that something had happened during his tenure in Moscow in the Mahoney days. Allusions to all sorts of dark stories had floated around Langley and out in the field for years. Mahoney was not saying anything from his fortress out in Minnesota or Wisconsin or wherever, and of course Carlisle couldn't be asked. One wondered, however.

"Just fine, thanks," Horn said. "Actually Christine was a little put out that our vacation was cut short."

"We'll make it up to her," Carlisle said earnestly, thus answering in Horn's mind at least the question of duration. "And to you. On that, Jack, you have my solemn word. In the meanwhile, I'm afraid you're in the hot seat. This Boyko, Vitali I., was your boy, after all. You created him."

"What was he doing in Helsinki?"

"Just our question, Jack, among a million others. What

indeed! He's not been active for years. What set him off all of a sudden? Any guesses you'd like to hazard on that score?''

"And who killed him?" Horn asked.

Carlisle glanced at Oestmann and Nobels, then blew air out of his mouth all of a sudden as if he had just run up a steep hill. "Who indeed? Oh, yes, who indeed?" he asked, his voice soft, almost reverential in the face of such a question after he'd asked one of his own.

Histrionics, Horn wondered, or was this the real thing? With Carlisle it had always been hard to tell, except that the man did get things done. And besides, no one came to Stockholm in January on vacation. Horn drank his brandy and set the glass aside.

They had gathered, according to Carlisle, not to pick over the bones of an old, dead agent, but to explore every avenue lest they be caught at some future date with their trousers down around their ankles as the fire bell sounded. There was a very real possibility that Boyko had decided to come over and had been killed for his attempt. But he would not have come empty-handed, which brought up the question of exactly what it was he had brought with him, if anything, and where he had gotten his information.

Who could know?

Normally it was the number two man's job in any station to run his agents. Stringers was their official title, but Horn preferred madmen, because that's what they were in his estimation. According to Nobels, none of the old networks were still active. They'd all been shut down, some of them years ago. And he would have been the one to know about any reactivation.

"We've got our own stringers these days. They're hooked more into the military-industrial complex and less into the low levels of government. Paper work can't hurt us near as much as missiles and guns."

"We neither want nor do we deserve a policy statement at this juncture, Dewey," Carlisle warned. "Let's keep to the question at hand, shall we?"

Nobels began to stuff his pipe with tobacco from a scuffed leather pouch. He nodded. "I've spent the last eight or ten weeks dusting off the stringer files, getting them into shape for the new man. I'm out of Moscow, officially, as of yesterday. I wanted to put the house in order so he could take over from where I left off without leaving anyone in the lurch, or any operation without a rudder.''

"We put Van Howard in there. Just came up from Athens. Good man. He'll do a bang-up job for us," Carlisle said into the momentary breach.

"The operations list is divided into two sections, of course, just as it was in your day in Moscow. Active files on the right, the inactive dossiers on the left. Except that nowadays the inactive list is twice as long as the other side.''

"More for the money?" Horn couldn't help asking.

Nobels and Oestmann both grinned at the bit of irreverence, but Carlisle scowled.

"Actually we're spending twice as much. The new routine now is to keep a loose watch on a select few of the inactives on a rotating basis.''

"Why?" Horn asked. "If they're inactive, surely they've been isolated as well. I mean, you do change the locks on all the doors when you kick out the tenant, don't you?''

"Not always possible, we've found," Carlisle put in before Nobels could reply. "You're not having that kind of a problem in Berlin . . . at least not to the extent they've been experiencing in Moscow. The KGB has been having its successes too, you know.''

"Boyko is one of them?"

Nobels had finished packing his pipe. As he lit it he nodded over the bowl. "Works with the Foreign Trade Ministry.''

"Did from the beginning.''

"Supervisory staff now. Comes and goes pretty much as he pleases. Last year alone he left the Soviet Union on seventeen separate occasions. Pimping mostly, for the foreign currency stores. A shrewd buyer, from what I gather. Comes in with a trainload of goodies practically every time he goes out. But that's not all." He settled back in his chair, a haze of blue smoke around his head.

"He's brought women back with him," Carlisle said.

"Prostitutes?" Horn asked.

"Exactly.''

"French, mostly," Nobels continued. "They seem to be popular just now. He brings along a half-dozen signed visas with him to Paris, picks up that many high-priced girls, whisks them back to Moscow for a long weekend of fun and games, and whisks them back out. Neat, clean, no one gets hurt, and everyone comes away happy.''

Was Anna one of those girls with a story to tell? Horn asked himself. It opened up a lot of interesting possibilities.

"No mention was made of any girls in Helsinki," Horn said.

"Not this time," Carlisle said. "In fact Boyko hadn't been out for more than forty-eight hours when he was gunned down, and he certainly hadn't moved out of Helsinki in that time."

"You were following him?" Horn asked. He was starting to get the feeling that not only was there a whole lot being held back from him, but that both Carlisle and Nobels were beating around the bush.

"No," Nobels said. "Bill picked up on him from this side."

"He had a KGB tail. We watch for those sorts of things," Oestmann put in.

"Just wait a minute here," Horn protested. "Are you trying to tell me that you have an old madman running French whores in and out of Moscow on a regular basis, to sleep presumably with high-ranking Soviet officials—because they're the only ones who could afford such little weekends, right? You're telling me that Boyko, the little procurer, coming and going into all these important bedrooms, is not number one on your very *most* active list? You're telling me that you've literally thrown away a gold seam? The entire bloody mine?''

"Easy now," Carlisle said.

"What the hell have you people been doing?" Horn asked angrily. He could feel his blood pressure rising. After all the work of setting up a network, when it finally began to pay off, and pay off big, they'd thrown it away.

"Boyko couldn't be trusted," Nobels said indignantly.

"What spy can be?"

"You don't know him like I do," Nobels said.

Horn turned to Carlisle. "What kind of a joke is this, Farley? Your people have apparently blown a perfectly good man, and then when he comes out you can't even protect him. Instead, you let his own people kill him."

"We didn't say that," Carlisle hastened to put in. "Not that, Jack. We have no idea who killed him yet, or why."

Horn was almost dizzy. The incompetence in the study was thicker than Nobels's pipe tobacco smoke. He glanced at the

Helsinki COS. "You said your people picked up Boyko's KGB tail. That right?"

Oestmann looked a little pale. "We lost him."

"The tail?"

"Boyko."

"If the KGB nailed him, they were working split teams and knew all about Bill's people," Carlisle explained.

"I think I have it now, Farley. Oh, yes, I think I see, all right."

"Now listen here, I don't have to take this prima donna crap," Oestmann sputtered, sitting forward.

"At ease, mister," Carlisle snapped. "Just hold it now."

Why was it, Horn asked himself, that so many in this business were filled with their little bon mots and homilies? Maybe it was the constant danger that fieldmen experienced, and all of them in this room had been there at one time or another, that caused every agent he knew to dissemble as an everyday routine of life. They all told stories to each other, and among themselves it seemed that every human possibility was reduced to a quip, or a clever bit of syntax.

"What do you want from me, Farley?" Horn asked. "For me to play detective? Find Boyko's murderers? And when the trail leads back to Lubyanka, then what? Shall I storm the prison walls for you? Is that what you want?"

"There was no reason for him to have been shot down like that," Carlisle said. He lowered his head and rubbed his eyes with the thumb and forefinger of his right hand. He was a man, he was announcing in his own way, who was cursed with too many burdens. Atlas, with the world on his shoulder, got tired from time to time. "But it had all the earmarks of a standard Center assassination."

"He got in somebody's way."

"Indeed," Carlisle said, looking up. His eyes were red and naked-looking. It made him seem somehow vulnerable. "A little indiscretion here, a loose lip there, might have done him in, I guess. *Might* have mind you. It's all I'm admitting to at this stage of the game. But on the other hand, Jack, think of the services he'd been providing for his masters. Trinkets and chocolates and bright little baubles to keep the wives and babushkas happy, and *poules de Paris* to keep Ivan sated. Killing him would be like cementing up the cornucopia. It certainly makes no sense from where I sit. Does it to you? Can you see the internal logic? I mean was Boyko such a grating little sleaze that they'd follow him all the way out to Helsinki so that they could have the pleasure of gunning him down under the real risk of prosecution? Does that drip with logic to you, Jack?''

Horn said nothing. It had been a letter *from* Anna. If she were one of Boyko's French tarts, it would mean she was being held within the Soviet Union. Boyko had presumably been taking the letter out, not in. But to whom had the letter been addressed? Who could help such a woman get out of the Soviet Union? And why had Boyko risked everything for her? Love? Or was something else missing here? The latter, he suspected.

Carlisle was watching him. He shook his head sadly. ''What I'm trying to say to you in my own sometimes oblique way, what I'm trying to get across to you, Jack, is the very real and frightening—at least to me—possibility that Boyko was shot and killed because he was coming over to us, coming to collect a debt of service, coming with something in hand . . .'' He hesitated and Nobles stepped in.

''With something that could blow our entire Moscow operation completely out of the water.''

Carlisle shot him a harsh look but did not contradict him. ''Do you see what I'm getting at, Jack?''

''He wasn't active and hadn't been for years, isn't that so?'' Horn asked.

''He knew a lot of names. Still. Contact routines, letter drops. They had their groups in those days, and some of them are still active in an offhand way, if you catch my drift.''

Horn didn't, but he held his peace. Who was Anna? What was Anna?

''On the other side of the coin, he presumably knew the bedroom habits of his masters, as you suggest. Powerful stuff, that. In this I will have to admit your logic. However, I still keep coming back to his early work for us. What if—now just bear with me a moment longer, Jack, please—what if all those years Boyko had been a double? Just suppose he had worked for you—for us—while reporting back to the KGB? What happens if for all those years he was making absolute fools of all of us? One hand waving in our faces while the other played nasty little tricks behind our backs?''

''So what, Farley? What's done is done. He hadn't been active for years. Must I keep repeating myself?''

''He knew too much,'' Carlisle said, sitting forward for

emphasis. "Or if he'd taken the tumble, if they'd brought him over to Dzerzhinsky Square and pumped his grubby little body full of drugs, and he spilled all his lovely little secrets, mightn't the KGB even now be infiltrating all our in-place networks? So he got cold feet, is all. Decided he owed us something, decided a dacha in Iowa was better than a bullet in the brain in Moscow, and he made a run for it. Only they're a lot smarter than that, so they followed him out and shot him dead. But they waited until Helsinki to see who his contact might be. Maybe get two for one."

"What happened back in Helsinki?" Oestmann asked softly. "Did you see the body? Did you speak with the investigating officers?"

Horn might not have heard him. His thoughts had turned inward, back to the old days of ten, fifteen years ago, then forward to the letter from Anna. Was there a bridge from the one to the other, with Boyko as the time rider? Did he know the risk he had taken? Did he understand that someone would be coming in the night to shoot him down? Was that why he had carried a pistol? Why hadn't he pulled it out? Why had he allowed himself to get into such a situation? From all that Horn remembered of Boyko—and he remembered a great deal, because he never forgot a single one of his madmen—he had been the slippery one who knew and played all the angles. But Boyko had been a devout coward, the kind who would, without hesitation or compunction, abandon the best-laid plan to take himself out of risk. He was careful for himself. "No one else gives a damn, you know," he would say. "We Russians have learned how to take care of ourselves. How else do you think we would have survived two bad wars, and an even worse reign of Stalin? No, my friend, we have had centuries of practice taking care, even while your Indians were running around Manhattan Island in loincloths." With Boyko, he thought, the answers—if they were ever found—would be neither simple nor pleasant.

He looked up and sighed. "I think you were absolutely right to call me, Farley. I think Boyko was on to something, and I think he was killed for it."

"He was not merely coming over?"

"I don't think so. No, I don't really think it is going to be that easy."

Carlisle sagged a little. He nodded as he sat back. "What

do you need, Jack? What do you want from us? Anything. Anything at all.''

"Will you be going in?" Nobels asked.

Horn ignored him, turning instead back to Oestmann, on whose turf this had happened. The Helsinki COS was a ruggedly built man a few years younger than Horn. A long scar ran from the right side of his mouth across his chin and then halfway up his neck to the base of his ear. Plastic surgery could have hidden the scar, but Horn had a feeling the man wore it as a mark of some sort of courage. Like the dueling scars of the last century. His eyes were cruel, his hair and his dress and his manner precise in a way that only a haughty Austrian could carry off.

"Boyko had a tail. Tell me about that. Right up to the shooting, please."

Oestmann hesitated, but then Carlisle nodded for him to go ahead. After all, they were all among friends here, weren't they?

Helsinki Station owed its primary importance to the simple fact that Finland and the Soviet Union were next-door neighbors. Finnair and Aeroflot exchanged flights on a regular basis between Helsinki, Leningrad, and Moscow, daily train service operated between the two countries, and the highway that crossed near the Soviet city of Vyborg was well traveled. Helsinki was the first Western capital most Russians encountered in their travels, and the city was becoming the Lisbon for the eighties in terms of intelligence activities.

Oestmann had a lot of legmen assigned to him. On the morning of February second, one of his teams reported the entry of two known KGB fieldmen on the direct flight from Moscow.

"We have a standard operating procedure in these instances: tail them, but do not interfere," Oestmann explained. "Usually they are merely passing through, but this time it was odd. They weren't in such a big hurry. Before long my people realized the Russians had followed one of their own people out."

"Was Boyko traveling alone?"

"Yes. We followed them over to the Hesperia, which is Helsinki's finest hotel, and then Boyko did the town, his baby-sitters in tow. The man was a regular dynamo. I don't think he ever slept. He knows a lot of the suppliers in town.

When he comes in they gather around him like moths around a flame because he always travels with Western currencies, and he throws a pretty good party."

"You knew Boyko, then?"

"Only by reputation, Mr. Horn. I've seen his photograph, but I've never personally laid eyes on the man." Oestmann's on-again, off-again formality was odd.

"This was the first time he came out with a tail?" Horn asked.

"So far as I know. We haven't made a habit of watching him. No intelligence value . . . to us. In that we would have required direction from Moscow Station."

"No bickering now, please. We have work to do, and a lot of miles yet to travel," Carlisle said boyishly. The sword evidently cut both ways.

"Did you think this time, because of his tail, that something might be up?" Horn asked.

"My best guess was that Boyko was going to abscond with Foreign Ministry funds. Such things have happened before. It wouldn't be unheard of."

"And your team was ready to accept him if he decided to make his move?"

"Only in the broadest sense of the term. We'd made no specific plans. We weren't all that certain, of course, and, as I said, my brief is quite clear on the subject: follow the KGB, but do not interfere. We've often gotten ourselves into quite a jam with the Finns because of an overenthusiastic station chief." Oestmann looked to Carlisle who nodded sagely for him to continue. "The Finnish government knows we're in place. And they don't like it. But as long as no one upsets the apple cart, nothing is said."

"That is why there is such a flap over his killing," Carlisle explained. "The Finns are a tidy lot; they don't like their streets bloodied."

"We kept one of our people at the hotel in case Boyko began to make his moves, but for the most part he did nothing but party for forty-eight hours."

"For the most part?" Horn asked. "What do you mean by that?"

"Just bear with us a bit longer, Jack," Carlisle said. "Please."

"As long as you were following his tails, you were following him," Horn said, trying a new tack.

"So we thought. On the night of his murder, the fourth, Boyko and his entourage spent the early part of the evening at the Adlon. It's a nicer nightclub on the Fabianinkatu. But at ten he suddenly splits from his crowd and makes his way back to his hotel. His baby-sitters tag along, of course, and back at the Hesperia it seems like they're all settling in for the night. Boyko has evidently run out of steam." Oestmann shrugged deprecatingly. "The next thing we heard, Boyko had been gunned down on the street half a block from the Swedish Theater."

"Barely thirty-six hours ago," Horn said.

"That's right . . ."

"Why was I called so quickly?" Horn asked Carlisle. "The timing doesn't seem right to me somehow." He glanced again at Oestmann, but the man seemed to have a clear conscience. He didn't seem to be hiding anything of importance.

"We would have gotten around to you sooner or later in any event, Jack," Carlisle said. "Bill put the first encounter on the wire with a query tag: 'Any significance to a defecting Boyko?' Showed up in my bin, naturally. I was working late that night—otherwise there would have been no action for another twelve hours. I queried Dewey, needless to say, and it is to his credit that he was so quick on the draw. He shot back that Boyko was on the inactives list he was watching. Which rang a bell for me. Something was happening." Carlisle pointed to his midsection. "I could feel it here, Jack. I hopped a plane to see if we couldn't set up some sort of a meet with him. But I was too late. My fault, actually. I should have been more specific in my instructions to Bill."

It was big of Carlisle to admit his mistakes like that, but uncharacteristic, Horn thought. Something else had happened . . . something else was surely going on here.

"It's a little odd, Farley, to my way of thinking, for the assistant DDO to haul himself all the way out here for a second-rate sleaze who hadn't been active in the old Moscow network for years, wouldn't you say?"

Again Carlisle blew air out of his mouth as if he were getting set for his morning aerobics. He and Oestmann exchanged glances. "We're going to hold nothing back from you, Jack. Absolutely nothing, do you hear? I want you to be one hundred percent on that score."

Horn didn't quite know what to say, so he said nothing.

"Boyko did more than just party in Helsinki. In fact he did

something very significant. He made a telephone call to Paris. To an old number, a very old number. The safety valve. Surely you remember.''

Horn could feel his insides knotting up. Once again he found himself being hauled back to his Moscow days, and it was as if someone had forcibly pulled him from a warm safe place into a maelstrom. A very old Paris number. The only number that could have triggered Carlisle to come all the way to Sweden on such short notice was the old network's safety valve, the emergency number. It was the Mayday channel. SOS. Help me now, I am drowning. Help me now, they're about to drop the bloody atomic bomb down my chimney. Help me now, this is a flash. Most urgent. Lives are at stake here.

"What did he say, Farley?" he heard himself asking. "There were a lot of good people in that network. Most of them are still out on the limb, exposed."

"I know. It's why I came as quickly as I could," Carlisle said. "Something must be done, Jack. Now. And you're the one to do it. You know them all. You can pick up their trail, find out what's going on."

"The old leads to the new, doesn't it? That's what has you frightened."

"There's a lot at stake here."

"Boyko wasn't much, as a man," Horn said, remembering. "Unreliable. Untrustworthy. But his product was almost always good. We could never fault that."

"No. Of course not. All your madmen were fine," Carlisle admitted impatiently.

"What did he tell Paris?"

"The number is no longer operational; per se, you know. Automatic switching brings it across to the incoming security desk."

"Recorded?"

"No. Unfortunately not from that line. And the woman who took the call isn't at all sure about his exact words, except that he was supposed to call back. He was specific about that. There would be a second contact."

"Did he call back?"

"No," Carlisle said, sighing. "Just the one call from Helsinki within six hours of his arrival. Just the one with a very strange message. Very strange indeed. No one has been able to make hide nor hair out of it."

"What was the message, Farley? Exactly," Horn asked. But he had a feeling he knew what it was.

"He said he had a letter from Anna. No last name. No details other than to say if he was put in contact with someone in authority, someone at the consular level at least who could make decisions, he would tell everything. And it was big, he said. Very big."

A letter from Anna, Horn thought. An enigmatic telephone message, and the last words of a dying man.

"Plug the gaps, Jack," Carlisle said. "Return to Helsinki or go to Paris or get yourself to Moscow, but whatever you do, find out what that nasty little man was up to that got him killed. There's more at stake here than even you can imagine."

Carlisle and the others had gone. Looking out an upstairs window that night, Horn could see the Stock Exchange building on the other side of Stortorget. The Swedish Academy met on the second floor where they decided each year who would receive the Nobel Prize in Literature. There was no lights on over there tonight; their work was done for the moment, whereas his was just beginning. He thought about Boyko in the early days. The kid had had a lot of street savvy; it was his upbringing. Even in those days no one particularly liked him, which was why he had warmed up so quickly to Horn's advances. Horn thought about the first little dances and approaches, the sly innuendos, the flirting that was common both to young lovers on their first meetings, and agent runners courting their madmen. Boyko's turning hadn't been difficult, as some of them had been; he'd practically jumped into their laps once he realized that he was wanted—that someone actually *wanted* him. Still, no one liked or trusted him in those days.

Finally, he had gotten himself dead. The problem was, how many others would go with him? How like a house of cards had the Moscow network become? How many bridges between then and now existed? How many fragile structures would topple? How high would the casualty list reach? And in the end he owed it to them, didn't he? He had promised them his undying loyalty. If ever they needed him, he'd said, he'd come. Youthful words. First loves were always the most intense, and at least for Horn the least easily forgotten. He'd thought about his first madmen often. In the night, alone, waiting somewhere with only himself for company, he would see their faces, hear their voices. As the years progressed the memories had not become any dimmer. "You're eating yourself alive," Christine had told him, making a rather accurate stab in the dark. "Forward is the only direction, son," Doxy said.

A letter from Anna, Boyko had told the Paris number. *A letter from Anna*, he'd told a cop in Helsinki with his dying breath.

The call from Washington so close on the heels of the Helsinki business had not come as much of a surprise for Emile LeBec. But it was annoying nonetheless because it forced him to accept the fact that he was going to be busy for quite a long while. And it was going to be dangerous. But he was being paid well. Almost too well.

His plane arrived at Stockholm's Arlanda Airport very late and he took a taxi to the Resien, a small, comfortable hotel downtown on Skeppsbron, registering under the name Renauld Entremont. There was nothing to be done this evening, which was too bad, because he preferred the cover of darkness. But he'd been told to wait until morning so that he would be absolutely certain of his target. He had a description, and he had even managed to come up with a photograph as well as a plan. So wait he would, for LeBec was a man who knew not only how to follow orders, but how to carry them out with dispatch and imagination. He had a flair for his work, and almost no conscience.

He spent a restful night, and in the morning arose early, showered and shaved, and dressed in a conservatively cut, obviously expensive business suit. With his briefcase in hand, he took a cab into Old Town, getting off a few blocks from the Stock Exchange where he merged anonymously with the morning traffic.

He reached Stortorget Square a few minutes before seventhirty. Although the business day had not yet begun, many employees had already shown up at the Stock Exchange, so the doors were open and no one paid any attention to another man dressed in business clothes and carrying a briefcase.

Looking neither right nor left, he marched down the corridor to the rear stairs, which he took up past the second floor to the roof. The heavy steel door was locked, but it took him only thirty seconds to pick the old brass lock and let himself out.

The morning was overcast and very cold. He slipped his knife between the door and its steel frame so that it could not be opened from inside, then cautiously approached the edge of the roof. He studied the traffic for a moment down on the square, and then let his gaze rise to the tall white house directly across. From where he stood he had a line to the upper-story windows, as he expected he would after studying the city maps and Stockholm Directory the day before.

He would have plenty of time. All the time he needed.

Stepping back away from the edge, he opened his briefcase and began to assemble his rifle.

5

It was a question of a visa. Horn's, under the workname
Jack Horton, would not be ready for another twenty-four
hours. During that time he was not to contact anyone outside
the Stortorget house, especially no one from Berlin Station,
and most definitely not Christine. All that would be taken
care of for him. In fact an emissary would be going out to
Berlin the very day that Christine and the children returned
from vacation. As Carlisle had explained on parting: "This is
a big thing, Jack. It's possible they'll be watching for you, or
someone like you to make a move. So we're going to have to
play by the old rules with this one. I don't want Christine in
any possible danger, nor would I suspect you want such a
thing. We're going to have to be very circumspect here. Very
circumspect indeed. You are no longer Horn, you are Horton,
a relatively low-ranking officer in the consular section on
rotation to Moscow. Bob Early is the COS. Capable man.
One of the very best. Tops. He'll help you set up an appropriate legend for yourself so that you can run around Moscow
without raising too many eyebrows. But it won't last, Jack. It
simply will not last, so you're going to have to shake a leg,
be quick about it."

The safe house was empty of staff this time around. The
solitude was surprisingly pleasant in the evening and early-
morning hours. It had been a long time since he'd been on his
own like this. Around seven he arose and showered while the
coffee brewed. From the second-floor sitting room he watched

the square coming alive with the day as he began to prepare himself for Moscow.

Late in the evening a courier had brought over the standard Soviet Union kit for new hands, incoming, which included the ubiquitous hardcover green volume from the State Department, *Handbook for the U.S.S.R.* Someone at the Stockholm embassy had gone to the trouble of red-penciling the table of contents for items of interest to a man such as Horn who had not been a Moscow habitué for ten years or longer. A lot of things should have changed in those years, yet reading through the underlined passages he began to get the feeling that Moscow would never change. Nothing was different—at least nothing on the broader level. Such concerns as détente or tensions because of Afghanistan were so topical that they could only be properly assimilated by what were termed on-site briefings, which he presumed Bob Early would take care of for him once he arrived.

Most obviously missing from the briefs that had been delivered to him were any mention, even in the vaguest of terms, about existing Moscow networks: the agents as well as their runners; the ongoing long-term projects; the latest bits of work; what was in and what was not. In fact not a single word was written about any aspect of the Agency's Moscow mission, an omission he found decidedly odd in view not only of the sensitive nature of his assignment, but also in view of Carlisle's repeated assertion to the effect that absolutely nothing would be held back from him. He was to be told everything, the light would shine, according to Carlisle, on every little nook and cranny so long as that was what he required.

It was the way all assignments began, though. Disjointed, loose ends everywhere, dark little secrets that once the entire picture was understood seemed perhaps only shabby and not so dark after all. It was a matter of assimilating everything at once, impossible, but really it was the only way. Which meant that incoming agents were almost always a confused lot.

"I smelled the coffee," Dewey Nobels said at the head of the stairs.

Horn turned as the outgoing Moscow hand came across the upstairs hall, shedding his coat and draping it over a stand. "I didn't hear you come in."

Nobels smiled, the gesture weak, false. "I thought I'd drop by for a chat before you went off to the hinterland."

"Does Farley know you've returned?"

"Farley is on his way to the airport. He's returning to Washington. But yesterday he told me to hold nothing back, not a single thing."

Nobels sat down across the small table. He glanced out the window at the traffic on the Stortorget as Horn poured him a cup of coffee.

"After a time you forget what it's really like on the outside," Nobels said wistfully.

"How long had you been posted to Moscow?"

"Three years," Nobels said tiredly. "Three damned, awful years."

"Where to now?"

"Home, on the Russian desk for at least six months, I suppose. Then I'd like to go someplace sunny for a change. Warmth. With big air-conditioned cars and silly television shows." Nobels shook his head. "Probably send me to Afghanistan." He noticed the stack of books and reports at Horn's elbow. "Doing your homework, I see."

"Not much there."

"I think you're wasting your time. I think the KGB did the poor bastard in. And it was about time, I'd say."

"You had something against him?"

"I never really knew him all that well, but what I did know was that he was a little opportunist who'd sell anything or anybody for a buck . . . and I do mean a dollar. Strictly a hard currency man."

"Quite a feeling to have for a man you only watch sporadically," Horn suggested mildly.

"Boyko has been easy to get to know. Not like some of the others."

Horn raised his right eyebrow. "Others?"

"Some of the old network, some of the newer ones. Not all of this goes back to your early Moscow days. There were other agent runners posted to Moscow."

"Including you," Horn conceded. "You must have had quite a busy three years what with establishing your own madmen, all the while watching for strays from the old business."

"I have a staff."

"Oh, I'll bet you do."

"Listen here, Mr. Horn, I didn't come by to be insulted."

"No offense intended, believe me," Horn apologized. He

was feeling a little mean this morning for some reason. "It's simply that I'm having a little trouble getting a handle on all of this."

"It's why Farley suggested I return."

"He did?" Horn asked, catching the man in a little white lie. The first of many, he suspected. Nobels had intimated that coming back here was his idea. "What did he suggest you tell me? What ground were we supposed to cover this morning?"

"Whatever you wanted to know."

He'd suspected all along that the delay with his visa was a ruse for something else. It had bothered him until now. The CIA had, for a long time now, maintained what was called a hopefuls list. On a regular basis, worknames and backgrounds were selected and visa applications were submitted to the Soviet government. As each visa was issued, the workname went on a very short list of hopefuls. Agents ready for rotation into Moscow were assigned the workname and background and were sent off. The Agency was almost never without its short list. Delays, therefore, were very rare. Carlisle had wanted Horn to settle down in isolation for a little while, give him a chance to smooth his ruffled feathers for the rough way in which Christine had been handled, and then the real work would begin. Oestmann, he suspected, had been included in the initial meeting purely out of courtesy for the fact that the assassination had taken place on his turf.

"It's been nearly fifteen years since I was in Moscow."

"Exactly."

"But nothing has changed," Horn said, laying a hand on the stack of books and folders. "Networks have been shifted around, of course, but I assume our goals are basically the same."

"Nothing is the same, Mr. Horn. Believe me, everything is different. It changed even in the three years of my posting." Nobels took out his pipe and looked into the empty bowl. "It'll be startling for you." He looked up. "A different game altogether."

"In what way?"

"The KGB is more sophisticated. In fact they're learning by leaps and bounds."

"The rest of the world hasn't exactly been at a standstill, you know."

Nobels gestured with his pipe for emphasis. "The computer age had come to the Soviet Union . . . or at least to Moscow.''

"Computers still need input. That takes legwork—watchers, listeners, men on the street. But what about Boyko? What's he been up to all these years since I got out?''

Nobels said nothing.

"You came here to tell me about him, didn't you?''

"Sure.''

"So why the reticence? What's going on that I should know about but that apparently has you scared silly? Has it to do with the French whores he was bringing in?''

"They'd be a gold seam all right, just as you suggested, but we've been told hands off," Nobels blurted.

"By whom?''

"I don't know. What I meant to say is that no one directly told me to leave Boyko alone. I inherited the situation. I watch him coming and going from the country, and that's it. Beyond that, we don't go much further.''

"How do you know about the women he brings in?''

"You'd have to be blind not to see it. He comes through Sheremetyevo as bold as brass with half a dozen girls on his arm. They disappear for the long weekend and then he shows up Sunday night to see them off.''

"So naturally you want to reactivate him. Here is a gold seam if ever there was one. Or at least it has all the makings.''

"We're too busy, I'm told. We've got our cups full, Dewey. Later.''

"Early?''

"He's got his orders too, I suspect.''

"From where? From whom, if not Carlisle?''

Nobels shrugged. He pulled out his tobacco pouch and began slowly filling his pipe. It was the standard pipe smoker's gesture when he wanted time to think, time to prepare an answer.

"Did you know this Anna?'' Horn asked. "Was she one of the Paris tarts?''

"No. Never heard of her.''

"Then you did know the names of some of his women. And, of course, that they actually were from Paris. I wondered about it.''

Nobels looked up, caught again in one of his lies. Only now his lies weren't so white. "A few of the names.''

"We have someone in customs?''

"Passport control," Nobels admitted.

"Then you know *all* of the names."

"There may have been one or two that slipped by . . ."

Horn laughed and shook his head as he got to his feet. Nobels looked up, the picture of guilt. What a rotten spy he made, yet from what Horn knew the man had a fairly decent reputation. Decent enough for the number two posting in Moscow. Horn went into his bedroom where he got a fresh pack of cigarettes from his bag. When he returned, Nobels was puffing on his pipe as he stood by the window, his back to the corridor. His shoulders sagged and his head was bent slightly. He looked a little like a man ready for sentencing in a court of law.

"You were working outside your charter, weren't you," Horn said.

Nobels nodded. He did not turn around. The day was overcast. The light from outside through the tall windows was very flat, making all the angles inside the room harsh and quite sharp, like a painting done with the aid of a ruler.

"What did you tell Carlisle when Boyko turned up dead?"

"What?"

"You must have had some explanation for your interest if Boyko was supposedly hands-off."

"I'd just gone through the old network files, just as I said, to get them ready for Howard. That's the truth. Boyko's jacket is among them. Gathering dust."

"Then what are you doing back here this morning, Nobels? What do you want?"

"I came to warn you."

"About what?" Horn asked. "Warn me about what?"

Nobels started to turn when the side of his head exploded. He was flung backward, crashing over the table, blood, bits of bone and white matter spraying the white ceiling. The table collapsed under his weight and his arms and legs thrashed and pounded the floor as if he were a swimmer desperately coming up for air.

Horn dropped to his knees below the level of the window through which the shot had been fired. Probably from the street, the thought passed through his mind.

Nobels tried to push himself up. "Boyko!" he bellowed, his voice high-pitched and ragged like a hysterical woman's scream, blood pouring from the huge wound just below his temple.

Horn scrambled across the room. Blood filled Nobels's eyes. He couldn't be seeing anything, yet he looked up at Horn, then collapsed backward with a big sigh, his head thumping on the polished wooden floor. He was dead and there was nothing for it. But why? Who had followed him here? What had he come to warn about?

Turning to the window, Horn could see where the bullet had penetrated the glass. The hole was small and neat, which meant, he supposed, that it had been made by a high-powered rifle. Anything slower or less powerful would have shattered the glass.

Nobels was dead. Why? What had Boyko been up to that was so important that an outgoing agent runner had to be silenced?

Getting to his feet, Horn cautiously approached the window, keeping well out of the line of sight from the busy square. He edged the curtain aside and looked out. The square was as before, traffic hurrying back and forth. There was no commotion. No police. No milling crowds, no fingers pointed this way. The rifle had been silenced. Probably shot from the window of a van, or the back of a truck. The vehicle would have stopped for just a moment. Or perhaps it had been parked below, waiting for the chance that Nobels would show himself at the window. A lot of luck riding on it. And the shot would have been incredible. It was more than a hundred yards down to the square. The rifle could have been tripod mounted, of course, but still the shot was a good one. There were no trucks or vans down there now, however. The one shot had been fired and they had driven off. Neat. Professional.

By whom? And why? And what was Nobels's warning? The implications were chilling.

Nobels had diminished in size as all men do at death. He was no longer a rotten spy or a good father or a mediocre lover or a bad driver, none of those. Now he was simply a dead man. Horn quickly went through his pockets, but there was nothing other than his wallet and passport, comb, handkerchief, a few hundred dollars American, a pipe tool, tobacco, and several boxes of wooden matches. Nothing else. No letters, no codes jotted down on a slip of paper, no notebooks, nothing. Nor had he been armed. He may have been expecting trouble, but apparently not of the violent variety. Yet he had seemed wary, frightened. He had come with a warning.

Horn looked again out the window down at the square. Boyko had been followed out of the Soviet Union, had telephoned the old Paris number, and had been shot down. Nobels had left the Soviet Union, had come with a warning about something, and he too had been shot down. Where was the common denominator? In Paris? In Moscow? With Anna?

Perhaps Nobels had been running Boyko after all. Perhaps it had been the simple elimination of a madman and his handler. Such things had happened before.

Whatever it was, Horn thought carefully, stepping around Nobels's body, everything was changed now. He went downstairs and called the embassy from the hall phone. Boyko and Nobels had been taken by surprise. Neither had expected he would be attacked. They hadn't fought back. Hadn't had the chance. Horn wasn't going to be so easy a target.

Carlisle had not yet left the country. They managed to catch him at the airport and get him back to the safe house before eleven. By then Nobels's body had been removed through the back door and taken by windowless van to the embassy. The upstairs sitting room had been cleaned, the table replaced and the window repaired, all without fanfare, all without fuss, all without attracting attention from the outside. Two teams on a rotating basis watched from the street, and everyone was instructed to stay away from all upstairs windows.

No one had asked him any real questions. Horn assumed Carlisle had given Stockholm Station its strict orders the moment he had arrived. Assistant DDOs and up did not thrive on outward notoriety. While he waited, Horn remained for the most part in the downstairs study where he'd been given his brief, and tried to work out exactly what had happened, and what might be happening. But there wasn't enough information to make any kind of reasonable assumptions other than the one that had flashed across his mind as Nobels was crashing over the table: whatever else was or wasn't so, Boyko had definitely reactivated himself, and had done so in a very big way.

"What in God's name happened here?" Carlisle fumed even before he took off his hat and coat.

Horn came out of the study. "They got to Nobels."

"They?" Carlisle snapped from the stairhall. "Who exactly are *they*, and how do you mean, got to?"

"Shot him dead, upstairs in the sitting room."

"Oh, Jesus Christ," Carlisle swore. He looked up toward the second-floor landing. Most of the others had already gone. Only the cleanup crew was left, and they were packing their tools. "Are we covered here?"

"For the moment. But I'd suggest another safe house be found."

"No time for wit, Jack," Carlisle said. He was shook. "Were they after you, do you suppose?"

"I'd been sitting in front of that window all morning. They were after Nobels."

"What in God's name was he doing back here? He was supposed to be on his way out. He wanted to do some last-minute shopping, then take the overnight to Washington."

"He said you'd told him to talk to me."

Carlisle's eyes narrowed. "I told him no such thing, Jack. What did he have to say?"

"Nothing," Horn said. "He didn't have the chance. He arrived, I poured him some coffee, and then I went into the bedroom to get a pack of cigarettes, when the side of his head suddenly disappeared and he was dead."

Carlisle looked at Horn's eyes. "Spare me the gruesome details. He didn't say anything? Not a thing? Not a hint? I've got a little secret I'd like to share with you? Nothing like that?"

"Not a thing. I think he was worried about his career."

"How do you see that?"

"Boyko was a gold seam. I think Nobels was concerned that such a gross mishandling of a valuable madman would not bode well for him back home."

"He was looking for mercy."

"Perhaps."

"Then who killed him and why?"

"Whoever killed him killed Boyko, and probably for the same reason."

"Dewey was running something on the side, then?" Carlisle said thoughtfully. He looked up and smiled wanly. "But what agent runner doesn't? You do, don't you? You've got your little secrets, Jacky. Even now. From me?"

They heard a clatter from upstairs and they both glanced up. "Cleanup crew," Horn said.

Carlisle was a man weighing a difficult decision. "Your visa will be ready within the hour. You're booked on the six o'clock to Moscow. Aeroflot. If you want to take it, that is. Back out, Jack, and not one person on the face of this earth would lay fault at your door. They would have to answer to me."

Horn would forever remember this particular moment, because it was so terribly important for his safety, his future, his life. "Two questions, Farley. First, was Boyko active or wasn't he? Was he still working for us?"

"No," Carlisle said, shaking his head for emphasis. He still stood in the stairhall. They'd had their entire conversation at arm's length. "I give you my solemn word. Nothing was held back from you, nothing at all."

"Secondly, were the microphones switched on during our briefing yesterday? Or last night? Or this morning?"

"No."

Horn didn't know whether he wanted to ask why they hadn't been. Recording safe house sessions was SOP. But with a straight face Carlisle provided the answer, however weak it was.

"It's none of Stockholm's business. The whole Moscow network has become like a huge house of cards, Jack. Rotten in some places right to the foundation. Any little blast of air will topple the entire works. A lot of fine people, theirs as well as ours, would fall with it. The casualties would be awesome. We'll keep the need-to-know list to an absolute minimum here."

"Take care of Christine," Horn said, but the moment the words left his lips he was sorry he'd said them to Carlisle.

Horn transferred to the Highway 18 Esso Motel, north of the city and only a short bus ride to Arlanda Airport, under the Horton workname. He had a late-afternoon tea and then on second thought a drink at the bar. He had left his old things at the safe house. The kit had already been delivered to his room at the Esso, which gave him the afternoon to familiarize himself with his new identity, and to get comfortable with it before he made his run at Soviet customs and passport control officialdom.

Throughout that afternoon and during the short bus trip out to the airport, Horn kept thinking about Nobels. He kept seeing the man's head exploding, kept seeing him falling to the floor, crashing over the table, blood pumping, his arms and legs thrashing. *Boyko*, he had called. *Boyko*, his very last word.

Boyko had called out something about a letter from Anna.

Curious, our last words. Horn wondered what his would be.

Already LeBec was regretting his decision to help in the containment, and yet he knew he had no choice. Indeed none of them had any choice. The alternatives were unspeakable, and would have consequences on both sides of the Atlantic. Serious consequences. Traffic around Arlanda Airport was quite heavy in the late afternoon, so that by the time he was absolutely certain of Horn's destination, he had to hurry to make it back into the city to the telephone exchange. He made it with less than a half hour to spare before the office closed.

His telephone call to Washington went through immediately. It was noon there. "He is on his way to Moscow."

"I suspected as much."

"I could have accommodated him . . ."

"Not yet, Emile, not yet. I must see what he does, who he speaks with. He will have a few friends there, believe me. I will make a few calls."

"And for me, monsieur? What do you wish now?"

"Follow him, of course. Will you need help with the arrangements?"

"In Moscow, yes. But not here. I have friends too."

6

A cruel wind blew across Moscow's Sverdlov Square. Anna huddled in a doorway of the Bolshoi Theater. At six it was already dark, the homeward-bound traffic very depressing for her, and she was convinced that she would die alone, perhaps even in prison. She was being followed these days. She was convinced of it. There had been two of them: one very tall and husky, wearing a workman's cloth cap pulled low over his eyes; the other not so big, and wearing a black fur hat perched on the back of his blunt head. She had spotted Fur Hat three days earlier as she was coming out of the theater. They'd practically bumped into each other, but he hadn't apologized. Instead he had turned on his heel and had practically run away from her. Yet that very afternoon, as she was stepping off the Metro, she saw him talking with Cloth Cap. When they looked up and realized that she was watching them, they turned and hurried away. She'd thought at the time to chase after them, but then had wisely decided against it. She had her appointment at the hospital, and besides, what in heaven's name would she have said to them had she caught up with them? And just now she was certain she'd spotted Cloth Cap on the trolley bus crossing Sverdlov Square toward the Moskva Hotel. He hadn't turned his head, but she was certain he had seen her huddled out of the wind.

Her letter to Jason. It was the only thing she could think of. They were militia and they were following her to see what other secrets she would divulge to Boyko. More than once she had thought about returning to the Arbat to see him, to talk with him, to make sure he had had no trouble getting the letter out. But each time she had thought better of it. He knew how to reach her if there was a reply. If indeed militiamen were following her, another meeting with Boyko would clinch their case against her.

"On at least two separate occasions, Comrade Chalkin, you were observed with the traitor Boyko." The charges would be very specific. Treason. Hooliganism. Failure of a state-trained and state-supported artist to maintain a proper behavior. This last was the worst. "The entire world looks at you, Anna," it would be said. "For you to break the law is a more serious crime. Your punishment, therefore, must be more serious."

In the few weeks since her illness had been diagnosed, and she had gathered the courage to actually write to Jason and then to arrange for the letter to be delivered, she had done a lot of thinking about her past, a lot of ordering. She thought about the clandestine nature of her meetings with Jason during the eighteen months they had been lovers. She'd been terribly paranoid then, too, except of course when she was actually at his side. Then everything seemed at peace. Perhaps, she told herself, she was simply becoming paranoid now. She'd initiated contact with her old lover and she had consequently become suspicious of everything and everyone around her. But, she wondered, trying to think logically, did she suspect she was being followed by two men because of her paranoia? Or was it *because* of that very paranoia that she had become observant enough to notice her followers?

She had stayed at the theater much longer than she had planned. And now the thought of the long walk to her apartment made her a bit indecisive. She did not want to go out into the cold, to commit herself to the wind that had in the past few weeks become more like a very sharp knife than any wind she had ever remembered in a Moscow winter. It was her illness, of course. But she was blaming everything on her illness. It had become her own personal scapegoat for all the troubles of the world.

There was no sign of the man in the fur hat, and for a minute or so she began to seriously doubt her own sanity. Had she really seen Cloth Cap just now on the trolley? Hadn't they always been on foot in the past? And just how many fur hats, or cloth caps for that matter, were there in all of

Moscow? Hundreds of thousands, perhaps. More likely millions. Moscow was a city of hats in the winter. She was being a complete fool.

"Everyone reacts somewhat differently to their cancer, Anna," Dr. Mazayeva told her on her last visit. "For some it is an enemy with whom they do battle. For others it is simply the great destroyer against which there is no defense, so they lay down and wait to die. For others it is a shame in their lives. They try to hide it from others, and eventually they even try to hide it from themselves by denying themselves their medications, denying even their visits to the hospital. In some extreme cases I have heard of people who are afraid that the entire world is filled with voyeurs. Everywhere they go they imagine people are looking at them, pointing their fingers: 'See there, that person has cancer!' If that happens to you, Anna, I must know. I can help. There are certain drugs . . ."

Anna knew what Dr. Mazayeva would say about Cloth Cap and Fur Hat. Of course Dr. Mazayeva did not know the entire story, did not know about Jason, or about the letter, or about Boyko.

The question now in her mind was, how long could she stand to wait? It had been fully twelve days since she had passed her letter to Boyko. Twelve days in which her imagination had practically run away with her. How much more of this could she endure? She understood that in the end Jason could choose not to return a message. It would be terribly dangerous for him, for all of them, in which case there was really very little she could do about it. But if only she knew, it would make these last months at least a little more bearable.

She looked around the corner again across busy Sverdlov Square. The headlights of the cars and taxis and trucks and buses, the streetlights, the lights on the theaters and stores, and beyond, the big red star on the Kremlin's Spassky Tower, were dazzling. A fairyland of brightness and gaiety. In a few days they would be opening *Spartacus*. Then Sverdlov Square would be even more alive in a glittering sea of lights and people and limousines. Party officials and diplomats from the many foreign embassies in town would be there. So would the Americans.

Anna had considered, over the past days since she had convinced herself that she was being followed, going to the American embassy and asking to speak to someone within the consular section. But each time she got to that point in her thoughts, she stopped cold.

"Yes, Miss Chalkin, in what way exactly can the American embassy be of assistance?" a smug clerk might ask her.

All the while militia would be outside with their little black notebooks. (Would they even allow her through the gates? she wondered.) Citizen Chalkin arrived at the U.S. embassy at such and such a time, on such and such a day, and month, for a purpose we cannot determine. It must be noted, Comrade Chief Prosecutor, that Citizen Chalkin is the very same woman who met with the traitor Boyko at which time she passed on this document. At that point, in Anna's mind, she could see the prosecuting attorney handing her letter to Jason up to the judges. Very damning evidence, comrade. There can be no doubt that despite what the state has done for, and given to, Anna Feodorovna Chalkin, despite even her uncle's high position within the KGB, despite all of her privileges she is a traitor and has been a traitor since October 9, 1975. Eleven years without confession, without a change of heart.

If she remained in the doorway she would freeze to death.

Uncle Stepan would know. But in order for her to ask his help, she would have to tell him everything. Her perfidy would break his heart. This was something she would have to do on her own.

Pulling up the collar of her coat, and clutching her shoulder bag close, Anna stepped out of the protection of the doorway into the full blast of the wind. The sudden sharp cold took her breath away, the interior of her nose instantly thickening as the moisture there froze. She started up Petrovka Street past TsUM, which was about to close, last-minute shoppers scurrying into the department store past the disapproving glares of the monitors. Away from the square it wasn't as bright, the traffic was less heavy, and there weren't as many pedestrians.

She had fantasized about Cloth Cap and Fur Hat for days. She couldn't keep herself from thinking about them; they were a part of her life now, no less a bridge between her and Jason than was Boyko. All part of the same circle that she had come to think of as deadly. Within the confines of her circle she would die. Cloth Cap, she fantasized, was basically a good man who nevertheless had never been able to gain the understanding of women, which was a tragedy since his father was dead and he had no brothers or uncles. Cloth Cap's mother, she'd decided, was happy to have been rid of him at an early age; her obvious relief at his departure still distressed him. And the one love of his life had married a bureaucrat, someone with an automobile and a membership in one of the secret private government clubs that were so popular. Fur Hat was more interesting in that he was at heart a very cruel man. He had killed his best friend when he was thirteen, had spent two years in Siberia for his crime, and when he returned to Moscow he completed his technical schooling and joined the militia. He was a sergeant inspector, and was probably cruel to animals as well. Their lives were like some ballets Anna had danced: tragic, dark, rare, and very imaginative.

She had to stop at Kuznetskiy Most as four army trucks, red stars on their canvas sides, rumbled past, the drivers ignoring the traffic signals.

Fur Hat was across the street. At first she thought she was seeing an apparition.

If they had wanted to arrest her, she thought, they would have come to the theater, or they would have waited for her at home.

She wanted Uncle Stepan. He would know what to do. He would be able to protect her, even if it meant she had to tell him everything. But his apartment was on Kalinina Prospekt, nearly three kilometers in the opposite direction, and getting past his security people would be impossible if he wasn't home, and even if he were, simply getting a message up to him might be difficult. But three kilometers for her just then was to the moon and back. Uncle Aleksandr was closer, but she did not want to get him involved if there was any danger. He was too kind, too gentle a man; he wouldn't know what to do. Nor did she want to go to Uncle Georgi even if she could; his apartment was farther away than Uncle Stepan's, in the Southwestern District near the river.

Fur Hat was just staring at her. He made no moves. It was as if he were a statue of a man permanently affixed to the street corner.

Glancing over her shoulder, she was in time to see Cloth Cap coming up from the square. His right hand came up when he saw her. Though he was nearly a block away, she could definitely see that he had something in his hand. Something small and dark.

Dear God, she thought, stepping back. It was a gun. There was to be no arrest, no trial. With the speed of light she realized all of that. A trial would be too great an embarrassment for the theater, not to mention for Uncle Stepan. KGB General Patrenko, the one with the traitor niece. They meant to assassinate her here and now on this empty street.

Fur Hat suddenly started toward her across the broad avenue. Anna looked wildly around her, panic starting to rise in her breast. Kuznetskiy jogged to the left toward Kalinina, but Fur Hat had already cut off that direction. Nor could she get back to the theater. It meant she could only go to the right. They had given her only one possible choice. But everything was happening too fast for her. She could not believe it. There were no cars or taxis now, no pedestrians. She was alone. Terribly alone.

She suddenly sprinted to the right, her still powerful dancer's legs and lithe body carrying her half a block before she begin to get a glimmering of what they were trying to do to her. They were herding her like an animal toward a trap. She stopped in mid-flight, her heart hammering. Dzerzhinsky Square was barely a block and a half distant. The Lubyanka prison was there. Just ahead. Very close. They were driving her toward it. Herding her. She turned. Cloth Cap and Fur Hat were stopped at the corner. They were looking at her. They were standing there, looking at her. Anna's breath came ragged from her chest. It was her illness. She still had much of her strength, and agility, but she no longer had the stamina. Cloth Cap again raised his right hand. This time he waved whatever it was he held. Waved it as if he were signaling to her. Stop, Anna, or I shall shoot. They wanted her to remain there. They were hypnotizing her. They wanted her to wait for them so that they could catch up. They wanted her to hold still so that they could come in for the easy kill.

Cloth Cap started forward.

Anna backed up a step, then turned and ran. There would be traffic on Dzerzhinsky. There would be witnesses. The story would get out. Uncle Stepan would hear about it. The assassination of a ballet star in front of witnesses could not go unnoticed or unpunished.

Her heart was pounding as she raced past stores and shops closed and dark now for the night. During the day this was a very busy street. Now it seemed to her as if all of Moscow had packed up and left, or had gone home where they were hiding behind locked doors for fear of their lives.

Once she looked back over her shoulder. Cloth Cap was still behind her. He wasn't gaining, she didn't think, but she could feel her muscles already beginning to knot. One year ago she would have been fine. She could have outrun a gazelle. She cursed her own failing body. She cursed the hospital and Dr. Mazayeva's calm solicitude. Most of all she cursed her own weakness for having written to Jason. What terrible things had she set in motion by that one foolish act? Why, she screamed in her mind, had she not let well enough alone?

She skidded around the corner on Dzerzhinsky Place head-long into the arms of a very large man who had just stepped out of a limousine.

"No!" she screamed, struggling against him. There were other people around. Traffic. "Help!" she cried. "Please, help me!" But he had a tight grip on her as she flailed her arms and tried to kick him.

"Anna!" the man said sharply. He pushed her back at arm's length.

She looked up into the concerned face of her Uncle Stepan, and she hiccuped.

"What is happening, child? What are you doing here like this?"

She looked over her shoulder. "They're following me!"

"Who is following you, Anna? Who is it?"

No one was there. Cloth Cap was gone. She could see all the way to the streetlight on the corner of Petrovka, but no one was there. Even Fur Hat had left.

"Who is it, Anna?" her uncle repeated.

She looked up into his eyes, and then sagged. Her heart began to slow. She could not tell him. She couldn't say a thing. She loved him too much to pass on this burden. Boyko was a traitor, and by association not only with him but with her Jason, so was she. Nothing could alter the fact that her uncle was a KGB general. Nothing, neither her love nor his.

"I think they wanted to rape me," she gasped.

"Here?" her Uncle Stepan cried in rage. "Here in Moscow?"

7

Thirteen years ago when Jack Horn left Moscow for the last time he promised his madmen that he would be back. At the very least he would watch out for their welfare, make sure they had someone capable of running their plays. But when the Company pulled him out they had taken him away cleanly. His talent scout back at Langley had warned him that there were to be no entanglements. No histories. In those days, and to a lesser extent still, you needed a mentor, someone to look out for you, an older hand. There were a lot of pitfalls for the unwary on the way up. The advice Doxy had given him was never to look back. "You can be damned sure, Jack, that the assistant chief of station before you wasn't looking over his shoulder to make sure you weren't screwing up his old territory. No virgins here, you know. And you did name them correctly after all: they are madmen. That's what they are. Traitors. Don't worry so much." He'd been young then, and quick to forget, eager to get on with it, impatient for new challenges. He was going to fix the world in those days. He had decided that he had made the correct decision in leaving the Church—though he wondered if he had ever really been enough a part of the Church in the first place to leave it. Still, from time to time in Athens, or Korea, or even Washington, he'd stop at the odd moment and think back to his very first network and his promise. Now, riding in from Sheremetyevo Airport in the embassy's staff Chevrolet, all those moments were catching up with him. "Pity the poor agent runner who begins to have a conscience," Doxy said. "He hasn't long to go after that starts."

So how had his madmen fared in the intervening years? He knew about Boyko, shot dead in Helsinki. But what about the others? Guzov, the timid one. Avdeyenko, the clown. Or Pupyshev and Sheshkin, the serious brothers at arms. How about Turalenko? He had been the only one in the group to possess a party card in 1975. Where had they all disappeared to, if the station was no longer running them?

The interior of the car was much too hot. Outside it was very dark, so there wasn't much to be seen except for the traffic ahead of them. A light snow was falling and the windshield wipers flapped back and forth in a soothing rhythm. The beat made Horn think of some folk tunes he had learned here. Part of what made him such a good agent was his apparently innate ability to rapidly and accurately assimilate a culture. While in Rome do as the Romans do. Easier said than done, but he had a facility with languages, he had a feel for people, and he had a natural homing instinct for the idiomatic expressions that made Germans German, that made Greeks Greek, and that made Russians Russian. "Live a hundred years, learn a hundred years, still you die a fool," Russians said. "The shortages will be divided among the peasants" went an adage older even than Stalin.

His flight had been on time, but they'd been held in customs and passport control nearly two hours before they were allowed out. He'd never found out exactly why. Kyle Pfeiffer, aide to the chief of the embassy's consular section—and number three man in CIA operations in Moscow—had been waiting uneasily. "I was set to give up on you, Mr. . . . Horton. I even hoped you wouldn't show at all." They'd tossed Horn's bags in the back seat of the Chevrolet and headed into the city. He supposed that the embassy had already been informed of Nobels's death, but he wondered to what extent they had been briefed on his own mission. Carlisle had said the present-day Moscow network was like a huge house of cards. Any little ill wind would blow it all to hell, and when it fell a lot of good people would go with it. One thing was certain: Dewey Nobels had not been exaggerating when he said everything had changed here. Already Horn was able to feel it.

"We only just got word that Dewey was dead. Christ, I

can't believe it. They said you were with him at the time,'' Pfeiffer volunteered.

"I was with him. He was finishing my briefing."

"No one told us a thing, you know. We would have appreciated a warning. Something. Anything."

"Not my territory, Pfeiffer." Horn was having trouble deciding about the man.

"I'm called K.W.," Pfeiffer said, glancing over. "Bob Early and a few others are waiting to brief you. Though heaven knows I suspect they'll be wanting more from you than you'll get from them." Pfeiffer was a long, thin man who seemed to be all arms and legs and knobby joints. His nose was huge and beakish, his eyes bulged almost comically, and his complexion was sallow. It was the miserable Russian winters that made them all look like anemic ghosts.

Horn could see Nobels falling to the floor dead. What was his warning?

Coming into a new duty station was difficult under normal circumstances. But coming in on emergency footing with a hasty legend that you hadn't had proper time to get accustomed to was dangerous as well as disconcerting. He'd been down this path before, though. Many times. Just because Boyko had been one of his old madmen wasn't the only reason Carlisle had called on him. Somewhere along the line he had become a fix-it man, a crystal ball gazer, someone who could come directly into a situation, see the forest for the trees, and see what they liked to call at the Farm "the anomalies." They'd called him back to New York seventeen months earlier when Yuri Yevchenko, the United Nations Soviet diplomat, had decided life would be better in the West than at home. They wanted someone fresh to take over, someone who would not be bedazzled by the stars, someone whom the foreign community around the U.N. did not know and therefore would not spot during the snatch. Within twenty-four hours he had laid out his scheme, had put his people into place, and had pulled it off. By morning Yevchenko was tucked away in a Connecticut safe house and Horn was on his way back to Berlin.

This was something different. There was a link between him and Boyko that was more than a casual relationship. And Boyko was dead. There was also an implied connection between him and Dewey Nobels. Horn would have been surprised to learn he had *not* been spotted at the Stortorget safe house as well. Moscow was a dangerous place for him. It was entirely possible they would simply shoot him dead; or at the very least they might corner him at the embassy until some sort of a trade could be worked out, his free passage for perhaps the release of one of their people from some Western prison.

"I'll be needing quarters someplace outside of the embassy," Horn said. "Freedom of movement. I suppose we've still got our bedbugs."

"The place is crawling with them, sir. Practically one in four employees is a Russian, and half of them are Second Directorate types. It makes it damned near impossible for us to get any work done. And as far as your quarters go, you can bunk with me if you'd like. I have a place just across the river. Your background won't hold up for very long, you know."

"What about you?"

Pfeiffer shrugged his shoulders, then sucked his lower lip. "That'll depend upon you, won't it. I mean there's a whole lot of breath-holding going on here right now. God only knows which way it'll topple, or who will topple with it. We'll just have to see. In any event, they know who I am."

"The entire station has been spotted?"

"I don't think so, sir. Not to that extent. We've still got a few aces up our sleeves." Pfeiffer concentrated on his driving. They were coming into the city, past some very old ragtag neighborhoods of leaning three-story buildings and tar-paper shacks in their ice. There wasn't much light here, though even through the snow they could see a general glow in the sky, and traffic had begun to pick up.

Horn felt a sense of déjà vu. It was as if in reality he had never been here before, though he was experiencing coming into Moscow for the *first* time again, as it were, in a dream. And the lessons he had learned the last time seemed distant and very remote, as if he had never really learned them but had only heard about them from someone else. He felt like a shy, country bumpkin coming to the great metropolis for the first time, one hand over his wallet to make sure the pickpockets didn't run off with it, and the other over his heart to ensure his virtue remained intact. His experiences in the parks and theaters, in the restaurants and nightspots, and his dual roles as embassy gadabout attending routine parties versus agent runner haunting Moscow's back streets and alleys—

why did all those kinds of appointments seem to take place on dark oppressive nights?—seemed equally distant, equally unreal to him, as if they weren't his memories after all. But Moscow would do that to you if you let it, Doxy had warned a million years ago. The city was like a New York or Paris or London with its own unique aura and its own inherent dangers. In New York you might get mugged, in Paris run over by a taxi, in London attacked by Teddy boys or some other toughs, but here in Moscow you were subject to arrest at any hour of the day or night. "You are a foreigner in a country that was practically born of foreign invasion. The Japs held Vladivostok, remember, until 1922. They'll be suspicious of you—that will never change—they will be afraid of you and they'll automatically assume that you are a spy, which in your case, of course, will be true. It won't make your job any easier, Jack." That from Doxy.

"I'll need to see Nobels's day books, his case files, and his active and inactive dossiers," Horn said as they crossed the outer circumferential highway, the Moscow Ring Road, the housing here newer and much taller, apartment buildings in clusters of ten- and fifteen-story towers.

"Early and the others were closeted with the entire shooting match when I left to pick you up." Pfeiffer looked over. "They're waiting for you to set them on the right path. Something about one of the inactives Dewey had been spotchecking. It could have been that one that blew up in his face. I don't know."

"I don't know, either, K.W., but he was one of my old boys. Nobels could very well have stumbled onto something. Does his name mean anything to you? Boyko?"

Pfeiffer shook his head. "Never heard of him. You were here before?"

"The old days."

"Well, everything has changed. Quite a bit, I'd say. Something new comes up every week. Fifteen years ago was another universe."

Horn hadn't mentioned a time period. He wondered where Pfeiffer had heard it.

They came in past the Hotel Ukraina where they crossed the frozen river onto Kalinina Prospekt, then took Tchaikovsky Street up to the U.S. embassy, which was housed in a dumpy-looking yellow brick building that had once been an apartment house. Soviet militia officers watched the front of the embassy on a twenty-four-hour-a-day basis. Americans with proper identification were allowed in and out with no trouble. All others had to provide adequate proof as to why they wanted to visit such an obvious nest of spies.

It was like coming home, in a way, Horn thought, because it was here that he had cut his first teeth, here that he had manufactured his first madmen. Had he come home to complete the circle? To die?

They dropped Horn's bags in Pfeiffer's office, then took the ancient, iron-gated elevator up to the third floor. No one was around at this hour except for the Marine guards downstairs, a few night desk duty officers, and the communications people. If things had changed with the Russians in Moscow, they certainly had not with the Americans in their embassy. The same narrow, dimly lit, overheated corridors led back to the same cramped, overstuffed offices. Even the same posters seemed to be tacked up: *The walls have ears. A lock unlocked is an invitation—who do you want at your party?* A Russian political slogan was pinned up on one of the bulletin boards: *Glory to Work!* It was someone's idea of a joke, but since less than twenty percent of all the Americans stationed at the embassy could read Russian, it was a mostly wasted effort. Pfeiffer knocked once and they entered the conference room.

"You're late," a husky man in shirt sleeves growled, looking up. Horn figured he was Bob Early, the chief of station. He had the look.

"Delay at the airport, Bob," Pfeiffer explained. He closed the door behind them. There were two others in the room.

"Well, just lock us in, then, will you?"

It was the same conference room, Horn thought, where he had handled dozens of briefings in his tenure here. Nothing had changed. The same screened security window overlooked the same dingy courtyard below where in the summer some of the younger staffers played softball. The wire mesh was tied to a white noise generator to foil attempts at electronic eavesdropping. The overhead fluorescents hummed to the same purpose. The long conference table was piled with file folders, ledger books, computer printouts, and a large stack of what appeared to be surveillance photographs. Early and the other two men did not seem pleased. This was an emergency, and they were the pallbearers who'd been given the unfortunate task of lugging away the dead bodies as and where they fell. In addition, Horn figured there had to be a little resentment that an outsider had been called in to take care of a problem rightly theirs.

Pfeiffer made the introductions. Bob Early had been COS for nearly three years. He'd been given an eighteen-month extension, but to Horn the man already looked shell-shocked. Another year and a half might do him in. He'd seen others in the business burn out because they hadn't known how to pace themselves; they had no idea of their own personal limits. To Early's left was Van Howard, the new assistant COS from Athens Station. He had loosened his tie but had not taken off his jacket despite the stifling heat. He was a pale little man with liquid eyes and very fine, very thin light blond hair. He looked as if he could be broken very easily. He also looked a little bewildered, as if he were an accountant whose calculator had been snatched from him. He didn't know what to do with his hands. To Early's right was Norman Siskel, the chargé d'affaires. The ambassador was in Leningrad at the moment and was not scheduled to be back in Moscow until the following week. Siskel was a prim, self-important little man in a three-piece suit with gold cuff links, a gold watch fob, and a club tie all knotted and snugged up. Horn decided that he did not like the man. He had a hunch the feeling was mutual by the way Siskel looked across the table at him.

"Was the delay at the airport on your account, Jack?" Early asked. He had no neck. His shoulders were like slabs of beef, and his wrists were nearly as big around as a young boy's waist. In his day he had been a wrestler and weight lifter.

"I don't think so."

"Well, we just can't know that for certain now, can we," Siskel said. His voice was high-pitched, girlish, petulant.

"I think we can trust Jack's tradecraft here, Norman," Early said, looking directly at Horn as if for confirmation. "I've reviewed his file; he's a good man. Comes with the highest marks, the very best recommendations." His expression softened. "He practically invented the game we're playing here, you know." He glanced over at the chargé. "You don't have to stay for this, Norman. The nice man has just come aboard long enough to pick up a few loose ends and tuck them away neatly." He turned back to Horn. "Isn't that so, Jack? Isn't that exactly your assignment?"

"Something like that," Horn said. They stood around the

conference table like nervous bridesmaids before the rehearsal dinner, not quite sure who was in charge, or what was supposed to happen next.

"Dull and boring stuff, Norman. Dull and boring."

"I'll stay," Siskel said.

"Suit yourself." Early waved them all toward chairs while he remained standing, though slightly bent, his meaty paws on the tabletop holding him up. "We're here to help you, Jack, in any way that we possibly can. I want you to know that right from the start. You will have our cooperation, our *complete* cooperation. But in return I am going to have to know what you are up to at every single moment. We understand that your legend isn't worth a tinker's damn. It won't hold up for very long. If it falls apart before you are finished and we can get you out of here, there will be some tough questions asked. I'll have to know which direction it'll be safe to steer Ivan. Agreed?"

Horn nodded.

Nobels had come back to the Stortorget house to warn him about something. Horn was unable to detect any signs of duplicity here at this table, however. No shifting of eyes, no hesitations, no shuffling, none of the indicators that he was being lied to except by Pfeiffer on the way in. Perhaps Nobels had been running his own show. If so, it still did not explain policy regarding Boyko. Hands off, Nobels said. It was the way things had been done here. Hands off the old madman. Why? Unless Boyko had still been active and was someone's little pet project, so sensitive a project that he was classified "hands-off" by the general embassy population.

Early had picked up a file folder. He tossed it across to Horn. "This is an index of Dewey's case files during his three years here. We've pulled the bulk of his stuff out of the main stacks going back six months. But I'll be damned if I can see anything in it. Leastwise nothing I didn't already have knowledge of."

Horn opened the file folder and glanced at a few of the entries, most of which were listed under case names alone. Somewhere there would be a key, a translation. They were never kept in the same place with case indexes. Never.

"Were you aware that he was investigating one of my old madmen?" Horn asked, looking up.

Early inclined his head. "Of course."

"Something to do with bringing in French prostitutes to service Soviet government officials."

Early grinned. "That, Jack, is nothing but conjecture. It was one of Dewey's pet projects. He figured if this Vitali Boyko was running hookers, there'd be a lot of very good info available. I told him hands off until we could prove independently that this wasn't another disinformation plot. That we weren't being led down the merry path. Such things have happened before."

"And?"

"Nothing. We looked into it. But nothing came of it. There was no way of us knowing if Boyko was working alone, or was working for the KGB."

"What was Nobel's reaction when you told him this?"

Early glanced at Pfeiffer. "It's dirty laundry, if you know what I mean. Dewey was a good man, but he thought he was better than he was. He wanted my job here. He told me flat out that I should be rotated back to the States so that he could take over."

"Who killed him?"

Early's eyes narrowed as he tried to take measure of exactly how Horn had meant the question. "That's the sixty-four-dollar question, isn't it?" He straightened up, placed his hands at the small of his back, and then stretched backward to relieve an ache. "I think that Dewey Nobels was probably running this Boyko . . . or at least he was trying to do so. I think whoever was pulling Boyko's strings got tired of the entire affair, or perhaps Dewey did stumble onto something, so they were both eliminated."

"A warning for the rest of us?" Horn asked softly.

"It could be construed as such."

"Then perhaps Boyko was a gold seam after all."

Early shook his head. "One of your people originally, wasn't he?"

"Were there any of the others from the old network whom Nobels might have been interested in?"

"There was nothing in his day books."

"But there was mention of Boyko?"

"At first there was. When Dewey got onto the notion that we should reactivate him."

"But then you told him hands off?"

"That's right."

"I still can't believe this has happened," Siskel said from his seat.

Horn was suddenly very tired. Yet he felt an alertness at a

much deeper level than mere conscious thought. It was almost a function of his self-preservation level, an instinct for survival, you could call it, where only an instinctual reaction could possibly save your life. Whatever came of this, he didn't think it would be very clean or neat.

"I'll need to see those records. All of them."

"Of course," Early said.

"I'd also like to see the results of your investigation into Boyko's background. The basis for your instructions to Nobels that Boyko was a hands-off property."

Early seemed a little less eager. But he nodded his agreement.

"And I'll need a handgun. Something small will do, thirty-eight caliber, perhaps. I'd prefer an automatic."

Early's face had become animated by degrees, and Siskel seemed thunderstruck. Howard and Pfeiffer didn't move a muscle. Horn didn't wait for any of them to reply.

"Boyko was shot and killed in Helsinki, and Nobels was shot dead in our Stockholm safe house. I won't become the third victim." He took off his jacket, loosened his tie, and rolled up his shirt sleeves. He reached out and pulled the first stack of files across. "I'd like something to eat, if that's possible at this hour. A sandwich would be fine. I'll be needing some coffee, plenty of it, black, no sugar. I'll need a miniature tape recorder, half a dozen blank legal pads, a dozen pencils, an embassy directory, a Moscow City Directory with a government index, and two runners to bring me files." He lit a cigarette, laying the pack and his matches on the table. He glanced across the room. "Oh, yes, I'll be bunking with K.W., so I'll be needing a car, something *without* diplomatic plates, please. And for tonight, in any event, a cot can be put in here for me, and my luggage brought up. I have fifteen years of catching up to do."

8

Horn's runners were just down the corridor. He had only to open the conference room door and poke his head out and they would come running, literally. A cot had been brought up, complete with sheets, a blanket, and a pillow. The sandwich someone had managed for him was roast beef and quite good. The coffee, however, was terrible: very black, very bitter, yesterday's brew. They had to get back at him somehow, after all. He had waltzed in there and taken over. Not Early and not even Siskel himself had made any headway with him.

From the beginning Horn concentrated on organizing the mass of data already gathered for him into some sort of a recognizable pattern so that he would be able to accomplish what needed doing. In the first place he needed to develop a complete measure of the man—his method, his successes, his failures, and his pride. Every agent runner had his pride and joy into which he lavished his most extravagant efforts. It was his upper limits, so to speak. And as such it provided a much better measure of a man than did his simpler successes. Another aspect of such a preliminary organization of any large mass of data was that the gaps would become evident. Only where there arises a discernible pattern can one be sure nothing has been left out. Random means exactly that, uncertainty. With the very best agents and agent runners, however, methodology was often so complex and varied that any sort of a routine was difficult if not impossible to detect. But Horn was not having that problem with Nobels. Dewey Nobels had been as regular as the sunrise and sunset, as predictable as the phases of the moon—which probably got him killed. He was a man of obvious faults, among which, besides his penchant for routine, was his unfortunate ego. He had wanted to be a star, and he apparently had never quite reconciled himself to the fact that he wasn't good enough.

In the main, Nobels had targeted the scientists and engineers and to a lesser extent the administrators of the Soviet Union's military-industrial complex. He had said as much back in Stockholm, and his records now gave paper evidence to the same. In the old days the agent runner who handled eight or ten madmen was considered on the border of reckless. How could one be expected to satisfy the special wants and needs of so many individual human beings? Five or six stringers was considered optimum. In the old days one concentrated more on quality than on quantity. The old adage was that one woman in the prime minister's bedroom would lay that country wide open faster than a standing army of five million men. There would be no secrets left. Of course that was in the political arena in which Nobels apparently had little or no outward expertise. Nobels, however, had developed a stable of more than one hundred stringers. As incredible as it seemed, each one of them produced for Nobels little bits and pieces that when taken as a whole on some computer program that had been devised for him, came forth with what could arguably be termed useful intelligence. Nobels had literally been everywhere, it seemed, in his cover as a special manufacturing trade representative. His cover job was to go around to all the Russian factories to which he could possibly gain access for the ostensible purpose of exploring trade agreements between them and their counterparts in the United States. In his role he had actually come up with many U.S.-Russian trade agreements, but he had also developed his amazing list of contacts: the engineers and the like in the research and development facilities of each factory he visited. From contact to a stringer status more often than not was simply a matter of a little chat. They were most eager, according to Nobels's own notes, to talk about their work, and he was most eager to listen to them. Nine months ago, Nobels even had the gall to reserve a hall at Moscow State University to which he invited R&D engineers from two dozen factories to listen to talks given by representatives from a dozen factories in the United States whom he had flown in especially for the convention. (At least in this operation Horn had some admiration for the man's creativity.) It was a smashing success from a trade standpoint, a sort of Goodwill Games of the manufacturing set. And it had already begun to pay off as an intelligence operation before Nobels left. The entire mechanism, including the computer program to handle the ever-growing mass of data, had been turned over to Van Howard. It explained in Horn's mind about the new man, the accountant type, the milquetoast. He wasn't expected to be an agent runner in the ordinary sense of the word; he was simply a computer expert adept at juggling vast amounts of information, useless or not.

The first few hours went by very fast for Horn. When he looked at his watch he was surprised to find that it was already after two in the morning. His eyes burned, his back was sore, and his mouth was foul from cigarettes and the bad coffee. He got up from the table and went to the screened window where he looked down. It was still snowing. Across the courtyard a light on a tall stanchion glowed yellow, with a halo around it. The window glass was thick and uneven, creating odd patterns outside. A fairyland it was, Horn thought, of a thousand years of strife and misery. Poetry was a national mania, the outlet for deep-seated feelings that went back dozens of generations.

There was more to Nobels than a man merely adept at gathering insignificant information, else he would never have begun his surveillance of Boyko or of the other madmen in the old network.

Moscow Operations is like a house of cards, Carlisle had warned him. He was beginning to understand what was meant by this. Nobels's stringers had no real background. He had gathered them far too fast for him to create the justification they needed. Horn suspected that in many cases, if not in most, Nobels's stringers did not even suspect they were doing anything illegal under Russian law. If one fell, however, by association everyone else would tumble as well. There would be enough good and loyal communists among them that Nobels would have been fingered as a spy, and the entire Moscow operation would come tumbling down around their ears. The devilish part was that there had been no way for him to quit, to get out.

Against this background, with this ineptitude raised to the highest and most dangerous order, Nobels had gone sniffing after the old network men. The real traitors. The real agents. The ones who had been so carefully discovered and cultivated and nurtured and handled, brought along slowly so that their complete cooperation was guaranteed from the very first day. Nobels had gone after them under the guise of economy, with dreams of glory in his head and stars in his eyes. They were to be his pride and joy, on which he would lavish his very best tradecraft.

Horn turned away from the window and went to the door. Among the files he had seen so far there had been only the scantiest of information on this aspect of Nobels's Moscow tenure. And it was in this direction, Horn suspected, that the answers would lie. Gloria Townsend, one of his runners whom the junior staffers called "Town and Country" for not so obvious reasons, came down the corridor.

"I'm going to need some files that aren't on my index," Horn said. The girl just looked at him as if he were speaking Martian. "Perhaps it would be best if you awakened Mr. Early. He'll know what I'm wanting."

"Dewey called it Operation Lookback," a tired, cranky Early explained. He'd thrown a sweater over his shoulders and had brought along a bottle of French brandy and two clean glasses. "He was reviewing the inactives. Wasn't official, of course. Leastwise not as an operation. Those days are done. But he wanted to play cloak and dagger. Got him killed. Your job, as I see it, Jack, is to calm down your old stringers. Make certain none of them goes on the warpath, because there's no telling what Dewey might have stirred up. Other than that, of course, he did a superb job here for us. Magnificent. He had half the industrial might of this country eating out of his hand. It was a sight to see him work." Early poured them both a drink.

"None of those files are here," Horn said.

"That's because there aren't any."

"Even if it wasn't an official line of investigation, surely Nobels kept some personal records. His day book at least. Apparently he spent a lot of time at it."

"Entirely too much time. But no, he left no records other than his day book, of course, and contact sheets."

"No contact sheets in my pile."

"They're on the computer, Jack," Early snapped. "You've got a great bloody pile of readout in front of you. Goes back six months. I can't see why you'd need more."

"There's not one mention of the old crowd in there," Horn said. He was tired but he figured he was going to have to gird himself for the explosion that Early was on the edge of.

"Then he must have written them out by hand."

"Did you see them? Do these contact sheets have your review initials?"

"The ones that came across my desk do."

"Which ones are those? Can you remember how long it's been? Was Boyko's name among them? What I mean to ask, Bob, is how long had it been since Nobels had contact with Boyko? Or were his contacts strictly at arm's length, merely surveillance efforts? And did he work alone, Bob? Or did he have a crew? You know, drivers, cameramen, researchers, perhaps street teams. Nobels did mention to me something about a source out at the airport—passport control, I believe he said—who was able to alert him each time Boyko came and went. I just want to get the whole picture before I walk out the front gate and put myself on the line." Horn lit a cigarette, then drank his brandy as he watched Early's face come alive. He decided the man would never make much of a poker player, and would probably have a stroke someday soon.

"Now just wait a goddamned minute here."

"I want the loose ends tied up," Horn said calmly. He was goading the man, but he couldn't say why.

"I don't know who the hell you think you are, coming in here like this, all high and mighty."

"Who else besides yourself had access to Nobels's day books and his contact sheets? The entries having to do with my old madmen?"

"Damn you . . ."

"I'd like to know just when the old network went inactive. I think that might be significant."

Horn was seated at the table piled high with file folders, ledger books, photographs, and computer readouts almost all exclusively dealing with Nobels's industrial espionage efforts. Early had remained standing across the table. His face colored now, and he slammed an open palm with all of his might on the tabletop, making the brandy bottle and glasses jump, the noise like a pistol shot in the confines of the room.

"I won't have this!" he roared. "I simply will not have this on my station! There are procedures. We have a going concern here that has nothing whatsoever to do with your cowboy tactics, and, mister, it works. It has been working for as long as I have been here, and it will continue to work as long as I remain. I will see to it that it does. You have my guarantee. Which means, in very plain English, Mr. Horn, that you will not be allowed to run around Moscow fucking with the system."

"A system, need I remind you, that got your assistant chief of station shot dead."

"My former assistant . . ."

Horn's mouth dropped open with the rank callousness of the remark. He suspected that Early was running very scared just now, to the point where he might be entertaining the notion that in some way Nobels's death would be placed on his shoulders. It made him defensive.

Early sighed deeply, and ran a hand across his face. He shook his head. "I didn't mean that. At least not the way it sounded, Horn."

"I know that. And I haven't come to upset the apple cart. I'm here to find out who killed Nobles and why. I think it's related to Boyko's assassination. If I can come up with more information about their connections with each other, I might have a place to start."

"Dewey was gunned down in Stockholm, not here. And Boyko was shot in Helsinki."

"Which tells me that something is still going on here in Moscow. Something important enough that they wanted to keep Moscow free of any kind of an investigation."

"Then they'll be after you."

"If they've made the connection, yes. In which case I'll know who they are and will have at least a clue as to what they're up to."

"You're on your own here, then," Early said after a moment's thought. "I mean from the standpoint that I can't offer you any effective protection other than to have you tailed."

"I don't want that. If I'm being watched, nothing will happen."

Early nodded heavily. "I'll look through Dewey's records again to make sure we haven't missed something. And I'll go through my files to see if I have any of his contact sheets.

Frankly, though, I can't remember any specifics. The inactives were very low on the priorities list, you know. And Dewey did send a lot of material across my desk."

"Did he work alone? On the inactives, that is."

"Yes."

"No driver?"

"No."

"Who else besides yourself would have had access to his contact sheets, or to his day books?"

"Archives, I suppose, but only after the operation became history. You might find some of it back a year, perhaps as recent as eight or nine months. Dewey wasn't one to share everything he was doing."

But he had brought a warning out of Moscow, Horn thought. A warning of what, or of whom? "I wonder, Bob, if you could tell me when the old network began to shut down. Has it been recently?"

"Heavens, no. It's been years. Long before my time."

"Was it shut down all at once? Have you any sense of that? Perhaps your predecessor might have said a word or two?"

"From what I understand, it just petered out, like a lot of other things around here. That would have been in the late seventies. Policy changed. New satellite technology, telephone intercepts . . . you know all of that. It was thought the risks of discovery probably outweighed the product. I'm guessing, of course, but I don't think I'm far from the mark. In any event they weren't exactly what you would call a trustworthy bunch."

"They were people," Horn said, remembering back. "I hope we didn't simply leave them in the lurch. They deserved more than that from us."

"I wouldn't know," Early said. He straightened up, shook his head, then went to the door where he hesitated a moment longer before turning back. "There is also the possibility that there is no connection between the killings after all. I mean Dewey was an effective operative—"

"He wasn't killed because of his industrial spying," Horn interrupted. "The KGB might have kicked him out of the country, but they wouldn't have assassinated him. Not for that, I think."

"No. I suppose you're right at that," Early said softly, and he left.

Horn poured himself another brandy against the long night still ahead of him, and turned once again to the scanty references in Nobels's day books to the inactives he had spot-checked around Moscow. The book itself was in the form of a series of ledgers in which the operative was supposed to mark down how he spent his time—where he went, who he saw, conversations he'd had, lunches and dinners, the prosaic as well as the extraordinary, his tradecraft, dates, addresses, frequencies, codes used—the day-to-day details of his life and work.

That was the theory, Horn mused. In actuality there wasn't an agent alive who was a hundred percent honest with his day book because it was a diary, wide open for later inspection. And spies, even bad ones, are more private than that.

There had been other Moscow networks over the past ten years or so to be sure, some developed for a specific project, others for the long haul. But there hadn't been a group such as Horn's madmen before or since. Nobels's day books contained references, though brief, to all of the inactive networks. It was to this mass of data, often in Nobels's own shorthand notation, that Horn turned now, extracting only the encounters Nobels had had with Horn's old crowd. The most frequent references were to Boyko—not surprising to Horn—and to Sheshkin. But almost immediately it became evident that something was terribly wrong—either with Nobels's method or with the old network. It wasn't complete.

There had been six of them, including Boyko now dead in Helsinki. Nobels had watched only three, however. Boyko, Yevgenni Sheshkin, and until about four months ago, Sergei Turalenko. There was no mention of the others, not a single line. Not of Vadim Guzov, the timid one who was always looking over his shoulder, and who stammered when excited; not of Leonid Avdeyenko whom they called the clown because of his antics; not of Ilya Pupyshev, the serious professor who along with Sheshkin had made an inseparable team within the network.

From the day books Horn plowed once again through the computer printouts, cross-referencing operational names from the index, still with no results other than Boyko, Sheshkin, and Turalenko. Nor were there any photographs or other notes. Nothing.

Had Nobels simply missed the others? Horn doubted it.

The man had shown his methodical mettle on other occasions. After all, even with the aid of a computer, running a hundred stringers was a feat of an organized man. No, Horn thought, something else had happened. Something that was worrying him.

He jotted down the missing three names, including for each as much background information as he could dredge up from his memory: birth dates, or at least months; places of birth; occupations; even product if he thought it might help in locating them. He added Turalenko's name and details, along with the notation that the man had evidently dropped out of sight four months earlier.

This time the youngster, Tom McKenzie, came running from the little alcove halfway down the corridor. His hair was red and his face was a mass of freckles. Horn guessed the Russians found him fascinating.

"I'd like you to find some information on these people. Russians. They used to work for me."

McKenzie studied the short list. "What sort of information, sir?" he asked respectfully. There was no telling what Early had told them about Horn. Gloria was watching them from the alcove.

"I'd like to know what's become of them, that's all. Current addresses if at all possible. Who they work for. Just anything at all that might help me locate them."

"Yes, sir."

"And with the last name, Turalenko, I'd like to know the significance of the time period four months ago. He seems to have dropped out of sight as well. I'd like to know why."

"Yes, sir," the young man said, and he scurried away.

The cot looked inviting, but Horn had begun to seriously worry about his old crew. Never look back. God, how many times he had heard it. Now it rankled. Of course we had to look back. How else would we learn by our experiences, how would we know to correct our mistakes? He poured himself another brandy and at the window stared out into the lonely night. If Nobels's day books contained little or nothing about Horn's madmen, his own memory was a lot more complete. He could remember recruiting each of them, from the sublimely easy Boyko who practically jumped at them, to the difficult, skittish Turalenko whose proudest possession in those days was his party card, and Sheshkin, a man who considered every aspect of his every move before he would take it.

They were compartmentalized, of course. Or at least they had been in the beginning. The only ones who knew each other at first were Sheshkin and Pupyshev who had been friends from their schoolboy days. Horn had wanted it kept that way for obvious reasons. But it was Boyko who had ruined that. The man was no one's fool, though he had done some stupid, risky things, but no one had guessed how far he was willing to go on a lark.

It was a night for remembering other nights. "We're brothers at arms," Boyko had said. "We should form a club."

It was a very dangerous thing to do, and Horn had told him that, but none of them left. They were, after all, curious about each other.

Boyko had done a little backtracking of his own, he explained, following Horn to his letter drops and then hanging around to see who showed up. When he had the other five nailed solid, he approached each of them in turn, offering them information about the Foreign Trade Ministry, arranging a meeting at his apartment. Horn was the last one to show up, and after their initial nervousness had faded, they had sung him a song. No one trusted Boyko after that, of course, but they were stuck with him and with each other. It was a loose arrangement, one that Horn had never reported in his own day books, but it was human. His madmen were real people, flesh and blood, all filled with emotions and hopes and dreams. He'd never allowed such a thing to happen since. He took precautions. But that group had been his start, and first loves were always special.

"Vitali didn't mean anything by it, do you think, Jack?" Sheshkin had asked.

Horn could remember that night in detail. He realized just how deep Sheshkin's intuitiveness ran when it came to people. "He was probably lonely. But it was a damned fool stunt just the same."

"He's lonely, sure," Sheshkin said, looking across the room to where Boyko was piling caviar on a piece of toast. "I can understand that."

"Are you alone, Yevgenni?"

"I have my family, Jack. You know this."

"But do you have friends other than Pupyshev?"

"Sure I do," Sheshkin said. He smiled and patted Horn on

the arm. "I wouldn't have pulled a stunt like this. I understand the danger we're under here. We could all be lined up against the wall and shot like dirty dogs."

"Does that worry you?"

"Sure."

"All the time?"

"No, Jack. Just sometimes. But sometimes I worry about getting run over by a bus. I worry about nuclear war, and about the Germans, and I worry sometimes about the Chinese. You see, I am a sophisticated, modern man: I worry about everything."

Boyko had come out of Moscow with a letter from Anna, and Nobels had followed him with a warning. There would be a lot of snow on the streets by morning, Horn thought. But in Moscow that was not unusual. The city wouldn't slow down one whit. So what had happened to his old crew? Boyko had been shot dead in Helsinki; had there been other casualties?

The telephone rang. It was Early from upstairs in his office.

"I was mistaken, Jack. I don't have a thing up here pertaining to your stringers. Apparently Dewey put his contact sheets, if he had any, in the computer program. Look again."

"I don't have them here," Horn replied patiently. "He mentions them in his day books, but there are no matching contact listings either in his own hand or in the computer printouts."

"Then the bastard never made them out. It was an unauthorized operation in any event."

"What was unauthorized, Bob? Spot-checking the old inactives, or following Boyko and his prostitutes around Moscow?"

"You know what I meant," Early growled.

"You told him to lay off Boyko."

"That's right."

"Then shouldn't there at least be contact sheets for his spot checks?"

"No encounter, no contact sheet. It's simple."

Early was lying; Horn could feel it now. But he didn't think there was any dark purpose to it. He figured that Early was merely protecting himself against repercussions. He was safeguarding his career. Not particularly admirable, but certainly not illegal.

Nobles had probably been the perfect sort of an agent for Early. Except for his business with Boyko, he made a great show of getting out a lot of work: tons of paper work, so many contacts he needed a special computer program to handle them, and an ongoing operation that even involved the private sector. Everyone was happy; everyone was satisfied. But now Nobels was dead. Someone had to pick up the pieces; someone had to clean up the mess.

"Don't forget my car and a weapon, Bob. I'll be leaving fairly early."

McKenzie still hadn't returned, so Horn lay down and tried to get some rest, but his thoughts were seething on Nobels and Boyko. What had Nobels found that he wanted to bring a warning about? And did it have anything to do with Boyko's death? Was there a connection, or had it been merely circumstantial? Nothing seemed certain now; everything seemed hazy, like the light on the stanchion down in the courtyard, hazy and dim with a halo obscuring its real purpose even further.

He also thought about Christine and the children. He decided that he would have to make it up to them somehow when he was finished here. Perhaps a trip home. Christine had been wanting a trip back for quite a while now, ever since her sister had written that their father was aging. He suspected that secretly she was worried about his health, worried that she was going to die before she could get back to see him. He would indulge her.

Gloria Townsend came up a few minutes after six, waking Horn from a troubled sleep. She had brought along a pot of coffee, fresh this time, and some sweet rolls. Her face seemed long.

"Tom is having a little trouble getting a lead on Turalenko," she said. "Coffee?"

"Sure," Horn said, rubbing the sleep out of his eyes. He accepted the cup.

"He seems to have dropped out of sight sometime in early October. No one seems to have any idea where. His apartment is vacant, and apparently no one is watching it. Mr. Nobels's logs were the last known references."

Horn sipped his coffee. "What about the others? What did you find?"

"They're all dead, sir."

Horn looked up at the girl, his breath catching in his throat for just a moment. It felt as if his heart had stopped. "Accidents?" he managed to ask. "Died in their beds? Executed? Murdered? What?"

"Accidents, as far as we can determine, Mr. Horton," the girl said. She had brought along her notes to which she now referred. "Vadim Guzov drowned on June 5, 1980, here in Moscow. A boating accident of some sort. Tom will be bringing up the details. Leonid Avdeyenko died of an apparent heart attack on April 19, 1982, while riding a bus, also here in Moscow. And two years ago in May . . . the fifteenth . . . Ilya Pupyshev was run over by a truck on Pushkinskaya Square, near the Moscow City Soviet Building. He was killed instantly, according to the reports."

Which left only Sheshkin, Horn thought, a sudden cold wind wafting across his soul.

LeBec had taken the late-evening flight back to Helsinki, a city he hated nearly as much as he hated Moscow. His contact met him with a car, had handed over his travel papers, and had driven him over to the Rantasipi Airport Hotel. He had a late supper of cold cuts and excellent cheeses with a bottle of good Finnish beer, and then had listened to the news in English on the television because it seemed as if he had been out of touch with the world for the past forty-eight hours. He lay down on top of the bedcovers and tried to sleep, but he could not. On an ordinary day he would have slept easily, thinking about his usual Sunday trip to the seaside with his wife and daughter. It was pleasant on the Côte d'Azure, not like here. "Can we go fishing, Papa?" Jeanne would ask. "Yes, we *may* go fishing," he would tell her, correcting her grammar, for he wanted her to grow into a sophisticated woman, like her mother. In that way she would stand a much greater chance of marrying well and thus be insulated from the vagaries of a world he believed had gone quite mad.

There were times like these, however, when he wasn't sure how any of it would turn out. Times like these during which he felt as if he were on a downward spiral. To hell. His mother, God rest her soul, would turn over in her grave. Yet he was a pragmatist if nothing else. A true believer in the facts of life. He did not make governments; he did not create ambitious men. He only served them both. And served them well. If he would admit to it, he thought of himself as a technician, a piano tuner whose job it was to make certain discordant notes were eliminated.

He arose at six, showered and shaved, then checked out of the hotel. He took the shuttle bus back to the terminal. Traveling under the name Philippe Girarde, a French historian, he boarded the Aeroflot nonstop flight to Moscow, which departed precisely at 8:00 A.M. The plane was barely half full, mostly with Russians returning home from business trips or winter vacations. The morning had been overcast, but they flew over it in harsh sunshine. The clouds stretched as far as he could see in all directions. They were cold. Frozen in place, not like the clouds over the Mediterranean. Here there was no softness, no warmth. But then he hadn't come on vacation, nor had he come seeking peace. This was not an ordinary day; he'd come only for containment.

They touched down a few minutes before ten. LeBec hung back, getting off last. He walked down the boarding tunnel, and then followed the last of the deplaning passengers to the arrivals and customs hall where they were made to wait for their baggage. A young man wearing civilian clothes and a cloth workman's cap came up to him. He had a feral look, LeBec thought. He was not an ordinary Russian. He'd seen the West.

"Monsieur Girarde?" he asked, his pronunciation terrible.

"*Oui,*" LeBec said. "Philippe Girarde."

"If you will just come with me, we have a car waiting."

"My luggage . . ."

"Will be taken care of. Welcome to the Soviet Union. We have a job of work to do."

Indeed, LeBec thought. They needed him even here, in Russia, because this operation was not sanctioned by the KGB. Nor could it be. There were much higher stakes.

9

The Soviet Union had adopted the Christian habit of closing down shop on Sundays. Disturbingly an increasing number of young people had taken this relaxation of standards as an invitation to join the old babushkas at church. No one knew how long this liberal attitude of tolerance by the government would last, but as long as it did, there were those who would take advantage. The snow had finally stopped, though the sky was low and gray. Most streets had already been plowed. Crews, a lot of them women with shovels, wooden pushers, and brooms, were cleaning some of the narrower side streets. By noon even the alleys would be cleared.

Down on the Moscow River when Pfeiffer and Horn crossed on the Borodinskiy Bridge, already whole families were skating on a broad path of ice that had been cleared by a snowplow. Cars crossed the ice, and a very large half-track truck, hauling a train of at least a dozen heavily laden sleds, lumbered downstream toward where the river bent around the Lenin Stadium. Pfeiffer had returned early to the embassy. Horn had cleaned up and changed clothes. Early had brought down a Walther PPK automatic pistol with one full clip of ammunition and a spare. "Save one bullet for yourself if you have to use the gun," the COS quipped over his shoulder. Early had also brought along a miniature recorder no wider or longer than a pack of cigarettes and only half as thick. Even if the instrument were kept in a coat pocket, the machine would

102

record conversations up to ten feet away. Each tiny tape could record continuously for three hours. The machine was state of the art.

They joined the sparse traffic on Berezhkovskaya Embankment road that followed the eastern loop of the river up toward the Mosfilm studios and past the university to Gagarin Heights where Pfeiffer had an apartment in a foreigners' complex. Moscow and its environs were mostly flat. Here, however, the land rose a little so that they could look back into the city, the onion domes of St. Basil's surrounded by apartment towers and the tall hotels along Gorki and Kalinina streets. In the flat gray light the scene looked two-dimensional, almost like a bad painting done on a dingy backdrop. Horn didn't think they were being followed, but of course he wouldn't know that for certain until he was able to get off by himself.

"I've managed to come up with a Ford Cortina for you," Pfeiffer said as he slowed down. They approached a long gravel driveway that led down to a cluster of four eighteen-story apartment buildings that looked new. "The car is in reasonable condition. Belongs to Bill Kurtley who lives in the complex. He's an engineer with Teledyne."

"Is he clean?"

"He's rotating back to the States. Scheduled to leave from Leningrad on Wednesday. We don't expect him back here. His company will be picking up the car later in the week."

"Do we have someone on him?"

Pfeiffer looked sharply at Horn. "Are you planning on getting yourself into trouble that fast?" They turned down the road.

"Just to be on the safe side. We owe him that much, don't you think?" It was windier here outside the central city. Snow whipped around the corners of the buildings and shook the bare branches of the birch trees. A dozen children played on the hill beside one of the buildings. They were probably American. But Horn couldn't tell from where he was. If Marc and Marney were in the car, they'd be clamoring to join the play. It would not matter one whit to them if the children were Russian or not.

"I'll speak with Bob first thing in the morning," Pfeiffer muttered.

They passed a pale green Cortina with civilian plates and a USA decal on the trunk lid. "That's it," Pfeiffer said. He pulled in behind the next building and shut off the engine. "Militia is out front. We'll go in that way."

"Take my bags up for me?" Horn asked.

Pfeiffer's eyes widened just a little. "You're starting out already?"

"Any reason why not, K.W.?"

"I just thought . . ." Pfeiffer dragged the Cortina's keys out of his coat pocket and handed them over. "I'm in eighteen-B, when you get back. Top floor."

"Leave word with your militiaman."

"He'll want to see your passport, but it'll be all right."

Pfeiffer seemed distracted. Early had probably told him to keep a close eye on his guest without being too obvious. They were all afraid of something here. They wanted to protect the status quo.

"How long will you be gone?"

"I don't know. It's possible I'll be on the run, in which case I'll try to make it back to the embassy. Do we have a fallback?"

Pfeiffer nodded carefully. "Do you know the Moskva Hotel?"

"On Marx Prospekt."

"That's the one. If you can't make it back to the embassy, go directly to the hotel. Room Four-seventeen for tonight. Starting tomorrow around noon it'll change to Seven-twelve. Mr. Pridgen. Stanley Pridgen."

In the old days they'd used the Sovetskaya Hotel out near the Hippodrome as a rotating safe flat. It was right under the noses of the KGB who of course had a monitor on the rooms. The theory was, if you wanted to hide someone, the best place was in a crowd. It was depressing to Horn, however, that the system had not changed even though he had been told repeatedly that KGB operations in Moscow had become much more sophisticated since his tenure. He suspected the KGB was playing the same game they were: if you want to eavesdrop, don't let on that you're listening any harder than normal.

"Bob will want to know," Pfeiffer said.

"Fine. I'll check with you later."

It took a long time for the little car to warm up, and when he finally pulled away and drove up the long gravel road back to the highway, he looked back and saw Pfeiffer standing out of the wind at the side of the building. He was watching the children playing, but he had a clear view of the driveway. Horn felt an oddness, driving off alone like this. Moscow had been such a long time ago, and now he was back. He decided he was going to have to be very careful with the car. It was his back door. At the same time, of course, it was his weakness. USA, the tag said. The decal made him foreign. He would be watched. By everyone. In Russia and especially in Moscow at the seat of government, there was an almost fanatical patriotism, a loyalty to the state that nearly bounded on the mystical. No matter how bad the situation might be in Russia, no matter if their leader was a Joseph Stalin who killed innocent people, the state had saved them from the rule of the czars, it had saved them from Hitler's Nazis, and it continued to save them from the yellow horde of Chinese to the south. Americans rooted for the underdog; Russians rooted for their government.

It had taken Christine exactly four months to come to hate the place. The Moscow weather. The crazy shopping in which you were required to stand in one line to pick out whatever it was you wanted to buy for which you were given a purchase slip, then stand in a second line to pay for the item at which time your purchase slip would be stamped, and finally stand in a third line to pick up your purchase—a loaf of bread could take an hour, two light bulbs half a day, and a pound of meat forever. Her husband's irregular hours. The militia guard outside their door—nearly every apartment building in Moscow in which foreigners were housed had a militia doorman, there ostensibly to provide protection—that made her paranoid. The odd characters who would sometimes stop them on the streets to offer them almost anything from icons to caviar in exchange for ballpoint pens, blue jeans, and American or British rock and roll records. Even the embassy teas, which as a consular section wife she was supposed to attend, bothered her. In her estimation they were prissy almost beyond belief, and were, in her words: "Very high on the back-of-the-throat gagging scale."

The coup de grace had come when she found out what Jack really did for a living. Her first clue had come out of jealousy, not hers, but the other consular wives' envy of her youth, her beauty, and, Horn supposed, her refreshing naïveté. (How often were the worst things precipitated by simple jealousy, he wondered.) Christine had come late to a tea and had overheard a snatch of conversation she shouldn't have.

The other women, embarrassed, he supposed, told her that she didn't have to wander around feeling so smug, so high and mighty, when the position her husband held was so obviously bogus. He might as well have been the janitor for all the good he was doing the consular section. "Some of our husbands actually work for a living. They don't skulk around opening other people's mail," one of them said. Christine hadn't quite known how to take what they were saying, but though she was naïve, she wasn't stupid. Jack was off somewhere for the long weekend with the ambassador, so Christine had gone back to their apartment and proceeded to take it apart stick by stick. Spring cleaning, she called it when she admitted to him what she had done. It was her excuse for prying. She felt terrible about what she had done, as if she had betrayed their trust in each other, but hadn't he been guilty of the same crime? She had found a couple of notes, a few entries for his day book, nothing in themselves incriminating —he had never gotten that sloppy with his tradecraft—but incriminating enough in Christine's mind in light of the insinuations that had been leveled at her at tea so that when Jack did return home, she hit him with all fours.

"I think you had better tell me what we are doing here in Moscow, Jack. I don't think I can take much more of it. Not without knowing."

They hadn't been married long enough for Horn to instinctively home in on what was ailing her. He was still guessing, but he was close. "Some of the other consular wives giving you a bad time?"

Christine stamped her foot in exasperation. "Don't talk to me about the consular section. That belongs to the State Department."

Horn hadn't had a chance to take off his coat or hat. He had dropped his bag at the front door. "So?"

"You don't. We don't."

"I see," Horn said very carefully now that he was beginning to realize what had happened. He let his eyes roam around the spotless apartment, lighting at length on a few scraps of paper lying on the living room table. His scraps. His notes.

"Who do you work for, Jack?"

"The ambassador."

"I won't hear it!" she shouted.

"Who do you think I work for, Christine?" The apartment

was swept for electronic surveillance devices at least once a week. But this kind of talk still made him nervous. It was the nature of the beast.

"I don't know. Maybe the CIA. Are you a spy, Jack? Is that what we're doing here in Moscow?"

"If I were? What then?"

"I was doing some spring cleaning. I found some things."

"Yes, I see."

"Goddamnit to hell, talk to me! I deserve at least that much." It was the first time she had ever used profane language. It shocked her as much as it had him.

"What exactly did they say to you?"

"They said at least their husbands didn't go around opening other people's mail. They said your job wasn't real. They said you might just as well be the janitor for all the good you were doing the consular section."

"Who was there at that tea, Christine? Who exactly said that?"

Christine stepped back a pace, her hand going to her mouth. Her eyes were wide, her nostrils flared as if she were having trouble catching her breath. She seemed more surprised than frightened. The fear, Horn suspected, would come later. It was inevitable.

"Can you tell me, Christine? It is very important."

"All of them," she said in a very small voice.

"The consular tea? That group?"

Christine nodded.

"There is no dishonor in what I am doing, Christine," he had told her. "In this you must believe me. You must have faith."

She nodded but said nothing.

"I think after tomorrow you will get more respect from that bunch," he said.

She had never spoken about it since, at least not until a few days ago in Innsbruck, but from that time onward it had been there in their marriage like a cloud, or more like a thin gray veil that ever so slightly blurred the edges of their relationship. Now that he was back in Moscow, all that and a lot more was being dredged up from the back of his mind, as if the mechanism for recall were totally automatic and geographically triggered. Come to Moscow to remember!

The sparse Sunday morning traffic worked as much to

Horn's advantage as it did to his disadvantage. Though he was highly conspicuous driving a car with a USA decal on its trunk lid, so would anyone who was following him stand out against the bland background. In Moscow you had to assume that there were only two kinds of people: those who were following you, which meant they were KGB, and those who were watching you, which meant they were the remainder of the population. He didn't mind being watched at the moment, but he did not want to be followed. Not so soon.

He headed along the south bank of the Moscow River, following it as it curved south, then northeast again in front of the Moscow State University, quiet now this morning, then up past the Academy of Sciences and Gorki Park already filling with families out enjoying the snow. Muscovites enjoyed the out-of-doors. It was at least one thing that Horn had in common with them. He drove without haste, checking frequently in his rearview mirror for any sign that he was being followed. But no one was behind him, and he began to get the feeling that his entry into the Soviet Union had rung no alarms, had raised no eyebrows. Fourteen years ago was a long time, and though the KGB had possibly spotted him at the Stortorget safe house before Nobels was killed, they were not after him now. Either that, he thought, or they were a lot better than he gave them credit for being.

Boyko and Sheshkin, according to Nobels's reports, now had apartments within a few blocks of each other just off Oktyabr'skaya Square. Horn made his first pass through the square in front of the Warsaw Hotel, driving up Dimnrova Street past the French embassy before swinging back again toward the Moskovsko-Leninskiy department store, closed now and looking more like a sweatshop-era factory of red brick, rows of small arched windows above the first floor, than a store. A trolley bus rumbled past as he made another broad circle past a sports field a half-dozen blocks to the south, finally parking around the corner from the Warsaw Hotel, near the Metro station.

An old grandmother with a child on each hand, ice skates dangling around their necks as they headed down to Gorki Park, stopped as Horn was locking the Cortina. "There are no shops open today," she said, her English pretty fair.

Surprised, Horn turned around and smiled. There was no one behind the woman. No one else. "I know that, grandmother," he said gently. In Russia everyone was a busybody.

"You are taking the children skating, I see. On Golitsinskiy Pond?"

"Yes," the babushka said, happy to be able to use her English, and pleased that a Westerner knew the name of the pond in Gorki Park. "This is such a fine car to be leaving it thus on the street."

"It is my custom to walk on Sunday mornings."

The old woman shook her head, then clucking in disapproval pulled the children after her as she waddled down the street. They had a long way to go to the park, at least three kilometers. Perhaps they had enough money to return on the trolley. Horn hoped so.

Calmly, reasonably certain now that he wasn't being followed, Horn headed on foot in the opposite direction from that taken by the old woman and the children, going across the square and down four blocks into an area of low apartment buildings on the Dobryninskayas, of which there were four in a square array behind the main street also called Dobryninskaya. By now, of course, the Soviet authorities in Moscow knew that Boyko was dead. Knew officially, that is. As soon as they had been informed by the Finns, they would have come to Boyko's apartment. Searched it, probably, and possibly even stationed someone to watch it. Horn couldn't imagine them *not* doing at least that much. Even if the KGB itself had killed Boyko—which was likely—they'd want to know who might show up to pick over his bones. It made what Horn was doing this morning terribly dangerous. It was possible the KGB would be coming after him in any event, and now he was showing up literally in the lion's den. Early would have an apoplectic fit if he knew.

At the corner of Dobryninskaya 3, Horn hesitated for a moment or two. The street was barely half a block long, narrow, lined on both sides by four-story apartment buildings in brown brick, shops shuttered on the ground floor of a few of the buildings. Eight or nine cars were parked half up on the curb, most of them tiny Zaporozhets, a couple of Zhigulis and one Moskvich sedan with its right fender bashed in. He was looking for a van or a truck, something enclosed from which a surveillance operation of Boyko's apartment could be maintained. At the very least he was looking for one of the parked cars to be equipped with an extra antenna. But there was nothing out of the ordinary here. Of course, the KGB could be in Boyko's apartment itself, or in an adjacent apartment, perhaps even in one of the apartments across the street. Horn expected them to be there, but he had no sense of it now. Usually he could feel the presence of a surveillance unit. It was part of the sixth sense that made him such a good fieldman. But he was getting nothing now, other than the almost poignant memory of Boyko and the others that night when they had all gathered together for the first time. Not here, of course, but being in such close proximity to an apartment that one of his old madmen had inhabited brought back the memories.

He would have liked very much to see Boyko's apartment. Look through his things. Short of that he had wanted to see physical evidence that the KGB was interested. But no one was in sight, and the risks entailed in approaching and entering Boyko's apartment now were much too great to justify any possible benefit. At least for the moment, he told himself, he would have to keep clear. He was disappointed, but he had other things to do now. This place would come later if need be. There were ways.

Horn turned and walked briskly up the intersecting avenue past the main street of Dobryninskaya, along a curious curved street lined with shops, a bookstore, and one small working-man's café, all closed, finally coming out on Zhitnaya, a broad boulevard that angled between the Warsaw Hotel on Oktyabr'skaya Square and the Moskovsko-Leninskiy department store on Dobryninskaya Square. There was some traffic here. A bus came by, followed by a taxi that angled toward him until the driver realized that he wasn't a possible fare, then three army trucks, the red star on their canvas sides, rumbled by. A few pedestrians were out too, enjoying the new snow that lent the city a clean, freshly scrubbed look. Sunday in Moscow, like Sunday in New York or Washington or Chicago or Los Angeles, was a family time. A day of peace. There were a lot of smiling, friendly faces here. Horn pulled on his gloves and swung his arms as he headed up the street because it was impolite in the Soviet Union to walk with your hands in your pockets. It was all coming back to him now, all the bits about this place, the customs, the habits, the tradecraft a fieldman needed to know in order to be successful, to stay out of the Lubyanka lockup, and to remain alive. He smiled as he walked, a man with not a care in the world.

•   •   •

Number 21 Zhitnaya was a dumpy-looking two-story building on the upper side of the boulevard, some sort of a private garage below and an apartment above. A door led into a narrow, dark alcove. The stairs were blocked by a heavy iron accordion gate that was locked. The door buzzer was on a brown, chipped wall, a tiny card announcing that it was the apartment of Yevgenni and Tatiana Sheshkin. There were no other cards. No one else lived upstairs. The stairhall was dirty. It smelled of cooked cabbage and boiled meat from upstairs as well as grease and oil from the garage just on the other side of the plaster wall. It was cold enough so that Horn was able to see his breath in the light from the open door behind him. For thirty seconds or so he hesitated from going the rest of the way in, from pushing the buzzer. From above he could hear music; either a radio or a television was playing. Sounded like a folk tune. Boyko and the others were dead or, like Turalenko, missing. Sheshkin was the only one of the old madmen left. The KGB had apparently fingered Boyko. Had they also cracked the entire old network? Had the others been killed, their deaths made to look like accidents? But why? Why now after all these years? And what about Sheshkin? Was he next on the list, or had he turned informer?

He let the door close, then went the rest of the way in and rang the buzzer. He heard it upstairs in the apartment. A moment later the music stopped, and the door at the head of the stairs opened. A slightly built woman dressed in a pale orange warm-up suit, her long dark hair held back by a headband, came out. She switched on a light.

"Yes?" she called down. "Who are you?"

"You must be Tatiana," Horn said in his best Russian. He smiled up at her. "I have come to see Yevgenni. We are old friends."

"You are foreign. British?"

"American."

She was visibly disturbed. "What are you doing here? We don't want anything from you."

"I would like to see Yevgenni. Just to have a word or two. Nothing more."

"He is not here. He has gone out."

Even from the foot of the stairs Horn could see that she was frightened. Yevgenni had evidently told her about the old network, about his control officer. Dangerous stuff to tell a wife. The taint of being a spy, a traitor to your own country, was forever. Marriages as often as not didn't last. And when they ended sometimes there was a lot of bitterness. But Yevgenni had been the conservative. His apparent trust in his wife—according to what Horn had managed to dig out, they'd been married only four years—was extraordinary.

"When will he be back? Would you happen to know?"

"Tatiana! Who is there?" a man called angrily from inside the apartment.

"Why are you here?" Tatiana whispered urgently. "Can't you leave him alone?"

"Are we heating all of Moscow, Tatiana?" Yevgenni shouted, coming to the door. He had always been a big man, husky, but he had put on some weight, especially around the middle. He'd been an excellent soccer player in the old days, if Horn's memory served him, and like so many former athletes Yevgenni seemed to hold himself as if he were ready to sprint a kilometer. He was dressed in a matching pale orange warm-up suit.

"Hello, Yevgenni," Horn said.

"I told him to go away," Tatiana said, her arm going possessively around his waist.

"I wish you hadn't come here, Jack. I have a wife, a party card, and a different job now. I don't work for the government anymore. Now I am a buyer for GUM."

"I know. I didn't come about that," Horn said. "And I won't stay long, I promise you both. No trouble."

Yevgenni sighed deeply. He looked at his wife and shook his head in defeat. "I should have known, Jack, shouldn't I have. This is about Vitali?"

"You've heard already?" Horn asked. "How? From whom?"

"Heard, Jack? Heard what?"

Horn had thought it possible that Sheshkin was working with the KGB, that this was a trap. Now he didn't think so. Yevgenni seemed genuine. They might be talking about the same person, but they were not talking about the same thing. He didn't think that Yevgenni knew that Boyko was dead.

"May I come up?"

Tatiana clutched at her husband. "No, Yevgenni. No. Send him away. We don't want him here. Someone will see. Send him away. Please."

"Just for a few minutes, I promise," Horn said. "This is very important."

Sheshkin disengaged himself from his wife's grasp, but he made no move to come down the stairs. "Heard what, Jack? What was I supposed to have heard about Vitali?"

"He's dead."

Tatiana gave a little cry. "Oh, hell," she said.

"Dead of what? How did this happen? And where, Jack?"

"He was shot to death in Helsinki a few days ago. It's why I came back. All the others are dead too, or gone. Turalenko disappeared four months ago, you know. He was a good party man. And now there is only you."

Yevgenni shuddered. He looked at his wife, then slowly came down the stairs. Tatiana turned and went back into the apartment. At the bottom of the stairs Yevgenni hesitated a moment longer before unlocking the iron gate. He looked into Horn's eyes. He was frightened, and just a little angry, and yet Horn could see that he had probably been expecting something like this to happen. He was the one to keep in touch with the others. The maiden aunt who kept the family intact, or at least kept informed of their fates and fortunes.

"You know about the others?" Horn asked.

"Yes, Jack, I knew about the others. But with Sergei it is not the same. He has gone to Irkutsk. There is a very good job there for him. They are building a new factory—to make wire, I think. He went as a construction engineer."

"Have you heard from him?"

Sheshkin shook his head. He unlocked the gate and shoved it back, then stepped aside so that Horn could come through. Then he relocked the gate and went first up the stairs. Horn unbuttoned his overcoat, then hurriedly transferred the tape recorder to an inner pocket of his jacket and switched it on. At the top he took off his coat, and just inside, Sheshkin took it from him and hung it on a hook.

The apartment was overheated, as were most Russian apartments in winter. Someone once explained to Horn that the Russians lived in heat now to make up for a national memory of decades when there never was enough fuel for heat. These days no one in Russia was going to freeze to death. A dining room and small kitchen were separated from a fairly large living room by an archway. A short corridor led back to two doors; Horn supposed they were the bedroom and a bathroom. The place was nicely furnished, some pieces of Danish modern, and spotlessly clean. There were no children, according to Nobels's files, so they would lavish their time and money on themselves and their apartment. It was only natural. And it was obvious that Sheshkin was proud of what he had.

"It's a nice place, Yevgenni."

"Sure, we work hard, Jack. I'm not afraid to admit it."

Tatiana had disappeared. In the bedroom, Horn suspected. It would be better that way, with her gone. She might do a lot of guessing afterward, and her husband might tell her a lot of what went on, but it would all be secondhand. And the less she knew about this business, the better off they'd all be. He wanted to tell this to Yevgenni, but he thought it would anger his old madman enough to make him uncooperative.

"She is a pretty girl, your Tatiana."

"Thank you."

Horn moved over to the window that looked down on Zhitnaya to see if he had been followed after all. Two men, one of them taller than the other, had just disappeared around the corner. There was no one else. Only the light traffic and the normal Sunday passersby. The boulevard was too wide for the few cars, and it made the city seem deserted. Sheshkin understood the tradecraft; he watched, holding his breath, waiting for the verdict. Horn turned back.

"It's clean."

"Did you think you would be followed, Jack?"

Horn shrugged. "This is Moscow."

"This is Moscow. That is correct, Jack. But this is not the old Moscow. Not your old Moscow. And I am not your old Yevgenni Ivanovich. Everything has changed. I work for a department store now. Not the government. Unless you want to know about nylons and rock and roll records and television sets, I can no longer help you."

"Someone assassinated Vitali in Helsinki. Everyone else is gone too, including Turalenko. That leaves only you, Yevgenni. I want to know what is happening. I also want to protect you."

"I cannot help you. I know nothing, except that all of us knew that Vitali would be killed sooner or later. By a jealous husband, by a party official who thought he knew too much, by the black market, by the KGB."

"It may have been the KGB."

"Yes, why?"

"He was running French whores here to Moscow. Maybe he got too big for his britches."

"He always tried to wear too big boots, Jack; this you know."

"When did you last see him, Yevgenni?" Horn asked softly.

"I told you that I was no longer in this game. I made that abundantly clear. I am a buyer for GUM now."

"Was it recently?"

Sheshkin shook his head. "A while ago."

"Weeks? Days?"

"Ten days ago, maybe two weeks."

"He came here?"

"Yes, he came here."

"When? During the day? At night? Did he telephone you first? See you at work? 'Hello, Yevgenni, let's get together.' Something like that?"

"He just came here the one night."

"Late?"

"Yes. In the middle of the night. I told him to go away. I wouldn't let him up. He was drunk. So I sent him away. Tatiana was upset. We argued all that night. And now your coming here hasn't helped."

"You sent Vitali away?"

"Yes, that's right. He was very drunk. Loud. I thought he was going to wake up the whole neighborhood. He called me a spy. He was shouting like a crazy man. It's no wonder he was killed." Sheshkin seemed then like a cornered animal against whom the odds were so overwhelming that he had simply given up. He would now accept anything that would come. He could do nothing else. He was helpless. It was written all over his face.

"But first you helped him, Yevgenni. You just didn't send your old comrade in arms away empty-handed, did you? I mean he came asking for something, and you gave it to him."

"I couldn't help it. He threatened to wake up the entire neighborhood, as I have already said. We would both have been arrested. So, yes, I helped him."

"With what? What did he come to you for?"

"He wanted the old Paris number. The emergency number. I remembered it. I remember such things, you know that: 723-86-21. In case there was trouble."

"Was he in trouble?"

"I don't know. No, I don't think so, Jack. He had another

hot deal he was cooking up. But this time it was sick. I told him so. I told him that he would sell his own mother. But he said she was already dead. I knew this. It was just an expression on my part.''

"Was it the French whores, Yevgenni? Was that why he needed the Paris number? It makes sense."

Sheshkin seemed to shrink a little. "No. At least I don't think so. I didn't know anything about that, at least not directly."

"He mentioned them to you?"

"Earlier."

"Then what was it this time?"

"It was a letter someone wanted him to deliver. On the outside, you know."

Horn glanced beyond Sheshkin to the corridor. Tatiana had come to the bedroom door. She was looking at them with her large, dark, liquid Russian eyes. She might have been crying.

Sheshkin turned around. "Go back in the bedroom, Tati. Shut the door. This is not for you."

"It is not for *us*, Yevgenni. Tell him to go away. Now. Before it is too late."

"Please shut the door. It will be just a minute. I promise you. On this you have my word."

"You shit!" she swore, slamming the door. It wasn't clear to Horn to whom she had been referring. Probably both of them.

"I've told you enough now, Jack. Please, it is time for you to go now if I am to save anything of my marriage."

"Who had written this letter?"

"He didn't say, Jack. Honestly."

"Her name was Anna. Anna who?" Horn asked patiently.

"Anna Chalkin."

"Who is she?"

"This I do not know. I thought her name was familiar to me. From the old days, you know. But I cannot remember. It was a letter from Anna Chalkin. That is all I know."

"Who was it addressed to? And why did Vitali need the Paris number? This I don't understand. The number was strictly for trouble of the worst kind. It was our Mayday channel, remember?"

"He wanted to sell the letter," Sheshkin said, hanging his head. "It was a dirty business."

"Sell it in Paris? To whom?"

"I don't know. He didn't tell me that part."

"Who was it addressed to, then, this letter from Anna?"

Sheshkin looked up. "That's the odd part, Jack," he said earnestly, as if he wanted to please. "It's the one part I don't understand. It was a letter to Jason, he told me. Vitali said it was addressed to Jason, and yet he said he didn't know who it was. Was it Mr. Jason or wasn't it?"

"Had he opened the letter?"

Sheshkin nodded heavily. "That was the sick part. He said Anna Chalkin has less than a year to live. She is dying. And she had to get this letter out to Jason."

"No idea who Jason might be?"

"No names."

"Or who Anna Chalkin might be?"

"Certainly not French, Jack. Someone from the past. Someone . . . I don't know."

"But Vitali thought he could make something of it. Money. Points. Whatever."

"I think so. He was very excited. It was the old Vitali that we knew at work. When I told him it was sick, his opening a dying woman's letter, he got mad at me. Called me a spy. Said she was a whore. She had spread her legs for a foreign prick and didn't even know his name. Those were his exact words."

The air left the room. Horn felt as if he were on another planet, such as Mercury or even the moon, where there was a vacuum, and where the sun always beat down so harshly that shadows took on real meaning, while the rest of the world was too bright even to look at.

"Could Jason have been a code name, Yevgenni?" Horn asked, careful now to keep his voice even.

"Yes, I thought this myself."

"Did you get any sense of who he might be, from talking with Vitali that night?"

"An American."

"At the embassy?"

"Yes."

"He wanted to sell this letter to someone in Paris?" Horn asked compassionately. Sheshkin was having trouble dealing with it. He suspected Yevgenni was thinking about Boyko lying dead on some Helsinki street. It was what Horn was thinking about.

"He thought it was important, you know. I could tell. It was to have been a coup for him."

"What else? What else did he say?"

"Nothing more, Jack, I swear. After that—after I gave him the Paris number—I came back up and shut the door. I watched from the window. I saw him leave. That was all."

This time Horn was sure that Sheshkin was telling the truth. The entire truth. He could see it in his old madman's eyes. He could also see the fear and the despair. So who the hell was Anna Chalkin, and who was Jason? And why had Boyko figured someone at the Paris number could help make him a score? It didn't make any sense, and yet there was a frightening, dark undertone that was beginning to worry him. There was a lot more yet than met the eye. An entire universe, he suspected.

At the door he collected his coat. Sheshkin followed him out into the stairhall and went down to unlock the gate. At the bottom, as Horn was buttoning up his coat, he turned back to his old madman.

"Does the name Nobels ring a bell with you, Yevgenni?"

"No," Sheshkin said thoughtfully.

"Early? Pfeiffer?"

Sheshkin shook his head. "I don't know anything anymore, Jack. I swear it. Not knowing has become my hobby, you know. I am sorry that Vitali ever came to me. I am sorry that I called Irkutsk—" He stopped himself, but it was too late.

"Turalenko?" Horn asked.

"Yes," Sheshkin answered reluctantly.

"He's dead?"

"He was electrocuted. An accident at the factory."

"When?"

"Two days after he got there, Jack."

Horn crossed the street and worked his way back to where he had parked his car by a roundabout way, stopping and starting, making sure he wasn't being followed. But he had the feeling someone was there. That someone was behind him. Someone was above, in one of the buildings looking down at him. Reaching his car he looked back over his shoulder. No one was there.

Horn was a very good agent. But like any mere mortal he had his weaknesses as well as his strengths. Among his strong points was his ability to inspire confidence. When Jack Horn said he was telling the truth, everyone believed him. His major weakness, however, if he would admit it, was that he cared too much about his madmen; he truly cared about them in a big, personal way. He remembered all of them; these in Moscow, being his first, were his most important. Only Sheshkin remained. He was afraid now, just as he was afraid about Anna Chalkin, about Jason, and about what it all meant, and how it would all turn out.

10

Horn drove back across the river, using the Krimskiy Bridge on the north edge of Gorki Park, half the city, it seemed, down there enjoying the day. Still it was Sunday, barely one, and the overcast was deepening, portending more snow. Zubovskiy Boulevard was a very broad, tree-lined thoroughfare, nearly empty of traffic at this hour. Driving along it he was beginning to get the feeling that he had been back for a long time. Perhaps he had never left. Here, the distinction between the present and his past was so subtle he was starting to get caught up in his old habits, his old routines. Going to see Boyko's apartment and then talking with Sheshkin had brought him back to the promise he had made the last time he left. He hadn't done much to keep it, though Carlisle would have no argument with his method to this point. But now he was heading toward forbidden territory. The State Department would undoubtedly have much to say about his mission if they knew, which they would eventually, and none of it would be complimentary to Horn's abilities or judgment.

On the west side of the river he doubled back, taking the broad Komsomol Prospekt all the way to where it jogged right, and then worked his way through a strange neighborhood of old churches that had been converted to museums, and past back courtyards in which tar-paper shacks seemed to sprout amidst piles of garbage and junk. Finally he emerged on the boulevard near the skyscraper Foreign Ministry on Smolenskaya Square. By now Edmund Clay would be very old, he thought. Seventy at least. From what he had heard, however, the man hadn't slowed down a bit. There was only a fifty-fifty chance he'd be in residence in Moscow. If not here, he would be in his Central Park West apartment in New York. His two homes. But not divided loyalties. "Shared loyalties," he'd once explained. If he was here he would certainly help; if he was here and the information Horn sought was within his capabilities, he would give his assistance.

Number 24 Arbat Street was next door to the Vakhtangov Theater. Like the theater, it was a low, one-story house that had once been used as a palace. This section of the city had once been home to the nobility. Curiously, the surrounding streets were all named after artisans, as if the wealthy had gathered their own workmen around them: Plotnikov (carpenter), Serebryany (silversmith), and Kalachny (pastry cook) streets were prime examples. Horn parked across the street and shut off the Cortina's engine. It struck him just then that he had spent a great deal of his career like this, watching for some sign that all was as it should be, looking over his shoulder, planning and endlessly replanning his every move as if he were playing a for-real game of chess in which he could not see the other player. Of course he knew that the other man was there, because all the pieces kept moving. Attacking. Retreating. But for the most part the opposition was invisible, which made the game all the more dangerous. The house was white brick with tall windows under broad overhangs. The arches above each window looked as if they were gilded with gold, and the wood trim and two small columns at the portico were freshly painted. The house itself was set well back off the street behind a tall iron fence. The front and side yards, what Horn could see of them, were rich with plantings, trees, bushes, and beds, covered now, that in a few months would blossom in a riot of colorful flowers. Now the yard was bare of any green, a dead black-and-white fairyland waiting for spring. Clay's hobby was gardening. His apartment in New York had been filled with growing things, and Horn remembered an expansive vegetable garden on the roof. He had always thought Clay would have been happier in the countryside, where he could have had acres of land, or at least could have constructed greenhouses.

It was an odd place to come looking for answers. A forbidden place. But here he would receive the unvarnished truth.

He got out of his car, waited for a bus to rattle by, then walked across the street to the tall iron gate. A polished brass plaque announced only the number and nothing more. He let himself in, the gate operating smoothly on its well-oiled hinges, went up the path, and mounted the single step onto the portico. A notice beside the door was in two languages, first Russian, then English, announcing that this was the residence of Edmund Rutger Clay. The buzzer was beneath the plaque. He rang it.

Edmund Clay had come to Moscow in 1942 as a young army captain to help with the Lend-Lease program, and he had never really left. He divided most of his time between Moscow and New York. He was a wealthy man by any Western standard, which made his fellow countrymen trust and respect him. But he had a genuine disregard for most material things, ostentatious things, and a proletariat's view of class, which made the Russians admire him. Much like his more famous counterpart in entrepreneurial pursuits, Armand Hammer, Clay dabbled in this and that. Sometimes he worked out a grain deal between American midwestern farmers and the appropriate Soviet ministries. Sometimes he worked out trades of soft technology, such as television in the fifties, and sometimes he traded on culture for no profit, as when the Philadelphia Orchestra played in Moscow, and the Bolshoi Ballet played in Washington. At other times Clay acted as a private messenger between the two countries. Sometimes the exact nuances of the meaning of a written communiqué, even a perfect translation, could get lost. Clay could straighten it out. He had been trusted by seven presidents since Truman, and by five Soviet premiers since Stalin. He'd been married nearly forty-five years, but his wife had died a few years ago, and even that had not slowed him down.

The door opened and an older, short, dumpy-looking woman wearing an apron over a print dress and a scarf on her head stood looking out at him. Her manner attempted to be stern, but her eyes gave her away. They were warm and soft, laugh lines at the corners. Her face was slightly flushed, as if she had either been drinking, or had been laughing, or both.

"Yes, may I help you, mister?" she asked in Russian.

"I would like to speak with Mr. Clay if he is in residence today," Horn said gently. "You may tell him it is Mr. Horn come back."

"He knows this name? He knows you . . . Mr. Horn?" the old woman asked, peering more intently at him.

"From a long time ago. Fourteen years."

"You are from the embassy?"

"No, just visiting an old friend."

The woman looked at him a bit longer, as if she were inspecting him for signs that he might be lying to her. Finally coming to some decision, she nodded and stepped back. "Come in, then, come in out of the cold, Mr. Horn," she said, switching to reasonable English. "I think he will see you. He might even tell you whatever it is that seems so important to you at the moment."

Horn stepped inside and the woman shut the door. The house was refreshingly cool, and very neat. A highly polished tile floor led through a broad entryway to a large central hall, the ceilings very high, opening at the back in celerestory windows that gave natural daylight to the pleasant space that was filled with hanging plants and statuary. A marble bench was placed in front of a small water pool that divided the central hall from the entryway and the remainder of the house. There was an air of quiet wealth here. An up-to-date fortune. From what he could see, Horn suspected the entire house was well and constantly maintained, no mean feat here in Moscow where long waiting lists and shoddy workmanship were the rule among the service industries.

"Wait here," the woman said, indicating the bench as she passed it. She disappeared through a doorway that led toward the rear of the house, her voice trailing after her. "I'll see if the old man will see you."

Horn took off his coat and carefully laid it on the marble bench. The tape recorder was still in an inner pocket of his sports jacket. He reached in and fingered the controls. Taping a madman was one thing, but recording Edmund Clay in secret, without the man's consent, was a horse of a different stripe. He pushed the record and play buttons and removed his hand from his pocket. It wasn't a business for the timid. His father had told him that very thing about becoming a priest. "Not really a job for the weak of heart, you know, contrary to popular belief. God loves the priest with nerves of steel. They're the ones who end up canonized." Being an agent runner was like being a priest in a way: you were father confessor and God all wrapped up into one; you set the rules, then listened to how they broke them. Always, though, in the end you gave them absolution. After all, they were your creations. You couldn't leave them in the lurch. As he had here.

"Have you had your lunch, Mr. Horn?" the old woman asked, coming back only as far as the doorway.

Horn stepped around the pool. "As a matter of fact I haven't."

"This way, then. You're in luck." She turned and shuffled off, Horn right behind her, down a broad, pilastered corridor in which were displayed a dozen paintings by well-known American and Russian masters, including one that Horn took to be a Whistler and another by Ilya Repin, the Russian who painted the Volga bargeman scenes. He suspected that all of them were originals.

The corridor opened onto a long, narrow room that ran the width of the house. Tall windows looked out onto what in the summer would be a wonderful veranda and a rear garden. Along the inner walls were floor-to-ceiling shelves stuffed with books and folios. In a far corner was a concert grand piano across from a grouping of overstuffed, comfortable-looking furniture. To the right was the entry to the kitchen, and straight across was a glass-enclosed breakfast nook that jutted out onto the veranda. It was furnished with wrought-iron chairs, a glass-topped table, and large serving cart.

Edmund Clay rose from where he was seated at the table. He was a bear of an old man with heavy limbs, thick shoulders, a broad barrel chest, and a huge head surrounded by an unruly cloud of white hair, making him reminiscent of a giant Albert Einstein. His face was square and honest, lined deeply and weathered from a lifetime of working in gardens under the blazing sun. His nose was large and his eyes were pale blue and penetrating. Here is an intelligent man, they seemed to say quite forcefully; here is a man who brooks no nonsense, and yet here is a man with an obvious sense of humor. His manner was that of a man who felt as at home talking to kings and presidents as he did with housekeepers and maintenance men.

"I'll get an extra plate," the housekeeper said, and she shuffled off to the kitchen.

"I remembered the name, but I didn't think I'd remember the face," Clay said. "But I'll be damned if I don't. Though you've aged a bit."

Horn came across the room. He shook hands with the old

man whose grip was rock solid. "You don't seem to have changed a bit, sir."

Clay's eyes twinkled. "Flattery, my boy, is the art of the statesman. Don't shit an old shitter; some of it is bound to splash back." He laughed at his own joke, and his laugh was so real and so genuine that it broke any ice there might have been between them, as if the years had meant nothing.

"I thought I'd stop by to say hello," Horn said.

Clay's smile continued, but his eyes narrowed ever so slightly in disapproval. He did not like flattery, and he had a long-standing reputation for hating lies and despising their bearers.

"You'll have lunch with us?" he asked.

"I don't want to get off on the wrong foot with you, Mr. Clay," Horn said softly. "I came for some information. I need your help."

"Marina tells me you are *not* from our embassy here."

"No, sir."

"Just in for the weekend?"

"Or a bit longer. I arrived just yesterday."

"Something of importance?"

"Rather," Horn said, and he noticed a softening in the old man's attitude toward him.

Marina, the housekeeper, returned with a place setting for Horn, and she laid it out across from Clay's. A look passed between them, and she turned on her heel without a word and went back into the kitchen, closing the door firmly behind her.

"I didn't mean to interrupt," Horn said.

Clay smiled and motioned for Horn to sit. "Doesn't matter now, does it, Jack. You came here with some questions that you thought only I could help answer. Well, maybe I can and maybe I can't." He shrugged good-naturedly. "Or maybe I can and maybe I won't. That will depend a great deal upon you."

On how completely honest he was, Horn thought.

It began to snow as they drank spiced vodka and ate caviar with sour cream rolled in thin buckwheat pancakes called *blini*. Marina brought them a variety of cold meats, cheeses, and salmon along with two kinds of hard, dark bread baked into tiny rolls. Clay was a man who loved to eat, and his appetite did not seem to be affected by his age. The falling snow lent a cocoonlike atmosphere to the little breakfast nook. From time to time Clay would look out across his garden and sigh, causing Horn to wonder if the man was pining for the spring and summer·yet to come, or simply because of the loneliness of the winter scene which could have reminded him of his advanced years. He'd once said that the only trouble with getting old was that all the great and truly good friends you used to be able to count on died on you when you needed them the most. Clay kept up a running commentary not only about the food they were eating, but about the fact that he was all but retired these days. Since the Second World War he had been a man in the middle of what made the world tick. It would be hard for such a man to give that up easily, Horn mused.

"I don't know if I can be much help to you, Jack," he said. "I don't keep my ear to the millstone like I used to. The basics haven't changed, of course. I don't mean to say that. But the personalities have." He poured them another drink. "What I am trying to say, Jack, is that I may have become a bit rusty over the years. That, and just lately your compatriots at Langley seem to be bolloxing things up, especially in Central America. Doesn't exactly inspire confidence in a man."

"I didn't come for that, sir," Horn said respectfully. "I'm looking for a bit of your memory."

Clay tossed back his vodka, then looked at the glass for a moment almost as if he wondered how it had become empty. It was an odd gesture, just then. Disturbing in some undefined way. As if Clay were losing his grip on reality, and that one little thing was a sign.

"I've lived a lot of years, Jack," he said with a wan smile. "Could you be just a bit more specific about what part you're after? Memories shouldn't hurt us. Not if we're honest about them."

Clay had changed after all. Horn could see it now, and the differences between what the man had been and what he apparently had become were saddening. It happened to everyone: the gradual aging process, the slowing down, the hardening of the arteries, especially the ones in the brain. He used to think that a lot of the apparent changes one saw in people as they aged were caused by an increasing cynicism that came with advanced years: the older one became, the more foolish everyone else started to look. When you were thirty the antics of a five-year-old child seemed of little or no substance—interesting to watch, but certainly you wouldn't want your life to be guided by a child. You didn't allow five-year-olds to play with loaded pistols. How different could it be for a seventy-year-old to watch the antics of young politicians and scientists and lawyers and doctors, men in their thirties and forties? Horn was the five-year-old in comparison with Clay. Was that it? Or were the changes caused by something else? Maybe Clay would admit to nothing other than a simple tiredness. Maybe one simply wears out after so many years.

"Eight, ten years ago. Maybe as long as eleven or twelve," Horn said.

"Here in Moscow? After you packed up your kit bag and skedaddled for the hinterlands?" Clay asked.

In the old days he had been the man of the mountain, the difference in his and Horn's ages even subjectively greater than it was now. Part of Horn's job at the embassy—his cover—was to act as adviser to, and in some cases as chaperon for, visiting American VIPs. In effect he was charged with keeping them out of trouble, specifically out of the hands of the KGB's Second Chief Directorate. He and Clay had spent some time together in Moscow for a year or so, and then again for a brief period in New York City. Clay had known, of course, what Horn's real job was, but it had never been mentioned between them, at least not in so many words, not in any specific terms, nor had it ever seemed to bother the older man.

"I don't know how soon afterward. It could have been a month, a year. I have no way of telling."

"I was back and forth a lot more in those days than now," Clay said.

"It's about a woman. A Russian. I'm trying to find out about her. Who she is. What she was doing in those days."

"And with whom," Clay said, his eyes locked on Horn's.

He had wanted to give Clay only a few bits and pieces. He had wanted to isolate the old man from as much of the nastiness as possible. But sitting across the table from him now, he knew that it wouldn't work that way. Clay was much too shrewd. Still.

"Her name is Anna Chalkin," he started softly. "She wrote a letter to someone called Jason. One of my old people took it out of the country for her, and he was shot dead in Helsinki for his trouble.''

"And you are here picking up the pieces, is that it, Jack?'' Clay asked, apparently unimpressed by tales of women and couriers and murder.

"We'd like to know what happened.''

"Does the name Anna Feodorovna ring any bells with you? It should. Bolshoi Ballet. Prima ballerina for a number of years. Just recently she was bumped upstairs as assistant artistic director. They say she is too old to dance; I'd say it is something else. She displeased someone, perhaps, though that would be hard to imagine considering her background. One of her uncles is a very important man.''

"It was her stage name?'' Horn asked. He did remember her on stage. Small, like most ballet dancers; dark, he thought he remembered, and very good.

"Her patronymic as well. Father and mother never married, though. He is in the merchant marine out of Vladivostok, I suspect. Katrina Patrenkova is her mother. Rare beauty, but she never married anyone as far as I know. Still lives and teaches in Leningrad. Quite a competent concert pianist in her own right. A fair painter, a sculptress. There was a grandfather somewhere in Anna's background, as I recall, who was a poet. Might have been Petr Chalkin himself. I'm not so sure about that.''

"How do you know so much about her?''

"I enjoy the ballet, Jack. The Bolshoi is just up the street, you know. And everyone here knows who Anna Feodorovna is, just as they know Ekaterina Maximova, or Alexander Goudonov or Mikhail Baryshnikov, if you will.''

"You said she has an important uncle.''

Clay nodded heavily. "General Stepan Patrenko.''

Horn sat back, startled. He knew *that* name. Patrenko was head of the KGB's First Chief Directorate, the most important division within the Soviet secret service. It included departments for everything from counterintelligence to an effective scientific and technical espionage service. A lot of things suddenly fell into place for him, yet the vistas that General Patrenko's name opened up were legion. The horizon never loomed so far away.

"To whom did she write this letter?''

"We don't know,'' Horn said, looking up from his thoughts.

"A code name. Jason. Evidently she and Jason were having an affair."

"She wants to get it started again? I can't believe she'd want to defect."

"She's dying."

It was Clay's turn to register shock. He shook his leonine head. "What a waste," he said softly. "What a pity. You have this letter? You have seen it?"

"No. Someone else has, though," Horn said. "Have you any idea who Jason might have been?"

"An embassy lad. Possibly even one of yours."

"Do you know who he was, then?" Horn felt a bright, very hot spark in his chest.

"No," Clay said, looking inward. "The word did get around that Anna was having an affair with someone from our embassy. That was nearly eleven years ago, I think."

"Shortly after I left."

"It wasn't one of those things that gets written about in the newspapers, of course. In fact there wasn't much noise at all. I only happened to hear something at the ambassador's Christmas party. Just a mention, nothing more, as I recall. It was all kept very quiet."

"Could her uncle have arranged this affair?"

"In order to spy on the embassy?" Clay asked. "I suppose so. But at the time he wasn't a general, you know, and his niece was a very important Bolshoi star, or just becoming so. No, I think it's something that may just have happened."

"Just like that?" Horn asked. "An American and a Bolshoi star meet and fall in love?"

Clay chuckled. "Your naïveté is charming, Jack, but certainly not very practical in this day and age."

"You're trying to tell me that those girls were for sale?"

"Heavens no," Clay said, raising his hand in a gesture of dismissal. "But young, good-looking women, whether they be movie starlets, or singers, or models, or ballet stars, don't live ordinary lives. They naturally associate with the rich and the powerful. Not counting the effects of simple ambition, chemistry can and does happen."

"He was an American."

"Those were the golden days of détente, remember, Jack? Everyone was pals. We invited them to dinner, they invited us to dinner. No one trusted the other, of course, god forbid, but at least for a few years there was more straight talk than bombastic rhetoric. It could have happened.'' Clay laughed again. "Hell, it did happen.''

"No ideas who he might have been? Even a guess?''

Clay looked at Horn for a long moment or two. "So you can do what? Run him down? Maybe he's someone important, say a U.S. senator now. What will you and your head-hunters do about it? String him up on the nearest lightpole because he dipped his wicket with a young Russian ballet star ten, eleven years ago?''

"One of my people was killed,'' Horn said. He was thinking about Boyko, and about Dewey Nobels, but it was difficult to maintain an attitude of indignant concern. Clay was sharp.

"Maybe one of his own people did him in. What was he doing in Helsinki in the first place?''

"He had legitimate business there.''

"Which did not include posting a clandestine letter.''

But he had called Paris. He had called to set up a deal. He had offered to sell them Anna's letter. Horn could not keep his dark thoughts away from the obvious conclusion. Anna Feodorovna had had an affair with an American. Whoever he was, he did not want to be contacted. He had killed a man to prevent it. But he was someone well connected with the old Paris number. The only problem with that line of thinking was that there were two anomalies: Nobels's attempt to warn him about something, and Nobels's assassination.

"You don't gun a man down in the street for that.''

"For what, then, Jack?'' Clay said. He sat forward, a different look coming to his face, a thoughtful expression, almost sly-looking, as if he were expecting to be told a nasty little secret. "What, then, Jack? What are you after? You think it was an American did one of your madmen in? Is that it? Which one of your old crowd was it? No, let me take a stab at it. Must have been the entrepreneur himself: Vitali Boyko. That who you're talking about? Was he the victim?''

Horn was shocked by what Clay knew. The existence of a network was a given. Networks had existed from the beginning of history, and would exist as long as there were people to spy on and spies to do it. But specific names were supposed to be a closely guarded secret. Exposing the names was like cutting the major arteries of a living entity. It was usually fatal. Even more shocking to Horn was Clay's use of the term "madmen.'' The intrusion was intimate.

"Bingo," Clay said without waiting for Horn to respond. "Boyko was bringing out Anna Feodorovna's letter. He probably called someone, maybe dropped a note in some hole somewhere, put a chalk mark on a bridge abutment, maybe walked down the Pohjóisusplanadi with a *Herald Tribune* under his right arm. I don't know the tradecraft, Jack. But the setup wasn't right. Someone didn't like the way it looked. Or maybe he wanted some money, lots of it, and his contact didn't think it was worth the effort. Blackmail hardly ever is, you know. So they shot him to death for it."

Horn simply didn't know what to say without making a fool of himself. If Clay knew that much, what else was there? Without at least a notion of the range of Clay's awareness, Horn would be walking into a trap no matter what he said. And it was no wonder most of his old network was dead if their secret was that insecure.

"His own people probably followed him out, Jack. They may have seen what they figured was a deal in the making, and they may have gunned him down. A *mokrie dela*, they call it. Isn't that the term? *Wet affair*. Means spilling of blood."

"Any of that is possible," Horn said cautiously. "The thing is, we'd like to know exactly what did happen."

Clay's eyes narrowed. "Was Boyko still connected with your people?"

"Not directly."

"Was he doing something else in Helsinki, then? Something for your side?"

Horn thought it curious that even a middleman such as Clay would say "your side" when referring to his own countrymen. "No."

Once again Clay's attitude seemed to soften. "I'm really very sorry to hear that about Anna. Most likely it is the reason she was promoted." He shook his head. "Tom Wagner was one of them."

"Senator Wagner?" Horn asked, startled. "Oregon?"

"He was one of the old bunch stationed here at the embassy. I remember because he was campaigning even then. His daddy told him that once he got elected to the Senate he'd want to be on the Foreign Relations Committee. Get to know the Russians on their own turf, and he'd be a natural for the job."

"He's chairman of the committee."

"He might not want his constituency to know that he had once bedded a young Russian ballet star, now, would he?"

"But you don't know that he was the only one?"

"There were others. Get yourself a staff directory for that era and see who was there."

"It wouldn't mean anything by itself. It would take someone such as yourself who was on the outside, someone who saw both sides of the fence. Someone who would know who was active socially."

Clay acknowledged the obvious. "What if I do find a name for you, Jack? What then?"

"It will be my starting point."

"And if I don't? Or if I decide I'm not going to get myself involved? What then?"

"I'll start with Senator Wagner and go from there," Horn said. But if there was a connection between Boyko's death and the deaths of the others in Moscow and Turalenko's in Irkutsk, there would have to be a Russian counterpart to Anna's American lover. Someone who worked with the American, someone who wanted to protect him. That thought had been steadily mounting in the back of Horn's mind. Maybe he was dealing with a traitor, with a mole at the highest levels of the government.

"Have you been to see Anna yet?" Clay was asking.

"No."

"I would suggest you approach her, if at all, with a great deal of caution."

"Because of her uncle?"

Clay nodded. "She has never married, nor has her uncle. They are very close. He's always watched out for her welfare."

"Would he have someone watching her?"

"I doubt it, though I wouldn't put it past him. He's a very careful man, a suspicious man."

"Do you know where she lives?"

"In town, not far from the theater. I'll give you her address before you leave. But I can't emphasize strongly enough to be careful around her."

"Do you know the general? Have you ever met him?" Horn asked.

Clay chuckled. He got to his feet. Horn followed suit, their lunch finished. "Of course I know him, Jack. As a matter of fact the man is coming here to dinner tonight. I'm having a few men in for a smoker. I introduced it to them, you know.

A little poker, some vodka, good Cuban cigars, a little chitchat.''

It was late, nearly midnight. Horn lay smoking a cigarette on the couch in Pfeiffer's living room as he listened to the recordings of his conversations with Sheshkin and Clay.

"Was he in trouble?" Horn listened to his own voice.

"I don't know," Sheshkin said. *"No, I don't think so, Jack. He had another hot deal he was cooking up."*

After he left Clay's house, Horn had spent the remainder of the day wandering around Moscow, getting his sea legs, soaking up the atmosphere, looking at the sights—the zoo, the planetarium, a couple of museums open on Sundays. He had his dinner at the Rossiya Hotel, and then wandered over to the Arbat to catch the big band show, simply another tourist having a good time. He had wanted some time alone, in any event, to order his thoughts. To come down from the events of Helsinki and Stockholm. Pfeiffer had let him in, but had restrained himself with a visible effort from asking too many questions. The apartment was dark now, and quiet.

He ran the tape forward to his interview with Clay. *". . . are you after? You think it was an American did one of your madmen in? Is that it?"*

He advanced it a little further. *". . . know him, Jack,"* Clay was saying. *"As a matter of fact the man is coming here to dinner tonight."*

Anna Feodorovna, Horn thought, listening to the voices in the tiny earphone, an arm to his forehead. Anna and her American lover, code-named Jason. A cause for murder? Would it turn out to be that black and white, or would there be something else attached to it? Spies, traitors, moles, collusions between the CIA and KGB? God, at times he was tired of it all. The dishonor.

On four separate occasions in the last twelve hours LeBec knew that he could have killed Jack Horn. That morning, when Horn had come walking, bold as brass, up the street in front of Boyko's apartment, LeBec had followed him with his gunsights from the apartment across the street. A little later he had followed Horn to the apartment of Yevgenni Sheshkin, where he and Markov had waited around the corner. His third clear shot had come from Edmund Clay's garden, and the fourth opportunity had presented itself there in the parking lot of the foreigners' building where Horn had showed up a couple of hours ago after his tour of the city.

But he had been told to simply observe and report for the moment. Do not interfere. Yet. But Horn was coming close. Horn was a good man. LeBec could feel it, and he had a good sense of these things.

He looked up as Vasili Markov opened the car door and climbed in. Markov pushed his cloth cap back on his head. "The bastard is still up there?"

LeBec nodded. He didn't like Markov, or the other man, Nikolai Drozdov, but they were organized, and knew their way around Moscow. For the moment, at least, he would have to use them. Only for the moment, because this situation couldn't last forever. Washington would have to be made to understand.

11

Anna had begun to see her family through the eyes of a dying desperate woman. She was having trouble giving them the time they deserved and expected. But where was Jason? Why hadn't he written to her? Why hadn't he at least made the attempt to communicate with her? He could have sent word back with Boyko. No one else would have understood, only her. He could have sent back a single word: yes. It would have been enough.

It was very late. The snow was thick and it looked as if it would continue the rest of the evening. Anna stood by a large window in a corridor of Uncle Stepan's apartment between the kitchen and the large pantry that led back to the dining room and beyond it, the living room. His apartment was in one of the old buildings on Kalinina Prospekt and was laid out like a very long railroad car. He'd lived there for as long as she could remember. As a child she sometimes pretended that she was on a train traveling to Paris. In the other room she could hear her Uncle Stepan's booming voice raised in song, and then Uncle Aleksandr and Uncle Georgi joined in. Their children were laughing and clapping. It was a very old song that the peasants used to sing, and it was somewhat risqué. Whenever the three uncles got drunk together they would sing it at the top of their lungs, lingering over the verse in which the young washer woman bends over her washtub and the local rascal, Afansi, lifts her skirt and "Does his washing in her tub!" At the chorus, which was filled with catchy innuendos and puns, everyone formed a line and danced forward until the end, when they formed a circle and the next verse began.

When she was little Anna used to love to sing and dance along, even though she didn't understand all the words. Some of her fondest memories outside of the ballet company were of nights such as these. But in the last few years she'd simply watched, content, if a little sad for a lost youth, to enjoy at arm's length her family's gaiety. Her true joy, she'd once told her Uncle Aleksandr, was when she was on stage and the music seemed to fill her entire body to overflowing. Then she danced, and there was no greater thing. Her uncle had wept at the time, and said it was the most beautiful thing he'd ever heard, and that he was never so proud as at just that moment to be her uncle. He had given her a big, sloppy kiss and then had hurried off, swinging into the chorus with his deep voice.

For the most part, though, she thought, leaning her forehead against the cool glass of the window, she had missed her youth. The memories she had of singing and dancing with her family, of times in the countryside, of sleigh rides, and horseback races, and boats on the river, and picnics and games . . . all of those memories she could count on the fingers of two hands. There simply had not been many days when she was allowed away from the theater—away from her dance lessons, away from her academic schooling, away from instructions on poise and the decorum befitting a rising Bolshoi star. Then, too, as she got older, she was expected to help with the lessons of the younger girls. It was a way of life, exciting and rewarding of itself, but she had no real family life except the occasional evening or the very rare weekend.

Now she was dying. No matter what happened she would never recapture a lost youth; no one could. But she would not even be able to grow old with her memories, nor would there be time in which to develop more memories to add to her meager closet.

Even more than that, however, she wanted only to hear from Jason. One word. Anything.

"How are you feeling, Anna?"

She turned and looked into the wide, kind eyes of Aunt Raya, Uncle Aleksandr's wife. "Just fine, Auntie."

"Well, you look a little tired to me, though not as peaked as you have been looking." Aunt Raya glanced down the corridor.

The singing was as loud as ever. "They're going to wake up the dead with that racket."

Anna laughed. "They're having fun."

Aunt Raya had to smile too. "That's the problem, Anna. When those three get together it's always time for a party. You can't get a serious word out of their drunken haze."

"You should be there with them. You have a pretty voice."

"Not for that song. Besides, I came back to talk to you. Stepan is worried about you."

"Uncle Stepan has always worried about me," Anna said. She hoped he had not talked to her mother.

"This time he thinks it is serious," Aunt Raya said, peering into her eyes. "He thinks you may be ill, yet you refuse to see a doctor."

Anna forced a smile. "A winter cold, Auntie. And maybe just a little bit of depression because of my dancing. Postmenstrual blues, sometimes." Her smile broadened. "Now *that* I cannot discuss with Uncle Stepan. I think he would have a heart attack, or perhaps faint. Then what would I do?"

Aunt Raya's smile was weak. "You should see a doctor. When is the last time you had a Pap smear?"

"Five months ago. It was clear."

"Have you had your breasts examined?"

"At the same time, Auntie. I know what to look for." There were no lumps in her breasts, but they were often sore, as were her armpits and groin. Hers was a different kind of cancer. She wanted to tell her aunt everything. But not now. Not yet.

Aunt Raya stepped back. Her eyes were shrewd, appraising. "You are looking a little better, Anna, but there is something, I think, that you are not telling us. Something you are holding back."

"Everything is fine, Auntie. Believe me."

Aunt Raya shook her head. She was a large woman, buxom with sturdy legs, a big rump, and thick arms the backs of which, if she held them just right, jiggled with excess flab and skin. Aleksandr was the joker of the family. She was the serious one. Besides Uncle Stepan, Anna loved and trusted her Aunt Raya the most. "I don't, Anna."

"For God's sake . . ."

"Your mother is coming in two weeks."

"She didn't say anything to me on Sunday."

"I talked to her. I told her I thought she should come here and spend a weekend with you."

Uncle Stepan provided the bluster, but Aunt Raya ran the family.

The song was over in the living room. Uncle Stepan appeared at the doorway, his face flushed with vodka and from the exertion, for he never sang at anything below full volume. A big wet smile was on his lips.

"Raya, chou-chou—you're not going to spend the night back here talking like two old hens, are you?"

Aunt Raya brushed Anna's cheek with her fingertips, then left.

Uncle Stepan watched her go, then turned back to Anna. He was wearing a thick, bulky-knit sweater that made him look even larger than he really was. He completely filled the doorway. A lock of hair had fallen across his forehead, which glistened with sweat. "How are you feeling, chou-chou? Are you going to come in and join us? Maybe do a little dance for us? We miss you, you know."

She didn't know how much longer she could hold on. But she did know that without her family she would not have lasted forty-eight hours.

12

Snow fell all across Moscow, lending a festive air to the great city, and Horn drove through it very carefully. It was morning and he had slept badly, dreaming that Clay was telling the KGB general about his madmen, showing him their photographs one by one, each photograph marked with a big red X for elimination, Horn's rubber-stamped signature at the bottom. He had awakened several times in the night in a cold sweat. When the gray dawn finally came he felt weak, helpless, in a way detached, wanting nothing more than to go someplace where the sun was shining, someplace warm and safe.

He pointed the Cortina toward town. He had had tea, bread, and cold salmon for breakfast with Pfeiffer. "Shall I tell Early that you'll be in later this morning, Mr. Horn?" There was to be a meeting at ten for all hands, standard Monday morning practice: "Gives us a sense of direction, a weekly evaluation of our net worth, product and all, and a précis of the book for the coming week." Horn thought he would be back if not in time for the meeting, certainly before lunch so that they could have their own little chat before the day took off in full swing. There was a lot that would have to be accomplished this morning, or at least the setup would have to be worked out in detail, and the orders signed. It was a matter of cooperation, which in turn was dependent upon the understanding of one or more principles between two or more men of like purpose.

He could remember each of his madmen in great detail.
Boyko had been the most flamboyant, the one who stuck out
brightest in the crowd. Sergei Turalenko had been the most
enigmatic. Each time they had talked he had prefaced his
remarks with his dissertation on love for one's country, especially the great Soviet Union, which once she realized the
errors of her ways, would rise powerfully to become the
savior of the world. He was in reality merely helping the
process. It was his means of dealing with the fact that he was
a traitor. That, and the demented meeting places and letter
drops he chose for them, were not to be forgotten. Funeral
homes and crematoria and forbidden churches and even ancient
cemeteries. They would meet at night in the worst possible
weather, under the most awful conditions. Turalenko was
punishing himself. They were his symbols, his flags, his *prix
de justification* for what he was doing to himself and his
nation.

Horn drove the long way around, crossing the river on the
Moskvoretskiy Bridge so that he would come nowhere near
Clay's home or Sheshkin's apartment. After yesterday there
was a possibility that either place might be watched. Early
would have to be convinced, he thought, that the sooner he
cooperated, the sooner Horn would be out of his hair. If need
be, he figured he would telephone Carlisle on the encrypted
satellite link, and have him apply a little pressure. Behind the
tall walls the Kremlin bells were tolling the hour of nine.
Traffic, both pedestrian as well as vehicular, was thicker
here than anywhere else in Moscow. The museums, the towers and walls, St. Basil's and the cathedrals, all looked
prettier, softer, more fairy-tale-like when lit at night, he
thought. Turalenko had been proudest of this spot. Horn
made it a point never to meet with his madmen here. He
thought it would have been pushing his luck with them too
far. Like a Russian spy master meeting his American mark in
front of the Lincoln Memorial.

Christine had been frightened badly here during their first
May Day rally. The crowds, the noise, the awesome display
of military hardware, and brass enough to sink a battleship on
the chests of the old men lined up for review had gotten to
her. She'd wanted to claim a headache that day, and a
cold—the day had been blustery and rainy, he recalled—but
he could not leave. He was required to be there and so was
she. They'd toughed it out, and later that night, alone in their

apartment in each other's arms, she had cried in fear and
dismay and confusion. He thought now about how he had
wanted to protect her against her worst fears. Ah, Christine,
he thought, you never admitted—but he had always suspected—
that your biggest anxiety in those days had been plain loneliness. He had his work, but she had nothing except waiting,
the toughest job of all for any woman.

He continued up the hill past St. Basil's and GUM, the
huge state-run department store, turning up toward Sverdlov
Square beyond the Moskva Hotel, an Intourist tour bus parked
in front, a few passengers gathered around it. He and Christine had been offered tickets aboard the Trans-Siberian Railroad, but she had absolutely refused to go, no matter the
intelligence potential. Nothing anyone said had budged her an
inch. At least her persistence was something to be proud of.
Someone else went, and the trip had been scenic but in the
end useless.

The Bolshoi was quiet at this time of the morning. A ballet
was in production, but nothing much would be happening until
this afternoon when the principals would begin showing up.
He passed up Petrovka and turned at the Budapest Hotel,
making his way to Neglin 2, the street Clay had given him
for Anna Feodorovna. The lane was very narrow, the apartment buildings all low, three and four stories. At the far
corner were a grocery and a small bakery. A newspaper
delivery man was putting up *Pravda* in a glass-encased public
announcements billboard. Anna's apartment was number 15
on the upper side of the street. He passed slowly, looking up
at the windows of her place. A light shone in one of them.
There were three cars parked along the street, their wheels up
on the narrow sidewalk. Still there was no room for two cars
to pass. Then he was passing the bakery in which a small line
waited for service, and he was around the corner. There had
been no surveillance that he had been able to make: no
suspicious-looking cars, no vans, no one on the rooftops, no
one waiting on the corner or in a doorway across the street.
Of course it would be a long-term surveillance, which meant
they'd have the apartment above or below or across the street
or next door. It would be when she was on the move that
she'd be the most vulnerable to interception. When she walked
with the crowds, nearer to Sverdlov Square, she could be
watched or even picked up without trouble. There was the
possibility, however, that she did not live alone, and that she

walked to the theater with a friend or friends. Or, since she
was assistant artistic director and a former prima ballerina,
would she deserve a car? The possibilities were many but not
endless. Nothing was endless.

He'd always been on the cautious side. Never a man with
his feet stuck in the mud, but he tried to make sure he knew
his options. He found himself thinking that Doxy would
understand what he was doing this morning, taking the first
measure. Vincent Doxmeuller, the "best damned data analyst
in the business, our side or theirs, bar none." And that from
the assistant DCI, no less. "More creativity in his little finger
than God Almighty Himself; took six days for Creation,
didn't it? There isn't a notion Doxy can't unravel in under
seventy-two hours." Horn turned back on busy Petrovskiy
Boulevard, merging with traffic.

Item: Eleven years ago, give or take a couple, a Bolshoi
Ballet star has a fling with an American stationed here at the
embassy. Never mind the introductions, never mind the sur-
face absurdity of the union, but what about the mechanics of
the thing? Had he run to her apartment when the need arose?
Had they gone to a hotel? Scratch that, not in a nation in
which it was illegal to rent a hotel room for *any purpose* in
the city in which you lived. Item: The American, code-named
Jason for some reason, moved on, and Anna Chalkin—stage
name Anna Feodorovna—spends the subsequent years pining
for her lover. Item: Said Bolshoi dancer's uncle is an important man in the KGB. A very important man. Item: Anna
finds out she is dying (who else knows?), so she pens a letter
to her Jason. For her courier she selects Vitali Boyko, possibly one of the least trustworthy of all the men in Moscow,
and coincidentally a man out of Horn's past. An intimate
past. Are you with me, Doxy? Am I missing something? Are
you noticing the holes that are starting to gape with embar-
rassing regularity? Hold on, it gets much worse.

Item: Boyko understands the score better than any of us, so
he goes to his old friend Yevgenni Sheshkin, the serious one,
the brains and memories of the old network, and bold as brass
asks for the Paris SOS number. Never mind that it's older
than Nero; never mind that these days no one has thought to
put a recorder on it. The number still works and Sheshkin
with great remorse (he called Boyko sick, remember?) hands
it out. Item: Boyko shows up in Helsinki where he makes at
least one call to the Paris emergency number. Did I say

at least one call, Doxy, or was I merely thinking out loud? Forty-eight hours later Boyko is shot dead. He's carrying a gun, which means he knows he's in danger, and his dying words are—to a Finnish cop of all people, a perfect stranger on a street corner, for God's sake—his very last words are "A letter from Anna." Christ on a cross, how melodramatic can we get? But then Boyko was the one with the flash.

The embassy was on the next ring road out. Horn waited until Kachalova Street before turning up through Embassy Row: Nigeria, Egypt, Brazil, Cyprus, Belgium, Iceland, New Zealand, Ghana, Sierra Leone, Tunisia, a dozen more within a few-block radius. More trees here. Limousines, diplomatic plates. A peaceful exterior while inside, the ministers of those countries and more plotted the wholesale slaughter of their fellow human beings in one region or another.

Item: The outgoing Moscow hand, Dewey Nobels, comes to Stockholm where he tells a tale about Boyko running French whores. He also comes with a warning, for which, or at the very least, *during which*, he is shot dead. Item: Five out of the six original madmen in the old Moscow network are dead. Item: Edmund Clay knows all about the old network in shocking detail, right down to Horn's nickname for his stringers. Item: It is Clay's belief that the Jason to whom Anna has written could be someone as important as a United States senator. Wouldn't that blow the lid off the kettle, Doxy? Wouldn't that make the headlines? Who cares about a former Russian dancer, or about the death of a Russian traitor? The assassination of a high-ranking CIA employee, though, that's a different story.

Turning the corner onto Tchaikovsky Street and parking his car a couple of blocks from the embassy, Horn wondered what he had hoped to accomplish earlier by driving past her apartment. Maybe to catch a glimpse of her, if he was to be truthful with himself. Now that he had come this far through the mine field of anomalies, he could feel his curiosity building. He remembered her as pretty and delicate yet self-assured, at least onstage. "A great leaper," someone had once called her. He hadn't appreciated the flip comment, but it had stuck after all these years. But what about now that she no longer danced, and that she was ill? Perhaps she was in a hospital. But there had been a light in one of her windows.

"He went to her apartment," LeBec said.

His telephone connection with Washington was very bad. Not one person in a hundred in the Soviet Union had a telephone, and even fewer had access to a telephone that was capable of connecting with a foreign trunk line. This line had been installed in Boyko's old apartment, which had become their operational headquarters. He felt odd about it. Nervous. Vulnerable.

"My God. Has he spoken with her? Did he go up, Emile?"

"No, he only went past. But it means he knows who she is . . ."

"He can only be guessing. He cannot know."

"Edmund Clay—"

"Is an old fool. Listen to me. You must keep with it. Watch him. Make sure."

"What if he makes contact with her?"

There was a long silence on the line. "Then kill him."

"What about her?"

"And her too."

Horn was early. It was only a bit past nine-thirty when he signed in at the embassy and asked that Bob Early be advised of Mr. Horton's arrival. The consular section occupied most of the first floor. It was the busiest division of the embassy, employing the most Americans as well as the bulk of the foreign nationals—in this case, exclusively Russians. This morning the main corridor and reception hall were busy with people scurrying back and forth, half of them with coffee in hand, the other half still dressed for outside, melting snow on their shoulders, stamping their boots on the rickety wooden floors. The supplicants and the bureaucrats gathered to do the business of international relations. Over all was the clatter of busy typewriters, the shrill ring of telephones, the bells coming by twos, the high-pitched whine of computers printing, and a hum of conversation, one voice raised in Monday-morning anger.

Pfeiffer leaned out of the elevator halfway down the back corridor, and holding the rattletrap iron gate from closing, beckoned Horn along.

"You're a little sooner than we expected," he said. "We're just about ready to get started. Bob asked me to settle you in my office. We'll keep it on the short side this morning."

"Thanks," Horn said. "But this might be something all of your people might want to hear."

They started up with a lurch. Pfeiffer looked at him. "Have you been up to something this morning?"

"I want to mount a surveillance operation."

Pfeiffer seemed a little relieved. "A Russian? KGB?"

"A civilian. A former Bolshoi Ballet star."

Pfeiffer smiled. They arrived on the third floor and he threw open the gate. He let Horn step off first, and they started down the busy corridor, the screened room in the opposite direction. "I'll pass it along to Bob. But I personally don't think this is something for the whole group."

Horn thought that Pfeiffer seemed a little more nervous than he had been earlier that morning. He wondered what Early had already said to him. It had to bother them, having an outsider whom they were responsible for, running around Moscow meddling in things that were none of his business. He was packing a piece, for God's sake.

"Her uncle is a KGB general. Head of their First Chief Directorate."

Pfeiffer stopped in his tracks. "You're talking about Patrenko. Stepan Patrenko."

"That's the one. His niece is Anna Chalkin, stage name, Anna Feodorovna. Has an apartment on Neglin Two."

"Who the hell is she?"

"One of Boyko's friends, possibly."

"And she might know something about why he was killed?"

"That's the ticket."

"But how the hell did you get that kind of information so damned fast, Horn . . . er, Horton? Yesterday, was it? Did you see someone? Talk to someone? I mean if you did, and he or she isn't on our list, we'll have to know. We'll have to know in any event."

"In the meantime, why don't you go fetch Bob? The sooner we get started here, the sooner I'll be able to leave."

Two young women came down the corridor, one of them Gloria Townsend, his runner from the other night. They both carried bundles of file folders.

"Good morning, Mr. Horton," Gloria said, passing.

Horn nodded.

"You're talking about a major operation here," Pfeiffer said, lowering his voice. "If she's a Bolshoi star, she's a fucking national treasure. Add to that her uncle's status. They probably have half the fucking Surveillance Directorate watching her."

"It won't be easy."

Pfeiffer laughed derisively. He was getting agitated. "Easy? It could bust us wide open. We've spent a lot of time and money achieving a low profile. Now we're finally starting to reap the benefits. Dewey was just one part of a much larger picture. Believe me. We've got stringers at every level of Ivan's military-industrial complex. We know more about running their factories than they do."

"Congratulations," Horn said dryly. He was starting to feel a little mean.

"What do you want to me to do? Just tell me. But don't let's mess with the niece of a KGB general. Tell me something else."

"We'll need at least three teams to cover her adequately. I want it begun right away. Today. Certainly before this evening. I want to know her schedule. I want to know who she sees, who her visitors are if any, and I want photographs of everything. If possible I'd like a monitor not only on her telephone, but on her apartment as well."

"Are you fucking crazy?"

Something had changed Pfeiffer in the past few hours. Given him a confidence he hadn't had the previous evening or earlier that morning. For a long ten seconds Horn said nothing. Then he stepped a little closer and lowered his voice to a conspiratorial level. "If you ever swear at or to me like that again, K.W., I shall knock you straight away on your arse. Do you understand me?"

Pfeiffer's eyes widened. He stepped back. "I . . ."

"I did not come here of my own volition. I am not on vacation. I am not here for pleasure. I was sent here by the Company in order to do a job. Which I shall do. Now, run along and fetch Bob Early for me like a nice man. I'll wait in your office."

Pfeiffer glanced down the corridor toward the screened room. Several men stood by the door, talking. "Last door on the right," he said. "I'll get him."

Pfeiffer's office was one of the tiny cubbyholes that looked down on the inner courtyard at the rear of the building. The radiator hissed and clanked, making the room far too hot. Horn left the door open. A government issue gray linoleum-topped desk was bare except for a telephone and a calendar desk pad on which there were no notes. It made him wonder what kind of a man Pfeiffer was. He didn't know of anyone whose desk calendar was free of doodles or notes or comments. Two file cabinets were secured with steel locking bars and professional-looking combination locks. A map of the European section of the Soviet Union was pinned up next to a Playboy wall calendar. Another calendar was taped to the side of one of the file cabinets. A telephone rang somewhere. Time was running out. A least it was for Anna. He wondered if she too were counting the days on a calendar as Pfeiffer apparently was.

"What the hell does he think we're doing here?" Early's voice rose in anger from down the corridor. Someone else said something, apparently in reply, another telephone began to ring, and a second later Early was at the door, his face flushed, his tie loose, and his cuffs unbuttoned but not rolled up.

"We have a job of work to do, Early."

"You're damned right we do, mister. And we're trying to do it. I just want to know what you have against us. I just want to know that."

"I need a surveillance team."

"So I'm told."

"Today. Now. Immediately."

"Would you mind terribly much explaining just who the hell you think she is?" Early demanded, his voice dripping with sarcasm.

"Is this room secure?"

Early started to say something, but he held off. He stepped the rest of the way into the room, closed the door and threw the lock, and flipped on the fluorescent lights. He nodded. "I'm listening."

"Her name is Anna Chalkin. She was a friend of Boyko's. I think she might know something."

"Correct me if I'm wrong, but you're here to investigate the assassination of one of ours."

"They're related."

"Blood brothers?"

"After a fashion."

"She was bedding one of them, Jack? Both of them? What, you tell me. Her uncle is General Patrenko. *The* General Patrenko."

It made Horn wonder just how far Pfeiffer's voice had carried in the corridor, or just how ignorant he was of ordinary security precautions.

"Neither," Horn said. "Boyko carried out a letter for her. He apparently was killed for it."

Early's eyes were bright. "To whom, Jack? What was the address?"

Horn thought he had been in this sort of a situation a thousand times before. It never changed, but it never seemed to get any easier. How much of the truth to tell was a subjective decision. "We don't know that," he said pointedly.

Early picked up on it. "We?"

"Carlisle and I. Boyko telephoned an old Paris accommodations number. Forty-eight hours later he was dead."

"One of ours?"

"I don't know."

"But it makes for some very intriguing possibilities, doesn't it? Makes you wonder. What's in this letter? Have you seen it?"

"No," Horn said, watching him.

"Wasn't on his body, then," Early mused. "Did Dewey know about it? Was he in on it?"

Wallace Mahoney, one of the very best minds the CIA had ever known, had told him once that live agents in the end were those who had worked very hard at providing themselves with back doors, with escape routes. Trust not, want not, that was the litany. Nobels's last act had been to call out Boyko's name. He had come with a warning. About what?

"I have to take him at face value," he told Early with a straight face. A big lie tempered with a little truth. "He was watching Boyko here; there's little doubt of that. But he was done. He told me that he wanted to go someplace where it never snowed, lie on the beach under a palm tree, get a tan."

Early nodded his wistful understanding. "Boyko was your stringer. The first are always the best, they say. You tell me, what was he doing in Helsinki?"

"Trying to deliver a letter."

"*Sell* a letter, Jack? A little blackmail? From what I know of your Boyko, he was capable of it. Might he have been doing a little dirty deal?"

"That depends upon what was in the letter," Horn said baldly.

Early smiled. "What did he tell this Paris number of ours? Who did he ask for? In fact, Jack, why aren't you in Paris with your investigation?"

"What do you mean, blackmail?"

"Come off it, Jack. Her uncle is a KGB general. Maybe they had the goods on someone. Anna would have been the innocent point of contact. Who'd suspect her?"

"Of being manipulated by her uncle?"

"Something like that. But why aren't you in Paris?"

"Anna is here."

"What did Boyko tell Paris?"

"Nothing. Just identified himself and asked to talk to someone about a trade."

"A trade for what? The letter for what?"

"He didn't say. Before a meet could be set up he was killed."

"Possibly by his own people. Could be a simple mistake. Wires crossed. Failure to communicate."

"Possibly."

"But the letter is important, isn't it. Maybe it's filled with juicy little secrets that Anna has gleaned from her uncle the great general. Why didn't Boyko bring it here, directly to us? Nobels was watching him. Wouldn't it have been more logical for her to hand the letter over to Boyko, and Boyko would hand it over to Dewey, and Dewey would bring the prize home to roost? He could have written his own ticket. They both could have."

"If it was a two-way street," Horn said. He felt he was getting a little nearer to the truth from Early.

"What?"

"Was Nobels merely hound-dogging my old madman, or was he working him? I mean had they established letter drops and signals and routines . . . tradecraft? Or was Boyko retired?"

"I don't know."

"You're chief of station."

"Not God!" Early flared.

Horn turned away and glanced up at the wall calendar as he took out a cigarette and lit it. "I suppose it came as a big surprise to you when Nobels announced he wanted to rotate home early."

"I tried to talk him out of it. He was a real asset here," Early said.

Horn turned back. Bingo, he said to himself. Nobels had come out with a warning, and Early had evidently developed a habit of lying through his teeth. Why?

"About my surveillance operation. I'll take up residence here, in the screened room again if the cot is still available.

I'll need Townsend and McKenzie as runners. You'll have to assign someone to coordinate the fieldwork as well as the development of the product. Photographs and tapes. It's all I want, along with, of course, her schedule.''

"For christ's sake, Jack, if you think this is Grand Central Station, you're mistaken. You can't hop a train here. Not that way.''

"What way, then?'' Horn asked patiently.

"Look, if Boyko's own people killed him and they've got this letter, then they'll be watching for us to do something stupid like going after the broad.''

"Then we'll know, won't we.''

"We'd know, all right. They'd bust us wide open.''

"They'd kick you out.''

"That's right,'' Early answered defensively.

"Someone else would have to be sent over here. New methods, new faces, new stringers even, but all with the same objectives? Intelligence? See what they're up to before they do it to us?'' Horn decided he did not like Early. The man was burned out. And besides, he was crude. No one called women broads these days. And no one had ever called a ballerina that.

"I don't need your goddamned lecture . . .''

"One of your people was shot dead too. Doesn't that bother you? Maybe you'll be next?''

"Maybe it'll be you.''

Horn didn't reply.

Early sighed deeply at last. He had fought a good fight but he had lost, and he didn't understand why. It was written all over his face. "Why this Anna?'' he asked plaintively. "Why her?''

"I don't know, Bob. But for now she's the only one left alive who knows anything.''

"You want to meet her. Talk to her.''

"When it's safe for both of us. Which is why the surveillance, of course.''

"And then what, Jack? Are you simply going to ask her who she wrote to, and what she wrote about?''

"Something like that.''

Darkness came early to Moscow at this time of the year. It was just seven in the evening, and it was still snowing in the pitch-black night. The storm had intensified, bringing with it

colder temperatures and a rising wind. From his office on the
third floor of the embassy, Horn was hearing tales about the
worst storm in years. Moscow was actually slowing down, an
event no one in the embassy had ever witnessed, or ever
thought he would witness. Horn was getting reports of power
outages, of automobiles stuck on Kalinina only to be brutally
smashed as they were pushed aside by huge snowplows, of
hundreds of people being stuck in the metro stations where
militia and Komsomol Youth for World Peace were setting up
kitchens, first-aid stations, and emergency shelters for those
people unable to make it home. The first of the surveillance
reports on Anna Feodorovna had straggled in slowly because
of the weather but steadily despite it.

They had managed to place a monitor on her telephone
after first sweeping the line to make sure the KGB wasn't
listening too, which they weren't. They had even managed to
place a small parabolic antenna on the roof of the building
across the street from her apartment. The sound reproduction
was not the best, but anything said within the apartment
would rattle the window glass . . . ever so slightly. The
equipment was sensitive enough to pick up this movement,
subtract electronically from it the grosser movements because
of wind or because of plows rumbling by on the street below,
and from the remains reconstruct speech. The voices would
be all but unrecognizable, but the words would be understandable. It was clear, however, that the rooftop position
was not very secure, even in the storm. It wouldn't last much
longer than overnight. By morning the risks would rise dra
matically. Two teams covered the Bolshoi Theater itself on a
rotating basis with cameras and wire recorders. Three other
teams, again on a rotating basis so that there would be less
likelihood of them being made, were out to cover any contin-
gency in Anna's route to and from the theater, or wherever
else she might go. They were alert not only for Anna's
movements, but for the possibility that she was being watched
by KGB legmen, her uncle's men, who would not take kindly
to American intervention on their home ground. "A very
sticky situation could develop out of this," Early had complained. "It has all the earmarks of a major explosion." Seated
at the conference table in the screened room now as the first
of the tapes and photographs began to come in, Horn himself
began to wonder just why it was he hadn't started with Paris.

He had the answer—he knew damned well there was more than whatever happened in Paris between Boyko and the accommodations number—but the question was there nevertheless. It had something to do with the old network, and with Early and Pfeiffer who were hiding something, and lastly it had to do with Anna. *A letter from Anna*, Boyko had told the Helsinki cop. *Boyko*, Nobels had screamed with his final breath. And now all the old madmen were dead, save one. The network is dead. Long live the network.

Gloria Townsend knocked and came in, laying three paper-bound volumes on the table before him. One was green, one was yellow, and the third was red. They changed colors each year. They were marked *Staff Directory, Embassy of the United States of America, Moscow, U.S.S.R.* The years were 1974, 1975, and 1976. Each was stamped top and bottom, SECRET. The CIA's staff positions were clearly labeled inside.

"These what you wanted, Mr. Horn?" she asked. They had dispensed with worknames in here.

He looked up. "Just the ticket."

"We have some supper coming up for you, and Pete Reynard, he's our photo lab chief, says you have another batch of shots coming up."

"Any luck on my secure line to the States?"

"They should be ringing up here any moment now, Mr. Horn."

He sat back and took the time to light another cigarette. She reminded him of his daughter Marney, or what he thought Marney would be like when she got to be Gloria's age—twenty-five, perhaps. He wanted to ask how she had got the nickname Town and Country, but he suspected it wasn't very complimentary, and he didn't want to embarrass her. He thought she had taken a liking to him, but then she was Early's girl, and there was no telling what instructions he had given her.

The telephone rang. Gloria looked at it.

"I'll need a little privacy," Horn said. "You might hold everything outside for me. I won't be terribly long."

"I just wanted to say that I'm all for you, Mr. Horn. Both Tom and I."

The telephone rang a second time.

Horn smiled. "Thanks, Gloria. I appreciate it."

"Well, I just thought you should know that someone here is on your side." She turned and left, softly closing the door.

Horn picked up the telephone. "This is Horn." He could hear a distorted echo-image of his voice rattling down the line. It was on encrypt, and bounced off a satellite direct to Washington. Moscow was at Greenwich Mean Time plus three, and Washington at GMT minus five. They were eight hours apart. It was a few minutes after eleven in the morning there.

Carlisle started immediately. "Are you coming home, Jack? Is it wrapped up out there already? Were we lucky this time?" He sounded unnaturally bright, as if this call were a distraction from some pressing, more immediate problem he was faced with.

"Not yet, Farley. In fact we've got a bit of a blizzard here at the moment. It's slowing things down. But I did manage to speak with a couple of old friends yesterday. They were helpful, though they raised a couple of questions in my mind."

"Oh?" Carlisle answered carefully. Horn could see him at his desk. He'd be sitting up much straighter now. He'd have a pencil and paper in front of him ready to jot down a note or two, though all of his calls were recorded. Always. Still, it's nice to be sure about the salient points, he'd say. Avoid the chance garble. A note sets it in your mind.

"I'm going to need some help from your end."

"Anything, Jack. Anything at all. Just name it."

"What's going on in Paris? Is there anything more on Boyko's call?"

"Just what I've already told you."

"There wasn't a second call? Boyko only called once?"

"Just the one call, Jack. Why? Have you come up with something else there in Moscow?"

"Possibly. What about our Stockholm people? Have they come up with anything about Nobels?"

"There may have been a car with Danish plates in the vicinity. A Mercedes, but no one can be quite sure. No one has found the car as yet."

"What was he shot with?"

"A suppressed twenty-two caliber. Very probably a short-barreled rifle, though the lab boys say it was hard to tell. There was a certain amount of distortion of the bullet when it passed through the window glass, and a massive distortion when it hit the . . . skull."

"Doesn't sound like a Russian weapon."

"No, Jack. No, it doesn't. Which doesn't mean a damned thing. Now, who have you been chatting up in Moscow? Mutual friends?"

"I talked with one of my old madmen," Horn said, hesitating for just a beat. The thought crossed his mind that Early could very well be monitoring this call downstairs in the communications center.

"From the old network days?" Carlisle prompted.

"He's the only one left, Farley. All the rest are dead. Boyko in Helsinki, three of them here in Moscow over the past six or seven years, and one of them in Siberia just last fall."

"What are you saying to me, Jack? Talk to me. Was Boyko working some deal? Something Dewey knew nothing about?"

"My old madman told me that Boyko had come to him a couple of weeks ago and asked for the Paris number. He had a letter he wanted to deliver on the outside."

"The letter from Anna?"

"That's right."

"Who'd she write it to?"

"I don't know that name yet. But I know who Anna is. She's the niece of a KGB general. Name of Anna Chalkin. Stage name, Anna Feodorovna. She is, or was, a Bolshoi Ballet star. Apparently she had an affair with one of our people here at the embassy ten or twelve years ago. I don't have the date nailed down yet."

"So now she sends him a love letter?"

"She's dying."

"We're all dying," Carlisle answered tersely. "So now she wants to put her past in order. Nothing so terribly wrong with that, except for her knowledge of Boyko's function."

"That, and the fact that he was shot to death, Farley. He didn't have the letter with him."

"He may have hidden it."

"It may have been taken from him."

"By this Anna Chalkin's uncle. Isn't that a possibility? Who is he?"

"Stepan Patrenko."

"Good Lord," Carlisle said softly. Even over the distorted circuit, Horn could hear the awe in his voice. "Stay away from that man, Jack. Don't tangle with him unless whatever you've got is ironclad. Hell, cast in platinum. He'll chew you up and spit you out with hardly a passing notice. The man has a reputation."

Horn passed a hand across his eyes. "There's a bit more, Farley."

"No, Jack. It's as plain as the nose on my face. Can't you see it as well? This woman sends a letter out of Moscow, using for her postman one of your old boys. An unfortunate choice for him, for all of us. No doubt Boyko steamed open her letter, realized that he had the mother lode, and agreed to take it out—though not for the reasons she wanted it done. Of course General Patrenko had him followed out of the country. I'm sure he watches his niece pretty closely. A fair assumption, wouldn't you say, Jack? What uncle in his position wouldn't do the same? But Boyko was in no real danger, at least not up to that point, not until he actually called the Paris number. He stepped over the line there. The KGB knew what he was trying to do, and they killed him for it. Simple as that."

"She had an affair with someone from our embassy."

"You've said that."

"She wrote a letter to him. Boyko took it out. He called the old Paris number. Two days later he was gunned down. *Two days.*"

"Now, just a minute here, Jack. Just wait a damned minute. I won't listen to what I think you're implying. I won't hear of it."

"Who knew about Boyko's telephone call? Who was privy to that information?"

"Stop it, Jack."

Carlisle was truly frightened. Horn could hear that now in his voice, and in the unusual brevity of his rejoinders.

"I spoke with another person here in Moscow."

"Another one of your stringers?"

"The others are dead, Farley. I spoke with Edmund Clay."

"Don't tell me that," Carlisle moaned.

"That old man had a lot to tell me. Too much, as a matter of fact. Farley, he knew about the old network. He knew enough to make a judgment about Boyko's character. He even knew—are you listening to me, Farley?—he even knew that I called my stringers madmen. How? Has he worked for us all these years?"

"He's always served at the administration's pleasure, you know that."

"Does he read our reports? Is he briefed?"

"He has weekends with the president, for God's sake! Of course he can see our reports! He can see anything he damned well pleases!"

Horn knew that the bitch goddess Cynicism was creeping up on him, but he couldn't help but wonder how much information the Russians passed on to Clay, and how often in the name of international diplomacy Clay had exchanged what he knew. But he was being unfair in a broader sense: Clay was a peacemaker, whereas Horn was merely a soldier. So what if a few of his ground troops here and there had become casualties? The wider issues were more important. Sacrifice the few to save the many. "He knew about Anna and her lover. He'd heard rumors."

"He told you that?"

"Yes, he did, Farley. Anna's code name for her lover was Jason. Clay said one of the possibilities was Senator Thomas Wagner."

"Oh, God . . ."

"Could Senator Wagner have heard about Boyko's Paris call? Is that possible?"

The line was silent.

"Farley?"

"He's been in Paris for the last two weeks, Jack."

How about that, Horn thought. "Could he have established a pipeline? Are we that loose?"

"Yes," Carlisle admitted. "But listen to me, Jack—we're talking nothing but circumstantial evidence here. Coincidence. It could mean anything."

Horn glanced down at the staff directories Gloria Townsend had brought him. Who else was a possibility? Clay had been terribly glib with Senator Wagner's name after so many years. Maybe he was jumping at shadows, but there was a terrible odor beginning to rise from all of this, and Horn was finding it particularly distasteful.

"Why was Nobels's assignment here cut short?"

"Who told you that?"

"Early."

"He had no business telling you anything like that. And in fact I'm surprised he would have said such a thing."

Horn was amazed at how agile Carlisle had become. "Why, Farley?"

"There was some bad blood between them. Early accused Nobels of trying to run a one-man show. Of being too much of a cowboy. Too reckless. And Nobels thought that Early was far too conservative to be COS of Moscow. They both requested that Dewey be sent home early. It was a mutual agreement."

Carlisle wasn't that soft. Something else had happened here. Something that concerned Nobels enough to bring out a warning. Yet his initial comments about Early had been favorable. Testing the waters?

"Nobels was trying to warn me about something when he was killed."

"What?"

"I was standing across the room from him. He was starting to warn me about something when he was shot and killed."

"Warn you about what?" Carlisle asked very softly.

"About Early," Horn said carefully. "Did Nobels suspect that Bob Early was in bed with the Russians? Is that why Early asked for an extended assignment? Is that why Nobels wanted out? Was that what he was coming to warn me about? Is that why you were so nervous about Moscow, about sending me here? Talk to me."

"We have absolutely no evidence to that effect, Jack. Now, dammit, you'd better listen to me and listen closely. Early is a good man. His product is without fault. Absolutely without fault. Nobels, on the other hand, was unstable. He was scheduled for a psychological evaluation the moment he hit Washington. He was upset about a lot of things. It was only natural for him to lash out in all directions."

"Then who killed him, Farley? And why?"

Carlisle's breath caught in his throat. "Perhaps it's time for you to come home."

"Is that what you want?"

"You're talking crazy."

"Maybe not. Maybe I'm just covering myself. Maybe I need someone watching out for my back. Just in case, Farley. A little insurance. You can understand that."

"Well, I just don't see the connection, Jack. I can't see it for Adam."

"Maybe there isn't any," Horn said tiredly. "Maybe we're

dealing with two separate cases here. Nobels and Early, and Boyko and the embassy. Or maybe there's nothing to any of it. Maybe I'm wasting my time. Maybe I should come home after all. Christine misses the States."

"But you don't think so."

"I don't know. We have a surveillance operation going on at the moment. As soon as it's clear I'm going to talk to her. I want to know who Jason is. I want to know why she wrote her letter."

"Maybe it's innocent."

"See what you can find out from your end, Farley," Horn said. "See who might have used the code name Jason. Meanwhile I'll have a look through the staff directories here to see what I can come up with."

"Christine and the children are just fine, Jack. I wanted you to know that. I spoke with them yesterday."

"Did you tell her where I was?"

"No, but she's a sharp woman. I think she's guessed. She'll be all right."

Horn didn't like Carlisle's tone. Something was too smooth in his voice, too sickly sweet around the edges. It gave him a cold shiver. "If something should happen, if this should blow up, I want my family taken out of Berlin. The East zone is too damned convenient. I want them taken back to the States if anything happens. The *moment* anything happens."

"Is it bad there, Jack? Is it bad there, do you think?"

"I don't know," Horn said. "But I suspect it's going to get worse."

The falling snow was beautiful. Alone for the moment with his own thoughts, Horn lit another cigarette and went to the window. Now it wouldn't matter if Early had listened in on his conversation. If anything happened, Carlisle was convinced enough to go looking in the right places. It was a comfort. Something.

Senator Wagner was in Paris, or at least he had been. It seemed terribly pat, though. Clay mentioned his name and within hours the same name came up again, in connection with Boyko. It was like looking a gift horse in the mouth, but for all that, Horn was skeptical.

Nobels had apparently suspected Early, and possibly Pfeiffer, of collusion with the Russians. It was a serious charge: with proof they'd be heading for jail, or defection. Without proof,

Nobels would be heading for the funny farm. Just the accusations, of course, would be enough to make a man such as Early gun-shy. Add to it the accuser's assassination, and the sudden appearance of a man with the blessings of the DDO, and even a man as pure as the driven snow would have to become jumpy.

Horn went back to the table where he opened the staff directory for 1974. He thumbed through the alphabetical section at the back of the book, under the *W*'s for Wagner. The man's name was not listed. Horn tried the 1975 directory with the same results, and then 1976 with no luck. Wagner had not been listed on the staff for any of those years, and yet Clay had been certain Wagner was one of the possibles.

Starting with the index for 1974, Horn went through each section that included a staff position as cover for a CIA officer. There were a lot of them, starting with the chief of station himself, who at the time was Sylvan Bindrich, listed as special assistant to the ambassador, all the way down to Porter, Thomas F., listed as a consular specialist as a cover, and a cipher clerk as his real job.

Wagner was not listed.

Bindrich was also listed as COS for the years 1975 and 1976. But Wagner's name appeared nowhere in those directories. Whether he had not been stationed in Moscow during those years, or his name for some reason had not been included in the listings, he was nowhere to be found.

Horn took out his tape recorder and found the specific spot in his conversation with Clay in which Wagner had been mentioned. ". . . *is the reason she was promoted. Tom Wagner was one of them.*"

"*Senator Wagner?*" Horn's own voice came out of the tiny speaker. "*Oregon?*"

"*He was one of the old bunch stationed here at the embassy. I remember because he was campaigning even then. His daddy told him that once he got elected to the Senate he'd want to be on the Foreign Relations Committee. Get to know the Russians on their own turf, and he'd be a natural for the job.*"

Horn reversed the tape.

"*. . . one of the old bunch stationed here at the embassy.*"
Horn stopped the tape. Wagner had been in Moscow, according to Clay, but his name had not shown up in the directories. Which was the more accurate source, he won-

dered, a dispassionate directory that could be doctored, or the memory of an old man whom Horn no longer trusted?

He ran the tape forward again until he found something else that Clay had told him. "*. . . He might not want his constituency to know that he had once bedded a young Russian ballet star, now, would he?*"

It was a little too pat for Horn. He rewound the tape again to the very beginning and listened to the entire conversation. Clay had an ax to grind. What was it? And against whom? Senator Wagner?

13

Horn had left the church because he thought he would be too confined as a priest. How can you counsel marrieds if you had never been married yourself? How could you make a difference in the world from a cloistered tower, within monastery walls, or behind the façade of stained glass? He was being terribly unfair, he supposed, but everyone had his own particular set of rationalizations that worked. The ones that didn't, you threw out, right? He remembered he had felt free for about twenty-eight seconds. The pressures of college left little time for true independence of spirit. The military certainly allowed no freedom, at least none of what he imagined freedom could or should bring. And the years that stretched back from this moment to the day he had joined the CIA seemed filled, ironically, with cloistered little offices, long, lonely vigils, heartfelt concerns about the souls and bodies of his flock. "We all have a cross to bear," Wallace Mahoney had told him years ago at the Farm outside Williamsburg. Wasn't there at least one moment in life when you began to feel a bit like Christ climbing Mount Calvary, the burden you were forced to carry very heavy and oh, so terribly unjust? He hadn't thought much like that lately, though, until just now looking up from his work at quarter to eight in the morning. The heavy wire mesh on the window and the strong door to the corridor were meant to keep out the eavesdroppers and the unauthorized busybodies. Weren't those security arrangements also designed to keep him in? Langley was the Vatican, the

DCI was the pope, and Horn was getting the feeling that a Protestant was hiding in the woodpile, and unless the place was torn apart no one would be able to find him.

Wasn't it understandable? he asked himself. Men had been making sacrifices for women from the beginning of time, hadn't they? It's what made the world go round. But they made colossal mistakes because of it. Mistakes, he wondered, for which someone would commit murder?

He glanced at the dozens of photographs on the long conference table. The room stank of sweat and cigarette smoke and the acrid odor of photographic developer and fixer. Horn was a one-woman man. He'd had a couple of high school sweethearts, but they'd been more like friends. At that time he was preparing himself for the priesthood, and he still knew what involvement with a girl would do to his resolve. Then, of course, he had met Christine and his resolve had changed. He fell in love not with Christ and the Church, but with Christine and their marriage. For the Church he had been prepared to move mountains and save souls. For Christine he set out to slay dragons and save men. There was something in Anna Feodorovna's face that seemed to represent a cross between both loves. And it frightened him.

The evening had been hectic. To this point he hadn't gotten much sleep. The theater had not canceled its final dress rehearsal of *Spartacus* despite the snow. Anna had remained there until nearly midnight, and then she had brought home to her apartment fifteen or twenty of the cast and production crew, where they had partied, loudly, and were still partying for all he knew. The first surveillance photos had begun coming in fairly early yesterday evening, and the audio tapes had been brought up hours ago. For much of the evening, Gloria Townsend and Tom McKenzie had sat with him listening to the tapes and transcribing anything Anna said, picking it out of the din of everything else that was happening at the theater. The first of the tapes from the party had been brought up several hours ago and Horn had taken a first run through them while his runners had gone off to get a bite to eat. There wasn't much of any use on the tapes. A lot of laughing and shouting and music. But the photographs were something else. Something completely different, and Horn found his eyes straying continuously back to three of them. One at the theater taken in imperfect light backstage at the end of a long, tall tunnel of curtain rows. Anna had just turned in response, perhaps, to a call, and a stray bit of light illuminated her face as if it were an ivory cameo in bas-relief from an ebony backdrop. Her cheeks were high and finely formed, her eyebrows dark and serious, her lips full and sensuous beneath a delicately sculpted nose, a slight broadening at the nostrils either as a natural feature or because of some reflex action to whatever was being said to her off camera. Her neck, what he could make of it in the dim light, seemed long and delicate. She would be well proportioned, he thought, or perhaps a bit on the flat side. Her skin would be pale, Moscow-winter pale, and he imagined that in the correct light, gentle blue tracings of veins would be visible here and there: in the calf of a leg, in an inner forearm, perhaps in the creases on either side of her nose, in the backs of her hands.

The second photograph that struck him had been taken outside, within a block or so of her apartment. She had stopped a moment beneath a streetlight with her crowd of dancers and production assistants from the theater. The entire scene seemed contrived; the lighting, the backdrop, the piles of snow and the still falling snow, their costumes—it was from an exotic play or an expensive movie. Anna faced the camera. Her companions had parted momentarily, as if in consideration for the shot, allowing a full view. She was dressed in a rabbit fur hat and coat, but despite the thickness of her outer garments he could tell that she was slight. He could also see—or was he merely imagining it?—that she was holding herself just then as if she were infinitely weary, tired from her travails and worn down, perhaps, by her illness. Horn found himself wondering, for her sake, why she had brought all of those people home with her. In her state he would have thought it better to be alone, to have a quiet evening of rest, of peace, of solitude. He wondered if she had surrounded herself like that as a defense mechanism against her loneliness and fear. It was natural that she would be frightened, not only of her illness, but because of the letter. She'd had no response. She would be anxiously waiting for a reply. Wondering. Hoping.

The third shot was the most recent. It had been taken barely three hours earlier from the van passing on the freshly plowed street below Anna's window. They'd snapped a half-dozen shots in quick succession. One was much better than the others. Anna was at the window. She had parted the curtains and was looking down at the street directly into the lens of the camera, which of course she couldn't possibly see. Here I am, she was saying. I see you down there, I know what you are doing, I know who you are, and I know what will happen now. She looked directly out of the photographic paper into Horn's eyes. He was on the street; she was above in her window. She was tired, she was frightened, and she was crying for help. Don't leave me. I need succor in my time of desperation. He was hearing her confession. And he was seeing her with Boyko, sweet-talking, slimy Boyko who could not possibly have appreciated her fineness.

He had turned off the lights and had lain down on the cot sometime after midnight. But he couldn't turn off his mind, so he had gotten up fifteen minutes later. "You won't do yourself any good if you don't get some rest, Mr. Horn," Gloria had said solicitously. She had taken it upon herself to become his patron saint. He thought that Christine would have approved; she was always looking out for his welfare, looking for the one point that would make him see things her way and take it a little easier, the one argument to end all arguments that would finally make him see the futility of his quest and make him give it all up. For what, Christine? he wondered. Give it up and do what? Become a banker? A social worker? An electronics technician? A Bible salesman . . . a priest?

"How long is this nonsense going to continue?" Early had asked, stopping in about two.

"As long as necessary. Getting cold feet, Bob?"

"No. But my people are. It's impossible out there."

"Just till morning. Or perhaps noon when she goes off to the theater."

"She's nothing but a has-been ballet star," Early said in frustration, but then another batch of photographs arrived and he stepped aside.

Gloria said nothing to Horn, but a look of understanding passed between them. Good girl, he thought. As long as she could remain subtle, and learn to distinguish the good ones from the ones who would stab her in the back, she would go a long way.

Putting the third photograph back with the others, Horn got to his feet. He stretched. It had been a long night. His shoulders were cramped, his back was sore, and his throat was raw from cigarettes. He was going to have to see her, of course. The timing would depend on whether or not her friends would leave her apartment before she went to the theater. If he could catch her alone, out in the open. . . . Even better than that, if he could catch her alone in her apartment, they could talk in privacy. He would be taking a terrible risk that she would turn him in or, at the very least, tell her uncle. But it was she who had had an affair with an American; it was she who had initiated contact with Boyko and who had sent out a letter with him. Horn didn't think she would be too particular about turning him in merely for asking her one question.

Of course it was still too early to know much about her schedule. "She probably showed up at the theater around noon, left it at midnight, and is now partying," Gloria had said earlier. "If she does that sort of thing every night, she's got more stamina than I do."

"It's just for dress rehearsal night," Horn had suggested. "Once they go into their full performance schedule, her nights will probably be more routine."

Horn went to the window and looked outside. A gray dawn had come finally. It was still snowing. Below in the courtyard, long, delicately sculptured sweeps of snow had drifted against the walls and into the corners. The city, what he could see of it beyond the compound, looked cold and forbidding. Plumes of snow swirled raggedly across the rooftops, gusted along the roads as if they were running a race, and billowed around the snowplows that were creating their own blizzards within the storm as they moved. Moscow was all but stopped. It gave him an odd feeling to see it like that from the embassy window. Once he approached Anna and talked to her and told her that he knew about Boyko and the letter, he would have to clear out. Moscow would be untenable for him after that. He decided he wouldn't miss any of it here, except for Gloria.

"You're going out to see her, Mr. Horn?" she had asked. "It'll be very dangerous."

"At least take along a backup, sir," young McKenzie had suggested. Horn had the feeling that the two of them might be lovers.

"Not to worry," he had said.

"What did she do? Is she a spy?"

Maybe she was, Horn told himself, watching the snow-plows. He felt as if he were seeing the city for the very first time, and probably for the very last time, and he couldn't decide whether that made him happy or sad.

"There," Gloria had said, sitting forward. "It's the fourth time someone has asked her if she's feeling all right." She rewound the tape.

Horn looked up from the photographs he had been studying. "She's ill."

"What's wrong with her?"

"I don't know for sure. But I think she's dying."

Gloria had let out her breath. She'd looked away for a moment, her lips compressed. "Well, her friends know it, or at least they're guessing."

"What does she say to them when they ask?"

Gloria had glanced at her transcription notes. "Female voice, I think she's called Natalia. 'Yuri is starting to worry about you . . .' A pause. '. . . Mother Anton says you're looking like a ghost.' Laughter. 'Anna, go look in a mirror if you don't believe me.' Anna's reply is a little garbled, but what I got from it was something about her period. It was heavy this month. And then she said for Natalia to mind her own business. That she was getting worse than Mother. . . . And the next was garbled, probably Mother Anton, though. I'm gathering that whoever he is, he's the Bolshoi's mother hen. Probably gay."

Horn had laughed. "What else?"

"Variations on the same theme," Gloria had answered, flipping through her notes. " 'Are you feeling well, Anna?' That from a man, no identification yet. Anna's reply: 'Mind your own business.' A woman's voice, no identification: 'Goodness, Anna, you look like a ghost. Yuri asked me to come talk to you.' Anna laughs. 'Yuri's job is to worry about all of us. I'm fine. A little run-down maybe—my period is heavy and this show has been working us all to death.' Reply: 'Well, maybe you should see the doctor, just to be on the safe side.' Anna's reply: 'In self-defense I'll do it. Let's get the show started first, and then we'll see.' "

Gloria wore a knit dress that did little to hide her buxom good looks. Her face was wide and honest, but there was a definite no-nonsense streak to her that made her look cute. A very solid girl. Once again Horn was reminded of his daughter. Except that Marney had led a relatively sheltered life. He didn't think Gloria had.

"What about at her apartment? At the party? How's she doing there? I wasn't able to pick out much."

"Neither was I. There's a lot of background noise, and they're having trouble taking out the wind-driven snow. Sounds like a chorus of kettle drums."

"Are they going to get out of there soon?"

Gloria had nodded. "It's four now. I wouldn't expect them to stay much more than another hour or so. There'll be the last hangers-on, of course. Certainly they'll all be out of there by seven or eight. Even Russians sleep sometimes, Mr. Horn."

Horn turned away from the window and glanced at his watch. It was just eight o'clock. He wondered what Anna was doing at this very moment. He sincerely hoped for her sake that her friends had left and that she had put herself to bed and was sleeping now. She was going to need her strength for what was coming. Boyko was dead. How much hope had she pinned on him?

He looked at the photographs on the table again, at the tapes and at Gloria's and Tom McKenzie's notes, then let himself out. The corridor was quite busy with staffers who glanced at him with quiet astonishment. They knew he was up here, but not many of them knew his name other than his Horton workname, and even fewer knew for a fact exactly what he was doing. Review old records so that he could better fit in, for all they knew. Some sort of an auditor, a few whispers had circulated. Someone has had his hand in the till, and Mr. Horton from Washington is here to find out who it is. It's a reorganization. State Department has ordered it because of Reagan's latest politics. How can we defend the SDI or aid to the contras or even our position these days on Afghanistan under the old regime here? The cobwebs are going to be dusted out of the corners and a lot of old, sacred cows are going to fall. Mr. Horton from Washington is the man who's going to do it. He's even got Mr. Early at his beck and call. There's talk that he and Siskel don't see eye to eye either.

In the rickety bathroom at the end of the corridor, Horn washed his hands, splashed some very cold water on his face, then combed his hair and snugged up his tie.

The door opened and he looked up into the mirror as Early came in. The COS hesitated when he spotted Horn at the sink, but then he came the rest of the way in. He went to one of the urinals.

"Gloria and Tom are bringing up your breakfast," he said over his shoulder. "I saw them in the commissary."

"That's fine," Horn said tiredly, his mind racing ahead. "You've been at it all night, then?"

"Yes."

"I ran into Pete Reynard. He tells me you're getting some class-A goods."

"Really good photographs, Bob," Horn said, turning away from the sink. "He has some very fine, very dedicated people here. You should be proud. This is a first-class operation. I want you to pass that along to your people. Tomorrow."

Early turned so fast he nearly sprayed the wall. Horn was already at the door. "Wait a minute, goddamnit!"

Horn hesitated.

"What are you talking about, tomorrow? What the hell are you up to now?"

Horn smiled. "I'm leaving this evening, Bob. I'm just about finished here."

"Leaving? When? How?" Early demanded, zipping his fly.

"Same way I came in, very nearly. I'd like your people to book me out to Helsinki. Something after six this evening, I should think would be good enough. They'll have the runways cleared by then."

"Then you found what you came looking for?" Early was becoming strident. It was obvious that he felt he had somehow lost what little control he had had over what he thought was an intolerable situation.

"Very nearly, yes."

"What the hell is that supposed to mean?"

Horn opened the door and stepped out into the corridor. A red-faced Early came right after him. Horn turned back and they were suddenly face-to-face. Early smelled of fear. It gave Horn only the slightest bit of satisfaction but absolutely no pleasure.

"You'll see my report before I leave."

"I'll see a hell of a lot more than that, mister," Early said, managing to keep his voice low. Their presence like this in the corridor was creating a bit of a stir.

Early was not in bed with the Russians. He was not a traitor. It wasn't possible, Horn decided, for anyone to be quite so obvious. Not and get away with it for so long. Nobels had been mistaken after all. He had probably been killed because of his association, no matter how loose, with Boyko. He'd been odd man out.

Gloria Townsend and Tom McKenzie showed up at the end of the corridor. Gloria was carrying a covered tray. They went into the screened room.

"Let me get my coat. I'll meet you up in your office. If you want to set up a call to Washington, it'll be all right with me." Horn glanced at his watch. "It's a bit after midnight there. Not too late for Farley."

"That won't be necessary. I never said that." Early was backpedaling. "But I'll ask Siskel to sit in."

"This is Company business, Bob. If you want a witness, ask Howard or Pfeiffer to sit in."

"This is my station . . ."

"Then I suggest you call Carlisle if you want your report from me," Horn said harshly. He didn't bother keeping his voice low. He started down the corridor.

"I'll expect to see you in my office, mister," Early called after him. "Within fifteen minutes. I won't be kept waiting."

Horn had to knock on the screened room door. Gloria let him in. "We brought your breakfast," she said, closing the door after him.

"I appreciate it, I really do," Horn said, "but there's no time now. I'll be leaving soon."

"The embassy?"

"Moscow."

"You're going home, Mr. Horn?" McKenzie asked, almost wistfully. He was seated at the table, back at work, a tape recorder's earphones around his neck.

Horn nodded. "I'm just about finished here, Tom. I'm going off to have a chat with Anna sometime this morning, and then I'll have to get out. It'll only be a matter of time for me, I'm afraid. Once she mentions me to her uncle the general, all hell will break loose."

A look of concern crossed Gloria's face, but McKenzie grinned. "You're going to cause some trouble, sir?"

Horn had to smile in return. "Something like that. But with any luck we'll all keep our skins intact, and Bob won't have a stroke."

Even Gloria laughed now, albeit nervously. "Have you found what you wanted?"

"I don't know yet, Gloria. But listen to me—I'm going to need some help."

"Anything," she said earnestly.

"Bundle up all these photographs, and any that come in today, along with the tapes and your notes. I want them sent out in the very next diplomatic pouch. For Your Eyes Only to Farley Carlisle. If need be, file the originals and send out a set of duplicates." Horn was looking directly into Gloria's eyes, willing her to understand that he was trying to cover his back.

She nodded, and he could see that she understood. In fact she seemed relieved. If he hadn't suggested it, she would have.

"Anything else?" she asked.

"Find out what time the Helsinki flight leaves Sheremetyevo . . ."

"Eight o'clock," she said.

"Confirm my reservation."

"Under your workname?"

Horn nodded. "I asked Early, but he might be busy. It could slip his mind."

"How will you get out to the airport?"

"I'll take a cab or something," Horn said, but he was looking down at the photos of Anna spread out over the table. He picked up one of them and looked into her dark, serious eyes. He could see that she was in pain, couldn't he? Pain from her illness, pain from not knowing what had happened to Boyko and to her letter, and the pain of separation all these long years from her lover, Jason. He could understand that, couldn't he? The separation from a love, or a lover? He slipped the photograph into his jacket pocket.

"Is there anything else, Mr. Horn?" Gloria asked, breaking into his silence as diplomatically as possible.

He looked up, appreciating it. "Who is the cultural attaché here in the embassy?"

Tom McKenzie sniggered. Gloria shot him a look of reproach. "Eric Parsegian," she said.

"First floor?"

"Fifth. Just down the corridor from the ambassador's office. He's a pet project of the ambassador's wife. And he does a fine job."

"Is there something I should know about him?"

McKenzie sniggered again but said nothing.

"Eric is a little strange. You'll see," Gloria said. "Not bad strange, just odd," she added.

"Early's office is on the same floor as well?"

"Opposite end of the hall."

Horn picked up his overcoat. The Walther was still in an inside pocket. He prayed to God he wouldn't have to use it. Not here in Moscow. Not now. He felt vulnerable in a small way, as if he had read his horoscope and found it bad. This had been a sad, grubby business from the beginning. He didn't want it to end in more tragedy than had already befallen them.

"Well, then," Gloria said. "It's been a pleasure working with you, Mr. Horn." She stuck out her hand. McKenzie had jumped up.

Horn took her hand in both of his and drew her a little closer. He kissed her on the cheek. "Thanks yourself," he said. He shook McKenzie's hand and then left.

Long good-byes had never done anyone any good.

The cultural attaché, or cultural affairs officer as he was sometimes called, was charged with the responsibility of keeping current with the arts and learning of his host country: the symphony orchestras, the dance companies, the theater groups, the singers and poets and writers. He was also charged with knowing what was happening in the arts in his own country, and then somehow affecting goodwill exchange programs and appearances. Cultural attachés attended every sort of function imaginable, many of which they themselves organized and conducted; they worked as masters of ceremony, as booking agents, as researchers, as barometers of what was good and what was not, and as talent scouts. The job was hardly appreciated. The Moscow embassy was no exception in that its cultural attaché had no staff and only the part-time use of one secretary.

"After all, Mr. Horton," Eric Parsegian explained, "bombs and guns and MiGs and tanks are terribly more important than the ballet, don't you agree?"

Parsegian was of medium height with an undistinguished but pleasant face, lovely blue eyes, and short but modishly cut blond hair. He had a few days' growth of whiskers on his face, however, and he wore no socks with his low-cut loafers, nor did he wear a tie. In fact his shirt had no collar that Horn could see, and the collar of his lightweight sports coat was turned up. Horn suspected the man's dress was state of the art. Marc and Marney had mentioned a television police show that took place in Florida in which the main character dressed that way. *Miami Vice*. The Don Johnson look. It was popular in Germany. Parsegian's office was a study in pastels and soft tones, startling here in Moscow, but comfortable for all its pretensions. A thick, pale-green carpet covered the floor of the large room. A glass-topped desk faced a very broad window that looked out across Tchaikovsky Street toward Embassy Row. A grouping of white, kid-glove leather furniture was arranged around a brass and glass coffee table. A couple of Picasso prints adorned the walls, leather-bound books were artfully arranged on highly lacquered bookshelves, and Tchaikovsky's Violin Concerto in D was playing softly from tall, freestanding speakers.

"It's a crying shame, but we do what we can," Parsegian complained. "All they want these days is that raucous rock and roll here, and back in the States, well, the Bolshoi once in a great while, and perhaps even the Kirov as long as it's not overdone, mind you, and that's it. *Finis*!"

"And your job is to make all the arrangements," Horn suggested. Parsegian was probably gay. Not outrageously so, but gentle and effeminate enough so that it was probable. Horn had learned the difference firsthand at a lot of Catholic retreats in high school and later in college. For a while he had even been categorized as one of the possibles; a few bloody noses and displaced teeth did wonders to quell such suspicions, though such physical acts in themselves meant absolutely nothing. At seventeen certain things were still black and white, however.

"Would you care for a cup of tea, Mr. Horton?"

"Thanks. But I've been up all night working."

"Brandy, in that case?" Parsegian asked, smiling.

Horn inclined his head. "If you'll join me."

"Of course." Parsegian got up from his desk and glided to a sideboard where he poured them both a generous measure of brandy into very expensive crystal snifters. "I'm very flattered that you decided to drop by," he said, returning.

Horn accepted the drink. "Thanks."

"From what I hear, you came along to study the more efficient operations here."

Horn looked blankly at him.

"For the promotion board?"

"Actually no. I came only to ask a few questions about something that may have happened here ten or twelve years ago."

"How interesting," Parsegian said, his smile broadening. "A little before my time, of course. But do continue—I'm all ears."

Horn took a sip of his brandy. It was very good. He sat forward and put his glass down. "I think you should understand something, Mr. Parsegian, from the very beginning. What I have to say to you this morning must be kept in the utmost confidentiality. I can have the ambassador confirm that if need be."

Parsegian's eyes widened, but he waved Horn's suggestion away. "You are a spook. Right here, in my office. Imagine."

Horn raised his right eyebrow. He wasn't sure what Parsegian was up to. The man was intelligent, but Horn thought that at least some of his mannerisms were affected for some purpose. So be it. "My life, in some measure, may depend upon your discretion."

"What can I do for you, Mr. Horton?" Parsegian asked, lowering his voice and dropping most of the pretense. He'd read something of the seriousness from Horn's manner.

"Does the name Anna Feodorovna mean anything to you?"

"Lovely girl. I've seen the film studies, of course. She's doing a creditable job as an assistant artistic director to Grigorovich himself. Doesn't dance any longer, which is a pity; she was very good. Something about her foreign travel passport being revoked."

Horn hadn't heard that part. "Do you know anything about that? The circumstances behind her passport being withdrawn, I mean."

Parsegian shook his head. "Afraid not. Before my time, as I've said. Her uncle has something to do in the government— maybe that was it. Or it could have been almost anything. Russians, as a group, are a bit on the paranoid side, if you hadn't already noticed."

"What else do you know about her? Husband? Boyfriends?"

"Single, though I can't imagine why. She has a certain attractiveness. All the dancers do, in a gaunt sort of way. And they usually marry each other. You know, the Ludmilla Semenyakas and the Mikhail Lavrovskys. Their little couplings usually—not always, mind you, but usually—end up as terrific duos onstage.''

''But not Anna?''

''Not Anna. Her father is nothing, her mother teaches the piano or something in Leningrad, but her grandfather, now he was someone special. Petr Nikolaivich Chalkin.''

Horn didn't know the name.

''Only one of Russia's greatest poets before the Revolution. He didn't do much afterward. Died during the Second World War, I think. He was the very first to tell the world that the Russian spirit was not only tragic, but that Russians loved to wallow in tragedy. It was a national forte.''

''They mustn't have loved him after 1917.''

''No,'' Parsegian said, smiling, appreciating the little bit of humor. ''For all we know it's the reason Anna was denied foreign travel.''

''The revolutionary spirit is genetic.''

''Close enough.''

''How did she get into the Bolshoi in the first place, with such a questionable past?''

''The Russians enjoy a lot more than they export. Especially when it comes to talent, Mr. Horton. Believe me, the Bolshoi in Moscow is different than the Bolshoi in New York. The spirit just isn't the same once they leave the motherland.''

''She deserved it?''

''She was good, I told you. Prima, not assoluta, but very good.''

''She may have had an affair with someone from this embassy ten, twelve years ago.''

''So what?''

''That doesn't surprise you?''

''Should it?''

''A young Bolshoi star and an American? It seems a little contrived.''

Parsegian laughed softly, his laugh a little high-pitched but genuine. ''I don't mean to poke fun at your obvious good nature, Mr. Horton, but the cock does rule the world, if you hadn't guessed.''

Horn was startled. He hadn't thought Parsegian would be that crude. But then this was the season for surprises.

''Oh, don't be shocked. It happens all the time. Every petty little engineer or visiting doctor or especially the bureaucrat with any sense of self-importance at all would like to stick it to a little foreign pussy. The younger the better.'' Parsegian flipped his hair back. "It shocks you, my dear man? Don't let it. The act is commonplace. Fish gotta swim, birds gotta fly . . . something like that. I can tell you about a thirteen-year-old—"

"Anna," Horn said.

Parsegian shrugged. "Sorry, but it doesn't come as a shock to me."

"How could it have happened?"

"Mechanically, are you saying? Or do you mean how did a nice girl like that meet a lecherous old bastard from this nest of Philistines?"

"Both."

"This isn't the police state that everyone in Des Moines believes it is, you know. You can still get a hotel room if you know the ropes. You can still find an apartment for a little tryst, a dacha, a house. Hell, do it on the museum floor after hours." Parsegian sighed. He sat back, cradling his brandy snifter in both hands.

"Had you heard anything about Anna?"

"No, I'm afraid not."

"Who was the cultural attaché in 1975?" There had been no real need to know that until now.

Parsegian's eyes narrowed a little. It was a question he hadn't expected. He started to say something but then thought better of it. He got up, went to a teak file cabinet built into the wall beneath one of the bookcases, and withdrew a fat volume bound in green paper. It took a moment for him to find what he was looking for. His shoulders sagged. He looked up, a bleak expression on his face.

"Yes?"

"Does the name Edmund Clay mean anything to you, Mr. Horton?"

Horn held himself in check. He nodded.

"His son Rupert was cultural attaché from 1974 to 1977."

"I didn't know that his son had been stationed here," Horn said. "I didn't even know he worked for the State Department."

"I knew him," Parsegian said softly. He looked again at the entry in the book, then closed it and replaced it in the file cabinet. He turned again to Horn. "About five years ago. In Washington. Before he was killed in a car crash."

"You knew him personally?"

"Yes," Parsegian said, leaving little doubt as to exactly in what way he had known Clay's son.

"Did he ever say anything about Anna, and whoever it was she had had an affair with?"

Parsegian shook his head. "We didn't talk about business. Not that kind of business, anyway. I was helping him on the senator's campaign at the time. We bounced back and forth between Washington and Oregon for most of that spring and summer, right up until the November elections."

"Oregon?" Horn asked carefully.

"Yeah," Parsegian replied, still back within his own memories. He came back and sat down behind his desk. "He was working for Tom Wagner. They'd known each other for a long time. They were old friends."

"Lovers?"

Parsegian laughed. "Hell, no. Wagner was about as hetero as they came in those days. They knew each other from before. I think they were old family friends or something."

"Clay never mentioned it?"

"It never came up." Parsegian spread his hands. "Then he was killed. It was tragic. He had a lot going for him. He would have eventually taken over for his father."

"He said that?"

"Yes," Parsegian said, lowering his head. "It brings back a lot of painful memories."

Horn waited a moment or two in respectful silence, and then he got to his feet. Parsegian looked up. "Anything else you can tell me about Anna?"

"Is it all that important, what happened that long ago?"

"Did you know that Senator Wagner had been stationed here about that time?"

"Of course. We used it in his campaign."

"Then you knew that he and Clay had worked together before."

"I said they were old family friends . . ." Parsegian stopped. An odd expression crossed his face. "You think that the American with whom Anna Feodorovna was having an affair was Tom Wagner? And that Rupert set them up?"

Horn nodded. "It had occurred to me," he said.

Bob Early had provided himself with reinforcements. Besides Kyle Pfeiffer and Van Howard, the new assistant COS out of Athens, Gloria Townsend and Tom McKenzie were waiting for Horn. When he came in they all looked a little guilty. Gloria was rooting for him; he could see it in her eyes. She was defiant.

"Dissecting the body even before it's dead?"

"I don't think that's funny under the circumstances," Early said from behind his desk. He motioned Horn to the remaining available chair across from him.

Horn sat down. "I'll try to make out my report for you this afternoon."

"I've called off my surveillance people. She's alone, in any event. The apartment is quiet."

"Good. I didn't want them getting in the way."

"I do not want you to approach her. She is hands-off."

"Yes?"

"Because of her uncle. If the KGB should find out that we have conducted a surveillance operation against the niece of their First Chief Directorate's top officer, we might just as well roll up the carpet and go home."

He'd been down this road before, this road of defiance. He wondered if he wanted to try again. He'd come perilously close on more than one occasion to losing everything he had worked for; he could remember some of the times but not all of them. Just recently, however, over the past couple of years, he had begun to see the world somewhat differently; his eyes were those of a man who had come a lot of miles. A father, a husband, a lover, an agent runner, and all the complexities of spirit that entailed. An ex-priest, fallen priest, almost priest. Bits and pieces that had hardly been worth a passing glance in years past now seemed to occupy an increasingly larger portion of his waking thoughts. His daily routines seemed to come less easily than they had in the past; even shaving in the morning sometimes seemed like such an alien task that he would stare at his face in the mirror, his hand raised, the razor poised, and wonder what in God's name he was doing there like that. Mid-life crisis? Or was it something else? Burnout, perhaps? It had all but sapped his patience.

"Is that all?" he asked.

Early was nonplussed for just a moment. It wasn't the response he had expected.

"I'll be gone on the eight o'clock to Helsinki. K.W. can bring my bags out to the airport."

"I want the gun I gave you," Early said.

Horn got to his feet, his overcoat over his arm. "I'll give it to K.W. tonight at the airport."

"I don't want you leaving this embassy, mister."

"Is that an order, Mr. Early?"

Early nodded. "Yes. It is."

"I'll make note of it in my final report. Please don't try to have me followed. It will make the situation entirely too dangerous for everyone concerned."

14

Horn had taken the ancient iron elevator down, signed out
at exactly 9:17A.M. and had hauled on his heavy winter coat and
hat. He had half expected Early, or at least Pfeiffer, to come
running after him, and he had been fully prepared for a big
scene in which he would have been tempted to relieve Early
of his position right on the spot. Whether or not he could
have gotten away with such an outrageous act, whether or not
Carlisle would have supported him, wouldn't have mattered.
It would have been something to work out after the dust had
settled. But it would have gotten Early off his back, and
insured just a few hours of cooperation. It was all he really
needed, after all. He figured if he could get away from the
embassy cleanly, Early would have second thoughts about
coming after him and would probably figure in the end that
the path of least resistance for him would be to allow Horn to
get off on the Helsinki flight. "I figured once we got him out
of the country, we could pick up the pieces," Early could tell
Carlisle. "Can't rake leaves in a windstorm."

It had nearly stopped snowing, and the wind had all but
died, but it was very cold. The air this morning smelled crisp
and clean, very nearly as neutral as the atmosphere within any
large city can smell. Horn hesitated for a moment just outside
the door. Two militia officers bundled up in their heavy
greatcoats and fur hats watched him. They were very young.
In the summer this was fairly pleasant duty, watching the
U.S. embassy. They could see the pretty secretaries coming

and going, catch glimpses of very important people, even catch a spy from time to time. Now, like this, however, there was very little pleasure in the job, it was far too cold, and it showed on their bleak faces. Had Horn been Russian, or even of questionable nationality, they would have hassled him simply for something to do. But he was so obviously American by the cut of his clothes, by his height and build, and by his open gaze toward them, that they turned away, and he headed on foot up the street to where he had parked the car. The snowplows had been busy through the night and into the morning. Tchaikovsky Street had been almost completely cleared. An army of old women was clearing the snow away from the few parked cars that had been buried by the passing plows. For each car they dug out, they attached a cardboard envelope beneath the windshield wipers, or to a radio antenna or door handle. It was a five-ruble fine for parking a car so as to interfere with the work of the snowplows. The fines paid the old women's salaries, though they had to split the money with the snowplow operators and the militia.

The engineer's car had already been dug out. The women had even cleaned the snow off the windows. Horn took the brown envelope from beneath the windshield wiper, stuffed a five-ruble note into it, sealed it, and walked back half a block where he handed it to one of the women. She gave him a toothless grin, stuffed the envelope into her ragged coat, and went back to work.

The car didn't want to start at first. But in the end, just before the battery was nearly worn down, the engine finally kicked over. Horn let it warm up for a long time as he watched down the street, the way he had just come. Traffic was finally beginning to move. A bus rumbled by and then two large dump trucks loaded with snow passed, heading for the river where they would dump their loads. No one had come from the embassy after him. It was something. Before he drove off he had to scrape the frost from the inside of the windshield with a credit card. Plastic snowscrapers were just as rare a commodity in Moscow as were good ballpoint pens and genuine designer jeans.

He made a U-turn and headed back past the planetarium and the Pakistani embassy. This was the Grand Boulevard, called the Sadovaya, and was on two levels, which eliminated crossing streets. Tunnel entrances for the lower level were at the major intersections. Tall apartment buildings lined the

broad thoroughfare that under normal conditions was busy
with traffic. More old women were working there, some of
them with blowtorches, melting the ice and snow from the
trolley car tracks. By noon the city would be fully back to
normal. The storm may have been unusually harsh this time,
but the way of life was common. In five minutes he reached
Tsvetnoy Boulevard where he turned south, crossing the
Petrovskiy where traffic lanes were separated by a wide strip
of grass and trees bare now against the winter winds. There
were playgrounds in the strip, open spaces, benches, and
even flowers in the spring and summer. The much narrower
Neglinnaya was not so well plowed. He had to turn back up
toward the Budapest Hotel where he circled the block so that
he could park on the lower side of the street which had been
cleared of snow, his wheels up on the sidewalk. He locked up
and walked around the block, passing the Ministry of Health.
Enough people were out and about now so that his presence
there at that hour wasn't unusual. There was a holiday mood
downtown. He had to wait until a snowplow rumbled up
Neglinnaya before he could cross, then he started down Neglin
2. These side streets had not yet been plowed. Long snow-
drifts blocked the road, though the more open avenues had
been in worse condition. Here the close-set buildings had
provided some protection from the falling snow.

At this point Horn was not in a hurry. Absolutely no one
was around now, though there were some footprints in the
snow right down the middle of the street, and one set of tire
tracks led from a dug-out parking spot to the far corner where
the driver had shoveled and pushed his way onto Zhdanova.
He passed Anna's apartment and glanced up at her window,
the very window in which her photograph had been taken from
the passing van. The curtains were closed, and Horn was just
a little disappointed, though he hadn't really thought about
what he expected. To see her still standing there, waiting for
him? She'd been up most of the night and morning entertaining her friends. She would be tired. She would be sleeping.
Leave her be, some voice inside of him said. Turn away,
leave, go to Helsinki and then back to Berlin. Go to Christine, now, before it is too late. At the corner he stopped,
crossed to the upper side of the *pereulok*, and then glanced
back at the roof of the building opposite Anna's. There was
nothing to be seen, of course—at least nothing to be seen
from there. No surveillance team, no parabolic antenna on its

tripod, no workmen, no chimney sweeps, no sightseers . . . no uncles. He trudged back through the snow, half expecting at any moment to hear the shrill bleat of a militia whistle, or someone stepping out of a doorway: "See here, what are you doing in this neighborhood? State your business." Fight or flight, our only choices in the end. At number 15 he stopped and looked over his shoulder. No one was behind him. He mounted the steps and entered the corridor, his breath white inside. The inside of the door window was thick with frost, and a long streak of snow from the wind had forced its way beneath the door and down the narrow corridor. Unlike Sheshkin's place, this building was very well maintained. It even smelled clean. The floors and stairs, except for the snow, were free of debris and dirt; the plaster looked new and was neatly painted a pale brown, with white-painted wainscoting to elbow height. Anna's name was listed under Chalkin, 2A, on one of the four mailboxes. There was no buzzer.

For a long ten seconds or more he stood just within the doorway listening to the sounds of the building, smelling its clean, pleasant odors. A motor was running below; a pump of some sort, he figured. Somewhere above he could hear music. Faintly. A woman singing. It was an opera, and it seemed somehow vaguely familiar to him though he could not quite make out the melody. He took off his gloves, stuffed them in his lefthand coat pocket, then withdrew the Walther automatic. He checked to make sure a shell was in the firing chamber, then put it back in his pocket. His chest was a little tight, but other than that a calmness had come over him as it usually did when he was in the field. It was adrenaline, he told himself, starting slowly up the stairs. Anyone could be up there. The surveillance team could have been spotted coming in or leaving. The monitors could have been discovered. The telephone tap made. The theater people who had come home with Anna last night could all have been plants. All of them KGB. Department Viktor, KGB. Experts in *mokrie dela.* Up there now to protect the niece of a KGB general. No one but a fool would bang on her door in the blind like this. A fool or a man with a definite death wish.

Reaching the first-floor landing he could hear the music quite plainly, and he recognized it; he'd listened to the thing hundreds of times during and since college, though his was a different recording, he thought. It was *Madama Butterfly.* And almost instantaneously with his recognition of the music came another understanding, this one at a much deeper level, this one beginning viscerally and working its way to his brain at an unknowable speed, even faster than déjà vu itself. Anna had put herself in the position of a Madame Butterfly. She had loved an American—had he promised her the sun and the moon?—who had left her, who had gone away to distant shores, to distant home fires and loves. Now she wanted him to return; now she wanted to tell him about herself, about what she had become, where she had been, with whom she had eaten and danced and spoken. She wanted her Jason to know everything there was to know about her, because if it were true that she was dying, there would be little else to know about her. She wanted to see him again. Her love, kindled ten or twelve years ago, had apparently not diminished. It may even have grown stronger, as often is the case in which fantasy becomes much larger, much more intense than real life. How much closer was the comparison between Anna and Madame Butterfly? He hoped not much closer. He hoped that she and her Jason hadn't had a child; he sincerely hoped that that was not the reason she had been denied a foreign passport. He hoped also that her dying had not been mentioned in the letter in a metaphorical sense, as a way in which she was telling her Jason that she was soon to commit suicide as Madame Butterfly had in the end. Puccini's opera was a tragedy. He sincerely hoped that he had not arrived in time to witness a real-life rendition of the story.

He went to 2A and listened at the door. All he could hear was the music from within. No movement, no conversation, no man's voice lowered, nothing to indicate that Anna had company. She was alone inside her apartment listening to *Madama Butterfly* while she waited for her Jason. What had Boyko promised her?

Horn raised his right hand, hesitated for just a moment longer before he finally committed himself, and then knocked, the noise unnaturally loud in the corridor. He imagined that the entire building's framework had shaken. If anyone had been asleep, he would be awake now. He thought, however, that this being a weekday morning, the apartment building would be mostly deserted, its tenants off at work. "Minimize your risks, boyo; minimize your exposure wherever you can," his instructors told him a million years ago. But "fear has big eyes," the Russians would say.

The music stopped abruptly as he was about to knock

again. He stayed his hand. Anna Feodorovna opened the
door. She wore a heavy velour robe. Her long dark hair was
pinned up in the back exposing her delicate neck and tiny
ears. Horn was struck by her sadness as well as by her
delicacy. She was smaller, more fragile than he thought she
would be, and yet he thought he could see a certain wiry
strength to her. Here was a woman of a thousand contradic-
tions. How many could he possibly know? He did understand
Jason, however. Oh, yes, he did. He took off his hat.

She looked beyond him into the empty corridor, then up
into his eyes. "Yes?" she asked cautiously.

"Are you alone, Anna?" Horn asked, his voice soft, his
Russian formal. "Have your friends left you? Have they
returned to the theater finally?"

Her eyes widened. She could hear his accent. "You
are . . . foreign?" She was afraid to say American.

Horn nodded. "I have come about Jason. About your letter
to Jason.'"

"Oh, dear God," Anna said. Her knuckles turned white
where she gripped the door to stop from falling down.

Horn knew that he would remember this moment for the
rest of his life. Her eyes were wide, like a tragic poem filled
with a hope that was nevertheless overshadowed by impend-
ing tragedy. Why wasn't Jason here, or at the very least,
Boyko? Who was this stranger?

He made sure the door was locked. They sat in her small
living room on bulky, overstuffed chairs. The apartment smelled
of smoke, and somewhat of liquor; other than that there was
no sign that a party had gone on all night. The apartment
wasn't as warm as most Russian places. It was well furnished
with what appeared to be very old, very substantial pieces. A
very large oil painting of a ballet dancer on pointe hung on
one wall. Horn immediately recognized that it was Anna
when she was very young, perhaps seventeen or eighteen.
She was very beautiful. Filled with confidence. Hopeful for a
bright future. Sure of her own growing power. The artist had
been very good; he had managed to capture all of that on
canvas. Anna sat now on the edge of her chair, her knees
primly together, her hands on her lap. She was still very
beautiful, Horn thought. But her feet were ugly, bluntly
misshapen; they were the feet of a dancer, proof that she had
worked all of her life at her art.

"He sent you because it is too dangerous for him to write," she said, as if she didn't believe it herself. "It has been weeks. I've sat here waiting, not knowing what to expect, not even knowing whether or not he got my letter." She got up abruptly. "Would you like some tea? The water is still hot."

"It is not necessary."

"You've come a long way to see me. We'll have some tea. Do you have a cigarette?"

Horn was struck by how much she reminded him of a frightened little child. He thought he could see that she was dying by the translucence of her skin, but then the painting showed the same glow. He got up and gave her a cigarette, holding the light for her. Her hands shook.

"I'll have a little lemon in mine, if you have it," he said without thinking.

She smiled. "In Moscow? In January?"

Horn felt like a fool. "Sorry."

"Don't be. Let me tell you, I am more nervous than you. This is a very big occasion for me, you know. What is your name?"

"Jack."

"Just Jack?"

Horn nodded.

"Perhaps we should be celebrating, Jack. It's never too early for champagne." She was puffing nervously on her cigarette. "But I've only the sweet kind. Jason never liked it. I don't suppose you would either, Jack. If only I had thought to buy some French wine. But one can't think of everything, can one? Especially not at times such as these." Her eyes were glistening, her entire body shaking now. "Christ, Jack, just tell me, is he alive? Is he all right? Is he happy?" Her nostrils flared. "It's just that it's been so long, you see, without knowing. Without having a single word. Nothing. I was finally going crazy without knowing."

"He is alive and well, Anna," Horn said, hating the lie. And yet it wasn't really a lie, was it? It probably had been Jason or someone acting on his orders, or someone protecting him, who had committed murder. At the very least Boyko's. Which meant Jason was alive, and very likely well. He could feel hatred welling up in his breast.

Anna closed her eyes as she took a very deep breath and let it out slowly. She smiled bravely. "Then I shall fix tea, Jack. Take off your coat, please. I'll just be a minute."

She went into the kitchen. Horn took off his overcoat, laying it over the back of his chair in such a fashion that he could quickly reach the Walther. He switched on the miniature recorder in his jacket pocket, then lit himself a cigarette. He went to the window where he parted the curtains just enough so that he could look down at the street. No one had come behind him. Besides the tire tracks, the original set of footprints down the middle of the street, and his own footprints in the snow on both sides, no one else had come. Nor could he see anyone on the roof across the street or in any of the windows, but that didn't mean anything. He would have liked to have run an electronic sweep over the entire apartment, to check for bugs. But Early's surveillance people had said that as far as they could tell, from a distance, her apartment was clean. It only slightly bothered him. Considering her background with an American lover, her association with the Bolshoi, the fact she'd been denied a foreign passport, and considering who her uncle was, he would have thought her activities would have been monitored.

Anna came to the doorway. "Jason didn't share my letter with you? You haven't read it?"

Horn turned around. "No, I haven't read your letter, Anna."

She seemed relieved, and then a little embarrassed. "But you have brought me a message?"

"Not exactly."

"No?" she asked, her face still wide and innocent.

"I've come to ask a few questions."

She was puzzled for just a moment, but then something dawned on her, because she brightened. "Of course. I understand. He will want to make sure, won't he."

She turned and went back into the kitchen. Her meaning was crystal clear in Horn's mind. Jason would have to make sure this wasn't some kind of a trap. A honey trap, they used to be called. Send a good-looking woman to get involved with the mark, take photographs and audio tapes of their liaisons, and then use them as blackmail. Now or twenty years from now. Like a fine wine, some operations gained in value and prestige with age. But was it really that simple? He sincerely doubted it, though he couldn't rightly say why except for the look in her eyes. She was an innocent. But Jason would have to make sure. She recognized that much in him. He was an important man. Ah, God, Horn wondered, what sort of *Homo sapiens* were we producing these days? Intelligent men. Beyond tool users. We had become abstractionists in very nearly the fullest sense of the word; we had come to think only of the essence of a thing; of its spirit, of its ideal, and not the actual object. People were portraits in our minds, not flesh and blood. Portraits could be sullied, so then we changed our perceptions, never fully understanding that real people could bleed real blood. Jason had used Anna as an abstraction—a Bolshoi dancer. He had disregarded the fact that she was Anna Chalkin, a little girl with ugly feet who cried real tears and was dying now. "Christ," he swore under his breath. "Oh, Jesus Christ!"

The tea kettle whistled and then stopped as she took it off the burner. She thought he had come as a front man for Jason in response to her letter. It meant he should know Jason's real name. He would have to proceed with care. She would frighten very easily at this stage.

Now that Anna thought she knew Horn's real purpose for coming to her, she was somewhat more relaxed. She sat deeply within her big chair, her legs folded beneath her as she cradled her glass of tea in both hands. There was an air of expectation about her, as if the lights had just gone down on the opening of a ballet and she was listening to the overture, enjoying it but impatient nevertheless for the curtain to rise and the dancing to begin. The apartment was very quiet, the light gray from the half-parted curtain.

"This mustn't become a case of mistaken identity," Horn said.

"Of course not. I'll do whatever I can to help. Did he give you a message for me? A letter? Something?"

Horn forced himself not to look away. "First there are some questions I must ask you. Some ground we will have to cover. I think we need to establish your identity beyond any doubt."

"My identity card? My internal passport? I don't have a driver's license."

"Documents can be manufactured."

"My friends—"

Horn shook his head, cutting her off. "It's important that we go over some very old ground now . . . common ground between you and Jason, that only you and he could possibly know."

She took a moment to reply. "I shouldn't have supposed it would have been easy, should I."

"No," Horn said noncommittally.

"He was always worried about that."

"About what?"

"Identification. Not passports or that sort of thing, but what people were really all about. We talked a lot. It was important."

"Yes?"

"About our families, our backgrounds. What we wanted for the future. We used to sit at night in the spring when the rain pounded on the roof, listening to music, drinking wine and talking. Just talking. Nothing to hide. No little tricks or practical jokes."

"When did you meet him?"

"The date?"

"Yes."

"October ninth," Anna said with conviction.

"Seventy-four?"

She shook her head. "Seventy-five."

"How can you remember the date so accurately?"

"It was my twenty-fourth birthday, Jack. Besides, I would never have forgotten that date. Never." She had looked inward for a moment. She blinked, focusing again on Horn. "Haven't you a significant date or two in your life?"

"Yes, I do. We all have. Where was it that you met?"

"At the theater."

"Backstage?"

"Yes."

"Who else was there?"

Anna's eyes narrowed. "Please?"

"There was someone else there that night? Someone perhaps who introduced you?"

She pursed her lips, thinking back. She shrugged her shoulders. "There were people. There are always a lot of people backstage after a performance. For the artist, you know," she added with a wistful note. "I don't remember anyone specifically."

"Americans simply come backstage at the Bolshoi and introduce themselves? The Bolshoi is very democratic?"

Anna laughed at the little joke. "I don't know."

"Rupert Clay. Does this name mean anything to you at all?"

She shook her head, but then sat forward a little. "Wait. Yes, perhaps I do remember the name. He was a homosexual, perhaps? With long hair, I think. A pretty boy."

Clay had been a handsome young man. He'd been compared in looks to a young Clark Gable.

"He is the one," Horn said. "Were he and Jason friends?"

She giggled. "Hardly, Jack. No, I would say. No."

"But they knew each other?"

"I don't know. Is he important, this other man?"

"You tell me."

"Jason had a way of asking questions just like you."

"And did you have the answers for him?"

"I don't know what you want of me, Jack. Tell me. I want to help. Believe me. But I don't remember this person very accurately. I'm sorry, but it is just so. I met Jason on my birthday. I think he was just there. Very tall, very handsome in evening clothes." She smiled. "He complained about the sweet Russian champagne. Someone brought him French champagne. He offered to share it with me."

"All that at the theater?"

"Yes. It was a party for me afterward. It happens a lot in the beginning of a show, and then at the end too. But especially at the end."

"How did Jason come by his code name?"

She smiled in remembrance. "He was Jason and I was his Medea. We were the Argonauts lost on a sea of mistrust and violence. But our ship was strong. He picked it."

It made Horn sick to think of how the son of a bitch had used her. She had been only twenty-four years old. A baby. And Jason had decided to play games with her. Another conquest.

"You know, the depth of his knowledge was amazing. He even knew about the dance, and about opera. Verdi and Puccini were his favorites, of course. Mine too. More melodic, not so strident. And when it came to concertos, well, Bartók was anathema to him. He called Bartók that 'peasant Hungarian who never really learned to play the piano.' I would laugh and laugh, you know. It was good for the soul, though sometimes a little hard on my tummy. I loved him because he loved our Tchaikovsky for all the right reasons. He told me once that Tchaikovsky did in music with our Russian folklore what the brothers Grimm did in words with German stories. It was what every Russian schoolchild knows. But it was unusual to hear it from an American."

"What happened after your birthday party?" Horn asked.

"I think it was a few days before I saw him next. This time

Ekaterina Maximova held a dinner party at the Metropole Hotel in one of their private rooms. There were at least a hundred of us, mostly from the theater, but some from the Kremlin, too, the old men who always were there.''

"And Jason?"

"We sat next to each other for the entire evening. Later, when we all went dancing, Jason and I never came off the floor. He was very good and very sure. Most men are usually intimidated if you are a ballet dancer. They think that you are too good for them, so they get nervous and stumble all over their feet, and yours too.''

"Didn't you attract notice?"

"Because I was dancing and talking for so long with an American?"

"Yes."

She shrugged. "I don't know. I didn't even think about it. I was too happy.''

"Did you two speak Russian, or was it English?"

"It depended, though his Russian wasn't as good as yours. Sometimes when . . . we were together, we would speak French. It was his favorite language, he told me. It was our language.''

"When you were together in public, such as the dinner party at the Metropole, he spoke in Russian?"

"No, on the contrary. In public he mostly spoke English. When he was required to use his Russian he pretended that he understood much less than he really did. He said it encouraged people to talk about him more openly, more freely than if they thought he couldn't understand.''

"But he did understand."

"Oh, yes, very well. His accent got in his way when speaking, but he could understand and he could read perfectly. Still, he preferred French. And so did I after a while.''

"What did you two talk about?"

She smiled. "Everything.''

"Music?"

"Of course.''

"World affairs?"

"Sometimes.''

"Sports?"

"Yes, that too.''

"America?"

"We really talked about everything, Jack. Honestly. Once in the summer we were in a boat on the river—''

"Which river?" Horn asked.

"The Moscow River," she replied. "It was at night, and we were alone up top; everyone else had gone below. It was very cold, I remember, because we had to cover up with a heavy blanket even though it was June. The sky was very clear and Jason began to tell me about the stars. The Big Dipper that pours into the Little Dipper so that you can find the North Star. There was a name for that star, but I can't remember now."

"Polaris," Horn said automatically. Christine was always asking him things. It was habit.

Anna looked at him, and nodded. "Yes, that's it. There was the hunter Orion, too, who loved Eos and was finally killed by Artemis. Orion chased the seven sisters, who were the Pleiades. Jason said they were the seven daughters of Atlas. That constellation looked to me like a very tiny dipper. But it wasn't."

She'd been sheltered by the state all of her life. Suddenly she had been thrown together with a worldly man who struck her as sincere. She had been seduced. It had probably happened within the first five minutes of their meeting.

"What happened after that, Anna? After your first few meetings at the theater, at the Metropole. Did you two have a special place?"

She blushed a little, the color coming high on her cheeks, and a splotch on her forehead. "I made him dinner at my apartment a few times."

"Here?"

"No. I had a place on Kalinina then. He came there, but we had a militiaman downstairs for security. Some important people lived in that building."

"And you were a prima ballerina."

"Not yet. But very close, Jack."

"Then what?"

"Is this necessary?" she asked tiredly. "Jason had a friend who was gone on weekends, and once in a while during the week. We were able to use his apartment up by the university. It was small, but very nice."

"Do you remember this friend's name? An American?"

"I never knew his name. But I don't think he was American."

"Why not?"

"It was not a foreigners' building. It was a haven, Jason

said. He was tired of being watched wherever he went. We always went to the apartment separately. We left at different times too. I would usually go first, and he would wait an hour before he'd leave."

"You'd stay the entire weekend?"

"Sometimes. Sometimes not. It depended upon what show we were performing. Sometimes I had only a matinee. Afterward I would come back to the apartment."

"He was always there?"

"Always, Jack. He was never even late. Not once. He was a very good man, very good to me." She put her tea down as if the glass had become an impossibly heavy burden. "It has been a very long time, Jack. What is going to happen now? Can you tell me that much?" Her eyes were wide, her forehead high, but even without makeup she was beautiful in the classic sense, as if she were a *haute couture* mannequin, elusive in some ways, untouchable.

"Where else did you meet?"

She sighed. "There is a family friend who has a dacha on the Istra River. You know this place, outside of the city?"

Horn nodded.

"His name is Dominic Shevchenko. I used to go out there alone sometimes when I wanted peace and quiet. I took Jason there and no one knew. It became our favorite place, especially in the winter."

"How did you get out there, if you didn't drive?"

"Jason would pick me up with his car by the Kazan Station, or by the Hippodrome, once by Gorki Park. He'd always drop me off at a Metro station on the way back."

"Do you remember his car?"

She shook her head. "Four doors, I think. It was no limousine, but it was a nice car. The heater worked."

"But you did go out in public from time to time."

"Yes. More at first than later."

"Then how did he introduce himself to you at the theater? How did he introduce himself in public, to your friends, to the maître d's at the restaurants?"

"Oh," Anna said. "As Ted Wells. I hated the name."

It didn't mean a thing to Horn. "That wasn't his real name."

She smiled. "Of course not. I don't know what you're trying to do, Jack, but I wish you'd stop it. He called it his workname. Our little secret. It was a game. To me he was, and will always be, Jason. I never knew his real name.'' She looked up. ''But you do, don't you?'' she asked softly. ''Has he aged badly? Has he gained weight? You can tell me that much, can't you? He did fifty sit-ups every morning. He was worried about his waistline. Is he fit now?''

Ted Wells, Horn thought. The name had the same initials as Tom Wagner. Coincidence?

''How did you know about Boyko?'' he asked.

''Jason told me, of course. How else?''

Jason had known about Boyko, then, and presumably about the network. The chain of connections was circumstantial, but it was there, it did add up, no matter how pat it seemed in Horn's mind. Edmund Clay, because of his connections, read the daily CIA Moscow summary. He knew about Boyko and the network, and it was very possible his son knew it too. The imagination was not stretched one bit to believe a father such as Clay would communicate at such a level with his son, especially if he had dreams of his son taking over. And finally, Rupert Clay was an old family friend of Tom Wagner's. In fact Clay had been stationed here in Moscow at the same time Wagner, according to Edmund Clay and according to Eric Parsegian's recollection, had been stationed here. They too could have communicated. And finally Wagner—Jason? —had told Anna. Told her what? Told her that his *workname* was Wells? Who used such terminology except the Company?

''Exactly what did Jason tell you about Boyko?''

''That I could reach him at the Arbat. It is a restaurant. His hangout. Jason told me that Boyko was not very trustworthy, that he worked for anyone who had money, especially Western currency. That I shouldn't trust him, but that if anything at all went wrong in my life, I could send a letter out with Boyko.''

''Did he tell you any other names?''

''No. And I was frightened. It was a very long time ago to think that Boyko would still be active. But he was.''

''Did you pay him anything?''

''No. He didn't ask. It happened too quickly. He was just there one moment and gone with my letter the next. I've been waiting ever since. He didn't come back. No messages came. Nothing. Not until you.''

''Why did you send the letter, Anna?'' Horn asked. ''Why have you written to Jason?''

She didn't move. She didn't say a word.

"Do you want to come to America? Do you want to defect? Is that what you want? Is that what you have asked?"

"You weren't lying—you haven't seen the letter, have you," she accused.

Horn shook his head.

"In fact you haven't even talked with Jason," she said. Her eyes had grown dull, her shoulders had sagged.

"Boyko is dead. He was murdered, Anna. In Helsinki. Whoever killed him took your letter."

She pressed the knuckles of her right hand to her mouth. She wanted to cry out. Horn could see that she was barely hanging on. Her letter had been her final hope. He'd just dashed it. But he wanted to help. "If I knew his name, if I knew who he was, I would tell him that you had written."

"It's too late, Jack. Believe me. Besides, I never knew his name. He was Jason. I was Medea. He will always be my Jason."

"Why did you write the letter, Anna?"

"Who killed Boyko? Do you know? Do you know why?"

"I'm not sure."

"But you have a guess?"

"He was trying to sell your letter."

She closed her eyes. "He read it?"

"Yes."

"Who was he trying to sell my letter to?"

"Someone in Paris. He had the telephone number."

Anna opened her eyes. "What telephone number? Whose number?"

"Our embassy in Paris. Isn't that where you sent the letter? Wasn't that the address?"

"No. It was a number on the Rue Gay-Lussac. He called this place an accommodations address."

"What was the number?"

"Twelve."

"Just twelve?"

"Yes."

"Where did Jason work, Anna? At our embassy? Was he in the consular section? Did he ever talk about his work? What he did? Any of the names?"

"I don't think I want to talk to you now. I think you should go away, Jack, before we both get into trouble."

"I'd like to find Jason for you, Anna. I sincerely would."

"Go away," she said. She got to her feet, her robe parting

slightly, giving Horn a brief glimpse of her wonderful dancer's legs, and she started toward the kitchen.

"I just came to help."

Anna stopped at the door. "Help with what, Jack? Me, or your investigation? Leave now, and I won't tell my uncle."

"Who might he be?"

Anna looked at him and smiled coolly. "You don't want to know, Jack. Believe me, you don't want to know."

"If you just had a photograph of Jason. A snapshot?"

Anna shook her head, then disappeared into the kitchen. Horn pulled on his coat, put on his hat, and let himself out. Moscow was done for him. Maybe the entire business was too. Maybe now it was time to go to Christine and the children and return to the States.

The snow had finally stopped. A few shafts of sunlight broke through the clouds to glisten on the fresh snow that covered the river ice and the roadways that had been plowed there. Horn had given himself plenty of leeway in case Anna would have been harder to approach. She could just as easily not have been at home, or her uncle or some friend could have been there. A dozen circumstances could have cropped up to delay him. Driving along the river across from the huge Kiev Station, he saw a family skiing on the ice. Snowplows and trucks were everywhere now, scraping, hauling, spreading sand. All of it made him think of when he was a young boy growing up in the Midwest. The way things were done in Moscow gave it an old-fashioned ambience. It was reminiscent for him of the forties back home. Not an altogether unpleasant feeling.

He drove back up to Pfeiffer's apartment where he let himself in with the key he had been provided. He fixed himself a couple of eggs and a thick slice of dark bread with a lot of butter. He couldn't find any coffee, so in the end he settled for a bottle of beer. They would not expect him to return here, so he figured he would be undisturbed through the afternoon. After taking a shower and shaving, he lay down on the couch in the living room and closed his eyes. He was bone-tired, but he kept seeing Anna; Anna coming to the door, her knuckles turning white where she gripped the door; Anna sitting on the edge of her chair, her knees together, while she patiently answered his questions. No matter what happened now, the situation could not possibly end up good for her. She was going to die and she would never see her Jason again. She would never again know the joy she must have felt in his arms. Too much time had passed for the damage to be repaired; too much distance separated them, and now murder had raised another impossible barrier. Twenty minutes later he got up, put the Walther and the empty tape recorder on the kitchen table, and packed his bags. He sat by the window smoking and watching the children play on the hill as he waited for Pfeiffer.

Has he aged badly? Anna had asked. *Has he gained weight? You can tell me that much, can't you*? In the end he simply had not been able to lie to her any longer.

It wasn't until after seven-thirty before LeBec finally reached Washington. He didn't understand the delays. First the foreign trunk lines had been busy, then his telephone was simply dead, and for one hour there was no answer. He was fed up. And just a little concerned that somehow he was going to be stuck here.

"He's been to see her," LeBec shouted into the telephone. "He's spoken with her. They talked in her apartment this afternoon. Hours ago!"

"Are you absolutely certain, Emile?"

"Yes, of course. *Merde!*"

"Then kill him. Finish it now."

"There will be repercussions. He spoke with Edmund Clay."

"Yes, I know. There are things I may have to take care of at this end. Clean up the details there in Moscow, Emile—all of the details—and then go home."

LeBec was frightened. For the very first time in his career he thought it was possible that he had made a grievous error of judgment. For now, at last, he understood that the man he had worked for and with over the last fifteen years was, in all likelihood, mad.

15

On the day that Horn had decided to stop studying for the priesthood and join the service instead, he'd taken a week off to run away. It was spring. He was driving a Mustang convertible in those days. With the top down he headed south from Georgetown, through the hills of Maryland and Virginia to the sand dunes of the Carolinas. The season hadn't really started yet, so he was practically alone in the beachside motel overlooking Pamlico Sound. The first couple of days he spent most of his time in his room, going out only for meals. On the third day, though, he walked along the beach, where he had begun to do his most serious thinking. Over the next couple of days he would stop at times to sit on the sand and stare out across the sound toward Cape Hatteras. Sometimes he took off his shoes and socks, rolled up his trouser legs to his knees, and waded in the chilly water. At other times he would take off running for all he was worth, as if he could somehow exorcise the devil rising in his head by the sheer physical act of movement. "The grass always seems greener," his father who was fond of platitudes used to tell him when a bout of wanderlust would strike particularly hard. "But every one of us carries the means of his own dissatisfaction. Wherever we go, it comes with us. Don't forget it." He hadn't. Not then. Not now.

Anna's photograph lay in the middle of the bed, her eyes following him around the hotel room, crying for help that he could not give her. He wanted to run, but he could not. The

photograph had been imperfectly dried, and it was already
starting to turn yellow. The corners had curled up from his
pocket, making the photo seem very old; Anna had come
from a very long time ago. She wasn't real, not now. Horn
walked around the bed looking at her face from different
angles, trying to get her voice out of his head, trying to see
only a photograph of a sad, beautiful woman, and not the
accusing eyes, the pleading eyes, begging for help. She would
die in Moscow, and her secret love would die with her. His
mistake had been in going to see her. In speaking with her
face-to-face. He did not want to compound his error now by
doing something stupid. Write your report, Jack, he told
himself. Leave it be. Christine is waiting.

He had arrived in Helsinki at eleven o'clock, and after
clearing customs had taken the shuttle across to the new
Rantasipi Airport Hotel. It was extremely cold here. Walking
from the shuttle bus into the hotel he had heard the jet engine
sounds from across the airport as if he had been standing right
on the runway; every noise, every smell was unnaturally crisp
and clean. He had registered under his Horton workname,
surrendering his passport for the overnight police check, then
had walked across the lobby to the courtesy booking agency
where he reserved and paid for a one-way ticket on the
morning's Finnair flight to Hamburg. He would make his
own connections from Hamburg back to Berlin. Mark Ryan
would be expecting him in any event. It was a safe bet that
Early had already complained vociferously to Washington
about him, so they would know that he was on his way back.
No one was going to like what he had to say. But it didn't
matter, did it?

He picked up her photograph and laid it facedown on the
bureau across the room. But even lying on the bed with his
eyes closed he could imagine she was looking at him, calling
him, beseeching him to help her become reunited with her
Jason. "You have an overdeveloped sense of morality and
responsibility," he had been told. His bishop had meant it as
a compliment. His Agency recruiters meant it as the very best
of attributes for a spy. But Wallace Mahoney told him that it
would be the bane of his career.

His room overlooked the airport. Each time the beacon on
the control tower came around white, then green, it flashed
on his ceiling. He'd left the television switched to the overnight news service channel, the sound off, the ticker-tape

words in green marching across the screen first in Finnish, then Russian, and finally English. There were no pictures or narration, only the words with music for background.

It was seven minutes after one. Horn waited for the digital clock on his nightstand to switch to the next minute. In Langley it was seven minutes after five in the afternoon. Yesterday afternoon. Early would have already sent his telex, perhaps he'd even called, but the fuss wouldn't have started yet. Not yet. These things took time. Like a pebble dropped into a pond, the waves started outward immediately, but it took a good amount of time before any kind of a reaction could be felt on the distant shore.

Leave it alone, Jack, he told himself.

Justice, constancy, mercy, and fortitude. Cornerstones of the priesthood, promises laid out in the ordination. *Justitiam, constantiam, misericordiam, fortitudinem,* and all the other virtues for St. Paul.

He reached for a cigarette, lit it, and after a moment sat up, swinging his legs over the edge of the bed. He'd been sweating, now he was cold. Someone had passed in the corridor, the shadow interrupting the line of light at the bottom of his door. In his head he was hearing the music of *Madama Butterfly* on the stairs to Anna's apartment. But it was bringing back other memories. College. Even Vietnam. His own marriage. Christ.

He got up and went into the chrome and porcelain bathroom where he laid his cigarette on the edge of the counter and splashed some cold water on his face.

Come back to me, Christine had told him in Innsbruck. Come back to me.

You had to leave before you could come back. But what if you'd never been there in the first place? he wondered. What then? How could you ever return? The thought frightened him.

He sat on the edge of the bed, switched on the night light, picked up the telephone, and dialed for the hotel operator. "I would like an overseas number," he said. "United States, Langley, Virginia." He gave the operator the area code, the telephone number, and his Horton credit card number.

In the old days he and Christine used to spend a lot of time reading poetry to each other. They were gentle times. Thoughtful times. "My portable feast," she called those days as a paraphrase of Hemingway. He wished it were then. But then the feast was portable, not reversible.

The connection was made and Horn asked for an extension.

He could see Nobles's head snapping back, he could hear the smack as the bullet hit his skull, and he could still hear the ragged scream: "Boyko!"

"Forty-two fifty-one," Vincent Doxmeuller said.

Horn recognized his voice. It seemed like an impossibly long time since they'd sat across a table from each other, drinking, talking, swapping stories. Doxmeuller was originally from Tennessee. He and his wife Donna had lived in Philadelphia where they had run a bookstore before he had signed on as an analyst with the Agency. Currently he was number one man on the Eastern European desk. Not quite the USSR, but close enough.

"Hello, Doxy."

"Is this who I think it is?"

Something was wrong. Horn could hear it in his old friend's voice. "Donna would recognize me, but then the two of us are very close." It was their old game.

"Where're you at, boy?"

"Are you on record, Doxy?"

"The line's clean for the moment. All hell is starting to break loose here. Carlisle has been upstairs in powwow with all the big chiefs since noon. I think they're going to drag you back for the unholy inquisition."

"I'm in Helsinki."

"Are you on your way to Berlin?"

"First thing in the morning, through Hamburg. Ask for my recall? Why? What's going on there?"

"I don't rightly know for certain, Jacko, but evidently you stepped on a few toes. You've been in badland, I'm told."

"Just got out. I need a big favor, Doxy."

"Gremlins?" Doxmeuller asked. They'd always thought that sooner or later the gremlins—meaning the opposition— would get the persistent fieldman. Sooner or later even the best made a mistake.

"Something like that," Horn said. "I need a name."

"From inside. Any possibilities?"

"Senator Tom Wagner is high on the list. He had some sort of a relationship, about ten or twelve years ago, with Rupert Clay."

"Son of the venerable Edmund Rutger Clay."

"One and the same. Wagner has been visiting Paris just lately."

"The significance of which you are going to explain for me in due course."

"Our man was stationed at our Moscow embassy in 1975. He used a code name, Jason, in reference to Jason and the Argonauts, and a workname of Ted Wells."

"Same initials as the good senator's. Was Wagner there at the time?"

"Apparently, though his name wasn't in the staff directory. Rupert Clay was cultural attaché at the time."

"The plot thickens."

"Whoever our boy turns out to be, he knew about my old network, specifically a Russian named Boyko."

"Who was most recently gunned down in Helsinki."

"Our man also knew my network's old Paris SOS number, 723-86-21, as well as an accommodations address I'd never heard of before. It's on the Rue Gay-Lussac. Number Twelve."

"Why Wagner, besides the obvious indicators?"

"Our man had an affair with a Bolshoi dancer, then rode off into the sunset. Before he left he gave her Boyko's name and contact procedure as well as the accommodations address to use if ever she needed him. She wrote him a letter, and sent it out with Boyko."

"Who called the Paris number and got zapped for his trouble on the same day Tom Wagner was in town."

"I spoke with Edmund Clay. He brought up Wagner's name. There may have been some vendetta between the two of them because of Clay's son."

"Who was as gay as they come."

"From what I gather, though Wagner apparently isn't."

"Tragic, unrequited love," Doxmeuller mused. "Has this anything, perchance, to do with friend Dewey Nobels?"

"Possibly," Horn said. "What does Carlisle say?"

"You haven't seen a Western newspaper or news broadcast yet?"

Horn focused on the television. A story about the blizzard that had swept across much of Eastern Europe and European Russia was coming across. He hadn't been paying any attention to the television. "No," he admitted.

"Nobels, it seems, was working for the Russians. He had been for years. His old control officer came over to us thirty-six hours ago. Spilled his guts. Times, dates, places, data. The entire shooting match. KGB did Nobels in. They thought he was going to blow the whistle.''

"I was with him in our Stockholm safe house when he was hit, Doxy. Did Carlisle tell you that?''

Doxmueller whistled softly. ''No.''

"He had come to warn me about something. Moscow Station is damned near in shambles. He and Early were at each other's throats.''

Doxmueller was silent for a few seconds. "Warn you about something . . . or *somebody*?'' he said. ''Get yourself back to Berlin and stay there. I'll see what I can dig up from this end.''

"The score is Gremlins two, Good Guys zero, Doxy. Watch yourself.''

"Just worry about keeping your own ass down, kid. And give whatshername a hug for me.''

He switched off the light and lay down on the bed again. He kept waiting for something about Nobels to show up on the news channel, but Finland and the Soviet Union were neighbors, and such news wouldn't do anyone any good. He couldn't sleep, although he was dead tired. His mind kept seething, going back time and time again to Anna—how she had looked, how she had sounded. It was over now, or at least his part in the business was finished. The rest would be handled by Doxy in Washington. They had enough information now, he suspected, to find out who Jason was. It made him sick to think that he knew Jason, that they might even have worked together.

Someone passed again in the corridor—Horn could see the shadow beneath the door—then he came back and stopped just outside. Horn waited a moment for him to move on, but when he did not he sat up in bed and held his breath to listen. Someone was out there. Making no noise. Himself listening. It could be nothing. Someone at the wrong door. He didn't think so.

Horn got carefully out of bed, his heart starting to thump, a hollow feeling rising at the pit of his stomach. He had no weapon. He'd gone into Russia clean, and he'd come out the same way.

Moving silently he opened the desk drawers beneath the television, in search of something, anything, even a letter opener. But there was nothing except for a ballpoint pen, some hotel stationery, and a room service menu.

There was a knock at the door. Horn looked up. What the hell did they think they could do here, like this? There was a chain on the door. Even if he opened it to see who was outside, they would be delayed in getting in because of the chain. They had to know it. Unless they planned on shooting through the door.

Whoever it was knocked again. More urgently.

Horn stepped over beside the bed. "Yes?" he mumbled, as if he were still half asleep.

"There is a message, sir," a man said in English. With a French accent. The desk would have called, wouldn't they?

He knocked again.

"Yes, yes," Horn said.

"There is a message for Mr. Horton."

Horn frantically scanned the room for something, anything he could use as a weapon. His eyes lit on the bedside lamp.

The man at the door knocked again. "Are you awake, sir? This is very urgent. You must sign for it, sir. From Washington."

"Yes," Horn mumbled. "Yes, I'm coming, for God's sake, just hold on." He unplugged the lamp and yanked the cord out of the base, careful to make as little noise as possible. He put the lamp down on the table and took the cord to the door.

The man at the door knocked again. "Are you coming, Mr. Horton?"

Horn slid open the closet door. Just inside, at the baseboard, was an electrical outlet. It was 220 volts. Taking care to keep the bare ends of the wire separated, he plugged in the cord, then flattened himself against the wall.

"Just a minute," he mumbled.

He deliberately made noise fumbling with the chain, and made even more noise opening the lock. With his left hand he turned the knob, expecting either the rush or a shot, and he yanked open the door as he brought up the live electric wires.

He had the momentary impression of a tall, dark man, his hat pulled low, raising a silenced pistol. Horn jabbed the wires into the man's face.

"*Merde!*" the Frenchman screamed, jerking backward.

Horn dropped the wire, grabbed a handful of the man's coat with one hand and the man's gun with the other, and hauled him inside, spinning him around as he slammed a knee into the man's groin.

The Frenchman went down hard, Horn twisting the gun out of his grip and stepping back to close the door. They'd already made too much noise. Someone would be coming to investigate. Horn expected that the Frenchman, shocked, kicked, and disarmed, would have given in, but as Horn turned back, the big man was jumping up, and he had no other choice but to fire, twice, the silenced shots hitting the man high in the chest, driving him backward, his arms akimbo, his head bouncing off the carpeted floor. And then he was still, his eyes open, dead.

Horn listened at the door as someone came down the corridor, stopped, said something to someone, then moved off. His heart was hammering, his breath short. First it had been Boyko, then Nobels, and now they'd come after him. Christ, it wasn't over. Not yet.

Turning back to the body, he quickly searched the man's pockets, coming up with a French national identity card and driver's license in the name of Renauld Entremont. There were photographs of a woman and young girl, evidently the man's wife and child, as well as a fair sum of money. In a jacket pocket Horn found a room key. Entremont, or whoever he really was, had a room just across the corridor. But how had he known to come to this hotel? This room?

He looked at his watch. It was still early. If they found the body, he might be delayed getting away. There would be questions, the police would become involved, and in custody he would almost certainly be killed. Jason's power extended this far. It was obvious.

Horn unplugged the lamp cord and tossed it aside, then listened at the door. The corridor was silent. He opened the door a crack and looked out. No one was there. Whoever had passed by had already gone. Stepping quickly across the corridor, Horn let himself into Entremont's room. He turned on one light, and went to the plain brown suitcase open on the stand, and went through the Frenchman's things. Wrapped in a sweater were two books on French architecture in the Soviet Union, a street map of Moscow, and an envelope containing a few rubles and some kopecks. Horn stared at the things for a few seconds, then looked up. Entremont had been in Moscow. He might even have come out on the same flight. But he had been there. Watching, following. "Christ," Horn swore, stepping back. It was possible that Entremont, and therefore Jason, knew that Horn had gone to see Anna. Now there was no telling what the man would do to protect himself.

Checking again to make sure the corridor was still clear, Horn dragged Entremont's body back across the hall, making certain he did not leave a trail of blood, dumped it on the bed, and covered it with the bedspread. He unplugged the bedside lamp and brought it to his room, where he switched it with the damaged lamp, bringing it and the cord over to the Frenchman's room. He wiped his fingerprints off the key, laid it on the bureau, then hanging the Do Not Disturb sign on the doorknob, he locked the door and went back to his own room.

It took him a half hour to clean the blood off the carpet. Entremont had died immediately and subsequently had not bled much. When he was finished, he took a shower, then got dressed and repacked his bag. It was nearly four by the time he tried to make a second call to Doxy. His old friend would have to be warned. Doxy would have to watch himself in Washington. They had no idea now who they could trust. The number rang and rang, ten times before Horn put down the telephone. Doxy was gone. Or he was unable to answer the telephone. Horn shuddered to think which.

He checked out at six and made it over to the airport in plenty of time for his flight, though he had become paranoid and constantly found himself checking over his shoulder. He got rid of the Frenchman's gun in a rest room trash container. In Hamburg he transferred to an Air France flight into Berlin, and as he rode a taxi from Tegel Airport to his home just off the Tiergarten in the city center, he began to get another frightening feeling, that something had happened to Christine. It was the very first time in his career that he was truly frightened for his family.

Christine had always wanted a house on the Wansee, or somewhere south of the Grünewald, anywhere but the place they'd landed downtown. Too much traffic, she said, too much noise and smelly exhausts, too much crime and not enough room for the children to play (never mind the Zoological Gardens and the Tiergarten itself), nothing was correct. Horn suspected that her real problem was the wall. They could see it from the windows of their second-story bedroom.

Once they'd even heard gunfire. But apart from her initial disappointment two years ago when they'd arrived, she'd never complained. And the children loved being at the heart of things. It was an adventure. If they wanted woods, they could drive to them on weekends.

The house was a three-story tile-and-steel fifties hodge-podge with a lot of Art Deco details. This part of Berlin had been completely knocked down during the war. Whoever got the commission for this block had built for the future. It was just a little sad now, even futile, Horn thought at times, but they had all three floors plus the basement, which gave them more room than most of the houses they'd looked at and for a lot less money. They'd had the room and finally the cash to hire a live-in cook and housekeeper to help Christine. The only real disadvantage was parking their car on the street.

It was a little before noon when Horn paid off the cabby and let himself in, setting his two bags in the stairhall and draping his hat and coat over the banister. He was trying very hard not to go off half-cocked. The house was quiet. It smelled clean and very fresh of flowers and ever so slightly of woodsmoke from the fireplace. Normalcy. Everything was all right here. It was a bastion. The children were off at school, of course, but the BMW was parked out front, which meant Christine was probably in the house, unless she'd gone off with Marta or Jane, her only two friends from the consulate. He looked up the stairs, then forced himself to go into the living room where he poured himself a stiff brandy at the sideboard, drank it down neat, and returned to the stairhall where he picked up his bags.

"Christine?" he called out, starting up.

"Jack? That you?" Christine answered immediately.

The relief was sudden and sweet. Everything was all right. "I'm here," he said.

She appeared at the bedroom door as he reached the head of the stairs. She seemed worried. "Mark Ryan is on the telephone for you," she said. Her hair was tucked under a checkered bandanna. She was dressed in a sweat shirt and blue jeans. It was obvious she was doing one of her spring cleanings, a job she tackled whenever something troubled her. With his career she'd kept their house spotless. She was obviously troubled now. "He just now called."

He put down his bags and they kissed. "Are you all right?" he asked.

"Just fine, Jack. But you look like hell."

"I haven't slept much in the last couple of days. What does Mark want? Did he say?"

"He said you'd be showing up here any moment. Something's up, Jack. Something is happening. I can feel it. He sounds . . . damned distant."

Horn looked beyond her into their bedroom. The telephone on the nightstand was off the hook. Ryan was waiting. "Anyone else call, stop by? Anyone?"

"No . . ." she started to say.

"Yes? A plumber, an electrician? Television gone on the blink?"

He could see understanding dawning in her eyes. "The meter reader," she said softly. "This morning."

"A new one?"

"Never seen him before. He had to check something in the basement. He had the plastic badge."

"Right," Horn said. He'd hoped they wouldn't come here. Even after Helsinki, though he'd been afraid for Christine and the children, he had still hoped they'd leave his family alone. They had nothing to do with it.

"What is it, Jack? Where've you been? What happened?"

Horn's mind was racing ahead now to the dozen possibilities he could foresee. He envisioned operations like mystery plots. The endings were the most important; they came to mind first. But the subplots and the complications were what made the game.

He lowered his voice so that there would be no chance of being overheard by Ryan waiting on the phone. "Listen to me, Christine, and don't argue, just do exactly as I say. Get dressed, go to the bank, and withdraw five thousand dollars. Go to the airline office and book yourself and the children out on the next flight to New York. Your dad can pick you up there. I want you to pack a bag for you and the children, make sure you have your passports, and then get the hell out of here. Take a cab—I need the car."

She wanted to argue, she wanted to protest, but she held herself in check by the sheer weight of what he was saying, and just how he was saying it. She nodded.

"Right now, Christine," he said. "And don't talk to anyone. No one."

She was frightened, but she nodded again, and as Horn went to the phone she was already getting out of her sweat shirt and jeans. She had learned at least that lesson very well over the decade and a half they'd been running around the world together, toting their babies and all their belongings with them. When the sailing is smooth, there's plenty of time for nit-picking, but when the captain says to jump because the ship is sinking, it's the moment for blind obedience, for instant action.

"Hello, Mark," Horn said into the telephone.

"What was that all about?" Ryan said. His voice was rough, with a Connecticut Yankee quality to it. He was fifty-three. He'd risen as far as he'd go, though Berlin Station was a plum.

"I've just now walked in the door. Hardly had the chance to take off my coat, and Christine says something is up."

"She's been nervous about you being gone, Jack. I think she probably guessed where you'd been. How was your trip?"

"Tiresome." He thought about Helsinki.

"Why don't you stop by this afternoon? We can go over your report. Langley is very interested."

"So I hear."

"Yes?"

Christine had pulled on a pair of pantyhose and was getting into her blue knit dress. The one he liked. He had a sudden strong urge to put down the telephone, tear off her clothes, and make love to her. It seemed like an impossibly long time since they'd been in each other's arms.

"I think I may have stepped on a few toes, Mark. I'll probably need your backing. I'd like to telephone Farley this evening. Around six. He'll be finished with his morning rounds."

"I'd like to know what's going on. Carlisle may have sent you off, but I was the one who had to sign your release. Which means it'll be me who has to answer—"

"Answer to whom?"

"Listen, Jack, I don't mind telling you that there have already been some questions. I stuck up for you, too, but now I'm out on a limb. I'd like to have a few answers."

"I haven't slept in two days."

"I'm not going to be tough. Get a few hours of sleep, take the edge off it. I can hear it in your voice, by the way. Get some sleep and then come in, say around three, maybe four.

We can talk. Whatever it is, Jack, no matter what, I think I can help.''

"Have you been given instructions?"

"Instructions? What instructions, Jack? What are you talking about?"

"I was under the impression that I was being recalled."

"Just where did you hear something like that?"

"If they want me in Washington, for heaven's sake, I'll be glad for the break. I wanted to see my mother in any event. A trip home would be grand. Christine would like to see her father, and the children have been clamoring for their grandparents." He was trying to sound normal.

Christine had stopped dressing and was looking at him. He waved her on.

"Where did you hear something like that?"

"Early threatened me with it. And just now Christine said that you weren't yourself. You tell me."

"Oh, well, I'm sorry. We all have our burdens to bear—you know how it is around here, Jack. If I was a little brusque with Christine, apologize to her for me. Please. Believe me, I meant nothing."

"You scared her half to death. She didn't know what to think." He was angling for time, the all-important commodity. Time for Christine and the children to get free, and time for Doxy to come up with something for him. He'd be returning to Washington, there was very little doubt of that in his mind, but he wanted to walk into Carlisle's office with the proof. "The truth shall make you free," the Apostle John said. *The truth shall make you strong.*

"Put her on. I'll apologize myself."

"It's not necessary, Mark. I guess I'm overreacting a bit myself. It *has* been a difficult few days. Especially when Nobels got hit."

"You know about that?"

"I was standing right next to him, Mark. You mean to tell me that Farley didn't say anything to you? It wasn't pleasant, you can have that much."

Christine had pulled the suitcases down from the closet shelf. She'd stopped again to look at her husband, her eyes wide with fright. She knew exactly what had been meant by the euphemism *hit.* She also had the sense to understand that he was stalling, and that frightened her even more. She was going to have to be strong. He figured she could do it, though. She'd once explained to him that there wasn't a woman alive who was incapable of moving mountains when it came to assuring the welfare of her children. Or a lover? Horn wondered, thinking just then of Anna.

"Not on an open line, Jack."

"Has Carlisle asked that I return to Washington?"

"No. And if you don't want to come in now, I'll be happy to come to you. We can chat, and that way you won't have to come in until tomorrow. You'll be able to get plenty of rest."

"No, it's all right, Mark. Just let me catch a few hours of sleep this afternoon, and then I'll be in to brief you. We can telephone Carlisle and get this thing straightened out. But I for one wouldn't object to a trip home. I could use it."

"Couldn't we all," Ryan said wistfully.

Christine was throwing things into her suitcase. She was angry.

"I'll see you this evening, then," Horn said.

"About six?"

"Maybe a minute or two later. But I'll be there."

Horn hung up the telephone and Christine whirled on him. "It's a shabby way to learn the truth," she cried.

He hurried across to her and drew her into his arms, holding her close. It was possible that their bedroom was bugged. The bedroom was the one room of any house in which it was most likely to overhear a secret. He didn't want to take any chances now. Not now. "It's not what you think, Christine," he said softly but urgently. "You're going to have to be very strong. No matter what happens, no matter what anyone says to you."

"What are you talking about?"

Carlisle had been less than honest with him about Nobels. Doxy said all hell was starting to break loose at Langley, and just now Ryan had not been himself on the telephone . . . a telephone that had been bugged. But by whom? Boyko had been a scumbag. No one on this side of the fence should have mourned his death, yet Horn had been sent immediately off to Moscow to plug the leaks. Carlisle's orders. Nobels had come to try to warn him about something, but he'd been assassinated and then was exposed as a spy by the Russians. And now they were gunning for him. Plots within plots. Edmund Clay had implicated Wagner as a candidate for Anna's Jason. The current Moscow embassy's cultural attaché had known Wagner and Clay's son. Early had been hiding something all along, and there was a lot of dissension in Moscow Station. Gloria Townsend had all but written it in chalk on the lavatory walls. And all but one of his old madmen were dead now. All since 1980—the year Wagner had been appointed to the Senate Foreign Relations Committee.

"Take everything with you now, Christine. Go to the bank, pick up the children, and then go directly out to the airport. I want you out of Germany on the very first flight. Go to London or Paris first if need be, but I want you and the children out as soon as possible."

"What about Hilda?" Christine asked. Horn hadn't seen her when he came in. He'd supposed she was in the kitchen.

"Send her to her brother's."

"I'm not going to leave you here . . ."

"Goddamnit, Chris, you have to do as I say!"

Christine's face was white. "Will you be coming to Washington?"

"Soon."

"We'll wait for you there."

"No. Go to your father's. I'll send for you when I think it's . . . time." Safe, he'd wanted to say. But she was beginning to understand now; he could see it in her eyes. She sagged a little in his arms.

"I don't like this," she said, tears glistening. "I don't like this at all, Jack."

He kissed her. "Neither do I, but it's important."

"I hope so. God, I hope so," she said.

He helped her finish packing, then brought the bags down to the front door. She called a cab, and while she was talking with their housekeeper, he hurried back upstairs and quickly searched the bedroom. The bug was in the handset. He recognized the unit. It was a new one, very sensitive. It could not only pick up telephone calls, of course, but even when the handset was on its cradle, the bug could pick up ordinary conversation. They'd gotten the new equipment less than six months ago. It meant Ryan or someone in Berlin Station had ordered his house bugged. Why? There were telephones in the kitchen, living room, and in his study as well. They'd be bugged too. The one on the third floor for their housekeeper was on a separate line, and probably had not been touched. The relay transmitter was most likely in the basement. They had taken a big chance coming up here. But Christine was gullible at times, and if the technician was at all quick on his feet, he could have come up with a plausible explanation.

For now he would leave the transmitters in place. In the end it wouldn't matter.

Downstairs Horn checked out front to make sure Ryan hadn't already sent his baby-sitters, but the street was clean as far as he could tell. When he came back into the house Christine stood in the middle of the stairhall, her coat on, waiting.

"Is it clear?" she asked.

She didn't understand about the bugs, not truly. It was better that she and the children were going, but suddenly he realized just how much he was going to miss them.

He nodded. The cab came a minute later. He picked up her bags and went outside. She followed him. The driver opened the trunk and Horn stuffed the bags inside.

"Passports? Bank book?" he asked.

"I have everything," she said, looking up into his eyes. "Come back to me, Jack," she said softly. "This time *really* come back."

"Count on it," Horn said. They kissed deeply, then he closed the trunk lid, she got in, and the cab drove off. He stood there wondering under just what circumstances he would see her again.

Horn needed a way out, the sophistication of the method dependent upon what Doxy would be able to tell him. If Doxy was able. Someone within the Company, or someone with close connections to the Company, had committed at least two murders and had attempted another in an effort to save his name. What else was he trying to protect? He was still powerful enough to command an organization that seemed just as effective in Finland and Sweden as it was in the Soviet Union. Yet Entremont, the man who had tried to kill him in Helsinki, had been French. Boyko had called the French number. Where was the connection?

His study was on the second floor next to their bedroom. He went up. At the head of the stairs he listened for a few moments to the sounds of the house. Hilda would be upstairs packing, probably wondering if she'd been dismissed and they'd been too kind to tell her straight out. But he could hear nothing.

Behind his desk he took down the print of the Wyeth

painting from the wall and closely examined the dial on the wall safe. It had not been disturbed; he would have bet anything on it. He opened the safe and from within drew out his escape kit. Money in German marks, a Beretta automatic with an extra clip of .38-caliber ammunition, and two passports, one as Hammer and one as Hansen.

Back in their bedroom he repacked his shoulder bag. If he was going to have to bail out, he'd be traveling light. There would be plenty of time later to come back for the rest of it.

Enough people knew that something odd had happened, was happening.

There were at least two explanations for every phenomenon.

No matter how arrogant Jason was, he wouldn't try anything now.

With a lever long enough, the entire world could be moved.

Who was Jason?

The afternoon became interminable. He stayed out of sight until Hilda had left the house, and then he went down to the basement where he found the remote transmitter. He did not touch it for the moment. Upstairs he fixed himself a light lunch, and then sat by the fireplace in the living room waiting for Doxy's call. Keep your ass down, kid, Doxy had said. He thought about his Moscow madmen dead now except for Sheshkin. He thought about Anna waiting to die. He thought about her eyes, her hair, her mouth. About four o'clock he dug out his recording of *Madama Butterfly* with Leontyne Price and put it on the stereo. The music enfolded him, transporting him into a universe in which it was possible for him to be in more than one time and place at the same time. Simultaneous universes. He was with Anna as she wrote her letter to Jason, and yet he was with Christine, through all of their early years of discovery together. They'd had so much, and Anna so little in terms of human compassion. He could feel a sense of pride in his own achievements, and yet a sorrow for Anna. In a way both emotions seemed right together like this.

> It grieves me thus to wrest
> From you all your illusions.

The telephone rang a few minutes after six. Horn jumped up, raced out into the stairhall and down the basement stairs,

and at the junction box ripped the remote transmitter off the
telephone terminal. He raced back up the stairs and picked up
the telephone on the fourth ring.

"Yes?"

"Edmund Clay is dead," Doxmueller's ragged voice came
over the long-distance line. It sounded as if he were in pain.

"Doxy?" Horn shouted.

"Run, Jack. Run!"

"Doxy?" Horn shouted again, but the line went dead. The
music welled up.

> It's nothing, nothing.
> I thought I was going to die, but it
> soon goes, like the clouds over
> the sea.
> Ah! Has he forgotten me?

PART TWO

16

By the end of their first week Anna and Jason were ready to go to bed with each other. He sent a note backstage at the intermission inviting her out after the show. Alone. For the remainder of the ballet she was as light as air, her leaps higher, her pirouettes tighter, more controlled, her pointes straighter, more refined than ever before. It was well past midnight by the time she had changed and was able to break free from the theater. She met him a block away, on the other side of Sverdlov Square so as not to attract undue attention, and they had driven directly over to an apartment building near the university—a friend's place, he told her. The apartment was small, but nicely furnished and not too warm. Jason carefully undressed her, and then himself, and they lay down together. It was better than she had imagined it would be; like his ballroom dancing, Jason's lovemaking was sure yet gentle. For the very first time in as many years as she could remember, she didn't have a single thought for the ballet as long as she was with him.

Her thoughts on this late evening were only of Jason as she walked up Michurinsky Prospekt in Lenin Hills, the weather clear but very cold, a group of young men playing with toboggans behind the university on the Olympic Village's hills; other students called to each other, and the traffic was heavy. Like this it was difficult for her to believe that anything had changed, that time had passed. She could feel the difference in her body, however. The malignancy was grow-

ing. This morning's nausea after the clinic was very real. No
denying it. And she was having a little trouble seeing Jason's
face. It kept getting mixed up with how Jack had looked to
her at her apartment yesterday . . . barely thirty hours ago, or
was it thirty years? She had moved through the rest of the day
and last night at the theater in a daze. Her letter had been lost.
It had never reached Jason. Boyko had been murdered for it.
Why? And who was Jack? What was Jack, to come to her
like that with his voyeuristic little questions? And she'd nearly
told Uncle Stepan, too. But in the end she had thought better
of it. She would have had to explain everything to him. She
could not.

The street rose higher through a neighborhood of low
apartment buildings in brown brick. The birch trees looked
naked and cold without their leaves. Much of this region was
built before the war, and it looked it. Across the field, back
toward the university, there were a lot of new high-rise
buildings, and off toward Mosfilm, the big motion picture
studio, there were a lot of very big buildings. But here there
was more tradition. In a measure, comforting. Nothing had
changed in the past ten or twelve years. Nothing would
change. Yet everything was different.

A narrow dirt path ran behind the building to a little
courtyard into which in the old days the women would throw
the slops. It wasn't much cleaner these days, though it smelled
more like diesel fuel than garbage or night soil. A covered
stairway ran up to a balcony that led to the apartments on the
second and third floors. A separate stairway from the front
attached the fourth-floor attic. Anna stopped. Someone was
looking down from one of the windows. She could see a
figure but she couldn't make out the face, merely that it was
white against a darker background. A very dim light shone
behind it. The image was spectral.

After a moment the figure moved away. Anna noticed two
children who had evidently been playing beneath an old piece
of tin they'd covered with snow in the corner of the courtyard. It was very late for them to be out like that, Anna
thought. Their eyes were wide, their clothes dirty, tattered.
They had poked their heads out of their snow castle and were
staring at her, wondering who she was, if she had brought
something for them, perhaps. Anna was sorry she didn't have
candy in her purse. When she went to Uncle Aleksandr's or
Uncle Georgi's she always brought candy for the children.

But she had nothing with her now. The children seemed to her like little lost deer, fawns in the forest. She didn't know what to say to them, how to act without frightening them. Her own cousins had come to think that she was strange. But she'd grown up isolated, with only the other children of the ballet company as companions. And now, being an old maid, she was afraid of children, she supposed. It made her sad. Some years back she had gone through a stage in which she had had elaborate daydreams about having children with Jason. She'd even imagined the pain of childbirth and how she had heroically withstood it, how she had thanked the doctors and the nurses when it was over. In fact she had put on a little show for the staff before her discharge, and one night months later the entire hospital had shown up at the Bolshoi with front row seats to watch their very brave little Anna perform. Her children, of course, were like little porcelain dolls, perfect in every respect, yet incomplete in her dreams as dolls usually are. Pretty perhaps, delicate, but not human. In her dreams she had one girl and one boy. She taught them to dance, while their father taught them about the world and about the stars and geography and history and science. Music seemed to be everywhere in those days, in her life, in her head . . . music, that is, besides the ballet. Everyone was singing as if in a comic opera; everyone was happy. The sun always shined. But then her dreams had faded. For a time she had tried to recapture the mood, tried to bring back the brightness, the joy, the music, but she could not. And when at last her dreams were completely gone they'd left behind a huge empty space inside her. Later, she supposed it had been her way of dealing with the realization that she would never have children, that she would never have a family.

The figure came back to the window above. Anna looked up, then turned and walked back out to the street. There was nothing here for her, of course. She hadn't really thought there would be, and yet this was where she and Jason had spent a good deal of their time together. This is where they had made love for the very first time, and for the very last time. Too, eleven years ago, she had walked away like this, forcing herself not to look back, and yet looking back and seeing his figure in the window above. She'd come looking for him, hadn't she? A fool's errand. The wanderings of a demented woman, just as the contents of her letter had been the ravings of a simpleton. A dangerous simpleton. But then

Jason would know what to do. He'd always had all the answers. This wouldn't bring him down. He wouldn't let it.

Anna found a taxi on Lomonosovsky Prospekt. She'd done this before too: walked down from the apartment where she caught a cab for home. Traffic was heavy downtown. After the storm no one wanted to remain inside. She sat back in the corner, only half listening to the beefy, red-faced driver tell her about the troubles he was having with his three teen-age boys who were hooligans interested not in school but only in American and British rock and roll music, blue jeans, smoking, and girls. There were two younger children at home. During the day they wore out his wife, and all night he worked driving taxis around the city, so there was no one to adequately supervise the boys. What was a man supposed to do in this day and age?

They crossed the river on the Kalininskiy Bridge, then turned left on Tchaikovsky Street. With traffic it was quicker this way to her apartment than going through town past Red Square. As they passed the American embassy, Anna leaned forward in her seat so that she could get a better look.

"Are you there, Jack?" she murmured. "Still?"

He was the only one who had offered to help her. Boyko was not to be trusted. Jason had told her that years ago. In any event Boyko was dead. But Jack was different. Jack had an honest face. She knew that she could talk to him. She had seen it in his eyes, the same quality that was in Jason's. He had come to offer his assistance, he told her. Her salvation?

But what did she really want? To be with Jason, of course. There was nothing else for her now. To die in his arms as if they were players in a real-life tragic opera. Jason had come to her here in Moscow, and their meetings had been discreet. Jack had come next to try to help her, but she had spurned his advances because she was frightened. So now it was up to her, wasn't it?

She sat back when they were past and closed her eyes. She'd been denied a foreign travel passport years ago because, she'd been told, she was a national treasure.

"Listen to me, chou-chou," Uncle Stepan had explained. "Because of my position in the KGB, and the fact that you are a wonderful dancer, we cannot afford for you to leave us. We cannot take the risk. You can understand this?"

It didn't really matter to her in those days, though had she guessed how her restricted travel status would affect her dancing career, she might have put up a fuss. She had her family. She had her dancing. And some day Jason would return to her. What need did she have for foreign travel?

"It will not be forever, chou-chou," Uncle Stepan promised. She was sitting on his lap in his office. They were drinking sweet champagne. "You will see. I promise. You will see."

It was up to her now. In the morning she would see about getting a foreign travel passport. She would make formal application. She might be denied initially, but she would not be ignored.

17

Now that he was on the run, Horn was hearkening back to his early days as an altar boy. In search of the correct morality. In order to find the right path. But the right choices were always a relative matter, no matter the facts of the situation: wasn't that the way of it? With only an ego for support, there wasn't much comfort.

He sat in his car on the Friedrich Strasse across from Checkpoint Charlie, watching a tour bus crawl through the complicated speed traps in the crossing. Traffic flowed in a steady stream parallel to the wall here, up Oranien Strasse; it was a little like the Ku'Damm in its stridency. There was a frantic measure to the beat of the city so close to the Eastern zone. On the other side the nights were a lot calmer.

Edmund Clay was dead. It was hard to believe even now after everything that had happened. Jason would be after Doxy too. Christ, where would it all end?

Horn had his own troubles as well. Jason would be coming after him with a vengeance after what happened in Helsinki. But so too would Mark Ryan. The moment the relay transmitter had been pulled out of its slot, Ryan's clock would have begun. They'd be coming in full force now. Probably an entire regiment, if Horn knew his COS. And rightly so. No telling what they had on their hands. He'd been to badland. Now Langley wanted him pulled in. What had happened to him over there? What has become of our Jack Horn?

Berlin was an island city. It had finally become an ancient

Rome surrounded by the Huns. Everyone thought the down-
fall was imminent. Everyone knew the city would not hold
out much longer. The pressures from outside the wall, though,
were starting to pale in comparison to the pressures within.
The simple fact of population notwithstanding, a moralistic
malaise had settled over Berlin. Horn had seen its growth in
the short time he'd been there. His madmen on the other side
sometimes shared a little pity with him. "When it's time for
me to come over, Jack, it certainly won't be to West Berlin,"
Nikolai Volodin told him. He was talking for a lot of the
others too, not just the transplanted Russians doing duty in
East Berlin, but for his disaffected GDR *Freunden* as well.
Still, at least outwardly, there was a touching faith in the
Republic here. Perhaps the wall would disappear someday.
Berliners were like the flame that is strengthened in pure
oxygen, a flame that, however, flares up to an early death.
The fire never burned so brightly as it did these days in West
Berlin. The parties, the private clubs, the garish cabarets, and
the flashy whores along the Ku'Damm all seemed to operate
at the speed of a supersonic jet. "Transporting us all to hell,"
as Hans Siegler, an unofficial spokesman for the Green party
said last month on Television One. "Either give Berlin back
to the German people—to all the German people—by international agreement, or tear down all the boundaries and let
nature take its own course." Even the wild-eyed kids didn't
believe in their hearts, though, that such a miracle was possible in their lifetimes. Nor did many of them even understand
what Germany had been about. They were too young, most of
them, to remember a whole Germany, a Germany unified in
war. These days they provided the white noise that was
actually a deafening roar at times, beneath which, or around
which, the real work was being done as a sort of rearguard
action.

     Where was the faith? Horn asked himself, watching the
brightly lit crossing. It was cold here, not as cold as Moscow
of course, but cold enough so that the chill penetrated too
deeply for comfort. He hadn't found faith since Vietnam, he
supposed. It wasn't going to be so hard to fight them now. He
was ready.

     Mark Ryan had ordered the phone taps installed. He would
be leading the search. Christine would have stopped at the
bank and then picked up the children before Doxy's call. She
would have looked back at least once, though. It was only

natural for her. He hoped she had not tried to telephone the house. Nor come back for some forgotten item—a piece of clothing, a scrap of paper, a toothbrush—a last look-see. God, Christine, just follow orders this time. Nothing cute or fancy, mind you. Just don't come back. Leave. Get out of Germany. He would not have the time to look over his shoulder. He could give her no help. Not now.

Ryan would expect differently, however. He'd expect that Jack would first see to Christine and the children. He'd never dream that Jack would run for the border so fast. Who would? Only Jason. It was galling to think of the power that man had. The arrogance. First Boyko, then Nobels, and now, incredibly, Edmund Clay. Horn still found it hard to believe. Anna's letter was Jason's Achille's heel. But who these days would give a damn if a man had had an affair a dozen years ago with a Russian ballet star? If anything, it might enhance a man's reputation. There was more.

The tour bus was through. Horn flipped on his headlights and pulled away from the curb, merging with traffic. He'd stopped long enough to hide his gun, passports, and money in the trunk. He'd been across dozens of times using his little rathole to bring and take items of interest, and the *Grenztruppen* had never even come close to finding it. This time was different, though. This time he was on his own. There would be no backup if he got himself into a jam. It made him think about Doxy, and he worried about his old friend.

The powerful lights at the crossing lent a violet cast to the no-man's-land. He passed the ATTENTION, YOU ARE LEAVING THE AMERICAN SECTOR sign, and rolled down his window as he slowed and stopped. A pair of East German border guards stepped out of their hut and came across to him where he was halted by the red and white striped barrier.

He had his papers out, which included his regular passport with East German visa, an international driver's license, and green insurance card. He handed them up to a stern-faced young man.

"Yes?" the soldier asked. "And the purpose of your visit"—he opened Horn's passport—"Mr. Horn?"

"The opera."

"Ah, yes," the soldier said. He didn't look old enough to shave. But the automatic rifle slung over his shoulder was deadly nevertheless.

The other soldier had brought over a mirror and light

attached at an angle to a long aluminum pole, which he used to search the undercarriage of the car.

"You will be leaving then, directly after the program?"

"Possibly. I may stop for dinner afterward."

"Yes, I see." The young man abruptly turned and went back to the guard hut. The other soldier came around to Horn's side.

"Please to step out of the car, sir, and open the trunk."

Horn shut off the headlights and the engine, got out of the car, and walked around to the back. He unlocked the trunk, opened the lid, then stepped aside. The soldier glanced at him, then shined his powerful flashlight in all the corners and behind the spare tire. He pulled the carpeting up and knocked on the deck with his knuckles.

"Yes?" he said, looking up. Horn suspected he didn't speak much English.

The young soldier went to the driver's side, opened the door, and began searching in the back seat. Horn straightened up the trunk carpeting, then closed and relocked the lid. The other soldier was talking on the telephone. Horn could see him through the broad windows, the light inside the hut yellow. He glanced over his shoulder at the American observation post fifty yards down Friedrich Strasse. One of the American soldiers had stepped outside and was watching the proceedings through binoculars. It was possible that Ryan had already alerted the crossing posts throughout the city. It might have happened just now. But no one had challenged him. There had been no roadblocks. No one waiting.

Here at the border crossing you were onstage, Horn thought. Under the lights. Everyone was watching. It was dangerous. You had to make certain you made no false moves, gave the East German boys no reason for alarm. *Alles ist in ordnung.* Four little words that meant everything was in order.

A blue Fiat pulled up behind Horn's BMW. A large man was at the wheel, an angry-faced woman beside him. They seemed very impatient. The man rolled down his window and motioned for the young soldier who had just backed out of Horn's car. The boy ignored him.

The soldier inside the hut put down the telephone, stood there for a moment, then came out. In his one hand he held Horn's papers. His other hand was on the strap of his automatic rifle. The big man in the Fiat stopped his gesturing. He sat back as if he were suddenly afraid. Horn stood next to his car. He braced himself as the young soldier came around to him. For a moment he wished he had carried his pistol in his pocket, but it would have been useless. Out of the corner of his eye he could see that the guards in the tall observation tower were looking down at the barrier. They were armed with machine guns.

"This is your favorite opera tonight, Mr. Horn?" the soldier asked. Horn could read nothing from the expression in the kid's face, but the question was one of the oldest in the books. No spy worth his salt would have fallen for such a trap.

Horn shrugged. He knew all the schedules over here. It was part of the game. "*Die Fledermaus* is amusing. Have you seen it, then?"

The young man shook his head. "*Alles ist in ordnung*," he said. He handed Horn his papers, then opened the leather purse at his hip. Horn dug for his wallet. It was the law that each time a Westerner came across the border, twenty-five marks had to be exchanged. Not so curiously, only hard Western currencies could be used. Horn gave him West German marks.

Afterward he drove slowly through the barrier. On the east side it wasn't so bright as on the west, nor was there anywhere near as much traffic. It was orderly here. Peaceful. But there seemed to be police on every corner. He turned immediately onto Leipziger Strasse and headed up toward the apartment way out on Griefswalder Strasse.

He'd spent a lot of time on this side since he'd been stationed in Germany.

It was almost like home to him now. Safer than the other side just now.

Their emergency system had been one of the very first things to be worked out. Horn always carried a couple of red thumbtacks with him when he came across. He drove across the Spree River, then up to Alexandria Platz where he pulled off and parked on Lenin Allee. He walked back to the square where he looked up at a bus schedule posted on a light pole. Making certain he was not being observed he quickly stuck one of the thumbtacks in the side of the waiting bench. The KGB's Horst Wessel Barracks wasn't far away. Volodin came by here at least once every twenty-four hours to check. The pin meant come quickly. "Is this necessary, Jack?" he'd asked at the beginning. "Absolutely, Nikolai," Horn had told him. "Someday it may be your only lifeline."

Or mine, Horn thought, walking back to his car, his coat collar up around his ears. This time he was the one who needed help. He wondered how much confidence this night would inspire in Volodin or his other madmen. Perhaps like rats they would desert what they perceived to be a sinking ship. He wasn't being terribly fair, he supposed. But then this was the season for perfidy and dishonor, it seemed. And murder.

He drove around the corner and then up Griefswalder, the traffic only a little bit heavier. There was a lot of new apartment buildings in this area. Housing had always been a problem in both Berlins. The eastern sector had always lagged very far behind the west, but the GDR was coming along nicely in at least that respect. Two of his East German madmen were proud of the fact, though they were disgruntled enough with the political situation that they could act as traitors. With his madmen these days, however, he maintained an arm's-length relationship compared to his first crowd in Moscow.

Of course Ryan would get onto him sooner or later, if he hadn't already. They'd have jotted down his car's license plate number, wouldn't they have? They'd know he was over here. Question was, what would Ryan do about it? Sending someone over would be like putting your hand into a beehive. You might get away with it, and then again you might not, depending if someone had stirred up the nest before your arrival.

The real problem, of course, was Jason. The man was a power. He had an organization. But where was it? What was it? Senators did have staff, but Good Lord, how dedicated could they be? Loyal enough to commit murder in the name of simple democratic expediency? Or, like politicians before him, had Wagner—if Jason was indeed Wagner—hired the Mafia or some other nefarious underground criminal organization for his own aims? In trade for what? Horn wondered. No matter which way it cut, the speculations were chilling. Anna, though, was the only one with the answers.

Horn turned off Griefswalder just past the huge Berlin Sports Forum in Weissensee. The region here was one of those very common in the eastern zone that had changed very little since the war. Many of the four-, five-, and six-story brown-brick apartment buildings that tightly lined the narrow, cobblestoned streets were still nicked and scarred by the Allied bombing and street fighting. Trees had grown up along the sidewalks as high as the fourth story in front of most of the buildings. A lot of cars and a few trucks were parked along the curb on both sides of the street. Nearly every window in this block was lit. The street seemed very domestic, very safe, even Western in a way. He drove slowly down a narrow alley where he pulled up at a garage. He jumped out of his car, unlocked the door, shoved it aside, and then got back behind the wheel and drove inside, cutting his lights and then the ignition.

He cranked down his window and sat listening to the ticking engine as it cooled. For just a moment, he told himself, he didn't want to be running. He imagined he could hear his own heart beat. For the most part it was very quiet in the East, he had found. It was something you forgot about until you were away from it for a while and then came back. The old-fashionedness, the quiet, the comparative domesticity of East Berlin reminded him, as did Moscow, of his youth in the forties and fifties in the Midwest. Listening to a truck passing on the street at the end of the very narrow lane, he was a little boy in Wisconsin, chasing after the iceman's truck, waiting for the gigantic, leather-caped figure to carry the tremendous block of ice into his grandmother's house, and then boosting himself up on the tailgate to steal the big slivers. The iceman didn't really care; he only chased after the boys to make it more exciting for them. He had nine children of his own. Was it time to go over? Horn wondered, surprised by the unbidden thought. Or were you just frightened silly about Jason and about what he was all about? I mean, how much confidence can you have in your leadership when they run around killing people willy-nilly to keep their love lives secret? Even Jack Kennedy didn't do that. Perhaps it was simple weariness. Christine wanted him to quit, or at the very least come out of the field. Most of his contemporaries, those still alive and those still with the Company, that is, were now chiefs of station, or manning one desk or another back at Langley. I'll leave at my own pace, and in my own time, he told himself and Christine. And certainly not at this moment. Not now. Not yet.

He got out of the car, locked the door, and then pulled the garage door shut, plunging the garage into darkness. By feel he unlocked the BMW's trunk and opened the lid, the trunk light coming on. Quickly he released the spare tire and pushed it aside, then unscrewed the jack from its brackets and set it aside too. The forward part of the tire well, unlatched and pulled upward, revealing a long, narrow space in the body just behind the rear door on the driver's side. Horn reached in and pulled out his leather shoulder bag, a plastic sack containing his money, his two passports and other papers, and his Beretta and extra bullets. Then he relatched the lid and reinstalled the jack and spare tire, wiping his hands on an old rag.

"The trouble in the West is lack of order," Volodin was fond of saying. "The state isn't nearly strong enough." He was a KGB captain stationed in East Berlin as training officer for the East German secret service.

"Or discipline?" Horn asked.

"That too. Just think, Jack, how many acts of terrorism occur in the West, versus in the Soviet Union. There has to be a reason, you know."

Horn locked up the trunk, shouldered his bag, and then opened the garage door a crack to peer outside. The alley was deserted. He slipped outside, closed and relocked the garage door, and headed down the alley.

"Police on every corner," Horn had replied without anger. The cardinal rule was never to lose your temper in front of a madman, unless you were doing it for effect.

"You have the CIA, Jack. The FBI, the National Security Agency, state police, county police, city police. Even a little farm village, from what I am told, has its own policeman who carries a gun and who knows everyone's name."

"Informers everywhere," Horn countered.

Volodin smiled. "There was a story last year, Jack—you read it in the newspapers, I am sure—about the little girl in California who turned her parents over to the police."

"They were drug addicts."

Volodin nodded sadly. "They were law breakers and the little girl did her American duty. Your country was behind her. So what about a little boy doing his patriotic Russian duty by turning in his parents for breaking the law?"

Horn started to protest, but Volodin, who had graduated first in his class in social psychology at Moscow State University, held up his hand.

"Breaking the law of our country, I meant to add, Jack. You have laws, we have laws. Sometimes they are different."

"There is a difference, Nikolai, between laws of the people, and laws that are imposed on the people."

"I don't know this difference. I think it means nothing."

Horn held back the obvious retort: Why, then, my friend, have you become a traitor to your wonderful country?

And now he was going to have to depend on Nikolai Volodin for his own salvation.

Their building was four doors from the alley entrance. Volodin had rented the fourth-floor apartment in his own name as a place for his trysts. He was married and had one child, but, Volodin had informed Horn, his son was an idiot and his wife was a shrew, and from time to time he found himself involved with another woman. Some of the East German girls were fascinated with the power of a Russian KGB officer. "They think Russians have big dicks, Jack," Volodin explained. "They are never disappointed with me." The arrangement was dangerous for Volodin, and especially dangerous for Horn. But they had agreed on this place as their emergency fallback. If the place was not safe, in Volodin's estimation, he would leave the front bedroom curtains open. They were closed this evening. Horn's signal that an emergency had come up was the red thumbtack on the bus bench, and his signal that he was in residence, and had not been followed, was a milk bottle in the kitchen window, clearly visible from the alley. Simple but viable tradecraft.

The apartment was very cold. Horn started a fire in the oil burner, then put the milk bottle in the window. The alley was dark and empty. The signals were in place, the car was out of sight, and now there was nothing left for him to do but hang on. He took off his heavy coat, and as the apartment began to warm up he went into the kitchen and fixed himself a bowl of soup and some bread and beer. Volodin had evidently been here not so long ago; the larder was reasonably well stocked, and there were four bottles of champagne left in the tiny refrigerator. When you're doing nothing but waiting, you become vulnerable, he thought. Your own doubts began to gnaw at you: someone may have seen the car with West German plates pull into the garage; Ryan wouldn't stop at the border but would come charging across like a bull in a china shop; or, worst of all, if Jason knew about Horn's madmen in Moscow, why wouldn't he know about the East Berlin mob? Perhaps Volodin was already sweating it out under sodium pentothol, or the electric prods. The variations were endless. He went back into the living room where he took out his gun, laid it on his lap, and then sat back with his feet up for just a little rest. It seemed like years since he'd slowed down enough to sleep properly.

Four times in the middle of the night, Horn woke with a start and padded around the apartment in his stocking feet, gun in hand, first to listen at the door, then to look down at the street and finally the alley from the kitchen window. But the city had settled down for the long winter's night. Something he was unable to do. His thoughts were bouncing all over the place, from Christine on her way home to Anna stuck in Moscow. From Mark Ryan in West Berlin and Jason wherever he was, to East Berlin, at least the second most dangerous city for him in the world. Morning came very dull and gray. It would soon snow; the sky had the look. He watched from the kitchen window as he had his coffee.

Volodin finally arrived at noon, red-faced and a little out of breath from the long climb up four flights of stairs. He let himself in and stood in the middle of the long living room looking at Horn seated at the kitchen table with the Beretta in hand. Volodin was a big, square-jawed Ukrainian who hated Germans—East or West—and justified his work for Horn with his desire to get back at the German people for what they did to his homeland and his people during the war. It was a very common attitude in the Soviet Union, even forty years after the end of the war. "A Ukrainian is slow to anger, but even slower to forget," he once told Horn. He wore a sheepskin coat and a fur hat.

"You are in very big trouble, I think," he said. "They are making a show of tearing West Berlin apart looking for you. But they know that you are here."

"How long do you have with me today?" Horn asked. Christine and the children were free. He was certain of it.

"All day if need be. I'm making snap inspections of our training centers. No one will complain if I do not show up. But what is happening with you, my friend?"

"How do you know that my people think I am here?"

Volodin shrugged at such an obvious question. "They are not watching the crossings, Jack. It is simple. If they thought you were on the run, and that you were caught in the western sector, they'd close all the exits. They have not. Ergo . . . they must have seen you cross." He came the rest of the way into the kitchen. "What is it, then, Jack? Are you here to tell me that you are defecting?"

"It's all a cover-up, Nikolai," Horn said with a straight face. He had put down his gun. He poured Volodin a cup of coffee. The Russian sat down across from him.

"So, a very elaborate cover-up, I think. Too elaborate, perhaps?"

"The stakes are very high."

"For everyone, Jack. Listen to me, Colonel Astayef has become interested. He would very much like to talk to you. I might even get a promotion if I brought you in." Astayef was the chief of the KGB station in East Berlin.

"I need your help."

"Hiding out in East Germany like a cowboy in the badlands is for you, I think, not a very good idea."

"I don't want to hide here."

"Do you want to return home, then, quietly?" Volodin asked. "What? You tell me, Jack. Speak to me."

"I must get to Moscow, Nikolai. Immediately. This afternoon if possible."

"You are not making a joke, I think."

"No, I am not making a joke, Nikolai," Horn said with patience. "I must get to Moscow. I came for your help. Can you do it?"

Volodin looked at him appraisingly. His big paws were curled around his coffee mug. After a moment he nodded. "It is possible, Jack. But once you are in Moscow there will be nothing I can do for you. You will be completely on your own. And if your own people are truly looking for you, your own embassy will not provide a refuge. It would be a very dangerous place for you to be now, I think."

"Will you do it?"

"Why, Jack? What is your prize?"

"I can't tell you."

Volodin sighed deeply after a few seconds. "Is your car in the garage around back?"

Horn nodded.

Volodin indicated the Beretta. "You will not be able to take that with you. How about a passport?"

"I have one for this."

"Is it any good?"

Horn smiled.

"I'm sorry," Volodin said deprecatingly. "Truly. I will

arrange for the necessary travel papers and tickets." He looked at his watch. "The evening Moscow flight leaves at eight. It gives me plenty of time. I will have to take your passport with me. And the gun. It will be too dangerous for you to have it any longer. What about money, Jack? Do you have enough?"

"I have plenty. Mostly West German marks."

"You will be welcomed with open arms. As an engineer, I think. Your marks are almost as good as dollars, or yen."

Horn stood up and went into the living room where he got his Hammer passport and the extra ammunition out of his bag. Volodin had come in with the Beretta. He pocketed the gun and took the other things from Horn.

"This is making you feel very naked and alone, my friend, I know," Volodin said gently. He laid a hand on Horn's shoulder. "But my own life has been in your hands now for nearly two years. Not an altogether pleasant feeling. I think you will agree by the time you arrive in Moscow. But there is nothing for you to do except trust in me, and in the end come back to us. Here we still have much work to do."

"Thank you, Nikolai."

Volodin left. A couple of minutes later Horn watched as the Russian emerged on the street below, climbed into his Fiat, and drove off. Now it would be a simple matter of who worked the fastest: Nikolai Volodin, Mark Ryan, or Jason.

Horn switched on the radio, and listening to some music, he fixed himself some lunch. At night the street below was lined with cars. During the day, however, it was mostly empty. Everyone was at work. The neighborhood had taken on a deserted, down-at-the-heels look. Around two in the afternoon it finally began to snow in fitful little flurries that wouldn't amount to much. By three he was beginning to think about Moscow, beginning to plan his moves, beginning to think out his contingencies. But he'd been taught that the very best field agent is the improviser, the one who makes up his own plays by his own rules while still on the run. Conform and get nailed, adapt and survive to play again.

18

Alone in the midwinter afternoon darkness, Horn waited for his salvation to arrive, yet half suspecting that something was about to blow up in his face. He'd been taught even before the Agency's school at the Farm outside Williamsburg that Jesus had been sent to earth to die on the cross for mankind's sins. Comforting under the right circumstances, but even as a boy he used to wonder when the next Jesus was going to arrive. By sheer numbers of population alone, not to mention the print and celluloid media, there had to be much more sin extant these days than at the end of the Roman empire. Where was our Savior? In Vietnam he'd found his savior, and it was himself. Not comforting, but certainly practical. His mood had darkened with the day. There was no news on the radio, and he felt cut off, isolated, which served to deepen his depression. He thought of Doxy and hoped that his old friend was safe. Doxy had sounded ragged, under siege . . . persecuted. It meant he'd stepped on some toes in Washington; he'd poked his nose where it wasn't wanted. It meant that Jason was in Washington, either that or his influence and power were in full existence there. He thought again about Christine and the children with a lot of guilt for leaving them on their own the way he did. Her father, who was a former lieutenant governor of New York, would look out for them providing she could get that far. He had a place on Long Island. He would know to surround himself and his daughter and his grandchildren with people, a lot of people, all of them

234

potential witnesses. He thought about the discussion he'd had
with his father-in-law some years ago, just after Marc was
born, about the business and about a family's vulnerability.
The old man was not dense; he understood fully. Horn also
worried about Mark Ryan and the others in the West. They'd
be sick at heart by now, believing that one of theirs was a
traitor. He thought too about Carlisle back in Washington
who was nobody's fool. Sooner or later the fiction would
break down. Sooner or later Carlisle would figure it out. The
trick would be to hold on long enough for that to happen, and
the whistle to be blown . . . or for Carlisle to be killed like
the others if he was stupid about it. He thought also about
Anna. He worried about what her reaction was going to be
when he showed up again on her doorstep.

The prayer just before the consecration, the holiest part of
the Catholic mass, came to him.

> Vouchsafe, Oh God, we beseech thee to make this
> obligation in every way, the blessed, legitimate, ap-
> proved, reasonable and acceptable sacrifice, so that it
> may become for us the body and blood of Thy dearly
> beloved Son, our Lord Jesus Christ.

The mystery of the mass. It had been so grand in the old
days. But then the real mysteries had become more important
for him.

Volodin swung past a few minutes after four. From where
he sat by the window, Horn recognized the car. There was
someone with him, though. Someone in the passenger seat,
and it looked to Horn like a woman. Volodin did not stop. At
the corner he turned left. Horn moved back a little into the
shadows of the room so that he could not be seen from the
road. Seconds later a plain blue paneled van came up the
street. The plates were western zone military. It was Sam
Morrison's vehicle.

Jumping up, Horn hurried into the kitchen where he pulled
the milk bottle from the window. He stepped aside as moments later Volodin's Fiat came down the narrow lane. "It is
not safe, Nikolai," Horn muttered. He'd come down the alley
to see, leading his tail once around for Horn to get a good
look. Seconds later Morrison's van passed below. But Volodin
was smart. He'd brought the girl along as cover. He'd been at
this game long enough to realize the score. Someone besides

Horn from Berlin Station would know the names of Horn's madmen. It was part of the drill, SOP. A logical target for Ryan, who knew Horn had gone over, would be his madmen. Volodin had come looking for Horn's signal, for the milk bottle, which meant he had a fallback.

Back in the living room Horn dug his Hansen and Horn passports out of his bag and pocketed them within the zip-out lining of his coat. He distributed his marks and his remaining American currency among his pockets, his wallet, and his overnight bag, then pulled on his coat.

Mark Ryan had sent the best available. Horn wondered, though, if old Sam Morrison was actually prepared to pull a gun and bring him back by force, or if he had come with the intention of merely talking. It was ridiculous to contemplate. You didn't pull guns on old friends.

Ten minutes later Volodin was back, parking his Fiat out front. Horn flattened himself against the wall and watched from the living room window. Volodin got out of the car, hurried around to the passenger side, and opened the door for the woman who was bundled up in a bright red ski jacket, fitted stretch slacks, and tall fur boots. He reached in the back seat and pulled out a bright red bag, then arm in arm they bounced across the street and disappeared below. Horn remained by the window. True to form, a few seconds later Morrison cruised by in the panel van. He looked up directly, it seemed, at Horn, and then he was gone down the block. Horn could hear Volodin and the woman on the stairs below, but he remained where he was. Ryan was a stickler for detail. "Never let even the most tarnished opportunity pass you by," he was fond of saying. A gray Chevrolet Citation turned the corner and came slowly up the street. The driver pulled in front of Volodin's Fiat and parked. Horn could not see who the driver was, or see if he was alone, but he recognized the car as one of Berlin Station's. Ryan had sent Morrison, but he'd also sent muscle. Horn got a picture of several large types from the State Department's Bureau of Political Security who'd been sent out last year because of the increased threats of terrorism. But they loved to get themselves involved in Agency operations. A lot of them were throwbacks to the days of the U.S. Information Agency. There were a lot of grudges still. Arm twisters, they were called. Jason's people?

Returning to the kitchen, Horn went to the window and

looked down. The blue panel van was parked in the alley. All right, Sam, he thought, if you have to be there, I understand. But just stay in your truck. Don't go exploring the parking garages down there. At this point they could have no solid proof he was up there. They had merely followed Volodin, hoping that Horn might have gone to him.

He went to the kitchen door and waited. Someone was just outside in the corridor, and he was certain he heard the woman giggle. Then the lock turned and the door swung open.

"Oh, fuck, it's you," Volodin said in Russian. The girl's eyes were wide. She hung back.

"I was just leaving," Horn replied in Russian, and he could see the relief in Volodin's eyes that he'd understood the necessary fiction.

"Oh, no, it is all right. Marlene is coming soon?"

Horn shrugged noncommittally. This was Volodin's show. He was going to have to play it his own way.

Volodin said something to the woman who was, Horn thought, quite attractive, with high cheekbones and lovely lips. She smiled uncertainly, but waited at the open door as Volodin came the rest of the way into the apartment, clapped Horn on the shoulder, and led him back into the kitchen.

"They have two teams on you, Nikolai," Horn whispered, but still in Russian.

"I picked out the blue van."

"It's around back. Gray Chevy Citation in front. But they can only suspect that I'm up here at this point."

"I've brought your things," Volodin said. He glanced around the corner at the woman. She was still in the corridor. He handed Horn a small manila envelope that Horn immediately pocketed. "Passport, visa, travel permits, tickets, and hotel reservations in Moscow at the Berlin. It is on Zhdanov Street."

"I know it," Horn said. Volodin had never been able to resist a small joke.

"I will leave her bag here. I'll tell her that we must have some drinks, perhaps a little *zakuska* for an hour or so, and then we will come back. Perhaps your friends downstairs will notice that we have not brought her bag with us, so we intend returning, and therefore you mustn't be here."

"They'll notice all right, but they might not buy it."

"Do you want your pistol?" Volodin asked, lowering his voice even more. "I brought it just in case."

"No," Horn said.

Volodin smiled bleakly. "I did not think you could shoot one of your own, even though they are convinced you are capable of murder."

"What?"

"Jack, were you in Helsinki recently? In the last day perhaps?"

Horn nodded. He knew what was coming.

"You are being accused of murder, my friend. A French historian."

"Renauld Entremont."

"Yes, this is the name."

"He tried to kill me, Nikolai."

"He was a friend of the Soviet Union. I think Moscow will be very dangerous for you, my friend, but I think if you are looking to prove your innocence, it may be better than here. Interpol is now after you."

The Frenchman had been a part of this business after all. There was now absolutely no doubt in Horn's mind. He'd been maneuvered into a position where he could be gunned down by the police without raising any suspicions on Jason. Shot trying to escape. Sorry. Jason, whoever he was, knew all the moves, knew Horn's every step.

"It'll work out in the end," Horn said, thinking more aloud than offering any assurances.

Volodin smiled again. "I hope so, Jack. I sincerely hope so. Now, have a pleasant flight, please. I will lead your former compatriots on a merry chase."

"Oh," the girl said.

Volodin spun around.

"Horn?" someone called from the corridor, in English. "Jack Horn?"

Volodin yanked Horn's Beretta out of his pocket and handed it to him. Then he pulled out a big Makarov automatic from a shoulder holster and barged into the living room. "What is going on here?" he bellowed.

Horn stood out of sight, just around the corner.

"We've come for Jack Horn. Turn him over to us and no one will get hurt," a man said. The voice was unfamiliar to Horn. He wasn't one of the station regulars. No one Horn knew.

Volodin laughed. "Need I remind you that you are in the

German Democratic Republic now? And there is only the one of you.''

"I would not want to hurt the girl, Comrade Volodin.''

"Nikki?'' the woman cried in alarm.

"I think that would be a very large mistake,'' Volodin warned. ''In any event it is, how do you say, a standoff?''

Volodin needed a distraction. Horn stepped around the corner. A large, dark-skinned man stood just at the living room door, his gun trained on the frightened woman, while Volodin's gun was trained on the agent.

"That won't be necessary,'' Horn said, the Beretta in plain view.

"Christ,'' the agent swore. He made as if to step back as he started to bring his gun around. Volodin shot him, the noise deafening in the confines of the small room, the man's chest caving in, his arms flying outward, and his body slamming backward against the corridor wall, a big splatter of blood behind him.

The girl had fallen down. She was trying to get up, blood all over her ski jacket. Volodin leaped across the room to her.

Security agents almost always traveled in pairs. ''Nikolai!'' Horn shouted.

As Volodin cleared the doorway someone fired three times from just below on the stairs, the first hitting him in the shoulder, spinning him around, the second taking off the side of his head just behind his left eye, and the third hitting the girl in the neck, destroying her throat and flinging her backward.

Horn dropped into a shooter's crouch, the Beretta up, safety off.

The second agent came the rest of the way up the stairs but held up just back from the door. Horn could hear him out there puffing like a steam engine, trying to catch his breath, trying to figure out what to do next. There wasn't going to be much time to get away from here. Sam Morrison would have heard the shots. He'd be watching the back, making sure Horn didn't come that way. But he would run the moment he heard the sirens. And he would be feeling bad about an old friend. The East German police would be showing up momentarily. Someone would have reported the shots.

"Horn?'' the agent called softly from around the corner.

Volodin tried to sit up. The agent fired two shots, the second destroying the front of Volodin's head. The man was

an animal. Horn's gorge suddenly rose. This wasn't Mark
Ryan's doing. Not this.

"You're not going to get out of here, Horn," the man
said.

"Jason sent you?" Horn asked, his gun trained on the
doorway. The man was just around the corner.

"You think you know? You don't know a fucking thing."

Horn pulled left and fired twice at the thin wall, six inches
from the doorframe. The agent cried out in pain and then fell
backward, crashing down the stairs with a huge racket. Horn
rushed to the doorway and cautiously peered around the
corner. The man he'd shot lay in a crumpled, bloody heap at
the first landing, his left leg broken at the hip and tucked
grotesquely beneath him. The other one, along with Volodin
and the innocent girl, was dead too. There was absolutely no
doubt of it.

"For what?" Horn muttered. To protect some madman's
reputation? More, he told himself. There had to be more.

Back in the apartment he grabbed his overnight bag, then
carefully stepped over the bloody remains in the corridor and
hurried down the stairs, stopping at the landing. This was the
real world. Kill or be killed. The building was very quiet.
The few at home at that hour would not be looking out their
doors. It was better not to see such things, better not to know,
not to become involved. In that respect they were people
under siege like those in any big city: New York, London,
Paris. On the ground floor he looked outside. The street was
as quiet as before. Directly across was Volodin's car and the
gray Chevy. Morrison had not come around to the front yet.

Pocketing his Beretta, Horn stepped outside, then turned
right, away from the alley entrance, and walked away. I'm
sorry, Nickolai. I should have warned you that Jason would
not give up so easily. Warned you that he is a monster,
inhuman. Boyko, Nobels, Clay, and now this at Jason's
bidding. He was angry.

At the corner, he crossed diagonally onto a narrow side
street that jogged over to Griefswalder, passing a church
behind which was a school, its tall brick chimney rising as a
black line in the darkening sky nearly as high as the church
spire. There was traffic here, big buses, trucks, a lot of cars
and taxis. He heard the first of the sirens in the distance.
Morrison would be bailing out at any moment, and it was

possible that he would come this way, taking the main avenue downtown where five of the seven checkpoints were concentrated in a few-block area. Streetlights had come on, traffic ran with headlights, the city was coming alive with the early evening, and even more sirens were converging here. Still Morrison had not come out. Schöenfeld Airport was about fifteen miles to the south, beyond Treptow. Getting there by taxi would take forty-five minutes, checking through security in the international terminal another half hour providing in the meanwhile no one put together the fact that Volodin had arranged the visa for the American engineer Hammer, and now Volodin lay shot to death in an apartment.

Horn crossed Griefswalder with the light where it met Wisbyer Strasse, and before the light changed, he motioned to the driver of an empty taxi on the far side. The driver flipped on her occupied light, and when the signal changed she shot ahead of traffic and angled to where Horn stood waiting.

Two police cars, their blue lights flashing, their sirens screaming, raced by and turned up the next street as Horn was getting into the taxi. Sam Morrison passed in the blue van, and he looked over, his eyes growing as he spotted Horn.

"Damn," Horn swore to himself.

"Mein Herr?" the driver asked, looking in the rearview mirror.

Morrison made the next light and turned right. He was going to try to circle the block and get back there. But he would have no idea where Horn was headed. Back toward town, by the direction he was facing. Back to the checkpoint. Back home.

"Schöenfeld Airport," Horn said. "And fast. I am late for my flight."

"Yes, of course," the driver said, and she pulled away from the curb, merging smoothly with traffic. She cut left on one of the ring roads that circled the city center, and ran down through Friedrichshain, then along the wall, the western sector barely four hundred yards away at times, past the Soviet War Memorial rising in a park along the Spree.

Twice Horn chanced a look over his shoulder out the rear window, but they had lost the blue van. Horn figured Morrison would be cursing himself by now for having come so close and yet allowing the situation to deteriorate and Horn to slip through his fingers. "Did you at least find out where he was heading, Sam?'' Ryan would shout. Horn could hear him. ''Did he come over? Did he rendezvous with another of his stringers? Did he go to ground in some other apartment we knew nothing about? What, Sam? Don't tell me that you lost him. Not that, Sam.''

The driver was an older, heavyset woman with short-cropped hair beneath a red scarf. She kept up a running commentary about how her mother did not think it right that a woman should be driving a taxi. The driver laughed. Her mother was still living in the dark ages. In the thirties, and even the twenties.

''Things are different now,'' the driver said. ''And it is better now, I think, even though my mother doesn't think so sometimes.''

They passed through the area of Treptow and then turned southwest, the highway generally following the contour of the wall, off now in the distance. The countryside was neat, pastoral, with farms and little farmhouses clustered together to share living space away from the productive land. The airport rose up out of the fields, its control tower and terminal out of place in such a scene.

The taxi fare, which was state-regulated, was ridiculously cheap. Horn resisted the urge to overtip. He shouldered his bag and walked into the terminal. A flight had just come in and the terminal was filling with people, some of them speaking Polish, but a lot of them speaking Russian. It was a few minutes before six, which gave him a full two hours before his flight was scheduled. Plenty of time for him to check in, but also plenty of time for someone bright to figure out that he may have run, that he may have gotten travel arrangements from poor dead Volodin, who had never trusted the West.

He crossed the main floor of the terminal to the rest rooms along the east wall just down the corridor that led to the security checkpoint leading into the international section of the terminal. Announcements came over the public address system in German, French, and English. It was just a little slur by the Germans against their masters the Russians, and their neighbors to the east, the Poles. The policemen and armed customs service officers looked up at his approach, and watched closely as he turned and went into the rest rooms. The Beretta felt as if it weighed fifty pounds in his coat pocket.

Two men were using the long urinal trough along one wall, a third was washing up at the sinks, and at least one of the toilet stalls was occupied. Horn went to the last sink in the row and set his overnight bag atop the large wastepaper container. He unbuttoned his coat and took his time washing his hands, splashing water on his face and then using a lot of paper towels to dry himself. The one at the sink looked up at him with a disapproving scowl, dried his hands on a single paper towel, then stepped around Horn to dispose of his soiled towel in the container. Both men at the urinal trough finished and went out, the one from the sink following right after them. Horn was alone for just a moment. He hurriedly pulled the Beretta out of his coat pocket, wrapped the weapon and the extra clip of ammunition in his paper towels, and stuffed the entire bundle deep in the wastepaper container. He was just straightening up when one of the airport security guards came in, looked at him for a long, appraising moment, his eyes flicking to the leather bag atop the wastepaper container, and then he went to the urinal trough. Horn grabbed his bag and got out. He was getting jumpy now. No matter what happened, he was a murderer. That was going to stick with him for a very long time. It wouldn't take the East Germans very long to perform an autopsy on Volodin and the others. They would discover that the American on the stair landing had been shot with a lighter-caliber weapon than Volodin's Makarov. It wasn't likely they'd be able to tell the make of the weapon because of the distortion the bullet underwent passing through the wall, but they'd have a fair idea of its caliber by the weight of the lead. The East Germans might not immediately know who killed the second American, but Ryan certainly would. And so too would Jason.

He turned away from the corridor that led down to the international section of the airport and walked across the busy terminal. The shops and restaurants were on the mezzanine above. He took the stairs up, stopping at the top long enough to lean against the broad aluminum rail to light a cigarette, a traveler weary at this hour. Moments later the security guard came out of the men's room, stood at the entrance to the corridor for a second or two, scanning the crowd, and then he returned and went back. Imagination, Horn wondered, or had the guard been looking for him?

The Hansa Haus Bierstube was located at the far end of the mezzanine. Horn sat at one of the tables from which he had a clear view of the stairs and a portion of the main floor below. He ordered a beer while he waited. The business at the apartment was finally beginning to hit him. Really hit him now. He had gunned down one of his own people. Jason's man, but an American nevertheless. He would have to answer to that charge when this was over. He hadn't stopped long enough to check the man's ID to find out his name. He'd have a wife, children perhaps. A mother, aunts, uncles. Christ. He ran a hand across his eyes and forehead. Nikolai had to have been half dead when he sat up. He couldn't have seen a thing, felt a thing. He had been no threat. Nikolai was dead already. Shooting him had been like desecrating the grave of an old friend. That agent would never have taken you across the checkpoint, Jack. He'd been sent to kill you. Sam Morrison would have ended up the unwitting witness. "Shots were fired, Mark. Jack had a gun, we knew that. Nothing else could have been done under the circumstances. He had two fake passports, and enough money to run. God only knows what he was up to. It was self-defense on our part. Nothing we could have done to prevent it." The worst part of it in his mind was what they'd tell Christine. The DCI himself spoke with the families of the Agency's fallen heroes. But Horn would be listed as a traitor. Maybe they'd stonewall it, tell her nothing. Maybe Sam would see her through, try to explain. So why was he doing this? Why was he pushing? What was he taking the risks for? No one had given him the orders to go as far as he had gone. He wasn't throwing himself at the front line on the command to charge. "We're all of us either a part of the solution or a part of the problem," Doxy would say. "No fence-sitters here, Jacko. Just remember that." Turn the other cheek and the bloody bastards will likely blow it off for you. Principles are such lovely things, he'd heard somewhere; too bad they're wasted on people. Or Gods. *Vengeance is mine,* the Lord said. *I will repay.*

He finished his first beer and ordered another, paying for both of them with the East German marks he'd gotten at the checkpoint crossing. While he waited he took out his Hammer passport from the envelope Volodin had handed him. Visas for East Germany, Poland, and the USSR were neatly stamped in the back. Volodin had also provided him with work cards for all three countries; he was a sewage plant design and troubleshooting engineer, according to his papers, enough of an innocuous occupation that he'd not likely be questioned about it. Volodin had arranged round-trip tickets on LOT, the Polish national airline, on its East Berlin to Moscow direct flight. The return date had been left open. With the tickets was a Hotel Berlin reservation confirmation telegram, crumpled as if it had been in his pocket for several days. There were also receipts for hotels and restaurants here and in Cracow. The paper work was all legitimate. Horn wondered where Volodin had come up with it on such short notice.

Sam Morrison showed up at seven. Horn hadn't seen him cross the main floor, in fact had seen nothing until Sam was there on the stairs. There was plenty of time to get up and leave, or move to the shadows in back. Sam wasn't here to search every single nook and cranny, every face. He'd merely made a couple of assumptions and was making a quick circuit of the airport, hoping for a little luck but not really expecting it. He was alone, as far as Horn could determine. And he would not pull a gun. Not here. Sam had come merely to talk.

Horn stood up and waved as Morrison came slowly down the walk, looking into the shops as he passed. He stopped in his tracks when he spotted Horn, but then he seemed to gird himself for something very difficult and he came resolutely, it seemed, the rest of the way. They shook hands, though it was clear that Morrison wasn't quite certain if he should.

"You're a surprising man, Jack," he said. "Are you meeting someone here? Flying somewhere? Laying a track? Can I help?"

He was a good man, Horn thought. He wouldn't go off half-cocked, but he was persistent. And he was intelligent. There weren't many lies he'd believe now. And yet lies might be what would save his life. It would depend upon how much he already knew or had guessed.

"I'm not a traitor," Horn said.

"I didn't think you were. Or at least I don't want to think it. But they've got some pretty convincing evidence to say you are." Morrison looked all in. He wasn't a fieldman, not really. He hated it away from his desk. "I'd like you to come back with me, you know. Mark is on your side. All of us are."

They sat down. The waitress came over and Morrison ordered a beer so as not to be conspicuous. She brought some big pretzels and mustard for the table. The *bierstube* was beginning to fill up now. The hum of conversation was polyglot, so no one paid any attention to their English.

"Have you heard from Doxmeuller?" Horn asked.

"No. Should I have?"

"I thought he might have called," Horn said softly. "Who ordered the taps on my telephone?"

"What are you talking about?"

"My house was bugged, Sam. Christine told me that a meter reader came by the day before I returned home. He put the taps on the telephone. I found the transmitter in the basement. One of ours, no mistaking it."

"I didn't know anything about it, Jack. I swear to you." Morrison shook his head. He leaned in a little closer. "What the hell happened back there, at the apartment? There were shots and then the *Polizei* showed up. Next thing I know I'm seeing you getting into a taxi three blocks away. Took me a bit to figure out where you might have run off to. This was just a lark. But what about Thompson and Guthrie? Their car was still parked in front when I got out."

"They're dead, Sam. Along with Nikolai Volodin and his lady friend."

All the air went out of Morrison. He sat back heavily in his chair. "Oh, Christ," he breathed, shaking his head again. "What the hell have you done, Jack? What in God's name are you up to?"

"Saving my own life," Horn answered him. "And yours too if you'll listen to me."

"Have you gone over, Jack? Is that it after all? Are you going to give me the spiel about how the West has decayed, how it's rotted from within, and that we're dying now? Communism isn't perfect, you'll admit, but you'll work hard to make it better. Is that it, Jack?"

"Don't be an ass."

"What the hell else are we supposed to believe? It's a little unusual to have your kids pulled out of school in the middle of the afternoon, and put them and your wife on a plane for the States with absolutely no notice to anyone. We'll have to pick up the pieces on that one for you. And then, when we want to talk to you, where do you run off to? The East zone, to your stringers, your madmen, and immediately we come by to say hello and ask what the fuck is happening with you, and World War Three starts.''

"Your musclemen were armed, Sam.''

"Of course they were.''

"Who sent them? Where did they come from? I don't remember seeing them at the station.''

"They flew in this morning. Langley sent them out.''

"They came up on us single file, Sam, and pulled a gun on the girl. Volodin shot the first one in self-defense. The second one shot him and the girl.''

Morrison's nostrils flared. "And then in remorse he turned his gun on himself?''

"I shot him, Sam, or he would have shot me. He had no intention of bringing me back.''

"I do, Jack. Come back with me. We'll work it out. You have a lot of friends. They're a bunch of trigger-happy hotheads over here, though. Mark should have known better. I told him as much. That'll count for something.''

"The same people who killed my old Russian madman killed Dewey Nobels in Stockholm. I'm going to find out who and why.''

"By running around East Berlin shooting your own people?'' Morrison blurted. He stopped himself. "But you're not staying here, are you, Jack? You're off somewhere, then. You're flying someplace.'' He turned and looked down into the terminal at one of the flight schedule boards.

"Go back while you still have the chance, Sam.''

Morrison turned back, his eyes round. "What does that mean? Are you going to gun me down too?''

Horn sat forward. "Use your goddamned head, Sam. There are two Americans shot dead in the stairwell of an apartment here. Lying right there with them is a KGB captain and his mistress. Someone may just have seen your van. Sooner or later the border will be closed for you. All hell will break loose here. Get out while you can.''

"Then come with me,'' Morrison said earnestly.

There wasn't a chance in hell that Sam would know how to handle the truth, Horn thought. He smiled sadly and shook his head.

"Tell me what you think is going on, then? Who killed Boyko and Nobels, and why? You must have some ideas. Something to go on. Something we could help with.''

"In Paris," Horn said, looking up.

"Paris? What's there?"

"Boyko called someone in Paris. An emergency number from the old days. Forty-eight hours later he was gunned down."

"One of our people did it? Is that your theory?"

"I don't know. Nobels had spent the last year following Boyko around. Boyko was running French whores into Moscow from Paris. When Nobels came out he was trying to warn me about something, or someone connected with Boyko."

"Could be a Russian did him in."

"It's possible, but I didn't find anything useful in Moscow, except that all of my madmen from the old days are dead."

Morrison looked down at the pretzels. "What about the Frenchman in Helsinki? Did you kill him too?"

"Yes, I did, Sam. With his own gun, after I took it from him."

Morrison nodded. "So, Paris is next?"

"I'm not going there directly. You can tell Mark that it wouldn't do him much good to try to intercept me."

"There are only two airports—"

"And a dozen train stations and bus depots, hundreds of highways and roads, and then there's always the river."

He hated leading his old friend around like this, but it was necessary. Doxy had gotten himself into trouble, and Sam wasn't half as capable.

"Paris is a big operation. Carlisle will send out half of Langley if need be. You know that. They're not going to let this ride. They can't. And Interpol is in on this now."

"I know," Horn said, and he stopped himself from adding: It's because of Jason . . . he can't afford to let it ride.

"So come back with me, Jack. We can work it out together. I can run your investigation for you. No one will be gunning for me."

Horn wanted to say, You're wrong, Sam, but again he held his tongue.

"I could pull a gun on you, force you to return with me."

Horn grinned. "No, you couldn't—not here. Besides, you don't carry a gun. They frighten you, remember?"

"Shit."

"Don't try to follow me, Sam," Horn said. He finished his beer. "Tell Mark what I told you. He can pass it along to

Carlisle. But I won't be very long. Once I know who pulled the trigger on Boyko and Nobels, I'll have a pretty fair idea why.''

He got up. Morrison jumped up too. He'd lost and he knew it. Horn could see it in his eyes, in his manner. He was trying to think of something else to do or say to change the situation. He did not want to return empty-handed.

"I'm afraid for you, Jack. It won't be very pleasant being on the outside, looking in. There will be a lot of experts coming after you who don't know you like we do. They won't give a damn. You'll just be another face that's gone over."

"It's my only chance," Horn said.

"What about Christine and the kids? Christ, have you thought about them?"

"Leave them out of it, Sam. Make sure Mark does too. Christine knows me; she knows I haven't gone over. That's good enough for her, if the rest of you will just leave her alone."

"I'll try."

"Do that, Sam."

Horn left the *bierstube*, alone. He went down the stairs and crossed the busy terminal. At the entrance to the international terminal corridor, he turned and looked back. Morrison stood at the rail above, watching him. The Paris fiction wouldn't hold up for very long, but he hoped that it would give him just a few hours grace.

Security was a bit of an anticlimax. He did not trigger the metal detector, and although the fairly large sum of money he was bringing with him raised a few eyebrows, he wasn't asked about it, nor was he asked about his occupation or why he was traveling to Moscow. Spies, of course, never set out to go to Communist bloc country from another Communist bloc country. His reservations at the LOT desk were in order, he was issued a boarding pass, and he stopped at a stand-up bar for a leisurely cognac to clear his head before his flight was due to board. Four East German businessmen, also on their way to Moscow, were joking and laughing loudly about their black-market dealings. From what Horn could gather from their conversation, they made this Moscow trip on a regular basis, and each time they went in, they brought American and British rock and roll stereo albums with them.

In fact, the one boasted to his friends, he made half again as much in record sales in Moscow as he did in his regular line, which was office equipment and furniture. He had built a house with the clandestine profits. Not one of them bothered to keep his voice down. They were not overly concerned, it seemed, about being caught.

When the boarding call came, he paid for his drink and walked across to the gate.

"I'll just keep this with me," he said to the stewardess, shouldering his bag as he boarded the jetliner. The plane was a Tupolev-154, which was the Russian counterpart to the Boeing 727 or the old Trident. It was half full. They took off ten minutes late, and as they banked left over the terminal, Horn imagined that he could see Morrison's long, sad face down there turned up to the black sky. He'd know then that Horn had lied to him. "You weren't going to Paris, Jack. You were heading off to Moscow." "You're right, Sam. But I lied for your own good. Stay back. Stay back." The East German businessmen from the lounge were seated together near the front of the plane. They'd brought bread and sausages with them, and they were still drinking cognac, passing the bottle back and forth. They were in good spirits and laughed and joked, and an hour or so out, they even began to sing some old army songs that the few Russian passengers aboard did not find particularly entertaining. One of the stewardesses tried to say something to them, but they laughed her off and continued, unabated. They'd broken out on top of the clouds. A half-moon shone from a star-studded sky over the fairy-tale landscape below. He'd always wanted to jump out and explore. Virgin territory, he supposed. His basic wanderlust. He had a seat alone, so he lay back, closed his eyes, and pretended to sleep. The stewardess didn't bother him after that. And he actually did fall asleep, he supposed, for a short time, because when they landed, his heart was racing and he was damp with perspiration, yet he could remember nothing.

People tended to see what they thought they should.

The KGB customs officers were the same ones from several days ago when Horn had last been through Sheremetyevo. He recognized them, but they did not remember him: his name was different, he wore a different coat, he wore no hat, and his name now was Jack Hammer, an American to be sure, but one who had worked in East Germany and Poland for the people, and who was here now to lend a hand to Russians. His reception this time was more toward the warm side of neutral. He was allowed through the preferred passport control, customs, and baggage checkpoints, and was finished in less than an hour. On the outside, looking in, Morrison had called it. Horn felt a little odd to be back like this. Getting out wasn't going to be nearly as easy, he suspected. A lot would depend upon Anna: if she would cooperate with him, if she would tell him what he needed to know—though she had told him she never knew Jason's real name, she could provide him with a description—he would bring it back to Washington to the president if need be. He still had a lot of friends in Washington who could arrange it. Christine's father could help. A face out of the past to which he could match a name in the present, along with a motive. He came down the ramp from customs onto the main arrivals concourse. It was very late. He was tired, his throat scratchy from too many cigarettes. And he was wary. This was *badland*. A name he and Doxy had used. He was the enemy here. There would be no Daniloff-like trade for him. Over the years he had done the Eastern bloc far too much harm for them to give him up so easily. A voice out of the crowd hailed him.

"Hello, Jack."

Horn turned as Kyle Pfeiffer materialized. He was smiling. His gloved hands were in plain view.

"Berlin Station?" Horn asked, disappointed. There was no use for a story.

Pfeiffer nodded. "They thought you might be showing up here." He looked around. "But, don't tell me, none of your pals are here to meet you, comrade."

"I'm not defecting."

"Very good. Then you wouldn't mind coming back to the embassy with me. Bob would like to have a little chat with you. In fact there are quite a number of people who would like a word or two with you." Pfeiffer's manner was oily.

"You're taking quite a chance, K.W."

"*You* are, coming back like this, you bastard."

"I'm a murderer, besides being a traitor. Or didn't they tell you?"

"What are you doing here?"

Pfeiffer was an idiot, but he wasn't in on any conspiracy. "Looking for answers."

"What sort of answers?" Pfeiffer asked. He seemed a little less certain than before. "You want answers, we'll give them to you."

They were beginning to attract some attention. Horn shifted his bag to his left shoulder and nodded toward the front doors. "Who'd you bring with you?"

"That depends on you."

"We're kicking up some dust here, if you hadn't already noticed. I think it would be a good idea if we got out of here. Now."

"That's just fine. But I warn you, Horn, don't try any funny business. Give me your passport, please."

"Don't be silly," Horn said, and he started across the main concourse. The press of people was already thinning. Theirs had been the last incoming flight. Within a half hour the airport would be closed for the night.

Pfeiffer came after him. "Just hold up there, Jack."

"Don't create a scene here, K.W. It won't do either of us any good," Horn said without breaking stride. One of the KGB's airport security people had come from his station by the duty-free Western currency shop and was talking with one of the Intourist hostesses at the information booth. They had been watching.

There was a long line at the taxi stand, and the first bus had already departed. The weather wasn't terribly cold, but it had begun to snow again. For some reason it depressed Horn. He turned on Pfeiffer.

"Just for the record, K.W., I'm not one of your bad guys. Beyond that, you don't want to know anything. Believe me."

"But you killed Josh Guthrie. Bureau of Political Security. East Berlin. Don't try to deny that."

Horn had caught the eye of one of the black-market cabbies parked off to the side. They only accepted cigarettes or hard Western currencies. They voluntarily paid a stiff city tax, so no one really minded them. The cab pulled up briskly.

"You don't think we're going to simply let you hop into a taxi, just like that," Pfeiffer said.

Horn put his right hand in his coat pocket as he turned in close to Pfeiffer. "If I have to shoot you here and now I will, but believe me when I tell you that neither of us would enjoy it."

"You wouldn't dare."

Horn smiled.

The cabby had jumped out and he came around to them.

"There will be two of us," Horn said in Russian. "The Rossiya Hotel. Twenty marks. West German."

"I think forty. It is very late, you know."

"Thirty," Horn said, keeping his eyes on Pfeiffer. The man was beginning to squirm.

"Forty, respectfully. There will be a long wait, as you can see."

"Thirty-five. Forty with the tip, then."

"Very good." The driver held the back door for them and stepped aside. Pfeiffer reluctantly got in, Horn behind him. The car was a Moskvich, spotlessly clean. The driver raced recklessly around the long curves, slippery now because of the light snow. Pfeiffer was scared. He wanted to look over his shoulder to see if his people were following them. So did Horn, but he made himself not do it. They were back there. He didn't doubt it.

"I thought if anyone would come out to meet me, it would be you," Horn said.

"What do you want here? What next?"

"I want to talk to someone from the embassy, K.W., believe me. But I'm just a little gun-shy at the moment. People I know get killed. Friends take potshots at me."

"You can talk to me. I'll listen. Christ, I promise you."

Horn patted him on the arm. "No need to worry, K.W. I'm not going to shoot you. Not right here and now, anyway. I'll talk with Gloria Townsend."

"All right," Pfeiffer said carefully.

"You'll have to tell her first that I'm innocent. That I'm not a traitor. I'll want her to repeat that back to me. Those words exactly so that I'll know you told her."

"I'll tell her. Where do you want to meet? The Rossiya?"

"Truck fatality square," Horn said.

"What?"

"Truck fatality square. Do you understand English? Did you hear me?"

"What the hell is that supposed to mean?"

"Send her alone, K.W. Just make sure of that, will you? This is my city, if you will rightly recall. If you set her up, if you follow her, I'll know, and you'll never find out what's going on. Noon, K.W. Alone."

• • • •

Losing Pfeiffer and the pair who had been following them was child's play. The Rossiya was a very large hotel, with dozens of entrances and exits. Before they realized anything might be wrong, he was four blocks away, and by the time they'd come around to the front again, he was already checking in at the much smaller, much shabbier Berlin Hotel on Zhdanov Street. For the remainder of that night he kept hearing *Madama Butterfly* in his head, the music rising nobly, drowning out even the incessant sounds of the elevator coming and going. In the morning, very early, he got his passport from the desk clerk and took a trolley bus across the river where he got off near the Academy of Sciences.

19

The morning was still dark. Streetlights cast long shadows as Horn walked across Oktyabr'skaya Square into Zhitnaya Street. There would be more snow soon; he could smell it in the air. Moscow was like a gigantic field exercise in which survival depended upon the application of proper tradecraft. How many times in the past had he done the exercises, and how many times like this had he pretended that it was all a game, that he could stop at any time he wished merely by raising his hand? They'll be using real bullets, Jacko, which will actually be the least of your worries, unless of course you're truly concerned about international balances. A top CIA fieldman is a plum well worth plucking intact with all of its juices flowing at their peak. Parade him around Red Square. Let the comrades watch his drugged, halting speech on the television as he tells them that he is guilty of spying against the *rodina*—the motherland—the most dastardly of all crimes. Be friends with the wolf, Party Secretary Gorbachev was saying about improving relations with the U.S., but keep one hand on your ax. It was the old Russian way. It was the same, though, in Washington and New York. The cold winds blew off the Potomac and East rivers as well as the Moscow. At forty-three he was a century old with a clarity of vision to see his own mortality as opposed to the immortality of youth.

Traffic surged along the broad boulevard. It was Friday, a workday. Pfeiffer and Morrison, he thought, were two men cut of the same cloth. They would like nothing better than to go to work in the morning and return home at night with nothing out of the ordinary in between. Looking forward to Friday, to the weekend, though not upset with a little overtime now and again, the odd Saturday assignment as OD, the occasional bit of midnight oil. What they and men of their ilk were deathly afraid of was the situation out of the norm, the operation that was skewed a few degrees to the right or left. Carlisle back in Washington was the same: don't upset the status quo, don't rock the boat, for heaven's sake. Clean up this mess, Carlisle would be shouting, and clean it up now! He'd changed; they'd all changed over the years. He thought about Christine and the kids, and hoped to God they were safe and sound by now with her father.

Yevgenni Sheshkin was getting ready for work. Tatiana let Horn up without any serious objections this time. She was finally resigned to what she had to consider madness on her husband's part, dealing with an American spy. "I'll get him," she said upstairs. "Do you want tea?" Her hair was up in rollers, her face pale.

"If it wouldn't be too much trouble."

"Oh, it is, believe me, mister." She shuffled back into the kitchen, her robe flapping behind her.

Horn unbuttoned his coat and looked around the living room. Nothing had changed. But this time he noticed there were a lot of books and stereo albums on homemade shelves, a bit unusual for a Russian apartment. Sheshkin had had good taste, though, even in the old days. Except for this now, he supposed his old madman had developed a happy life for himself.

"I thought maybe you had gone," Sheshkin said, coming to the door from the back. He was bare-chested. He was drying his hair with a big towel.

"I need your help, Yevgenni."

"I'm out of the business. I have told you this already, Jack. Believe me, I am a loyal Communist now. I go to meetings. I meet my quotas."

"What I am asking betrays no one. You must trust me in this. Have I ever lied to you? Yevgenni? Have I?"

Sheshkin had always been slow to come to decisions, and often slow even to make talk. But he was not a stupid man; in fact Horn had always found him to be quite intelligent. He was simply a cautious man. He was a methodical but sometimes inspired chess player.

"Stretched a few things now and then," Sheshkin said.

Tatiana came in with Horn's tea in a glass with a metal holder. She looked at her husband, shook her head, and went back into the kitchen, softly closing the door behind her.

"This is not doing my marriage any good, you know," Sheshkin said.

"I'm leaving soon."

"Moscow, Jack? For good this time?"

"Sure."

"When, Jack? Can you tell me this exactly?"

"Tonight. Tomorrow. Sunday at the latest. But I'll need your help first. Will you at least listen to me?"

Sheshkin glanced at the kitchen door. He put the towel around his neck and perched on the edge of the couch. He didn't want to come any nearer to Horn than need be.

"I need a car, or a small truck," Horn said. "And papers for me and a woman. Travel papers, exit permits, registration, insurance."

Sheshkin laughed. "A truck? Papers? Where are you planning on driving?"

"Helsinki. We are farmers. We are going to buy Finnish seed for the spring planting."

"That is a very long way from here, Jack."

"Finnish seeds are very good."

Sheshkin smiled. "Is that all you want me to do? Get you a truck and papers for you and some woman? You have found this Anna who has written the letter? She is important to you? You want now to smuggle her out of the country? Your embassy can accomplish this, I think, easier than it will be for you to drive all the way to Helsinki. Tell me something else, Jack. Almost anything else. For such a thing we would need a lot of money. A great pile of money."

"How much?"

"A lot, Jack. I don't know. Ten thousand rubles, perhaps. Less in foreign currency."

"What if I told you that the truck would not be lost? Perhaps it would not even leave Moscow?"

"What?"

"We would need a place to hide the truck for a couple of days. A parking garage, perhaps an old shed. Anywhere. It would not matter the exact location, though I would have to see the truck. See where it is parked."

"And the papers?"

"They would have to be legitimate, for me, and for a small woman."

"You wish to have a truck to drive to Helsinki, but it will not leave Moscow. You want papers, too, and will they remain here in Moscow?"

"No. As soon as we have them we would go. I promise you. I can give you a few thousand West German marks. No more."

For a minute or so, while Horn sipped his tea, Sheshkin sat thinking about the problem he'd been handed. He lit a cigarette. "This can be done, by tonight."

"What time?" Horn asked, suppressing some of his excitement.

Sheshkin shrugged. "I will get off early. Come back here, let's say at eighteen hundred. How about photographs?"

"Do what you can, Yevgenni. We will adapt."

"You say she is a small woman. Dark?"

"Yes. Long black hair. Dark eyes."

"Short, tall?"

"About Tatiana's height."

"Russian? Ukrainian? Armenian?"

"Russian, I think."

"Scars, Jack? Marks? Tattoos? Is she a tattooed lady?"

Horn had to grin. "I think not, Yevgenni." He put his tea down and got to his feet. "Do you want the money now?"

Sheshkin's eyebrows rose.

Horn took out three thousand marks from an inner coat pocket and laid the money on the table. Sheshkin looked at it but made no move to reach for it.

"If you need a little more, it will be all right," Horn said.

Sheshkin nodded. "Get out of here now, Jack, or I'll be late for work."

Ilya Pupyshev had been struck down and killed by a truck in May of 1985 on Pushkinskaya Square up around the Rossiya Cinema and the Soviet Supreme Court. Gloria Townsend had dug out the information and brought it up to him the last time. He hoped she'd make the connection from the message he'd given Pfeiffer for her. He did not think his cover was going to hold up very long here in Moscow. He felt rushed. Yet he did not want to approach Anna prematurely, not until everything was set, until he had all of his ducks lined up in a neat row. If she remained on schedule, she would not be going off to the

Bolshoi until around two-thirty or three. That gave him two and a half hours tops from the moment he was supposed to rendezvous with Gloria. A hundred and fifty minutes, give or take, in which to convince Anna that she had to cooperate with him. Too much was at stake for her to balk. Too many people had been killed. The prize he was going to dangle in front of her nose was a ticket out. Back to the States . . . to her Jason, face-to-face.

From Sheshkin's apartment he walked down to the Warsaw Hotel and managed to find a cab to take him back across the river to the Metropole across from the Maly Theater. There he had a breakfast of poached salmon and boiled eggs. The dining room was three-fourths filled with American businessmen and journalists with their Russian friends and counterparts. He'd taken a risk coming here like this in the open, but he wanted to see if Bob Early had raised the alarm yet. Apparently he had not, or if he had done so, he had not thought to post anyone where an American was likely to show up.

Afterward he walked up to the Berlin Hotel, where he made certain no one had disturbed his things. He'd taken the usual precautions with his toilet kit, with the towel half over the tub in the bathroom, the closet door slightly ajar, the fold of his socks into which he had placed a half-empty pack of cigarettes—a particularly enticing target for a KGB legman here on the search. The fold of his socks around the pack was practically impossible to duplicate exactly. No one had been in his room. Yet. But it could not last. The fiction could not hold up much longer. Jason, by now, knew that he was here. *Jack Horn has come to Moscow. He is back on your trail.*

At eleven he took a cab up to the Hermitage Gardens, all but closed now at this time of the year, and he walked slowly back to Pushkinskaya Square, the first flakes of snow beginning to fall, the city fully alive now, and bustling and happy despite the gray, overcast, very cold day. "Live and scratch," the Russians said. "When you're dead, the itching will stop." He was beginning to feel pressed. Early wouldn't let such an opportunity pass, and neither would Jason. Both of them had probably read the book on him. It meant they probably knew his tradecraft.

"In the end," Wallace Mahoney had told them in training at the Farm, "your tradecraft becomes your signature. And by your signature you shall be known. Take care it does not kill you someday.''

The square began where Gor'kogo Street crossed the first outer ring road, the Bulvar, which was divided by a wide strip that in the summer was green with grass and trees, and colorful with flowers, but now was white and gray with trampled snow and bare branches. On the right a big bronze statue of Russia's greatest poet, Aleksandr Sergeyevich Pushkin, stood at the entrance to a nice park. On the right was the huge Rossiya Theater. The *Izvestia* newspaper building was just across the street, and behind the cinema was the Novosti Press Agency's headquarters. The square was very busy with pedestrians and traffic. This was one of the major arteries of Moscow. Horn walked past the cinema, checking out ahead and on both sides, stopping to turn back as if he had forgotten something or perhaps had gotten himself lost, looking for the telltale signs that he was being followed or that observers had been set in place or a combination of both. But an army could have successfully hidden here. Yet it would take only one good man—well trained, disciplined, and nervy—to make a quick pass for the hit. A silenced handgun, a knife, a poison dart, or a dozen other more esoteric means of dispatch. They'd expect him to come early, to check it out. The possibilities were beginning to make his skin crawl.

He took a last, long look back across the square, then hurried around the corner past the Stanislavskiy Musical Theater to the Tsentralnaya Hotel where he had two vodkas and a small plate of toast and caviar. In Russia one never drank vodka without eating something. This was not a hotel normally frequented by Westerners. He stood out a little, but he figured he was reasonably safe.

Just at twelve, he walked out of the hotel and found a cab coming up Gor'kogo Street. "I'm meeting someone on the square. Probably near the statue," Horn told the driver, a bulky woman.

"Ah, yes, is she pretty?"

"Maybe not so pretty. But we have an understanding."

The driver laughed. At the corner they made the light and turned right onto the square. Horn immediately spotted Gloria Townsend at the base of Pushkin's statue. She wore a long, light brown leather coat with matching sheepskin-lined hat and tall boots. She was stamping her feet in the cold. The snow was falling more heavily now.

"There," Horn said, leaning forward. "In the sheepskin hat and brown coat." He scanned the crowds. There were no obvious plants.

"But she is very pretty, and married too, I think," the driver said, pulling sharply across two lanes of traffic.

"Her husband just might be nearby," Horn said. "He has a terrible temper."

They pulled up. Horn opened the door and beckoned urgently. Gloria hadn't seen him come up in the cab. When she spotted him, she stiffened and then pointedly made a move as if to look over her shoulder into the park. It took only a half second, then she skipped over to the cab and jumped in, red-cheeked and out of breath. Her eyes were very wide.

"Gorki Park," Horn told the driver.

They took off and he and Gloria sat back, their heads close as if they were lovers sharing their secrets. "Who's back there?" he asked, keeping his voice very low.

"K.W. and a couple of heavies you never met. They just arrived. Early is mad, and the circuits to Langley have been running nonstop since last night. They want you, Mr. Horn, real bad. They'll stop at nothing."

"Has Mr. Carlisle called from Washington?"

"I don't know. But they're saying you're a traitor."

"I'm not."

"I didn't think so, but I'm glad to hear you say it."

"Pfeiffer didn't give you my message?"

Gloria looked at him blankly. Pfeiffer hadn't passed it along. He had been confident enough in his ability to orchestrate Horn's arrest. The man was a fool, a dangerous fool. He turned in his seat and chanced a quick look back. Usual traffic, nothing more. They were passing the Central Telegraph Office. Pfeiffer and his legmen had been caught flatfooted.

"Why did you come back, Mr. Horn?" Gloria asked.

"I don't want you involved, except as an innocent bystander. Or as innocent as I can keep you." She was a tough little girl, but she was going to come under a lot of pressure. "When you get back you're to tell them that we rode around while I tried to convince you that I am innocent. I came back to Moscow because I wanted to find out who killed Edmund Clay."

Gloria's eyes widened a little. She hadn't made the connection, though she'd apparently heard about Clay's death.

"Tell Early I want to set up a meeting with him on Monday. Red Square, in front of the Lenin Mausoleum. Noon. He's to come alone, no funny stuff this time."

"He said he knew something was wrong from the moment he briefed you. And there was something about you questioning Eric Parsegian about Clay's son—he said it proved what you were all along. Everything else you'd said and done was just a smoke screen, a whitewash for your real motives."

"It's not true, but he can keep believing it. Makes things easier for me." Horn looked up. The cabby had been watching them in her rearview mirror. She smiled. A lover's co-conspirator, he wondered, or would she go to the KGB to report that two suspicious Americans had had a secret conversation in her cab?

"He'll want to know what else we talked about."

"The same thing over and over again. Don't give him too much. But we're going to have to meet one more time. I need a gun."

She glanced nervously at the cabby, then pulled a gun from her coat pocket. It was beneath the level of the back of the front seat. The cabby could not see it. Horn took it and a spare clip of ammunition and stuffed them in his pocket. She'd guessed he'd need a gun. She'd come prepared. It was the same Walther PPK that Early had given him. "Good girl," he mouthed the words. She grinned in appreciation.

"Anything else, Mr. Horn?" she asked, just a little self-importantly. "I mean, do you need some money or anything?"

"Do you have your passport with you?"

She nodded.

"I'd like to have it. Can you get along without it for a week or so? Afterward you can claim you lost it, or it was stolen on the Metro."

"Is there someone else here? Someone you—"

"Don't," Horn warned, touching his finger to her lips. "You may tell them almost anything except this, Gloria. If they press you, give them a little tidbit. About my madmen all being dead. Or about the gun. You brought it along for protection—you were afraid of me, after all, just a little—and I took it from you. But nothing about the passport. Nothing."

They'd crossed the river down from Red Square and the cabby took the river drive, probably because she thought it was more romantic.

"It's the only thing that is vital for me. Do you understand?"

"It's Anna, isn't it. You've come back for her."

It was the obvious conclusion. He smiled at her. "I'll need a little time before that comes up."

She carried a shoulder bag. She opened it on the seat between them, and took out a cigarette and lit it. Horn reached in and took out her passport, pocketing it. Their eyes met and she returned his smile, putting more confidence into the gesture, he was sure, than she felt. She had put herself on the line for him; her career and possibly even her life were in jeopardy now. The gun she might be able to explain. The same with her missing passport. But together they spelled conspiracy.

The cabby let them off at the Krymskiy Val entrance to the park, a big grin on her face as Horn paid her. "She is very pretty, and a nice girl too. Treat her well, you."

"I will," Horn said, laughing.

He and Gloria walked into the park until the cab was gone, then they went back out to the cabstand to wait for another cab to come along. She was shivering. Horn turned up her coat collar.

"I'm from Florida," she said. "Can't quite get used to the cold."

"When is your tour up?"

"In the spring."

"And then?"

"Home, I think. I'm getting a little tired of this." She turned and looked up into Horn's face. "Sometimes it's hard to tell what's right, and who is doing right. The bureaucracy stinks, you know. Mostly they're worried about how they're going to look, how it will affect their lousy GS ratings. Retirement benefits is the subject of endless debate in the cafeterias. But you're different."

Horn smiled. "Maybe not such a great recommendation."

A cab came across the Krymskiy Bridge and Horn waved it over. There were a lot of people out and about. Already several couples had lined up behind them for cabs.

"Why do they call you Town and Country?" he blurted. He didn't want to hurt her, yet he wanted to know.

She laughed lightly. "I have expensive tastes, Mr. Horn. Sometimes too expensive."

He didn't understand. The cab came up and he opened the door for her.

"Town and Country?" she said. "The magazine with all
the nice things in it? I get it sent here to me."

Then he did understand, and he felt a little foolish. "Oh."

She laughed again. "You thought it meant something else,
didn't you?"

He nodded.

She reached over and kissed him on the lips. "Good
luck," she said. "Maybe we'll have a drink together one of
these days." She got in the cab, Horn closed the door for her,
and she was gone. He watched for a minute or so, but then
another cab pulled up and he got in.

"The Kiev Railway Station," he told the driver. They
expected him to go west. He'd begun to lay his track. It was
the logical route. So he'd go south.

Trying to leave the Soviet Union was probably a foolish
idea, Anna thought, looking across the living room at her
Uncle Stepan. Her illness seemed to be in remission today.
She felt better than she had in months. Most of the soreness
was gone, she had eaten a big breakfast, and already she was
thinking about lunch before the theater. Uncle Stepan, his
back to her, stared out the window. He still wore his great-
coat and he hadn't even bothered to take off his hat. His
shoulders were hunched. Anna felt as if she had stabbed him
in the back by applying for a foreign travel passport. He'd
found out about it soon enough. Her name was flagged, he'd
explained, because she was the niece of an important general.
That had been said to her matter-of-factly, because Uncle
Stepan had never been puffed up about his own position. He
had a job to do. "We all have jobs to do," he used to tell
them. "Our people count on us to do our best." His disappointment, though, was her death certificate. She would die
here after all, in Moscow, without having seen Jason one last
time.

"It cannot be done, chou-chou," he said from the window.
"Not now, not during the season. Perhaps by summer, perhaps next fall."

There probably won't be a summer, she thought. And
almost certainly not a next fall.

Uncle Stepan turned around. "What did you say?"

She managed a weak smile, and she shook her head.

"I never coddled you. I never will. You were raised to be
strong. Now, my little chou-chou, it is time for you to begin

repaying the state for what it has given you." His manner softened. He shook his head sadly. "What is it out there that you are after, little one? What are you pursuing?"

I can't tell you, she thought. It would break your heart if you knew my secret, all the years.

"If you insist, of course, you can create quite a stir. But that is all, believe me."

"No, Uncle. I wanted to see Paris, perhaps. London. Rome. Not too much to ask, I'd have thought, considering."

"In the summer I'll see what I can do. Maybe we will go together."

There won't be a summer, she wanted to scream. She wasn't sore, but she was still a little tired, dragged out.

"Can't you wait that long?"

"Of course. Maybe it wasn't such a good idea. I've never even seen Leningrad properly. Not really. Mother wants me to come see her. Stay for a few months."

"What about your father?"

She thought about her father. He was only a vague outline in her mind. She never knew him. "He would come here if I asked, I think."

"Maybe you should ask. You should know him. Despite everything . . . he is a good man. An honest man. Now that shipping is all but shut down out there for the winter, maybe you should send for him."

For just the briefest of moments, Anna thought she could read what was in her uncle's eyes, and it seemed to her that he knew she was going to die very soon. It was a second sight vision she'd had for just that instant, and it left her shaken. They knew who she was at the Clinical Hospital, of course. Dr. Mazayeva could have telephoned Uncle Stepan. Or her uncle could have had her followed. It had been a few days since she'd seen Cloth Cap and Fur Hat, but they could have been working for her uncle. They could still be out there, following her a little more discreetly now. That night on the street when they'd chased her, she had lost her gloves. Thinking back she figured that the object one of them had held up and waved at her could have been the gloves. Uncle Stepan had brought them around the next day, saying they'd been found at the theater. He never said by whom, nor had she asked.

"I've talked with someone about you," he said a little

sternly. "They say it may be an early menopause. I want you to see the theater doctor. He will recommend a gynecologist."

"What does my father coming here have to do with it?"

"You've been upset lately. Working yourself too hard . . ." Anna tried to protest, but Uncle Stepan held her off. "Let me finish, Anna. Not only have you been working yourself half to death these last few months, but you've also been chastising yourself that you are no longer dancing. It is depressing to me to see you like this. You are promoted one day, and on the very next you begin to mope like a sick cow. It doesn't make sense. It is not healthy. Your Auntie Raya and I have decided we will have a family reunion. Your mother will come up from Leningrad, and your father from Vladivostok. You have some cousins on your mother's side living in Gorki whom you have never seen."

"Auntie Raya said nothing to me."

"It was supposed to be a surprise. But then you went and applied for a foreign passport." He shook his head. "What's an uncle to do? I had to tell you, thus spoiling the surprise."

"When?" Anna asked. She felt flushed with embarrassment and sadness that her uncle would do such a thing for her merely to cheer her up.

"Soon, chou-chou. We thought in the beginning of March. You will be between productions at the theater. We could make it the entire week, you know. The dacha is ours, of course. Your mother can stay here with you, and your father with me. That's up to them. And there will be a special guest. A very large surprise. What do you say?"

"Have you talked with my father? Is he coming?"

"Yes, and your mother too. It might be good for them to see each other, incidentally."

She'd had fantasies about that possibility for as long as she could remember. But then she'd had a life of fantasies: about her parents, about the ballet, and in the end about Jason, the only man she'd ever truly loved.

Uncle Stepan came across the room to her and took her in his massive arms. She came willingly. She'd always liked Uncle Stepan's smells, his caresses, and his powerful but surprisingly gentle embrace. It was a warm, protected place where nothing could possibly happen to her. If she was sick, she wanted her uncle. If she was lonely, Uncle Stepan would cure her blues. If she was weary or frightened or confused, her KGB uncle knew the correct words and just the right gestures to make her see the foolishness of ever being frightened. The only things she'd ever hidden from him were her illness and now her deep-felt, tragic need to look one last time on her Jason, to hear his voice, feel his touch. She shivered.

"After the theater tonight we will have dinner together. Raya and Aleksandr want us to come over. I told them we would. It'll do you good, I think."

Anna nodded. "Will you be there for the show?"

"I can't, chou-chou. But I will pick you up just after the last curtain. If I am a minute or two late, wait there for me."

"Of course, Uncle," she said. She reached up and kissed him on the cheek.

"Get something to eat before you go in this afternoon, though. It will be a late night," Uncle Stepan said, and he left. She went to the window and looked down at the street. His big Zil limousine was parked in front. A minute later he appeared, his driver leaped out of the car and opened the back door, and Uncle Stepan climbed in. Anna waited until the car had turned the corner at the end of the block, then turned away from the window, her eyes beginning to fill with tears.

"Oh, Jason," she cried. "Is there no hope, then?"

20

You have to understand, Doxy, that not all of us have clear-cut reasons for every single thing we do. Sometimes our actions are spontaneous. Like prizefighters, if we were reduced to thinking out every punch, counterpunch, and block beforehand, we'd get nowhere. We'd be lying in a heap at the feet of some instinctual animal. Sometimes we're led by our own innate sense of right versus wrong.

Horn stood at the end of Neglin 2, telling himself that his only viable option at this point was to turn around and run. It had been General Patrenko coming from Anna's apartment. He'd recognized the car first: the fender flags, red with two stars, marked a general's car and the license was a KGB series. And there had been no mistaking the general himself. He was a large man, his stride purposeful, his driver properly obsequious.

Horn had studied the ordination ceremony for the priesthood. It had been his banner, his goal, to prostrate himself before the altar and listen to the bishop, kneeling at the faldstool, chanting the litany of the saints, asking for help from them all.

> From all evil, Deliver us, O Lord.
> From all sin, Deliver us, O Lord.
> From Thy wrath, Deliver us, O Lord.
> From a sudden and unprovided death, Deliver
> us, O Lord.

From the snare of the devil, Deliver us, O
Lord.
From anger and hatred, Deliver us, O Lord.

The ceremony went on for a long time, comforting in its
regularity, in its predictability, comforting too in that divine
intercession was being sought, and they all believed it was
possible. He'd memorized every word by the age of fifteen. It
had made his parish priest proud, but a little sad too.

"First should come your faith, Jack," he said on the day
that Horn left for Vietnam. "All else is secondary. Please
never forget that."

He never had, though he hadn't been able to keep it.

He started down to Anna's apartment. It was already a little
after one. She'd be leaving for the theater soon. Out here like
this he felt very naked. At any moment the general could
decide to return. He'd forgotten something, some last instruc-
tion. Too, he could have set up a surveillance on his niece. A
guardian angel to watch over her. At this moment their
gunsights could be on his back.

The street was empty of all but a few old cars parked half
up on the narrow sidewalks. He crossed over to the upper
side, and at Anna's building hesitated for only a moment
before he let himself in. For a long while he stood just within
the doorway, watching through the narrow frosted window at
the street, and listening for the sounds of the building. But the
corridor was very quiet. The place could be deserted, or its
people frightened. He could imagine ears pressed to every
door listening for the sounds of an altercation. They'd mop up
the blood soon enough. Watch yourself. Move carefully.
Even at this late hour there was a way out. He wanted nothing
more than to listen again to Doxy's eloquent denial of faith.
There was no such thing as the antichrist, was there?

He climbed the stairs to Anna's apartment, taking care to
keep his tread light, weight on the balls of his feet, alert to
sounds and smells and movement. He wondered why it was
so quiet today. That bothered him a little. Maybe Anna had
already gone. Maybe the general had evacuated the building so
that when the confrontation came, no innocent bystanders
would get hurt. Not General Patrenko. Not him. The man's
reputation was hard. Merciless. Horn pulled the gun from his
coat pocket, checked to make sure the safety was in the on
position, cracked the ejector slide back just far enough to

confirm that a live round was in the firing chamber, then let it back slowly. At the top he stood a moment before going down the corridor. The carpeting was worn but very clean. He hadn't noticed it the first time. He took a deep breath and let it out slowly. He was being foolish. At her door he put the gun back in his pocket, hesitated a moment longer, then knocked.

Anna came almost immediately. She was dressed in a long gray wool skirt and a silk blouse with puffy sleeves and a tall collar that buttoned high on her thin neck. She wore stockings, but she hadn't put on her shoes or boots. Obviously she'd been getting ready to leave for the theater. She looked elegant.

"Oh, God," she said. She turned absolutely white. "I thought you'd gone forever."

"I've come to take you to Jason."

"I can't go with you."

"You must."

She turned and walked away, leaving the door open. Horn stepped inside, closing and locking the door. He went to the window and looked down at the street. Nothing had changed. No one had come after him. He looked across to the opposite roof line, but there was nothing to be seen there either. All of Moscow was deserted. Here and now was theirs alone. He turned back. Anna stood at her bedroom door watching him. She wore a little foundation, a little mascara, and a little lipstick, but still she was pale. She was beautiful, but not from this century, he thought. He suddenly remembered how she had looked on the stage. It had been a lot of years ago, but he could recall her grace, and her form, her slender body well muscled; there had been an aura of confidence around her like the halo of an angel Tintoretto might have painted, filled with dramatic highlights and shadowings that imparted a deep emotion with no necessity of movement or sound.

"My uncle was here."

"I saw him on the street," Horn said. "Can you leave the theater early? Five o'clock? Six?"

"And then what?"

"Meet me at the Kiev Station. Our train leaves at nine."

"For Kiev?" she said with a laugh.

"Odessa. Then by boat to Istanbul. I have friends there."

She put a hand to her mouth. "I can't," she said softly.

The words were coming to him now, he wasn't proud of what he was doing to her. "You cannot afford to wait, Anna. I know that you do not have the time."

She turned away, the movement sudden, her shoulders hunching as if he had wounded her, which in a large way he supposed he had. Ah, Jason, he thought, what have you done to her, you bastard? What measure of a man are you to have done this? He had to be aware even now of what he had wrought.

"Jason is shy—"

"No!" she cried out, without turning back.

"Yes, Anna. It is because of your uncle that there can be no direct contact. You can understand that. Your uncle cannot afford it and neither can Jason. It leaves only you. It is your decision."

"What do you want here?"

"To take you to Jason. To get you out of the Soviet Union."

"I don't have a foreign travel passport."

"I've made arrangements," Horn said gently. He felt like a heel.

"My uncle is expecting me for dinner after the theater."

"By then we will be long gone. But leave word for him. Tell him that you were tired, and that you preferred to come directly home and sleep. Tell him that you will talk to him tomorrow. We will be out of the country by then. There will be nothing he can do."

Anna turned back; she was angry. "It is my uncle we are talking about. I will not deceive him!"

"You have told him about Jason, about me?"

She was frustrated. She stamped her foot. "What are you doing here? You don't know Jason—you don't know me! What do you want of me?"

"To take you to him."

"Why?" The single word was a cry of agony, a cry for help. She was a drowning woman clutching at straws but fearing that whatever she reached could not possibly support her. She was a woman dying before she'd had the chance to fulfill the single most important aspect of her life, and she was crying for help. *Why* are you here? Give me a compelling reason for trusting you. Tell me that Jason has waited for me all these years. Tell me that by running away from my life here, I will not be betraying my country, my ballet company, but most of all tell me that I will not betray my uncle. And it was a good question, wasn't it, Doxy? he thought. What was the good answer?

"Because I care," he said simply, and because he couldn't think of any other reason he had come here.

"About what?" she snapped.

"About you, and what you have gone through these last years. About your letter and about the fact that some very good people who have worked for me, or with me, have been killed."

"Jason is not a murderer."

"I didn't say he was, Anna. But someone very important does not want you to see him. They have tried to kill me for coming here like this."

He hadn't intended telling her all of that, yet it was only right that she be made aware of the risks they'd be facing by running off.

"If I go with you, someone will try to kill us? Are you saying that to me?"

He felt as if he were losing her. "They won't be expecting us to show up in Turkey. They'll expect us to run for Helsinki, or perhaps Stockholm, the western border."

"Who are *they*?"

"I don't know, Anna. But I think Jason can tell us. He will have the answers."

"He always did," Anna mumbled. She looked up. "Are you a spy, Mr. . . . ?"

"Hammer. Yes, I am."

She nodded. "Then it is very dangerous for you to be here like this, Mr. Hammer, isn't it."

"Yes, it is," he admitted.

"And yet you took the risk. You came back."

"Will you come with me?" he asked. "There'll be no returning, of course. But you will see Jason, I guarantee it."

He could see a softening in her eyes, and he could see her fear as well.

"My uncle came here today to tell me that I could not have a foreign travel passport. He said that I could not leave the Soviet Union. I applied for a passport yesterday." She hugged herself as if she had just felt a chill. "It's very strange, then, you coming to me like this so soon after my uncle's visit. I mean, to tell me that you have a passport for me, and that we can leave. Just like that. I cannot believe it, and yet I know it is true. Like my illness, you see. I don't really believe it, yet I know it to be true."

"What do you have, Anna?" Horn asked softly.

"Leukemia."

"There are cures."

She shrugged. "Perhaps, but not for me, at least not from my doctor. Not here in the Soviet Union in any event. There are miracle cures in the United States?"

"I don't think so, but you will be looked after. If anything can be done for you, Anna, anything at all, I swear to God I will make damned sure it happens."

She closed her eyes. "My uncle also came to tell me that he has planned a family reunion for me. In March. My father and mother will be there. Aunts and uncles, even cousins I've never seen before."

"Will you come with me?" Horn asked again.

"Cousins I will never see if I leave." She opened her eyes. "Do you have cousins? Do you see them regularly?"

"When I'm in the States."

"The States," she said carefully. She was trying a new word on her lips.

"The train leaves at nine. I would like you to be there no later than seven. The Kiev Station. In front, by the main entrances."

"I was practically raised by my uncle. He is a very good man. Your enemy, I think, but a good man. He sees things. I think he knows that I am dying."

"Can you be there, Anna? Will you be there tonight?"

"I think you should go now, Mr. Hammer," she said tiredly. "I must get ready for the theater."

He had lost. He tried to search for words. "Anna?"

"Don't be too disappointed," she said. She walked past him, unlocked the door, and opened it. "Good-bye, Mr. Hammer."

He had run out of words. There was nothing for him to say to her. She would die here in Moscow. This month or next, by fall certainly. He wanted to reach out to her, to touch her soul, to make her see. He wished that somehow he could make her see inside his mind, make her understand what was at stake. But he could not. At the door, he hesitated a moment longer, then turned back and looked into her large, beautiful eyes. "I'll wait for you. At the depot. Seven o'clock. Please . . ."

"Good-bye, Mr. Hammer," she said, and Horn finally turned and left. Halfway down the stairs he finally heard her door close.

•   •   •

A half hour later the music rose around her, all but drowning out the sounds of the flushing toilet. Anna felt weak, her stomach tender, the bile sharp at the back of her throat, the taste of vomit still strong in her mouth. She rose up and looked at her pale reflection in the mirror over the tiny, cracked porcelain sink. Her hair was down a little, a bead of perspiration on her forehead. She ran the cold water onto a washcloth, wrung it out, and pressed it against her feverish forehead.

> You love me so much, tell me softly,
> just ''Yes'' or ''No'' . . .
> is he alive?

Waiting was easier than saying good-bye, she thought. She wanted to return to that luxury, that of waiting, but it was no longer possible. Her medical tests lent testimony to that. Time was no longer hers to spend; she had squandered her life. *What waste, what waste we're guilty of! What ragged edge of our personal universe do we approach when! At the very end we see what has been! Yet what could have been?* She remembered the lines, but not the Russian poet.

> It is all over for me now!
> All is finished! Ah!

Anna looked deeply into her own eyes as she listened to the end of *Madama Butterfly* from the living room stereo. *Be brave*, Butterfly's maid, Suzuki, sings.

> They want to take everything from me!

She left the bathroom in a rush, the music swelling again, her heart suddenly racing. *Make the sacrifice*, Sharpless, the American consul, was singing as she switched the stereo off. ''No!'' she gasped. She would not let herself sink to the level of Butterfly, so in love, so heartbroken that she'd been asked to give up everything that was dear to her—in Butterfly's case it was her son, in Anna's her family—that she would commit suicide as the only honorable way out. *With honor dies he who cannot live honorably*, Butterfly sings nearly at the end. Anna knew the words by heart. She'd listened to them over and over again, lived them each time in her heart of hearts. No ballet, even for her, came so close to such personal tragedy. Ballet was fantasy; for her, opera was real. "Oh, Jason," she cried, her heart breaking.

She was late leaving her apartment. It was after three o'clock, and by now it was snowing quite hard. Traffic was slowed because of the slippery roads. She'd decided to walk instead of calling for a theater car, something she'd been doing a lot of lately. It seemed to give her the time on the way to the theater to don her mask of ease and contentment, concealing her real feelings. And on the way home from the theater it gave her time to come down, to relax, to reach inside of herself to some inner flame that needed nurturing after having glowed so brightly for so long.

Cloth Cap passed her in a dark gray Zhiguli two blocks from her apartment. She was so startled by his sudden appearance after an absence of two days or so, that she stopped like a fool in mid-stride, her mouth hanging open. Passersby looked back at her, wondering if something might be wrong. She barely noticed them. Turning, she looked back the way she had come. Fur Hat was barely ten paces behind her. He too had stopped, and people surged around him as if he were an immovable boulder in the middle of a broad fast-moving stream. The falling snow blurred his features, but she could see his cruel eyes. They seemed to have a terrible life of their own, evil, with a deadly intent.

The light changed. She turned and hurried across the street, slipping and nearly falling twice. The clean new snow covered the dirty, salt-melted slush. Snow stuck to the windows of a shop that was closed. Anna could see one mannequin inside the window, but the rest of the shop was in darkness. She'd bought something there once, but for the life of her she could not remember what it was, or why it had come to mind at that moment. Perhaps it was a scarf. In the next block she looked back. She could no longer see Fur Hat, but she knew that he was back there. She could practically feel his dirty eyes on her back, boring into her skull, undressing her, seeing her secrets. He knew, for instance, about her illness, just as he knew about Jason and about the American who had come to see her twice. She scanned the passing traffic, looking for the gray Zhiguli to make another pass, but she also searched the face of each driver. She would not put it past Cloth Cap to suddenly come up with another vehicle. He was as cunning as his partner was cruel. She was sure of it. But there was no sign of him now either.

A militia officer was suddenly in front of her. "Is anything the matter, madame?" he asked politely.

Yes, everything, Anna wanted to scream. But she stepped back and shook her head. "No," she said. "No, thank you. I thought I saw someone I knew, you see." She half turned her head. "Back there. In the crowd."

"Was this person bothering you?"

A few people had stopped to watch and listen. An old babushka was clucking her tongue. Russians were busybodies, but they liked to help.

"No, of course not," Anna said. "I must get to the theater now. I am late."

"Can't you see she will be late?" someone called from the gathering crowd. "Let her be."

The militia officer ignored them. "If you are certain, then, that there is nothing I can do to help . . . ?"

"Nothing. Nothing, thank you," Anna muttered.

The militia officer touched his hat and stepped aside to let her pass. The small group parted for her. "If you are late, explain it to them. They will understand," the old grandmother said. Anna nodded, then lowered her head and raced down the street the last couple of blocks to the Bolshoi, her heart hammering so hard her side was aching by the time she arrived.

And still it was the same afternoon, though it was nearly dark now.

Horn was being followed. There were two of them. He'd picked them out a couple of blocks from Anna's apartment, and he had led them on a merry chase for a half hour around Moscow's inner ring section before he finally shook them. He stood just across the street from his hotel now, in front of Detsky Mir, Moscow's largest children's department store. KGB headquarters, known as the Center, was just around the corner in the Lubyanka prison. There were uniformed officers seemingly everywhere downtown. He had gotten the impression that it was his own people following him. Something about the tradecraft—the way they worked in pairs, one by car, the other on foot, sometimes switching—was reminiscent of what they'd been taught at the Farm. He thought he might even have seen Pfeiffer in the same embassy staff Chevrolet from the first time at the airport, but he had caught no more than a glimpse of the car and driver as it turned the corner by the Moscow City Soviet Building. Horn had dropped back around the corner onto Gor'kogo Street, expecting Pfeiffer to be coming back around the block, but the Chevy was nowhere in sight. Nor had he recognized any other cars or vans. The two legmen behind him had dropped out of sight by then too, and he had returned to his hotel to repack and get some rest. Minutes ago he had ducked out the back way, crossed the street at the end of the block, and had entered Detsky Mir from a side entrance, following the crowd out the front doors, then sidling off to one side, away from the lights. He'd felt spooked upstairs. And he'd been right. Someone was there, watching, parked in a gray Zhiguli sedan just behind the cab rank in front of the hotel. He was alone. Horn thought he might recognize the man as one of the legmen from earlier that afternoon. He was husky, but his face was impossible to see because of a dark cloth workman's cap pulled low over his eyes. The plates were not American consular, but that didn't mean much, and they were not a KGB series he recognized. Gloria Townsend told him that two new people had come with her to the square. Jason's people. They'd probably watched Anna's apartment until he showed up. Either he had lost them, as he thought he had, or they had some way of tracing incoming Americans to Moscow hotels, possibly through passport control. It was likely they had someone in KGB who passed on the information. This was Jason's city. And he'd have the unwitting cooperation now of Early and Pfeiffer.

The light changed at the corner. Horn stepped away from the building and hurried with the crowd across the street, keeping his eye on the man wearing the cloth cap in the Zhiguli. The man had hunched down in his seat and had laid his head back, evidently preparing for a long vigil. But they hadn't posted anyone in back. They'd been smug enough to think they hadn't been spotted. One man outside, and possibly one man in the lobby would suffice. They thought he was still upstairs in his room. They wouldn't move until they saw differently. They'd want to take him out in the open when the odds were more with them. A simple snatch and run operation, possibly, or more likely a straight hit. No one wanted to corner him, not after what had happened in Helsinki and in East Berlin. They'd be wary, but they'd also be trigger-happy. The book called the situation "unstable."

He walked back down to the broad Marx Prospekt, which was connected to Dzerzhinskogo Street at one end and Sverdlov Square at the other. A truck rumbled past, spreading salt and sand. Traffic flowed unconcernedly around it. The snow was coming down very heavily now. By midnight, he figured, the city would slow down. By morning, if it kept up, only essential traffic would be moving along the cleared snow emergency routes.

Come back to me, Jack, Christine had said. *This time really come back to me.* He'd been drifting over the past year or so, hadn't he?

She would be in New York with her father by now, he thought. Jason wouldn't dare try anything against her, and certainly he wouldn't try anything against them unless he could first communicate his intent. A trade, Horn. You, for the lives of your wife and children.

He and Doxy had discussed the concept at length one evening ten thousand years ago, the involvement of a man's family. Doxy had been one of Wallace Mahoney's students in the old days; he'd made a career out of it there for a while, he'd admitted. "The man was the very best, bar none," he said. "His wife is dead, his children and even his grandchildren were killed because of the business. Only his son John was left in the end."

The notion wasn't unknown.

If the prize was great enough, who wouldn't use it?

Not me, Doxy. I have honor.

Bullshit. When your back is against the wall, Jacko, you'll use the bloody hydrogen bomb on the nunnery, and don't kid yourself.

They are innocents.

No one is innocent: the terrorist's bible.

The Intourist Hotel stood on the corner of Gor'kogo Street and Revolution Square, where the Central Exhibition Hall and Alexandr Gardens were located. It was barely four o'clock and he had time: too much time now, too little tonight. He went into the basement bar and ordered vodka and a plate of *pirozhki,* caviar, hard-boiled eggs, cheese and bread. The place was already filling up, but it was not as busy as it would be later in the evening. Russians loved late-night dinners and outings. At midnight the hotel's various private clubs and bars would be packed. He sat by himself at the end of one of the long tables. A group of young American women sat at the other end with their Intourist guide. They were singing songs, first an American country and western tune, and then a Russian folk ballad. They seemed to be having fun. Horn envied them their uncomplicated lives. Another group came in a half hour later and took up an entire section of the bar. Evidently they had just come in from the airport and their rooms were not yet ready, so they had to wait there. There was some good-natured grumbling, but no one really seemed to mind. They didn't want to offend their guide, a young, pretty girl in a blue skirt, white blouse, and red scarf beneath her coat. Horn smiled at her when their eyes met, and she shrugged, thinking that he was somebody from the hotel.

He left, finally, at five, hunching up his coat collar as he stepped outside into the blowing snow. The wind had come up a little since he'd gone inside, though the temperature had not yet started to seriously drop. It was all a game, wasn't it, he told himself as he headed back up toward Sverdlov Square past the ornate Council of Ministers Building, and beyond it the lights of the Bolshoi. Sometimes, like now, the timing got a bit tight, and there came a point where there was no longer any room for error, but it would all work out in the end. He'd been on other field assignments. Only never before had the enemy included some of his own. He was having a difficult time dealing with it. Take a cab back to the embassy. Tell them everything. Carlisle would know what to do. They'd ferret out Jason, they'd stop him. Wouldn't they?

If anything, traffic was heavier now; most of the offices had apparently let out early because of the snowfall. It was the start of the weekend, and the city seemed to have taken on a gay, holiday mood. This was the second major snowfall in less than a week, and Muscovites were making the best of it. Horn thought they would have to get to the train clean. If they could do that, that one simple act, everything else might fall into place for them. But the variables over the next few hours were ominous. He wanted to call Christine, to hear her voice, to make sure that everything was all right. He wanted to call Doxy to make sure his old friend was safe. But not this time. He was on his own this time.

The gray Zhiguli was still parked behind the cab rank when Horn got back. He could just see the back of the man's head, the cloth cap still pulled low. He passed the car in a rush, keeping his eyes straight ahead, and entered the hotel. Crossing the broad lobby to the elevators he did a quick scan of the

people. The hotel was putting on a buffet for someone. A
knot of people were gathered to one side around a bar and a
long table loaded with hors d'oeuvres. Moscow hotels had
picked up the custom from American businessmen and diplomats traveling and working here. In the elevator he turned
and looked out across the lobby. As the doors started to close
the driver of the Zhiguli came up to a man wearing a fur hat.
They looked directly at Horn, and then the elevator doors
closed.

They were the same ones who'd followed him from Anna's
apartment; he was sure of it because of the hats. They were
being stupid about it, of course, and they didn't even know it.
Right now they'd be wondering what the hell happened. They
thought he'd been in his room all along. Amateurs, he wondered, or just overly cautious? The next few hours would tell,
providing he could keep them off-balance.

Upstairs he hurried to his room, let himself in, then chained
and locked the door. They wanted him, but first they'd want
to know what he was up to. The setup was perfect. Made to
order. Sometimes they fell into place like that, he told himself
as he finished packing his single bag. He picked up the
telephone and called the front desk.

"This is Hammer in Eight-oh-seven. I'm checking out.
Please have my bill ready for me."

"Of course, sir. Is something wrong?"

"No," Horn said. "Everything is fine." He hung up.

The only danger would be for Sheshkin, but they both
understood that a clear and present danger for him already
existed. All of Horn's old madmen, except for Yevgenni,
were dead. Someone had gone after them. KGB? It didn't
make much sense. If the KGB had wanted to put the screws
to an old network, they'd simply arrest the principals, not
arrange accidental deaths. It was Jason. It had to be Jason all
along. He was insane. Yevgenni's only chance was for Horn
to break the man by taking Anna to him. Yevgenni would
have to survive on his own, somehow, until then.

At the door Horn hesitated for just a moment. Once he
walked out of this hotel the chase would be on. There would
be no way of stopping it even if he wanted to. And someone
would get hurt. There would be no way around that, either.
For what, dammit? Why? What the hell had the man tried to
hide all of these years? It made him sick to think about it.

The corridor was empty. The elevator was stopped on the

fifteenth floor. Horn stepped out of his room, his leather bag over his left shoulder. A few feet from the elevator he glanced left into the floor maid's room. The smaller man with the fur hat stood just inside. Their eyes met, and Horn deliberately put his right hand in his coat pocket, his fingers curling around the grip of the Walther. The gesture had not been lost on the man, who stiffened slightly and stepped back as if to say, Not here, Horn. Not here and not like this.

Carefully, Horn turned away and walked to the elevator where he pressed the button. He turned and looked over his shoulder. The man had come to the doorway and was looking impassively at him. He wore a dark overcoat with a matching fur collar. But his coat was buttoned. Unless he too carried a gun in his coat pocket, he was at the disadvantage.

The elevator doors slid open, and Horn stepped aboard the car. "Are you going down?" he asked the man in English.

The man hesitated for just a moment, but then he nodded and joined Horn.

"Lobby?" Horn asked pleasantly. He pushed the button and the door closed.

The man nodded but said nothing. He looked up at the floor indicator as they started down. Horn stood to his left and slightly behind him. He'd wanted the man to speak; he'd wanted to hear him saying something. As it was, there was no clear indication of his nationality. American, Horn thought from the cut of his clothes, but he couldn't be sure.

"It looks as if it will snow all night," Horn said in Russian.

The man in the fur hat didn't say a thing, nor did he turn around.

"But it is the weekend, so no one really cares, don't you agree?" Horn asked.

At the lobby the doors slid open and the man stepped off first, glanced back at Horn, then walked away. Horn watched him cross the lobby. He stopped near the doors, turned, and looked directly over at Horn. We've gotten this far together, he was saying. You have your bag, now let's see what comes next. I am a patient man.

Horn went to the desk where his bill was waiting, paid with West German marks, then turned and strode across to where the man in the fur hat stood, passed him, and stepped outside. The man's colleague was waiting behind the wheel of the gray Zhiguli. This time he had the engine running, the wind-

shield wipers flapping. It was dark now, and the snow was
falling even harder than before. It was going to be difficult
for them to keep up with him, and they knew it.

Without bothering to look back—he knew the man would
be directly behind him, which is where he wanted him for the
next hour—Horn hurried to the corner, crossed with the light,
and walked past Detsky Mir to the Metro entrance on Marx
Prospekt. The streets were filled with people now. Downstairs the Metro station was crowded. Horn waited out in the
open in clear view for his train to come. When it pulled in, he
stepped aboard, chancing a quick glance over his shoulder.
Fur Hat was getting on too, but the other one was nowhere in
sight. He'd probably stayed with the car, which meant they
would have some means of communication with each other.
Useless underground, of course, but once they went topside
again by the Warsaw Hotel, just down the block from
Sheshkin's apartment, Fur Hat could call his partner. The
new field transmitters were small and very powerful, easily
spanning the city if there weren't many obstructions between
the sending and the receiving sets. Horn had used them all over
Berlin with success.

He had to transfer at Novokuznetskaya, and Fur Hat stayed
right with him, the train crowded enough so that both of them
had to stand.

It was nearly six by the time Horn emerged from the Metro
station on the corner up from the Warsaw. Oktyabr'skaya
Square was alive with people and traffic. Two big Intourist
buses were parked in front of the hotel. It looked as if
something big were happening there. I'm sorry, Yevgenni, he
said to himself as he started across the square to Zhitnaya
Street. I'm leading them to you, and for that I am sorry, but
these are the rules of this particular nasty little exercise. I
didn't invent them, and now there is nothing else I can
possibly do. In any event, Jason would have come after you
sooner or later. What sort of hate would have come into
Tatiana's eyes after that was anyone's guess, but he figured
she had a lot of it stored up for some reason. Many Russians
did.

A snowplow rushed noisily by as Horn reached Sheshkin's
building and went in. He thought he saw Fur Hat across the
street, but in the blowing snow and darkness he couldn't be
sure. He rang the bell, and Sheshkin, dressed for the out-

doors, came immediately. His wife said something from inside the apartment, but Sheshkin closed the door and hurried down the stairs. He unlocked the gate and came through, relocking it.

"The papers were not so easy, but I got them," he said breathlessly.

"Do you need more money?" Horn asked. They were keeping their voices low.

"For the truck, no. I got you a paneled van. It could make it to Helsinki, I think. Insurance papers, everything are with it." He took a small bundle of documents out of his pocket, one of them a Soviet foreign travel passport, and handed it to Horn. "For these I will need an additional one thousand marks. I am sorry, Jack."

Horn opened the passport. It seemed genuine. The photograph was not a good one, however. It showed a dark-haired woman who was heavier than Anna, and not nearly as pretty. But the resemblance was close enough, he thought, for Anna to cross any border, providing no one was actively searching for her just then. The name was Nadesha Neznayeva. She was forty-five, had been born in Kiev, and lived now in Moscow.

"It is the best I could do on such short notice, Jack," Sheshkin said. He was nervous.

"This woman is not a dissident? The KGB is not looking for her?"

Sheshkin was pained. "Jack, please, I would not do this to you. Believe me. The passport is legitimate. It will pass all the tests."

"It'll be fine," Horn said softly.

"Of course it will. The connections I have now are all legitimate. All on the up and up. But I must warn you that these papers will only hold up for a few days. Maybe longer, but there is no guarantee."

Horn dug out a thousand marks and handed it over. Sheshkin immediately pocketed the money.

"The van is not far from here. I will take you to it. There is enough gas to get you only halfway to Leningrad, but that is a moot point, isn't it? The van is good only for two or three days, like the papers. After that it will not be safe. That was the deal, wasn't it, Jack? You aren't going to run off with it?"

"I won't move it," Horn promised. "But I don't want you

coming with me. Give me the keys and tell me where it is parked. I'll leave the keys in the ashtray.''

Sheshkin wanted to believe him. Horn could see it in his eyes. At least that much had not changed in the past ten or fifteen years. But his old madman had a wife now, a responsible position that even allowed him foreign travel now and then, and privileges at GUM that were denied the average Russian. That was all in jeopardy now.

"You have to trust me, Yevgenni," Horn said.

Sheshkin suddenly glanced toward the street door. "There is someone out there. Is that it, Jack? Have you been followed?"

Horn nodded when Sheshkin turned back to him. He held out his hand for the key.

"Goddamnit, Jack, what have you done to me?"

"Nothing, if you keep your head. Stay clean. Go to work, come home, go to sleep, have friends over. Do nothing out of the ordinary. You will be all right."

"And if the KGB comes in the middle of the night with their . . . methods?" He was afraid to say arrest or drugs or torture.

"Then tell them that Boyko was a friend, and that I came here and blackmailed you. Give them that. It is a CIA plot against the *rodina*."

Sheshkin looked up the stairs in real fear now for what he could lose. The walls all over Moscow had ears. It was the baseline assumption.

"The keys, Yevgenni, and you'll never see me again."

"That's what I'm afraid of, Jack. Truly. Maybe I'll never see anything again." He dug a single key on a crude wire fob out of his pocket and handed it over.

"Where is it?"

"Zatsepa. Just a few blocks from here. South of Valovaya. A small brick shed. One window is stuffed with cardboard in back of a bakery. There will be no one there now. The mother has died, and the family has closed the bakery for a few days until the funeral in Gorki."

Horn managed to produce a smile. "Thank you, Yevgenni."

"Don't come back, Jack. In all honesty now, you will not be welcome here any longer. Not by me, not by . . . anyone. It is becoming too expensive to know you." Sheshkin was pessimistic and frightened because of it. "I hope it is worth the trouble, this woman. I sincerely do."

• • •

The real clock had started now, Horn thought as he emerged from Sheshkin's building. He didn't know if he could shake Fur Hat before Cloth Cap in the Zhiguli showed up. Nor did he know if Anna would show up at the train station. And after that the future was an even more amorphous gray mass with dangers hidden in the uncertain fog. He turned left on Zhitnaya and hurried up to Dobryninskaya Square where he crossed the street past the Metro station and continued to where the main boulevard changed to Valovaya. This was part of one of Moscow's ring roads. In a few blocks it would change again to Zatsepskiy as it turned north, and then to Krasnokholmskaya before crossing the river. A dozen street maps of Moscow showed a dozen subtle variations on street names. There were so many heroes of the Soviet Union that there weren't nearly enough streets, avenues, and squares to accommodate them. In three blocks a street could change names three times, yet so many of the smaller back streets and lanes were given the same names, distinguished from each other only by numbers as *pereuloks*. Zatsepa, a couple of blocks from Sheshkin's apartment, was still another variation. Its name was nothing more than a shortened version of the main avenue, several blocks away and not connected. For a foreigner, Moscow could be very confusing.

Horn had no trouble finding the shed. Inside was a dark brown windowless van in reasonably good condition. The garage smelled of age and decay despite the cold temperatures. One corner was filled with a jumble of old sheet metal, wire, and some cardboard. There was no light.

He watched through a hole in the cardboard that covered the single window for a few minutes until Fur Hat showed up, poking his nose cautiously around the corner of the building that housed the bakery. The windows upstairs were dark. Horn could see the vague outline, through the snow, of another building about a hundred yards away. It looked almost like a factory, with rows of dormers and something that might have been a crane rising above it. The bakery building seemed to lean into the wind forlornly, as if it were making a concerted effort not to fall down. Fur Hat would be waiting desperately for his partner to show up, but it was a long drive across the river from downtown, especially in this weather and the evening traffic.

Turning back, Horn took off his gloves, set his bag down,

and went to the driver's side of the van. He touched the door and the window, and then opened the door, purposely making sure he was getting his fingerprints over everything. He got behind the wheel and started the engine. It roared to life immediately. He let it run for a full thirty seconds, then shut it off. Leaving the key in the ashtray, he got out and went back to the window. Fur Hat was still there. Horn could just make out the dim outline of his figure through the dark, blowing snow. He picked up his bag, shouldered it, and then made a production out of opening the main door, acting as if it were frozen on its hinges, giving Fur Hat plenty of time to get out of sight. Then he walked back up to Valovaya without looking back, his head low into the wind, his collar up.

Fur Hat now had a difficult problem. He could follow Horn, to see what happened next, or he could remain on stakeout at the shed until his reinforcements came. He had to have heard the engine. Horn was planning on making his escape by road. *He didn't leave his bag, I saw it on his shoulder, but I thought the van would be the most important consideration under the circumstances. It was his escape.*

The Metro entrance stood on the corner next to the Moskovsko-Leninskiy department store. Horn passed just beyond the overhead lights, and in the shadows he stopped and looked back. The sidewalk was empty of all but a few pedestrians braving the horrible weather, though traffic was still quite heavy. There was no sign of Fur Hat. He'd apparently opted to remain at the shed, expecting that sooner or later Horn would have to return to it. Thank you, he thought, charging back to the Metro entrance and ducking down the stairs. In evaluating two possibilities, the fieldman must always use his imagination and intuition. Lines directly out of the bloody book. Fur Hat hadn't the good sense to change his hat, let alone realize he'd been diddled.

It was time now, Horn thought, to get the hell out of Moscow.

21

At a few minutes before seven-thirty, Kiev Station was alive with a sea of humanity speaking a dozen different languages, dressed in a dozen different regional costumes, and smelling of a dozen different combinations of odors. Four merchant marine sailors sat on the floor near a stand selling kvas, tea, and beer. Two of them played a fierce game of chess, the other two plus a small knot of bystanders noisily kibitzing. They passed around a bottle of vodka. All of them were quite drunk. Entire families from grandmothers down to infants in arms waited for the nine o'clock train. In the Soviet Union all trains departed exactly on time, but already an hour and a half before departure an excited hum rose to the ornately frescoed ceilings. A lot of passengers carried baskets of food, bottles of tea, and of course vodka. The food on most Soviet trains was usually quite good, but it was expensive. It was much cheaper to bring your own, supplementing it at the stops where depot vendors would come out to sell everything from cigarettes to meat pastries, wine, vodka, and sometimes even sausages. A samovar was kept going by the porters in each car.

Using the passport Sheshkin had supplied him in the name of Neznayeva, as well as his own in the name of Hammer, he'd purchased two first-class round-trip tickets to Odessa, first class known in the Soviet Union as "soft class" because they would be given their own private compartment with pull-down beds and a private washroom, just like on Western

trains. They were scheduled to return next week. It was a
vacation. More smoke screen. In the first search they'd be
looking mainly for the one-ways out of the city. The round
trips would come under scrutiny later. Every hour would
help.

But Anna had not come.

Horn had waited by the front doors on the main square
until quarter after eight, then thinking it possible she may
have arrived early and was looking for him at the trackside
gates, he'd made a rapid but thorough search of the entire
terminal. She had not come. She was not here. And to have
her paged would create far too much attention.

He could go alone, of course. He'd worked Odessa when
he'd been stationed in Moscow, and he'd seen the entire
European and Near Eastern reports on a daily basis. There
were ways to leave Odessa by boat to Istanbul. West German
marks were a powerful persuader. Hard Western currencies
could buy a lot of cargo in Istanbul that could be sold back
home for huge profits. A little risk added spice.

Jason would know that too, though, he kept telling himself.
Jason had been a step ahead of him all the way. The van on
Zatsepa Street wouldn't hold up for very long. Perhaps they'd
already gone to Sheshkin and taken him apart. Horn had seen
the look in his old madman's eyes; it wouldn't take much to
defeat him. A gun at Tatiana's head, for instance. They'd not
only have the van, but they'd have the Neznayev passport as
well which would lead directly back to Anna. Always it led
back to Anna. Poor little artistic Anna who'd fallen for an
American . . . what? Spy? Diplomat? Politician? Business-
man? What or who had Jason been? What are you, Jason?
Horn asked silently as he scanned the faces of the passengers
coming by taxi, or on foot out of the snow. Huge halos
glowed around the lights. The square looked like a lavish
stage production about Father Frost. Who are you? What in
God's name do you have to hide after all these years?

If they broke Sheshkin, they'd go to Anna. Even if they
didn't go after Sheshkin, they still might figure on watching
Anna. They'd done it before. Maybe Early was crazy enough
to try it.

Horn glanced at his wristwatch one last time, then made his
decision. He had come too far to turn around now and leave
empty-handed. Jason would track him down eventually and
eliminate him as he had the others. There would be no way to

fight back. There were no weapons other than Anna. Without
her he had no hope.

He left the station and caught a departing cab that had just
brought in an elderly couple. He ordered the driver to take
him posthaste to the Budapest Hotel, which was just around
the corner from Anna's apartment. Most likely she would be
at the theater. She said she wouldn't be coming tonight. But
what would he say to her if she was at her apartment and still
unwilling to leave with him? Please let it be that simple, he
told himself. Don't let Anna become another Boyko or Nobels or Clay or Doxmeuller. Not after all this, not after all she
had endured.

They came up Arbat, past Clay's house, dark now like a
tomb, and beyond the Praga restaurant they turned up the
center ring boulevard that led around the Rossiya Cinema and
the square where he'd picked up Gloria Townsend that afternoon. They had to stop twice to allow snowplows working
four abreast to clear intersections, once at Kachalova and the
second time at the entrance to Pushkinskaya Square. They
drove around a long line waiting in front of the cinema.
Though it was snowing heavily, the weather was quite warm
now and the crowd seemed good-natured. Maybe he was late;
maybe he was charging into a trap, he thought. He could
think of at least two: one set by Jason and his fieldmen, and
the other set by Anna's uncle, General Patrenko. The consequences of either would be fatal.

Turning the corner at Petrovka, they passed the Algerian
embassy down a narrow street that angled back to the ring,
and three blocks later turned the corner and pulled up in front
of the Budapest Hotel. Horn paid the red-faced driver, who
had evidently been drinking vodka all day, and went into the
hotel. He waited just inside the lobby until the cab left, then
he stepped back outside and hurried up the street to Neglinnaya,
acutely conscious that he was running out of time.

The street was deserted. Horn crossed in the middle of the
block, and at the corner of Neglin 2, he forced himself to
slow down, to wait in the shadows as he tried to penetrate the
snow and darkness into the windows of the facing buildings,
to the rooftops, and through the dark glass of the few cars still
parked on the narrow side street already half buried in the
new snowfall. But there was no movement. Nothing out of the
ordinary. No fresh tracks in the snow. No cars or trucks with
too many aerials. No dark limousines.

There was a light in Anna's window. It was snowing harder here for some reason, and his purpose suddenly seemed remote. He couldn't envision himself dragging a screaming Anna out of her apartment and across town to the train station. Their escape would demand her full cooperation. But why take the risk? He had asked himself that question dozens of times. Then he thought about Clay and the others, and especially about Doxy, and he went across.

Directly across from her apartment, he stopped in mid-stride as he saw shadows pass her window. There had been two figures. One much larger than the other. Anna, and who else? Horn backed into the darkness of a doorway. Someone was up there with her. Her uncle? The general was a large man. Would he have traveled incognito, without his car and driver? Or had Jason finally sent his people there to finish what he had begun a dozen years ago—Anna's destruction?

But there was no time left. Not now. Horn took out his gun, hurried across the street, and let himself in. He closed the door softly and listened. From somewhere he could hear music, and someone talking and laughing. Normalcy. His heart was hammering.

Then he heard the sounds of a scuffle from upstairs. He took a step forward, cocking his head to listen. A woman cried out, the noise brief and very sharp as if someone had clamped a hand over her mouth. The music suddenly stopped.

"Christ," Horn swore. He raced up the stairs, his overnight bag banging against his side until he reached the third-floor landing that opened to the right onto the corridor, where he pulled up short.

The building was quiet now, suddenly too quiet. Light spilled from beneath Anna's door. His hand was sweaty on the Walther's grip. His breath was ragged.

Horn approached her door, dropping his overnight bag behind him.

"Where is he?" a man said from within her apartment, his voice soft but distinct. He was a Russian.

"I don't know!" Anna cried out. "I don't—"

"Keep your voice down, bitch, or I'll cut out your eyes. Where is he?"

Horn's hand was shaking as he switched off the Walther's safety and tried the doorknob. It gave. They hadn't locked the door. A mistake, or a trap? How many were inside? Just the one. Another? He gently pushed at the door, easing it carefully past its latch, then, taking a deep breath, he suddenly shoved it the rest of the way open.

Anna was sprawled on the couch, a large man in a cloth workman's cap standing over her, a knife in his right hand in front of her face. Horn recognized him as the one who'd followed him, the one who'd driven the gray Zhiguli. Anna's blouse was torn, her skirt was hiked up around her narrow hips, and blood trickled from her nose. A rage rose up unbidden in him. His slaughtered madmen, Nobels's last hoarse cry, Doxy's final warning, the look on Christine's face when she'd gotten into the cab against her will and left, the attempt on his life in Helsinki, the death and mindless destruction in his East Berlin safe house, everything he'd done for the Company and for his country over the past twenty years, and all that he had given up—the church, a normal home life, even Christ—it all came to him in a piece, along with Jason's mad arrogance and Anna's plight.

"Here I am, you son of a bitch!" Horn snapped in perfect Russian.

Cloth Cap looked up over his shoulder, his eyes growing wide. "Fuck your mother," he swore.

"Put down the knife," Horn said, raising the pistol and cocking the hammer.

The Russian flinched with the noise of it in the quiet apartment. Then his eyes narrowed. "You won't get out of here, Horn. No way. We know about the van."

"Who sent you? Was it Jason?"

Anna tried to shrink back, but the Russian's left hand was clamped on her bare shoulder, the point of the knife still hovering just above her face.

"Put down the gun and the girl might live."

There was no time now. Their only escape was the train, and only if they could get to it cleanly. Where was the one in the fur hat? Downstairs? Waiting outside?

Someone was below the stairs. "Anna?" a woman called out.

The Russian's eyes flicked toward the corridor at the same moment Anna kicked out, shoving him off-balance. Horn fired, catching the man high in the right shoulder, spinning him away from Anna, sending him stumbling over a lamp table with a loud grunt of pain and rage, the noise of the gun shockingly loud in the narrow confines of the apartment.

The woman below in the hallway screamed.

"You stupid bastard!" the Russian shouted, clawing in his coat for his gun.

Horn took one step into the apartment and fired a second shot, this one hitting the Russian in the chest, just to the left of the line of buttons on his coat. A big geyser of blood shot up, the man's legs crumpled, and he fell back on the carpeted floor, dead.

"Oh, God!" Anna cried.

People were shouting downstairs. A door slammed.

Horn reached Anna in three steps, hauling her off the couch onto her feet. "We have to go, Anna! Now!"

She looked up into his eyes. For just a moment she seemed incapable of speech.

"Anna!" He shook her.

"In the bedroom. My suitcase."

Horn led her around the body and into her bedroom. A cheap cardboard suitcase lay open on her narrow bed. It was filled with her things. She *had* come home to pack. She had changed her mind.

His instinct was to turn and run as fast as he could go, get away before Fur Hat arrived, before the militia was summoned, before the KGB was notified and General Patrenko pulled out all the stops. The city would be sealed as only cities behind the Iron Curtain can be sealed. There would be no train for them to Odessa, no van to Helsinki, nothing but Lubyanka and death. Defeat. Better men than he had gone down in tamer circumstances.

Horn closed the suitcase and did the clasps. He helped her on with her coat and hat and boots, then took the suitcase and led her back through the living room, past the dead man, and out into the corridor. The building was ominously quiet now.

"Are we going to Jason?" Anna asked, her voice small.

In the distance Horn could hear the first of the sirens. Someone had already called the militia. They had truly run out of time.

Horn grabbed his bag and they started down the stairs. Then Anna heard the sirens.

"What is it?" she cried, holding back.

"Is there another way out of here?" Horn demanded. He wasn't going to get cornered here. Not like this, not now.

"It's the militia!" she said.

Horn shook her roughly. "You must help me, Anna! Can we get out another way?"

"Jason?" she whimpered.

"Anna!"

She blinked. "Yes," she stammered. "From the basement. In the back, there is a courtyard."

They hurried the rest of the way downstairs. The sirens were much closer now. There were a lot of them. He figured they were just around the corner. Anna led him through the back corridor to a narrow door that opened on rickety stairs into the dark basement. At the bottom they were in complete darkness, but Anna seemed to know her way. She took his arm and led him around what felt like piles of boxes and crates.

The first police car pulled up out front. They could hear the car doors slam, and then someone was at the front door, booted feet in the corridor and on the stairs. Someone was shouting something.

"This way," Anna said softly in the darkness.

They stumbled up a short flight of stairs, and then Anna was pulling open a steel door and they were outside in a dark narrow courtyard that was piled with snow-covered trash. Horn carefully closed the door, and together they crossed the courtyard, slipped between two buildings, and came out on Neglin 3.

There were even more sirens converging than before. Horn started right, back toward Neglinnaya, but Anna stopped him.

"We won't find a cab that way, I don't think. Not tonight. And the Sverdlova Metro station is too far."

"I don't have a car."

"We can take the Metro at Dzerzhin'kogo. They won't think to look there."

Moscow was her city. It hadn't been an act upstairs. She'd not been part of the setup. "I have our tickets."

"How much time do we have?"

Horn didn't bother looking at his watch. "Not much," he said. At the corner of Zhdanova Horn glanced back and thought he saw someone on foot passing beneath the street-light. But then the shadow was gone.

"What is it?" Anna asked, stopping.

"Nothing," Horn said, catching up with her. They continued the rest of the way down to Dzerzhinskiy Square in silence, passing the Berlin Hotel again, and around the corner from Detsky Mir, lights everywhere, traffic heavy in the snow, they entered the Metro station. Before they disappeared below, Anna took a long, last look at the Bolshoi Theater on the far side of the square, and Horn thought she shrank a little inside her coat; her shoulders seemed to settle, her head bowed, and it seemed as if her illness had suddenly flared up within her.

All the way across town, Horn got the feeling that they were being watched. But there weren't many people on the Metro that evening, so it would have been difficult if not impossible for a legman, even a good one, to hide himself. Their car held ordinary Russians: grandmothers, soldiers drinking, a few bureaucrats going home late from their offices, two whores from the square probably going to the train station to try their luck.

Anna had become withdrawn. They had to transfer at the Lenin Library station beneath the Alexandr Gardens, but she didn't say much. They had a two-minute wait. Horn led her down the long, vaulted, trackside platform, and at the end he suddenly turned back. No one stopped abruptly behind them. No one looked away. No one was following them. Yet the feeling that they were being tailed would not go away. Several times he reached into his pocket to feel the Walther's grip, though it wasn't as comforting a feeling as before. He might have felt foolish about it, but not after what had happened in East Berlin and in Anna's apartment.

Their train came and they stepped into the lead car, sitting directly across from the door. A half-dozen other people boarded their car and sat down. Above, it was night, the weather was terrible, cars and buses were slipping and sliding their way behind snowplows, and some along virgin streets, and parties were beginning. Below in the Metro it was perpetual twilight, always neat and orderly. A militia officer got aboard just before the doors closed. Anna stiffened next to Horn, and he shot her a warning glance. The militiaman was very young, and Horn thought he might be a little drunk. Obviously he was off duty, on his way home, perhaps. He gazed with open admiration at Anna, and scowled at Horn. A few minutes later he laid his head back and fell sound asleep. One of the old grandmothers clucked her tongue, and Anna sat back in the seat.

They stopped at the Kropotkinskaya station where a few more people got on. Horn watched their eyes. But they were no threat. More ordinary people homeward bound on a Friday night. Too poor to take a taxi, and perhaps too tired to really care. Still, Horn could not shake the feeling. He was spooked, as they said in the trade. Paranoia. An occupational hazard. Anna was holding his arm. Her grip tightened, and he looked down at her. "This is our stop coming up," she said softly.

"Are you all right?"

She looked into his eyes, and finally nodded. "I think so."

Their train stopped a few minutes later at the Kiev Station. They got off and Anna led them to the far end of the platform. There were two exits, she explained; one led up to the street, and the other led directly into the railway terminal above. They took the latter. There were more people here than downtown, most of them getting on the Metro. A train had probably just come into the station. They could hear the public address system as they neared the top. Horn shifted her bag to his right hand and looked at his watch. It was already quarter to nine. They had barely fifteen minutes to get to their train.

"Your name is Nadesha Neznayeva. Can you remember that?"

She said the name, and then nodded. "What about the photograph?"

"It's not very good. But it will do, I think."

"What if it doesn't?"

"Then we'll see, won't we," he said, a little more harshly than he intended. His adrenaline was pumping. It was an old Russian trick, a quirk of their nature, to let the escapee nearly make it before the KGB would swoop down for the arrest.

At the top he pulled her aside and gave her the passport. She opened it and looked at the photograph, wrinkling her nose. "If they arrest us, what will happen to you?" she asked.

"I don't know," Horn said. The station was very full now, and noisy. Everyone seemed to be in a hurry. "Are you ready, Anna?"

"Nadesha," she said. She managed to smile. They started across the broad concourse to the far side where stairs led back down to trackside. Horn had his passport and their tickets out as they reached the iron gate blocked by a half-dozen armed militiamen. Several other passengers were going through at the last minute. There seemed to be a sense of urgency, but the militiamen were taking their time. Soviet trains were never held. For anyone. But militiamen had their work to do too.

An older officer with a pockmarked face glanced at Horn's tickets and then at his passport. He handed them back and took Anna's. Horn didn't think he looked very carefully at the photograph, because he immediately closed the leatherette booklet and handed it back. He nodded toward the stairs.

"Be quick, then, or you will miss your train."

"Thank you, comrade," Horn said, and taking Anna's arm with his free hand, they hurried down the broad stairs.

Most of the cars on the long, silver train were already closed. Theirs was three behind the electric locomotive. An iron roof ended about a hundred yards down the track; a curtain of moving snow and darkness marked the edge. They had to show their tickets and passports again to another militiaman at the bottom. This one looked up sharply from Anna's photograph, his eyes narrowed. "This is not a very good likeness."

Anna shook her head and shrugged depreciatingly. "I am sorry, comrade."

The militiaman turned his gaze to Horn for a few seconds, but then he handed back their papers. "The train is about to leave. The next time come sooner. Have respect for the workers here who are not so fortunate as to take a holiday in the middle of winter."

There was no porter when they boarded, so they had to find their own compartment. Almost immediately the train began to pull out of the station. Horn locked their door, and Anna stood by the window, holding the curtain aside so that she could look at the station and the people sliding away from them. It was the end of Moscow for her, and it weighed heavily. He could see it in the way she held herself. This was just the very beginning. He wondered how she was going to hold up.

22

They had not brought any food. It was very late and the dining car was closed. There would be no meal until morning. Horn had gone out to try to find them something to eat while Anna cleaned up and got ready for bed. She sat cross-legged in the lower bunk staring out the window, though there wasn't much to be seen except for the slanting snow. Occasionally they'd pass a light off in the distance, and they had passed a few dimly lit villages, but most of Russia, she was discovering, was dark. The snow had not let up, and for some reason, though she had always loved snow in the past, tonight it made her morose. It was as if the snow were covering her life or, more accurately, covering the tracks she was making by running away from her life. Behind her was the Bolshoi, and her friends. Behind her was her Uncle Stepan and Auntie Raya and the others. Behind her too was her existence that had until this night been safe, comfortable, orderly, neat, with no surprises. Not even the announcement that she was dying had come as a complete surprise. Behind her was the body of a dead man in her apartment. She'd heard his pain and confusion that he was dying. She would hear that for the rest of her life; the picture of the blood erupting from his chest was seared indelibly in her brain. And ahead of her? The unknown. Jason, perhaps, but the unknown for all of it.

She knew something about the superficialities of the West, because Jason had told her about Washington and New York and California. Since then she'd watched for books and even magazines about the West, and she had talked backstage with foreign visitors. In the West there were more cars, more taxes, more crime, and except for China and India, more people. There was unemployment, inflation, illiteracy, and resentment, she'd been told, against a system that was exploitive. She'd been told about poor souls in the large cities—New York especially—who were called street people, who forever roamed the streets without an apartment, even a room, in winter as well as in summer, every single thing they owned carried with them in a paper bag or wire basket with wheels. She glanced at her suitcase. It was all she had now. But in the West were fashions and supermarkets, and television and movies, and places like Disneyland and warm winters—even warmer than Odessa. There was light. Unlimited travel. Consumer goods that would dazzle anyone's eye. And there was Jason.

Anna had done a lot of serious thinking about Jason over the past days. Even more thinking than she'd done in the past dozen years, and she wasn't all that certain any longer that she could really remember his face with any accuracy, or that even if she could, he hadn't changed beyond all recognition. Her fantasies were coming true, but all of a sudden she didn't know if she would be able to handle them.

A green light flashed past the window and Anna reared back, startled. A second later an explosion of station lights passed her window, and then there was darkness, which left her blinking. They'd passed another village. She was just a little surprised they had not stopped.

Life was a compromise, she'd been told. Her own, for instance. She'd been assured nice apartments, very good food, and the privilege of dancing onstage with the finest ballet company in the world. For that she had been required to give up any semblance of a normal life. She'd given up her parents, although perhaps her father had given her up beforehand, and she'd given up most chances at meeting boys other than dancers, ordinary boys from the university, say. She was allowed to shop at the foreign currency stores, but she was told what she would dance, how she would dance it, when she would dance, and where she would be allowed to perform. Her dancing partners were selected for her. She was free from any financial worry, however, but her life had been chosen for her, minute by minute, day by day. Sometimes she thought even her uncle had been in on the stifling conspiracy, though without him she didn't know how she would have possibly managed.

After she had written the letter, and had given it to Boyko for delivery, she had gone through a period in which she felt a great deal of guilt. She had betrayed her country. She was a traitor to the great *rodina*. She could hear Uncle Stepan's pained voice about how she had turned her back on the very state that had given her so very much: her dance, her friends, her privileges, in fact her life. She was glad that she would not be seeing her uncle's face when he found out. She would not be facing her Auntie Raya either. She didn't think she could.

Gradually, however, when she thought that there was little or no hope for her, she had come to remember something that Jason had once told her about the differences between the Soviet Union and the United States. In America, he'd told her, there is freedom of choice. In Russia all choice is made by the state. In America if something is not prohibited by the law—if an act is not mentioned specifically by law—then it is presumed to be legal. In Russia the opposite was true. It was every party boss's warning that the West was untamed, that without proper rule of law society runs amok. No one is safe on the streets, and choices become so bewildering that half the people in the United States are psychotic by the time they are twenty. But she believed Jason's explanation—that human beings were meant to choose. And remembering it, in small measure, had assuaged her guilt.

Then Jack had arrived, and the guilt had returned mixed with the faintest of hopes that it would be possible after all for her to see Jason. Only it made her sad. She didn't know if she would be able to fit in. Perhaps she *would* go insane. She was very much afraid of dying alone. At least in Moscow she would have had her family. But in America there was no one for her other than Jason. What if he rejected her? She could not go back. She would die alone, perhaps on the streets of New York City. Of course she would write letters to everyone back home. Tell them that all went well with her. Assure them so that they would not worry. In her mind she had already begun to compose exactly what it was she would say by way of explanation for her . . . *defection*. That's what it was. She wasn't a spy, but she was defecting: giving up her country in favor of another; giving up her life for one that would be totally alien; giving up her home ties for an uncertain love. What a fool she had been. Yet from the very first moment she'd laid eyes on Jason the choice had not been hers, all of his rhetoric to the contrary. She would be dead as far as her family was concerned, and after the funeral Uncle Stepan would try to comfort the others. "Chou-chou has gone to America to a lover she hasn't seen in more than twelve years," he would say, his eyes filling with tears, his massive Georgian head lowered. "We have lost her forever because there is no coming back." If only they had warned her. If only they had explained. "He is probably married, and has children. Oh, chou-chou, what do you think he will do with a poor little dying girl? Don't go. Please, just don't go."

Anna was no longer seeing the slanting snow, nor the occasional light outside the railroad car. Instead she was looking inward. She could not go back, of course, so she wanted to remember Jason as he had been so that she could imagine how he had become. In so doing she began to dredge up from her imperfect memory exactly how it had been between them during the eighteen months they had had together.

The dining car was five back from the engine, separating soft class from the rest of the train. A sleepy porter was just cleaning the tables, a cigarette—mostly cardboard filter— dangling from the corner of his mouth, his white jacket stained and dirty. A party was in progress the next car back; even over the roar of the train their singing could be heard. The windows were all dark now in the night.

"We didn't bring food," Horn told him. "My friend is very hungry."

The porter didn't bother looking up.

Horn took out two twenty-mark bills and laid them on one of the dirty tables. "Perhaps just a little something to eat and drink, comrade, if it wouldn't be too much trouble."

The porter reached over and scooped up the money, then turned and disappeared in the back. Horn turned in time to see a face in the window of the far connecting door for just an instant before it disappeared. He had the uneasy feeling that he knew the man. But he could not be certain from where, or when. He raced to the door and threw it open, his right hand in his pocket, his fingers curled around the Walther's grip. But there were only two men in workmen's clothes smoking and drinking on the enclosed connecting platform. They looked at him as if he were someone in authority.

"Was there someone here, comrades?" Horn asked, forcing a calmness to his voice.

One of them shrugged. "Just us."

"No one came through? Just a moment ago?"

The other one shook his head. "Just us."

He had known the face in the window, but he didn't know from where; the face was vague, his memory unclear. He turned and went back. The porter had brought a package of bread, a very small piece of cheese, an even smaller piece of sausage, and two bottles of dark beer. He'd laid it on one of the dirty tables in the middle of a big spill of soup. He'd picked Horn's accent as foreign, and had probably gotten the food from the garbage.

The compartment was dark when he returned, and for a moment he thought Anna had already gone to sleep, but then he saw her sitting on the lower bunk, staring out the window. She was dressed in a long flannel nightgown and her hair was pinned up. She'd washed her skirt and blouse and had hung them over the washroom cabinet door. She smelled a little like lilac. It brought Horn back a little to his grandmother.

"I brought something to eat."

They were moving quite fast. The sounds and motion of the train were hypnotic. "Do you have a cigarette?" Anna asked, her voice distant.

"Aren't you hungry?"

"A little. But I'd like a cigarette first."

Horn laid the package down and lit them both a cigarette. She turned away from the window. He sat down on the end of the bunk.

"Are you all right?"

– She managed a slight smile. She seemed particularly pale in the darkness. "Do you do this often, then, Jack?"

"Do what?"

"Take defectors across the border."

"I've done it before. Not very often."

"Is it always the same?"

"What do you mean?"

"Do they always feel remorse? Are they sorry?"

"Sometimes. At first. But usually not afterward."

"They don't think about their homes?"

"I'm sure they do, Anna. But it will be a better life. You

will see. There are other dancers in the West. Nureyev.
Baryshnikov. Makarova. Others.''

"And they dance in America?''

"They are very famous and well loved there, and in fact by
most of the world.''

"But I won't dance," she said, turning away momentarily.

"Perhaps you will.''

"I'm dying," she flared.

"Maybe you can be helped.''

"Oh, don't do that to me, Jack!" she said earnestly.
"You said yourself there are no miracle cures. The best
doctors are in the Soviet Union.''

"But we will try.''

"Against my will?''

"No.''

"Then it doesn't matter, you see. But I will hold you to
your promise to take me to Jason.'' She sat back, her legs
curled up behind her, and she blew smoke out her nose. "But
you haven't been honest with me about him. I can tell.''

They had not yet reached Kiev, but had stopped at a small
town. It was after three in the morning. The snow was finally
beginning to taper off. It looked very cold outside. There was
a lot of activity on the station platform.

Anna had eaten some of the bread, most of the sausage and
cheese, and had drunk most of one of the beers. She was
smoking a lot, but not really inhaling. Her face in the harsh
light from outside seemed to be the product of a modern
sculptor, all planes and angles, but delicate and very beautiful.

She told him that she had gone to see the old apartment
where she and Jason had had many of their meetings, and
about the two children she'd seen playing there in the dirty
courtyard. She'd been upset by them. It was very late and
they should not have been outside.

He knew without asking that she was sorry she'd never had
children. Now, no matter what happened, it would be impossible for her. But there was an even greater sadness within
her, even beyond the fact she would remain childless, even
beyond her knowledge that she was ill and would soon die.

"Tell me about Jason. In order for me to bring you to him
I'll have to know something about him. What he did at the
embassy, for example. What he looked like.''

"I don't know what he did at the embassy. And in all these years he's almost certainly changed."

"Was he tall?"

Anna nodded. "Like you."

"Dark? Light? Blue eyes? Mustache?"

"His eyes were his best feature," she mused. "They were understanding. He had dark hair, but there was a little gray in it. We laughed about it. He was too young for gray."

"How old was he?"

"I don't know. How old are you?"

"Forty-three."

"He was younger than you. But he knew things, like you. He used to tell me about the stars, and about navigating a big boat across the ocean. He was very proud of the navy."

"He was a naval officer?"

"No, he was a civilian."

"But he had been in the navy? He told you that?"

"I suppose he had been. When he was younger. I think he was an officer."

"Did he tell you where, Anna? What ship? What stations?"

"What difference does it make?"

"Probably none."

"Maybe he was in submarines. He talked about them once. He said that we had come from the sea, and that in the very end our destruction would come from the sea as well."

They were passing through the outskirts of Kiev. It was morning. Anna had gotten up, had switched on the washroom light, and was splashing some cold water on her face. Horn could see the outlines of her legs through the material of her nightgown. They were long in comparison with her torso. Dancer's legs. She turned and caught him looking at her.

He looked away. She switched off the light and sat next to him on the lower bunk. She'd been like a frightened deer earlier—skittish, suspicious, ready to bolt at the slightest provocation. Now she was overloaded, her senses burned out, her flight-or-fight mechanism shut down. Like the condemned man at the very end accepting his fate and walking calmly to the gallows, Anna seemed ready to accept whatever might come.

"Now you will tell me about Jason," she said.

"I don't know who he is."

"But you said Boyko had been murdered. You think Jason was responsible?"

"I think it is a possibility, Anna. But listen—"

She cut him off. "Why?" she asked in anguish. "Does he hate me, then?"

"I think he is afraid of you."

"Because of my uncle?"

"That, and something else. Something you might know. Something he may have told you that you still remember."

She thought about that for a moment. "Then he is someone important in your government? And for him the memory of his Moscow whore would not be so good for his career. Is it as simple as that, Jack?"

God, he wanted to reach out for her, take her into his arms and hold her so that nothing or no one could hurt her. Ever. He didn't think he had ever hated anyone more than he did Jason at this moment. The incredibly arrogant bastard. What he had done to a little Moscow ballerina, a rising star of the Bolshoi, was worse than murder. His ordinary victims' lives were over; the suffering for them was at an end. Quickly. But Anna had been made to endure the pain for all of these years with no respite.

They were coming deeper into the city. The snow had stopped but the sky was overcast, though it showed signs of breaking up. They had not gone to breakfast. Anna's eyes glistened. It was too much for her, and she was breaking. Horn felt even more sorry for her, and yet perhaps she finally needed to break down, to once and for all feel truly sorry for herself with good reason, and perhaps even feel anger toward Jason who had abused her so.

"Boyko took your letter with him to Helsinki. He was being followed by the KGB. He managed to slip away from them and he made a telephone call to a Paris number. He told them about your letter. At least we think he did. Forty-eight hours later he met someone in the middle of the night, and he was shot to death. Your letter was taken from him."

"What Paris telephone number?"

"A very old one, for emergencies. In the old days Boyko worked for me. I gave him the number."

"But there was no telephone number. I gave him no number. I gave him the address in Paris. I simply wanted him to post my letter. Nothing more. I've told you this."

"Jason gave you this address?"

Anna nodded. She looked out the window as downtown Kiev slid by, the circus off to the east, and the spires of St. Sophia beyond.

"He told you about Boyko? He gave you the address?"

"Yes." Her voice was soft; she sounded very weak. "Maybe it was someone else who killed Boyko. Maybe the KGB. Maybe they thought he was a traitor."

He had read Anna's letter. Boyko knew the score. He knew about the other madmen who had died. Was it possible he had been trying to contact his old control officer? He'd used the SOS number. Had he been foolish enough to think that Horn would still be waiting around after all those years for a call from one of his madmen? If so, who had intercepted the call? Only someone who had known Horn and his old network could have made any sense of it.

"Someone wants to kill us before we get to Jason," Horn said. "It is either Jason himself, or it is someone who wants to protect him. Either way it's because you know something they are afraid of."

Anna looked at him, her lips pursed, tears welling in her eyes. She didn't want to believe him, yet he could see that she did. After all these years there'd be no Jason, no happily-ever-after. She was nothing more than a game piece in some sort of dark contest.

23

The express train to Odessa took twenty-three hours, and from the station on Privokzlanaya Square, Horn and Anna took a cab to the Krashnaya Hotel overlooking the Ukrainian Writers Association of Pushkin. The feeling that they were being followed had continued to grow in Horn, and by the time they reached their hotel he'd become quite jumpy.

It was warm compared to Moscow, in the forties, and the sky was clear. This was the western gate of the Soviet Riviera, and although the high season was May to October, the particularly harsh winter up north had driven a lot of people south. They took the seaside promenade road up the hill overlooking the harbor. Several big ships were in port. A lot of pedestrians were out. Many of the shops were still open despite the lateness of the hour. Traffic was heavy in spots, and moved slowly. In addition to Moscow, Odessa had been Horn's city in the old days. Sheshkin and Boyko both had made trips down here for him. This was the Black Sea and the very edge of the Crimea. Nowhere except for Siberia was there more irreverence toward the Kremlin than here. Merchantmen regularly sailed to western ports: Piraeus, Alexandria, Marseille, Vienna, Naples, and Istanbul. They saw things and heard things, and brought their attitudes back with them. Though every ship that left every Soviet port carried her political officer, they too were men. And corruptible. They passed a cannon mounted on a tall wooden carriage, and saw another statue of the poet Pushkin who had spent some years

here in exile. Primorsky Boulevard intersected Pushkin. At
the far end was a large, ornately designed building that once
had been an important palace. Russians were glad of their
great Communist experiment, but there was hardly one among
them who didn't gaze at times with fond envy at the old
residences of the wealthy. Horn paid the cabby with a few
rubles from Anna, and they mounted the steps to the hotel
lobby. Before they went in he paused and looked across the
square, but there was nothing to be picked out. He looked for
familiar faces or even shapes from Moscow and from the
train, but there were sufficient people and traffic to make any
sort of recognition impossible. He saw an Intourist bus coming down the hill and it pulled around the circular drive to the
hotel. The Krashnaya was not one of the newer approved
hotels in Odessa, so he knew that the bus passengers were not
Americans or Western Europeans. They were probably Poles
or Hungarians or Albanians, for whom this would be the lap
of luxury. He took Anna's arm as they entered the broad
lobby. A string quartette was playing Tchaikovsky on a raised
platform. Horn figured it might take him twenty-four hours to
arrange passage for them. It would depend upon how much
things had changed here. In the meantime they would have to
lose themselves in the crowd. They would have to be anony-
mous, not all that difficult if they remained out of sight, even
for an American traveling with a Russian woman. Not in this
day and age. Not unless her uncle the general looked beyond
Moscow for his missing niece. Not unless they had, in fact,
been followed. They made for the front desk. "We'd like a
nice room overlooking the harbor," Horn told the clerk. He
handed over their passports and travel cards and filled out a
registration card. The clerk looked disapprovingly at Anna,
but when Horn paid in advance for three nights with West
German marks, his attitude underwent a dramatic change. He
assigned them a room with a shower-bath and wished them a
nice holiday.

"We don't wish to be disturbed, you understand," Horn
said. Out of the corner of his eye he saw that Anna was
blushing furiously.

The clerk understood.

Their room was pleasant, if not large or clean by Western
standards. They were on the eighth floor and could see across
the square all the way down to the Potemkin Stairs and
beyond, to the harbor. Horn ordered up a couple of bottles of

champagne, a bottle of vodka with ice, some caviar, and a
tray of light snacks and desserts for their supper. A large
closet contained drawers and a bar for hanging their clothes.
An ornate writing desk and two chairs were placed in front
of French doors that led to a tiny balcony overlooking the
city. Anna went into the bathroom while Horn made a quick
check of the room. One microphone was in the base of the
telephone, a second was beneath the wallpaper behind a very
bad painting over the bed, and a third was in the fake crystal
light fixture above the writing desk. He didn't touch any of
them. He wasn't surprised that the room was bugged. At least
a few rooms in most Soviet hotels, and all rooms in some,
were bugged. Hotel staffs were instructed by the KGB to
place foreigners in the bugged rooms, though the transmitters
were not always monitored twenty-four hours a day. He took
off his coat and pulled the curtains aside so that he could look
out. Now he could see that there were four big ships in port.
One appeared to be a Greek cruise ship; the other three were
cargo ships, two of them Russian. In the summer and fall the
port was a lot busier, and securing passage out was therefore
much easier. He'd worried, though, that there would be no
ships in port. He looked at his watch. It was a few minutes
before nine. They'd slept most of the day on the train, so
even without the adrenaline pumping, he would have been
wide awake. Anna came out of the bathroom. She had changed
into a pair of blue jeans and a loose sweat shirt. She wore no
shoes. Her feet were callused and misshapen from years of
ballet. Horn hurried across to her and pulled her into his
arms, his lips close to her left ear.

"The room is bugged," he whispered urgently. She stiffened in his arms. "It's all right. But I'm Jack, nothing more,
just Jack. And you are Nadesha. No last names, nothing
about the train. We're lovers here for a holiday. Do you
understand?"

Horn drew back. Anna was looking up at him, her lips
moist, her eyes wide. She nodded, and Horn smiled. He
pointed to the picture over the bed, then to the telephone, and
finally to the light fixture. Again she nodded her understanding.

"I ordered our supper and some wine, darling," he said
brightly.

"That's good. I'm starved," Anna said. She stepped away
from him. "I'll just be a minute." She went back into the
bathroom and closed the door.

It worried him that he had such a strong feeling they were being followed, and yet he had been unable to pick up their tail. Either his tradecraft was slipping, or he was becoming too jumpy for his own good. But he simply could not suppress the feeling. He listened at the door for a moment or two, then undid the latch, waited a moment longer, and yanked the door open all of a sudden. No one was there. The corridor was empty. But if someone had followed them, he reasoned, they wouldn't need to watch the corridor. Two men—one in front, one in back so they wouldn't make the same mistake they had made at the Berlin Hotel off Sverdlov Square, and again at Anna's apartment—would be sufficient. Unless they were herding him.

He shut the door and locked it, angry at himself. He would have easily picked out one or two following him. If they had wanted to become truly invisible, they would have had to have fielded three, maybe four teams. The cabbies. The porter on the train. The dining car personnel. A cop on the corner. A passenger in the tour bus that had pulled up out front. It took only a couple of hours by air from Moscow. They would have had the better part of an entire night and day to set something up in Odessa. If Jason had foreseen his movements, it would be possible. If Jason had the personnel. If Jason had the cooperation of the KGB. A lot of ifs, yet Horn could not shake his over-the-shoulder itch.

Someone knocked at the door. Horn yanked the Walther out of his coat pocket.

"Yes?"

"Room service."

"Just a moment," Horn said. He jammed the gun in his pants pockets, pulled off his tie, unbuttoned his shirt and pulled it off, then at the door slipped out of his shoes. He let the waiter in.

"Good evening, sir—" the waiter began, shoving the wheeled cart in. He stopped in mid-sentence, his eyes widening a little.

Horn turned. Anna stood at the bathroom door. She was nude. Her shoulders were small and rounded, her breasts small and very high, the nipples tiny, almost like a boy's. Her legs were long, ending at a tiny patch of very dark pubic hair. Her stomach was flat.

"Oh," she gasped. She hung there at the open door for a

long moment, her eyes flitting from the waiter to Horn and back. Then she closed the door.

"It's all right," Horn said. He knew what she had done.

The waiter, just a little flustered, rolled the cart the rest of the way in and set it up by the window beside the writing desk. He opened the champagne with a nervous flourish, his eyes glancing toward the bathroom door. When he was done, Horn thanked him and gave him a generous tip.

"We don't wish to be disturbed, my friend," Horn said. "You can understand. It would get around the hotel."

The waiter leered at him, and nodded. "Yes, of course," he said at the door. "If you should want anything, sir, anything at all, my name is Rem." He left. Horn locked the door.

Anna came out of the bathroom dressed again in her blue jeans and sweat shirt. She couldn't look directly at him. "Supper has come, I see."

"Are you all right?"

She laughed. "Why shouldn't I be, Jack? Don't be silly."

She seemed brittle. She was very embarrassed. Horn thought she was beautiful, and very brave just then. He poured her a glass of champagne. She drank it all at once and sheepishly held out her glass for more. He poured it.

"It's going to be a very gay holiday, Jack."

She was trying very hard. "You are very beautiful . . . Nadesha," he said. Part of it was the fiction for the microphones, but most of it was the truth.

She blushed a little. "Maybe not so beautiful." She drank her champagne. He poured her more.

"I think so."

She wanted to dispute him, but he put his finger to his lips and nodded toward the microphone above the writing table. She drank her champagne and again he poured her still another. She wanted to get drunk, and on an empty stomach she would probably succeed. But he'd been fooled on that score by Russians before.

"I'm going to go out for a little while, darling," he said.

She looked at him in real alarm.

"I would like to find some cigarettes. Some American cigarettes. I don't think they have them in this hotel."

"Is it necessary tonight?"

"Yes," Horn said. He moved to where he had tossed his

shirt and put it on. Anna brought him his tie and shoes. She reached up and brushed her lips against his cheek.

"Where are you going?" she whispered urgently.

"To the docks. Will you be all right here?"

She glanced at the light fixture and nodded. Her cheeks were flushed, her breath came short. She was frightened again, like a doe. He could see the wildness in her eyes. She'd led a very safe, secure life to this point, and now she was running off toward an uncertain future with an American spy. She was dying, but that fact had not affected her sense of obligation, of duty or responsibility, nor he supposed would it ever, not even at the end. He decided that she was an extraordinary woman. How different her life could have been. Should have been.

"Be careful," she mouthed the words.

He pulled her close. At first she resisted, but then she came into his arms, her body pressed willingly against his, and they kissed deeply. He was afraid of hurting her, and he felt absolutely rotten about what he was doing, but she clung tightly to him as if she wanted this too.

"Oh, God," she said, when they parted, and he agreed with her. Yes. Oh, God! And now what was to become of them?

It was after ten and Horn was confused and angry. He was on the move now, away from Anna, and he had a very specific thing to accomplish that would take all of his wits. Yet he could not stop thinking about her, seeing her face, feeling her lips against his, her body against his body. From the very first moment he laid eyes on her he had suspected that none of this was going to work out to anyone's satisfaction, neither his, nor the Company's, and least of all hers. What had happened tonight at the hotel was no one's fault, he kept telling himself. It had just happened, perhaps out of pity on his part for her illness, for her grief. At least a little of that. Jason was an American who had hurt her beyond all reason, and in some measure, he supposed, he was trying to make up for it, trying to give her a little comfort, some reassurance that it would all work out in the end. But he was a liar, wasn't he? He'd spent his life lying. Because it sure as hell wouldn't work out in the end—it couldn't—and that was one of the reasons he was angry.

"Plug the gaps, Jack," Carlisle had said at the Stockholm

safe house before Nobels had been gunned down. "Return to Helsinki or go to Paris or get yourself to Moscow, but whatever you do, find out what that nasty little man was up to that got him killed."

We know what he was up to, though, Horn thought. We know who killed him . . . or at least by code name we know his killer. But what we don't know yet, Farley, is the why. What was Jason hiding?

"There's more at stake here than even you can imagine," Carlisle had warned. The words were coming back.

More at stake? What more, Farley? What were you trying to tell me in your oblique way? Was it a warning? Where was he supposed to find fault with Boyko's tradecraft? The man had been trained by the best. He'd seen a lot of action in the old days. Had he become rusty, then, after all these years, with his trust? He'd gotten out of the Soviet Union with Anna's letter and he'd been carrying a piece. That wasn't so easy. He'd even set up his meet in a spot loaded in his favor second only to Moscow itself. Helsinki was Boyko's town. The border was just a quick jump away if he found himself cornered. He'd had friends in the Finnish capital. Nothing to worry about there. The odds had been loaded in his favor. Yet he had let himself be lured to a late-night meeting, and had allowed himself to be shot down. Even at the end he had tried to get his revenge, though. Give him credit for that much. *A letter from Anna*, he told the Finnish cop. His very last words. But if he'd been seeking simple revenge, it meant he knew who had done him in. He knew that someone would be coming looking for the letter, looking for Anna. And when they came, Anna would lead them back to Jason if she could be convinced to help. Had Boyko suspected even at the end that his old mentor and control officer would be the one to take up the quest?

"The whole Moscow network has become like a huge house of cards, Jack," Carlisle had warned him. "Rotten in some places right to the foundation. Any little blast of air will topple the entire works. A lot of fine people, theirs as well as ours, would fall with it. The casualties would be awesome."

Who was he talking about? What was he talking about? *A lot of fine people, theirs as well as ours.* Were we working with the Russians, then? Was that what Farley had meant? *The casualties would be awesome:* Nobels, Clay, Doxmeuller. Was that awesome enough, or did Jason want even more?

The only way to find out, Horn thought, was to ask the man face-to-face.

He had come down the broad Potemkin Stairs that led to the harbor, and had walked a couple of blocks over to a section of the waterfront that contained most of the merchant seamen's bars and clubs. He had taken care with his own tradecraft getting there: doubling back; stopping and starting; taking a bus, then a cab, and finally another bus. Though he hadn't been able to shake the feeling that he was being watched, he had at least convinced himself that it was unlikely he'd been followed. He stood across the street from a place called the Octobrists Club, which was housed in a two-story brick structure that had once contained the customs shed in the days of the czars. The new customs house was back by the Potemkin Stairs and the funicular railway. This club could have been on any waterfront in any port. It was run-down and shabby, and from inside he could hear music and loud voices raised in song, and argument, and drunken pronouncements about everything from vodka to women, from soccer to the weather. The languages were indistinct, but the content was understandable nevertheless. The windows had all been boarded up and were plastered with party posters: "The Party and the People are United," "Glory to Work," "Long Live the Soviet People, Builders of Communism." Left of the entry were three glass-encased bulletin boards that contained *Izvestia*, the party newspaper. The glass in all three was cracked.

Two men in rough workmen's clothes came down the block arm in arm and entered the club. Horn crossed the street, took one last look back toward the stairs, and went in. The noise and the smell hit him simultaneously, bringing with them a lot of memories, as well as Boyko's assessment of the first time he'd been there: "They're a bunch of filthy peasants, Jack, but how they can drink, how they can love a skirt, and how they can kill for anything that glitters." He'd had a lot of admiration for them. The club was long and narrow, the ceiling high. A bar ran most of the length on the right, with tables facing it. At the far end of the room, three teen-age boys and a girl with orange hair were playing rock and roll music on electric guitars, an electronic keyboard, and a tambourine. No one seemed to be paying any attention to the music, but everyone seemed to be enjoying it.

He went to the bar, ordered a beer, and sat down. The

bartender was a big, rough-looking Armenian with biceps the size of a normal man's thighs. Horn paid with a West German hundred-mark bill. The bartender was impressed. He made the change, and when he laid it down on the bar, Horn pushed it back at him.

"It's all right, my friend. I might need your help someday."

The bartender pocketed the money and poured them both a glass of cognac from the back shelf. "It's French," he said through his teeth.

Horn drank it down and forced a smile. "I can tell," he said. "Quality stuff."

The bartender drank his. Horn pulled out a second hundred-mark bill and laid it down.

"This time let me buy."

The bartender nodded and smiled. He poured them another, then pocketed the money. A few of the men at the bar were looking at them. They'd seen the transactions. One of them licked his lips. "Everyone ends up at the Octobrists sooner or later," Boyko had told him. Some things never changed.

"I see there are four ships in port tonight," Horn said pleasantly as he took out his cigarettes. He took one and offered the pack to the bartender.

"Six," the barman said, taking the pack. "Two up at Sukhoi Liman. Loading tractors for our brothers in Bulgaria."

"I saw the Greek liner."

"It just came in. Here for another two days. A lot of cheap bastards. Crew's been restricted. It's just as well. You can't trust those Greeks."

"How about her first mate?"

"A regular *puffta*, you ask me. Been in here once. Plenty for me. They practically ran him out." He nodded toward one of the big tables.

Horn glanced over his shoulder. A dozen burly sailors, most of them drunk out of their skulls, had four whores with them and were having a great time. Aside from the music, they were contributing the most to the general noise level. One of them had opened his fly and a whore was fondling him. One of the others had his arm under another girl's skirt. A lot of them were beating time to the music on the table with vodka bottles.

"They're off the *Pride of Leningrad*, that bunch," the barman said. "Some pride."

"Depends on what you're looking for."

"Me, I'm looking for a little money. Maybe buy a new car someday. Take a trip. Maybe see the world. But I'm going to keep my nose out of trouble. The future is his who knows how to wait."

"Istanbul is nice this time of year."

"Don't like the Turks. But I know what you mean."

"They're people all the same."

"Maybe," the barman said. He tossed back his cognac. Horn followed suit. The barman left to make a sweep down the bar. When he returned he picked up their conversation as if they hadn't been interrupted. He smelled money, but he also smelled trouble. "Take those two over there," he said.

Horn looked over. Two husky men were seated in a booth along the far wall. They were watching the show. They wore business suits, and looked out of place. Horn hadn't spotted them when he came in.

"KGB, if you ask me," the barman said, watching Horn's eyes.

Horn held himself in check. "Regulars?"

"Since yesterday, but I've seen them in here before. They after you?"

Horn grinned. "They'd have arrested me by now if they were."

The barman had been there before. He wasn't convinced. "Istanbul is a very expensive town from what I hear."

"There are two of us."

"What are you, a nest of spies?"

"The other one is a girl. An American."

"You too?"

Horn nodded.

"Your Russian is pretty good. But you say those two aren't after you?"

"They may be, but I don't think so."

The barman thought about that for a moment. "It would cost a lot of money. More of the BRD stuff if you've got it. Less questions than American bills floating around down here. The prick teasers in Moscow like that stuff for themselves."

"How soon would a ship be leaving?"

"When would you be ready?"

"Now."

"Five thousand."

"You'll take your share out of it. I wouldn't care for any

surprises. I still have a few friends around who would consider it a pleasure to clean up after me.''

"I cannot guarantee the other end. Your reception in Istanbul, you know what I mean. The watch would turn its back so you could jump ship. After that you would be on your own.''

"Fair enough.''

The barman looked at Horn for a long, appraising second or two, then poured him another cognac. "How much do you have with you now?''

"Half now, the other half when we dock in Istanbul.'' Horn glanced down the bar. At that moment no one was paying them any particular attention. He pulled out a wrapped stack of West German hundred-mark bills from his inner pocket. "Twenty-five hundred,'' he said, handing it across, shielding his movements with his body. The money disappeared instantly in the barman's jacket.

"If there is any trouble, you will die.''

"Wouldn't do détente any good,'' the barman grunted, and laughed. He turned and walked away from Horn, busying himself at the far end of the bar. A minute later when Horn looked back, the barman was gone. Someone had splashed water on the girl singer's T-shirt, and her nipples stood out as if she were not wearing a thing. The men were loving it. The pair the barman had identified as KGB were applauding and whistling enthusiastically. Horn figured they were either very good, or they were amateurs. Either way they could prove to be dangerous.

He listened to the music for a while. The kids weren't very good, but what they lacked in talent they more than made up for in volume. They were punk rockers, and therefore hooligans, antisocial elements. As long as they caused no real trouble, nothing would be done about them in a place like this. In Moscow it would be a different story, but this wasn't Moscow. It was possible, Horn told himself, that the KGB was there merely to check up on the band. It was hard to believe that two days ago the KGB had been able to predict that he would show up here. It was stretching Jason's powers too much. So it was a coincidence. But he did not like coincidences.

Another bartender brought him a fresh beer and tried to pour him a cognac, but Horn declined the liquor. The bartender shrugged indifferently. "With as much beer as you've had, it's a wonder you haven't used the pisser yet," he said, and he moved off.

Horn took his time. He watched the music for a little while longer, then glanced back down the bar where the second bartender was deep in conversation with one of the whores who had come over from the big table. The KGB types were still glued to the performance onstage. He slipped off his barstool and made his way back to the men's room. It was a long, narrow hall with a trough in the floor along one wall, and two toilets in the open at the far end. A few men were using the trough. Horn went to the far end and started to urinate. The big bartender came in almost immediately and stood next to him.

"It is set, my friend. The *Pride of Leningrad* sails at six in the morning. You and your girlfriend are to show up just at three. The border patrol pricks will be in the back getting themselves a complimentary piece of ass. Go aboard and get below. Someone will show you where you can stay."

"What about the ship's political officer?"

"Another prick who can rot in hell. He'll be busy. But believe me when I tell you that he is a son of a bitch, so you will have to keep out of his way. She'll make two stops before Istanbul—Constanţa and Varna. You'll have to keep out of sight the entire time, but especially while you are in port."

"How about food?"

"It is not a pleasure cruise, but you will be taken care of," the barman said. "Now, turn around and look over at the door."

Horn did as he was told. A small, rat-faced man with short-cropped hair, dressed in a filthy dark blue jacket, stared at him for a long time, and then he left.

"It will cost you an additional five thousand in Istanbul, though, not twenty-five hundred," the bartender said, zipping up.

"Why?"

The bartender's eyes were narrowed. "Someone is looking for you and your girlfriend. The word is out. But the bastards are too cheap to make it worth our while."

"The two out there?"

"Maybe, maybe not," the barman said. "But they will be taken care of. Just make sure you don't lead anyone to the ship with you. If you do, the deal is off."

•   •   •

Horn took his time getting back to the hotel. No one followed him. With far less traffic on the streets at this hour, he
could be absolutely sure.

Anna was sitting by the window, staring out at the night.
None of the food on the big tray had been touched, but she
had drunk all of the champagne. Her eyes were bright, and
her face was a little flushed.

He took her into the bathroom where he closed the door
and turned on the shower and the water in the sink to muffle
their voices. "We have to be at the ship at three this morning," he told her. Anna just looked at him. "They're looking
for us already."

"My uncle."

Horn nodded. "But they're not looking very hard yet.
They might not even know for sure that we're out of Moscow."

"He won't give up."

"No."

"He won't stop even after we get out. He will follow me
forever." She shook her head and turned away. "And I don't
know what I'll say to him when he catches up with me. Or
what will happen when he and Jason come face-to-face again."

Horn stared at her. Her sloping shoulders. Her bowed head
and long neck. Her slight frame. Her uncle knew Jason. A
KGB officer had known that his niece was seeing an American who was at the very least in those days a diplomat, and
very probably a spy. Where was this leading? What else was
there to know before it was over? Horn decided he had never
known a thing about trust or faith. Not really.

24

The Krashnaya Hotel was in a respectable neighborhood, so that by one in the morning traffic was all but nonexistent on the streets and Anna waited with Horn across the square, her knees a little weak, her heart fluttering, the plastic airline bag he had bought for her loaded with her few belongings and slung over her shoulder. They had crossed the square but had pulled up in the lee of the Pushkin statue when Horn had spotted the blue Moskvich sedan. It was hard for her to consciously realize just why she had come to Odessa with him, yet she understood that her forgetfulness just now was a simple defense mechanism. She was defecting. She was a traitor. He pulled her further around the base of the statue as the Moskvich came down Kondratenko and pulled up in front of the hotel.

There were two men in the car. The one behind the wheel waited while the other jumped out and went into the hotel.

"They're the same two who were at the club where I arranged our passage," Horn said, watching across the street. "The bartender thought they were KGB. Could be your uncle sent them. They showed up a couple of days ago."

"Did they follow you here?" she heard herself asking.

"They couldn't have."

"Maybe it's merely a routine check, Jack."

"I don't think so," Horn said.

"What about the boat?" she asked. "Will they follow us there too?" But if he answered her, she wasn't at all sure she

heard him, because she was listening to the sounds of a
winter sleigh down the frozen Istra River below Dominic
Shevchenko's dacha, how the dull plodding sound of the
horses' hooves on the snow changed to a sharp clatter on the
bare ice, and the sleigh's runners scraped and slipped side-
ways. She was also listening to the music and the singing and
the poetry, especially the poetry that always went on out
there, and the dancing sometimes too, the ballerina's hard-
toed slippers thumping delicately on the wooden floors. She
could see the rippling muscles in the premier danseur's thighs
as he moved and leaped in graceful, flowing arcs. Sometimes
she'd had erotic dreams thinking about their derrières and
bulging codpieces as they kneeled on stage and bent backward, their arms out in supplication.

Those were the things she was leaving as a defector, and
she wanted to tell Horn just that. Yet how could she describe
a sound or a smell or an evening, let alone a feeling, an
attitude . . . a heritage if you will? The lights are low, the
fireplace flickers. In the flue Anna can hear the fierce winter
winds blowing across the chimney, through the eaves, around
the windows. Someone has managed to obtain an edition in
Russian of Pasternak's *Dr. Zhivago*. Anna's uncle, perhaps.
The KGB captain. They're reading from the poems of Yuri
Zhivago: *Magdalene. As soon as night comes my demon
springs up out of the ground./ That is the price I pay for my
past./ They come, those memories of vice,/ And fall to gnaw-
ing at my heart.* Apocryphal, the visions? Or had she gotten
her sense of timing confused? In the midst of the music and
celebration she sees Jason, tall and sure and handsome, strid-
ing across the room toward her, his arms outstretched to meet
her leap. He is a magician because not only can he foretell the
future, he can bend and change it to his own will. Back and
forth they seem to race between summer and spring and then
winter. From the dacha to the theater and back to the apartment. Their apartment where they had privacy and laughter
and, in the end, tears. Another poem of Zhivago's comes to
her, and it makes her cry a little as it always does: *Guests
come until dawn/ To the bride's house for the celebration,/
Cutting right across the yard,/ Bringing their own music.*

They're at the theater. Everyone is in costume. Jason, sure
as ever, is directing the entire production under the watchful
gaze of her uncle. Looking at her through pince-nez, he
announces that Maximova is more beautiful than little Anna

Feodorovna, but that Anna has more soul and therefore will be his forever. Trumpets sound, the kettle drums roll, and the orchestra begins the wedding march. But Anna is watching from the wings. It is her show, but she has not been invited to participate.

The attendants line up to the left and right of the Russian Orthodox priest. Jason, magnificent in his scanty costume from *Spartacus*, shakes the hand of his best man, whose face Anna cannot see, and then delicately kisses each of the bridesmaids on the lips. The priest intones: "In Heaven and on earth, join these two in holy matrimony . . ." The audience applauds suddenly, rising to its feet, the orchestra thunders its triumph, the attendants file stage left and right, singing gloriously as they depart, and Anna and Jason together now march down the flower-strewn aisle out to a magnificent summer's day of sun and gentle breezes.

"Can we go to Washington now?" Anna asks as they leave the cathedral. "Or California. I would like to see San Francisco, I think."

But Jason does not give her an answer. He is holding the door of a grand carriage from the State Armory in the Kremlin, six white horses chomping at the bit, liveried footmen resplendent in red and gold waiting to whisk them away. Even for Anna the entire production is becoming a bit too much. She would like another rewrite, another rehearsal.

"I told you that I would come for you, Anna," Jason tells her. He is somehow older and more mature, and yet he is ageless. The entire world is ageless. "No more waiting, Anna. I am here."

They embrace. She can feel his strong but gentle arms around her, feel his breath on her cheek, the tenderness of his lips, his body against hers. All the way through Moscow in the carriage they are joined together, their bodies intertwined, the crowds along the street cheering for them, especially in Red Square, and somehow Jason the magician has brought them to their apartment, where they make love. But then there is the remainder of their lives together to consider. It bothers her that she cannot see into the future as clearly as he can. She doesn't have the power, and the union is unequal because of it. He is always smiling, she sees that ever so clearly, but she can see nothing else about what will come. He assures her that everything will work out. But she begins to have her doubts. Jason has brought a bottle of French champagne. It is a little too sour for her because she is used to the sweeter Russian variety, but she drinks it to please him even though the wine gives her terrible heartburn. Our Father Who art in Heaven; God, please let this be so. Cosset and protect us.

"Come give us a kiss, Anna," Jason says, grinning. "Quite a ceremony, don't you think?"

But that part isn't real. She knows it. She keeps getting her fantasies mixed in with her memories. Their relationship was a lot more physical than she hoped it would be. Yet they talk. Late at night, after lovemaking, when he is nearly asleep and he thinks she is too, is her very special time. She is wide awake with the excitement of her relationship, and she watches him drift slowly off to sleep. She listens to what he has to say, not understanding one tenth of it. He talks about submarines, about displacements and disbursement lines, about effective strike zones and throw weights, and the Nuclear Diffusion Blanket Theory, and about other boats or perhaps people called Nimitz and Forrestal. The words do not matter to her, only that he is speaking so that she can watch his lips move.

"You talked in your sleep," she says, and for the very first time something she has said gets a definite reaction out of him. He is angry, though he denies it. He tries to hide it from her, but she can see.

"About what, darling?" he asks, sleep leaving his eyes over tea. "What sort of nonsense did I babble in my sleep? Not another woman?"

"About boats, I think."

"You think?" He hoots. "But exactly what did I say?" He is trying to cover his alarm. "Don't be shy. We can't be shy with our clothes off. It's sort of silly."

He had a bit of hair on his chest and it excited her. The end of his penis was shaped differently than the only other one she'd ever seen, and she asked him about it. Circumcision, he'd called the operation. It wasn't clear to her why such an operation was performed, though she'd heard it was common among Jews. He fondles her breasts, and she lies back, her eyes closed. She is alive with the pleasure of his touch. His lips are on her nipples. She feels the cry building in her throat as his tongue slides down her belly, and even farther, to her secret spot. Oh, God! Oh, Jason!

"What sort of things did I say, Anna?" he asks.

It is the only time in their relationship that she is hurt—except of course at the end—by something he's said or done. She cries violently, the sobs wracking her body. And it hurts her even more that he does not try to comfort her. Instead he waits patiently for her to calm down. "To see the light of reason," he is fond of saying. Finally, of course, she does see the light and realizes that she is being a complete fool. A lot of what he has said in his sleep could be dangerous for him. He works at the American embassy. Naturally he would be concerned. "Loose lips sink ships." She had heard that one on a war drama on television, or perhaps her mother told her that her father said it. "You were talking about submarines," she says.

Jason smiles. "Oh, that," he says offhandedly as if he'd thought it might have been something *really* important. But it is; she's convinced of it.

"I didn't hear much anyway. You were mumbling," she says. "And snoring too." Trying to inject a little lightness.

Jason rises to the bait. "I do not snore. But you do!"

They are nude in the bed. Anna jumps up, her shoulders back, her hands on her narrow hips. "Ballerinas do not snore!" she declares.

"All Russians snore. And fart!"

She shrieks with laughter and falls back into bed on top of him, beating on his chest, and then kissing his nipples, and his neck and the cleft in his chin, and finally his lips, her tongue darting into his mouth. And she can feel his response. He is growing larger, and already she is moist. She simply cannot get enough of him. When he is inside of her, big, hard, filling, she thrusts her hips up to his. She wants to swallow him whole, take his entire body into hers.

"Did I ever mention any names that you can recall?" he asks her.

She gets a severe case of gooseflesh. Oh, Jason, she cries inside. Now it is spoiled. Tonight is ruined. "No," she lies. "Never."

Horn had taken Anna's arm and had led her away from the square. She was shivering and he was a little afraid for her. They kept away from the streetlights until they turned down Lastochkin Street past the Odessa Opera House, its ornate façade unevenly lit so that wild shadows played across the neighboring buildings, and shafts of light obliterated the stars.

He kept looking over his shoulder, half expecting to see the Moskvich behind them. The Octobrists might have been luck, or coincidence, but not the hotel. Not on the same night.

He was starting to get the feeling that they weren't being followed as much as they were being herded like animals toward a trap. Someone was directing their options, keeping one step ahead of them at all times, opening and closing the proper gates to make sure they moved along some predetermined path.

But there were too many options in Istanbul. Too many friends.

Moscow would have been easier, safer. It was General Patrenko's city.

Here in Odessa too.

Or aboard the ship at sea.

Too crude? If he had learned one thing about Jason so far, it was that the man was anything but crude.

A late-night tourist cafeteria stood on the corner near the top of the Potemkin Stairs, across from the funicular railway. During the day it served as an outdoor café. At night, however, everyone moved inside. Horn directed Anna inside. The place was nearly full, mostly with passengers and crew from the Greek cruise ship. A youngish man with a pockmarked face played tunes on an accordion. He was set up in a corner. Four bottles of ouzo were stacked on a chair next to him. Every now and then he'd stop playing, take a big pull at one of the bottles, and then start up again. Everyone clapped and sang. The club was filled with a boozy bonhomie, and although the official Soviet view was against such gatherings, the militia would look the other way, and the party would probably continue until dawn.

They found a couple of seats at the end of a long table near the back. A few bleary eyes turned their way, welcoming them, thinking they were from the ship, but then a young man jumped up and began dancing on one of the tables at the front and everyone cheered all the louder. Horn got them a bottle of wine and a couple of glasses, paying at the cashier, an older, rotund woman with a big red face and a nice smile.

"Quite a party," he said.

"All Greeks are degenerates," the woman shouted, laughing uproariously. "But their money is good."

Horn had to agree. Back at the table Anna was staring at

the musician and the dancer, her head cocked a little to one side.

"Are you all right?" Horn asked, pouring their wine.

She dragged her eyes away from the front of the room. "This is Greek music? It is good, Jack. I like it. But what are we doing here?"

"We have to wait somewhere until it is time."

She nodded seriously. "But, Jack, our passports are back at the hotel. Have you forgotten this?"

"We're leaving them. I have new ones for us." Horn leaned a little closer, though no one was paying them the slightest attention. "You are an American now. Your name is Gloria Townsend. Can you remember that?"

She actually smiled. "That is ridiculous. I can hardly speak any English."

"It doesn't matter, Anna. Just don't say a thing to anyone. No matter what happens."

She glanced again at the dancer. "Who is this Gloria Townsend? Do we look very much alike? The other passport was not very good, you know."

"This one is worse. But no one will be looking very closely at your photograph, believe me. Tell them you lost weight." He handed it to her under the table, and their fingers touched. Hers were cold.

"I'm a little frightened of what will happen to us," she said.

"I have friends where we are going. They will help us."

"Friends who will look the other way while you sneak a Russian girl out of her country?" She looked at her wine, then picked up her glass and drained it. Her hand stopped. "What about the two men who entered our hotel, Jack? Do you know them?"

There was something in her eyes all of a sudden. A warning. "What is it?"

"Don't turn around, but they are here. At the door."

Christ, Horn thought. "What are they doing?"

"Talking with the old woman where you pay."

"Have they spotted us yet?"

"No," Anna said, shaking her head. "I don't think so. What is happening, Jack?"

Horn's mind was racing. "Stay here until exactly two-thirty, and then walk directly to the stairs and take them down to the quay. Can you do that?"

Anna clutched at his arm in real alarm. "Oh, God, Jack, don't leave me like this. I don't know what I would do if—"

"If something happens—if I don't make it back to you—telephone your uncle and tell him that I kidnapped you, but that you escaped. He'll protect you."

"I can't."

"You must, Anna," Horn said urgently. He picked up his overnight bag, got to his feet, and without looking back walked directly away from the table. In the noise and confusion no one noticed him until he got up to the cashier, and then both men looked up, startled. They were both dressed in dark, poorly cut suits. One of them wore a woolen scarf.

Horn smiled at the cashier. "Good evening," he said. He brushed past the men and stepped outside. Immediately he turned left and crossed the square in front of the Sailors Palace, his heart really pumping now. Traffic was very light, even down here. A few cabs hurried past, but the buses had all stopped running more than an hour ago. At the head of the long flight of stone stairs that led all the way down to the harbor, he hesitated long enough to light a cigarette, and as he did he contrived to take a quick glance back the way he had come. He had already decided that if they had not come after him, he would go back. Her uncle might protect her, but there was no telling how far Jason's insanity might extend. But they were both there, just across the street, watching him. He threw away his match and hurried down the stairs, keeping to the right, the harbor spread out below. The *Pride of Leningrad* was docked several blocks to the southwest, past the Octobrists Club, behind a tall security fence. From where he stood he could see the ship. It was bathed in lights. Booms loaded cargo for the six o'clock sailing. At the bottom he turned east, past the new customs house, beyond which was the older section of the Port of Odessa, a rabbit warren of streets and back alleys. Tourists seldom if ever came down this way. Intourist guides would never allow it, denying in fact that such a place existed anywhere in Russia, and the few who came alone were warned to stay away from the area as well as the dangerous catacombs.

The two behind him might be fools; they should have taken him immediately. Yet something at the back of his mind nagged. It was too easy. Turning a corner he managed another quick glance back. Both of them were three quarters of a block back now, not even bothering to hide their presence or their outward intent. He turned right again, his step quicker as he worked his way nearer to the water's edge and the old seawalls and wharves. The buildings were mostly unpainted, severely weathered brown wood. Boyko had known a prostitute here. He'd wanted Horn to come along once. Between them they could have had a party. A *Ménage à trois*. Boyko had always gone in for the odd, the perverse. It had been his strength, and ultimately the weakness that had gotten him gunned down.

A tall wooden fence blocked off a narrow courtyard to the right, halfway down the alley. Horn ducked through the gate and from inside watched through a separation in the boards. The two men came around the corner in a run and pulled up short. Horn took the Walther out of his coat pocket and clicked the safety selector lever to the off position as they started down the alley. He glanced over his shoulder. Three houses formed the junk-strewn courtyard. No lights shone in any of the windows. The houses could have been deserted, but even if they were not, there would be no trouble, he thought. Not here. There was no love of the system here. A light from the street elongated the two men's shadows. One of them reached into his coat and brought out a gun. "Don't be stupid," the other one said. Horn's grip tightened on his. He heard their heels on the pavement. "Did he come back here? Fuck, it's too dark," one of them said. They were Russian. Any doubts Horn might have had on that score were dispelled hearing them. The one with the gun grunted and turned directly for the gate. Horn stepped back, his mouth suddenly dry. He remembered some of the words from the sacrament of extreme unction for souls in immediate danger of death. It was a part of the catechism, a part of the routine of the fieldman. Deliver unto Christ that which is Christ's. His memory was imperfect, but he felt the sense of it now. "What are you doing there?" the other one said, stopping in his tracks. "He may have gone in here, you pig," the first one answered, his voice shockingly close, just on the other side of the fence. Horn flattened against the boards as the gate opened and the man cautiously stepped halfway through, then stopped. His left shoulder was less than two feet from Horn's gun hand.

"Well, you stupid bastard?" the one outside called.

"It's darker than a whore's cunt in here."

Horn very slowly raised his pistol so that the barrel was

inches away from the side of the Russian's head. "Comrade," he said softly.

The man jerked as if he had been shot, and he turned right into the muzzle of the Walther, his eyes going wide as saucers when he realized what was touching his face. His mouth opened.

"Cry out and your brains will be splattered all over the alley," Horn said calmly though his heart was thumping madly. He wasn't this cold-blooded.

"Horn," the Russian choked out his name, and he stepped back as he brought up his gun.

Horn simply could not believe his ears. For a seeming eternity he was frozen, with absolutely no control over his muscles. Then another part of him concerned with the instinct for survival shoved aside the significance of the single word and he pulled the trigger. The Walther bucked in his hand, the shot sounding more like a toy pistol than a real one, and the Russian's head jerked violently to the left, a huge spurt of blood gushing out the side of his head, his eyes filling with blood, blood pouring from his nostrils and ears.

The Russian kept falling and falling down a long deep hole. All that had happened since the Finnish cop had pulled back the plastic covering to reveal Boyko's countenance in death came rushing up at Horn with the force of a tidal wave, shoving him into a corner of hopelessness. Jason was the puppeteer pulling the strings of his marionettes. He was a trusted American. He had been Anna's lover. He had the confidence of his government at the highest levels, which he had betrayed for all of these years. The future was suddenly dismaying in its fatal complexities. It's what Jason had done to everyone that was so despicable. So without human reason or emotion.

Horn stepped quickly over the dead Russian and out into the back-lit alley, oblivious of his own safety. The second Russian stood flatfooted ten feet away, his eyes wild with fright as he clawed in his coat for his gun.

The abyss was there, staring them both in the face. In less than a second Horn raised his pistol and fired two shots point-blank into the Russian's face, the first destroying the bridge of his nose and a portion of his right cheek, the second blowing away the top of his head as he went down.

Horn stepped back, horrified at what he had just done, at what he was becoming. He was a spy, not an assassin. An intellectual, not an animal. Yet in the space of a couple of days he had killed five men. He wanted to throw away his gun and run off, never look back, return to Christine and the children and sanity. But then he remembered the necessity of luring these two back here in the first place, and he remembered Clay and Doxy and all of his madmen, and he came around. Pocketing his gun he listened with one ear for the sounds of sirens as he gathered the dead Russian by the arms and dragged his body through the gate, dumping him inside the courtyard beside the other one. There was a lot of blood. It seemed to be everywhere. And a terrible stench arose from one of the corpses. "The meek will never inherit the earth," Doxy would say. "But they'll damned sure be buried in it." Horn forced himself to slow down, to go through their pockets, finding at once their identity cards in cheap plastic wallets. The light was too dim for him to read the names, but the red border and the hammer and sickle superimposed over the photographs was unmistakable. They were GRU agents—Soviet military intelligence—not KGB. Not militia. He kept staring at the identity cards, trying to pin something to their significance. GRU agents were supposed to go after military intelligence. Tactical scenarios, war plans, technical data. What the hell were they doing here? Why them?

"Horn," the one had said before he died.

Closing the gate firmly behind him, he walked out of the alley on legs of rubber, trying to figure how likely it was that the port would be closed up tight the moment the bodies were discovered. If there was anyone in the houses back there, they would be telephoning the militia by now. They had stayed out of it as long as there was danger, but now they would be good Soviet citizens doing their duty. It was only natural. An odd, disconnected sense had come over him. He was fighting it. He'd felt this way once a lot of years ago when he was on the run in Prague. Only then he'd been a lot younger, and a lot less sure of what he was doing. But he hadn't just killed two men in cold blood. "For this is my body . . . For this is the chalice of my blood . . ." The words of the consecration. The mystery of the mass, for life everlasting, for the love of Jesus Christ Almighty, the Son of God. *Pax tecum* . . . peace be with thee. *Et cum spiritu tuo* . . . and also with thee.

He was on the move now. There could be no further hesitation, or all would be lost. He would be lost. Anna would be lost. Christine, Marc, Marney. All life. His madmen. Moscow. Washington. "The troubles we encounter in life are almost all of our own making," his father had told him. "Our existence is God's choice, but our style is our own." He wanted peace but it wasn't possible now. He walked through Old Town, avoiding the main thoroughfares, avoiding the lights, avoiding people. He was calm, if not composed, but time dragged and it seemed forever before two-thirty.

At first he didn't see her and he thought she hadn't come, that something else had gone wrong. But then he spotted her in the doorway of an ice cream shop, wrought-iron chairs piled on top of three tables in front. A canvas-covered truck rumbled past on its way to the docks. When it was gone, Horn crossed the street. Anna stepped out of the doorway to meet him and she came immediately into his arms.

"I didn't think you were coming," she cried, kissing his cheeks, his chin, his lips. "I didn't think you would be here."

"Were you followed?"

"No. I don't think so, Jack. But they were watching me in that place. The cashier and all the drunks at our table. They thought we'd had an argument and that you'd left me. They wanted to come looking for you."

"But they didn't."

"No."

"Are you sure?"

"I think so. Are you all right, Jack? What about those two men?"

"They're dead," Horn said softly, taking her arm. "I shot them to death in an alley not one kilometer from here." Somehow it was important that he tell her the truth.

"Oh, Jack, it must have been terrible for you," Anna said. And of all the things anyone could have said to him at that exact moment, they were exactly the words he needed to hear.

His mother said he was a sensitive child. His father had despaired for a few years that he would ever turn out all right. Finally they'd all accepted his wish to join the priesthood, and no one thought he was a homosexual for it. Later he'd learned that that had been his father's greatest fear. Yet his father had wept when Horn had quit the priesthood and had joined the service for Vietnam.

• • •

The security gate that led onto the quay where the *Pride of Leningrad* was being loaded was ajar. Horn and Anna slipped through, passed the lit but deserted guard hut, and walked directly to the ship's boarding ladder that angled down from amidships on the port side. There was a lot of activity around and on the ship, but no one paid them the slightest attention. At the top of the ladder the same small, rat-faced man who'd appeared at the men's room door of the Octobrists Club was waiting for them. Without a word he led them belowdecks to a tiny cabin just above the waterline. He had a terrible body odor and Anna shrank back from him. At the door Horn slipped the man five hundred marks. "There will be twice that much for you, a little extra special consideration, when we dock in Istanbul." The man pocketed the money, glanced at Anna, smiled ever so faintly, then turned and left, leaving a bit of his odor behind in the six-by-eight-foot cabin.

25

It was a few minutes after six o'clock in the morning. The sounds of loading cargo had stopped more than an hour ago. Now the ship's engines were turning over at dead idle. Horn could feel the vibrations through the soles of his feet on the bare steel floor. Anna lay asleep on the narrow bunk, the rough wool blanket up to her neck. One hand delicately positioned at the side of her head, her lips slightly parted. Her sleep was troubled. From time to time she whimpered, though she never cried out. A curtain covered the small porthole. Horn had drawn it back and looked outside, but from such a low angle he couldn't make out much except for the bottom of the dock, the pilings, and the underside of the ship's boarding ladder. Besides the single small bunk, their cabin was equipped with a tiny chest of drawers bolted to the deck, a heavy steel chair, and a built-in closet for their clothes. A tiny compartment contained a fold-up sink and a toilet on a raised platform. The hot water out of the tap was extremely hot, nearly steam, and the cold was lukewarm. He was splashing some water on his face when the ship lurched. He went to the porthole in time to see the dock sliding away, the lights on the quay suddenly harsh, throwing long streaks across the black water.

Someone knocked at the door, and Anna sat straight up in bed, clutching the blanket to her chin. Horn reached for his gun and clicked off the safety. Anna's eyes were wild, her long black hair in disarray.

"Da," Horn said.

No one answered.

Horn listened at the door for a moment or two, but he could hear nothing other than the dull rumbling of the engines. He glanced back at Anna, then holding the gun behind his back, he unlatched the door and carefully opened it. The corridor was empty. Someone had left a wooden box at the door. Steam rose from a large tin pitcher of tea. There was some bread and a small bowl with butter, a plate of small pastry squares sprinkled with powdered sugar, and two bottles of vodka.

"What is it?" Anna asked.

"Breakfast, I think," Horn said, pocketing his gun and bringing the box in. He relocked the door.

"Have we left?" Anna asked, suddenly aware of the engine sounds and the motion.

"Just a minute ago."

"No one has come? We have made it, Jack? We're actually going?"

"We're not out of the harbor yet, but we're on our way."

She threw the blanket back and got out of bed. She looked out the porthole. "Oh, God," she said very softly. "I'll never see Russia again, will I?" She sagged. "My home. My family. The Bolshoi."

"Anna?" Horn said, wanting to go to her.

She turned around. "What have I done, Jack?"

"What was necessary."

"For whom?"

"For you. For Jason. For your uncle and me."

She looked out the porthole again. They were picking up speed. The entire city was laid out along the hills. The Greek cruise liner was ablaze with her in-port lights even though it was very early. "We're really on our way, Jack?"

"Really."

"Then I won't look back," she said. He could hear the fatalism in her voice. What will be, will be. What is, is. Life is unbearable, the Russian said, but death is not so pleasant either.

Already they were far enough out into the bay so that the ship was meeting the swells of the open sea, the bow rising up gently, slewing a little to the left, and then falling off as they slowly rolled right. Washington was still a long way

off, halfway around the world, Horn thought. And Jason
would not give up. Not this easily.

"I want to tell you something, Jack," Anna said. "Something about Jason that I don't think you understand. Is it all
right?"

Horn sat in the chair facing her on the bed. She was going
to offer up a defense. He didn't move. They'd finished
breakfast and on her suggestion he'd poured them both a stiff
measure of vodka. He was down to three cigarettes, but he
didn't really mind.

"I don't know his name, and that is the truth. I can't give
that to you. But I can tell you about him. Do you believe
me?"

"Yes."

"It was in the winter, you know, after New Year's Eve.
We'd been doing *Romeo and Juliet*. I was dancing the lead in
the matinee. Nina Timofeyeva was Juliet in the evening. Do
you know the story?"

Horn nodded.

"It is a beautiful story about two children who simply do
not understand love, though they think they do," she said,
obviously remembering clearly. "It is a tragedy. 'When you
dance this role,' Nina told me at the beginning, 'you must
believe that yours is a tragic love of youth: misunderstood,
misdirected, and certainly misspent. Only in this way will
you be able to bring to the role what it needs, what it
demands so that your audience will believe in you.' I was
studying for this role for five years. I danced every segment a
thousand times in rehearsal hall, and even more in my sleep. I
read Shakespeare and Lavrovsky and Prokofiev until I could
do the *opera*! And there are films of when the company first
did the ballet in New York in the spring of 1959. We'd all
studied them for so long that any of us in the corps de ballet
could have participated as understudy. But I'd never been
picked for that role until then. I was not ready, though I'd
done *Giselle* and even once, the dying swan in *Swan Lake*—
you know, the swan that Maya Plisetskaya did so well, there
were always three encores. *Don Quixote, Sleeping Beauty*.
Others. Do you know, Jack, what it means to be denied a
specific role, no matter its importance?"

Anna was talking now about what had been uppermost in

her life before Jason. She was animated. He merely nodded again, not wishing to disturb her mood.

"None of us liked it. But we all knew what it meant. Most of the corps never dances beyond the corps. Not even matinee. Suddenly that winter I am handed the role of Juliet on a silver platter. Matinee, but the role nevertheless. I have improved. 'Anna, something has come to your dancing that has never been there before.' It is suddenly universal. My family is proud of me, my friends are happy. A little jealous, but happy too. It doesn't happen to everyone, Jack. But it has happened to me, and I do not even have to rehearse. It's not necessary. Not in the tenth scene, not in the eleventh or the twelfth. I have the passion, they say. Everyone is amazed except for me. Because I know what has happened to me."

"It was 1976," Horn said.

"Yes." Anna smiled knowingly. "I'd known Jason barely four months and already my life had changed. I wasn't dancing any better, mind you. At least technically I wasn't. But I was feeling the story. I understood poor Juliet. I suddenly knew what she was capable of."

"Did your friends at the theater know you were seeing an American?"

"They knew we'd danced together at the club, and we'd all had dinner backstage. But no, our relationship was secret. It had to be that way, Jack. And we were very careful about it, though as I've said, Jason was often around after our performances. But so were a lot of other foreigners, including Americans. He knew a lot of the company."

"Did your uncle know that you were seeing him?"

Anna chose to ignore the question. She sipped her vodka. "Jason was happy for me. My life would begin to have meaning, he said. It was up to me, and others like me, to bring art and beauty into the world. But none of it would be worthwhile unless I gave absolutely everything that I was capable of giving."

"You'd been told that before," Horn suggested.

She smiled. "Oh, of course. But those were just words. With Jason it was different. He understood. He really understood."

The sun streamed through their porthole. The morning was beautiful. They'd crossed the outer bar and now the ship settled into her sea routine. Horn had placed the wooden box and empty tea container out in the corridor like shoes outside a hotel room door, or a tin plate outside a prison cell. He estimated they were making between fifteen and twenty knots, which meant they'd raise the port of Constanţa on the Rumanian coast sometime in the late afternoon or early evening, unless his recall of geography was way off.

"He sat me down and talked to me about passion, Jack," she said earnestly. "About ardor, intensity, excitement, love of an idea or an ideal. You know."

"But you understood that, Anna. As a ballerina, you must have known devotion."

"No, Jack. Not until Jason. I had no idea what love or passion were. I had my craft, but I hadn't gotten my art. Not until then. For that I have Jason to thank."

The afternoon turned dark as they progressed south, and it began to rain. They had an overhead light, but Horn didn't bother to turn it on.

Their lunch was a passable borscht with a couple of bottles of beer and some crusty bread. Anna devoured hers and a portion of his. She seemed to be on the mend at the moment. Building her strength, though there remained a fragility about her that he thought would never change.

He had waited out in the corridor while she took a sponge bath and washed out a few of her things. When she let him back in she wore one of his shirts, and nothing more, her bare legs curled up beneath her where she sat huddled in the corner of the bunk. She'd washed her hair and pinned it up. She looked fresh and clean and young, and even more delicate and fragile than before. He noticed for the first time that her ears and nose were tiny, making her eyes seem huge and dark and very round.

Horn slept a little in the chair. Whenever he woke up Anna was looking at him.

It was raining very hard and it was pitch-black outside when they docked at Constanţa. Their supper was late and when it finally came was nothing more than bread and cheese with a bottle of mediocre red wine. Anna didn't seem to mind. Afterward they finished the last cigarette and Anna lay back in the bed and fell asleep. Around ten Horn covered her up, averting his eyes from her body where the shirt had hiked up around her hips. He closed the curtains over the porthole. There was a great deal of activity throughout the ship. They did not leave until well after midnight, and he had to think it out before he understood that the day was Monday.

Anna woke up a couple of hours later because of the motion of the ship. Her eyes seemed to glow of their own fire.

"Maya was ill for the last performance of *Romeo and Juliet*, and her understudy had pulled a muscle, so I was asked to dance. I think it was on purpose."

"You'd already danced a matinee?"

"Yes, but I'd agreed to do it just the same. Because of it I was later elevated to prima ballerina. It was my break. They told me about it after my first performance, and I could have gone onstage that very minute."

"Were you able to get a message to Jason?"

Anna smiled and shook her head. "No, but he was there anyway. I think he must have heard something from one of the others. It was going to be a very big night. Brezhnev himself was going to be in the audience. The house had been sold out for months."

"And you danced it."

"Yes, of course. And I believe it was my very best performance ever. I received three standing ovations. The orchestra stood up in the pit and tapped their instruments for me. The director came onstage and personally presented me with roses, as did Maya, and finally Brezhnev himself came up. They brought a chair for him, the orchestra began again, and with the heart of Russia onstage I danced my solo from the second act. Afterward he came to me, put his arms around me, and kissed me on both cheeks. He was a wonderful man. He reminded me of my Uncle Stepan."

"You must have been frightened."

"I was floating, Jack. I don't think I felt anything. I kept looking for Jason. My uncles were there, all three of them, and my Auntie Raya. My mother had come from Leningrad, and except for my father my whole family was present. Maya had arranged all of it for the matinee, and at the last minute she told them they would have to stay for the evening performance. How she found them seats I'll never know. But she did."

"Did you ever see Jason that night?"

"Oh, yes," Anna said, laying her head back on the bulkhead, her hands folded on the pillow on her lap. "There was a party backstage, of course. The entire company was present. There was champagne and caviar, and a few members of the orchestra came to play for us. The theater was very big and empty that night, but for us onstage we were the entire world. We were our own island universe in a sea of darkness.'' She smiled. ''Jason came up to me and kissed my cheek. He told me that I'd danced wonderfully. That I'd finally brought art to my craft. Someone took exception to his remarks, so he apologized, but I knew what he meant. It hurt a little that he was being so formal with me. I wanted to take him back to my dressing room and make love with him right then and there. I knew that's what he wanted more than anything else. All the rest of that evening he avoided me, though. He wouldn't even look my way. If I suddenly turned and caught the corner of his eye, he would turn away. I didn't know what to think. By the end of the party I was frantic. He didn't love me anymore, he hated me, he thought I had done poorly. A million dark thoughts raced through my mind. You can't know, Jack.''

''But he couldn't have been so open. It would have been dangerous for him.''

''I know that. But at the time I wasn't thinking so clearly. Everything was so terribly confusing. There were so many demands. So many people wanted to talk to me all at once. My uncle kept introducing me to old men who wanted to shake my hand and kiss me. It was always like that after a big show, but this night it was special because it had been *my* show. Had I a poison kiss I could have eliminated half of our military command and most of the Kremlin, I think.''

''But Jason wasn't himself, and you were hurt.''

''Not hurt, maybe just disappointed. I wanted to share my triumph with him. But I understood that he was protecting me.''

Another thought occurred to Horn. ''Was Brezhnev there, at your backstage party?''

''For a short while. It was a great honor.''

''Did Jason speak with him?''

''Of course,'' Anna said. ''Jason knew more party officials than I did.''

In the pitch-dark she was talking, her voice soft, intimate, as if he were eavesdropping on her dreams. Everything she said meant one thing to her, but a completely different thing to Horn.

"I took a taxi to the apartment afterward, and he was there," she said. "He didn't even get mad that I'd taken no precautions. It was that kind of a night."

"And you made love?" Horn said without really knowing what the question had to do with anything. Except for some reason he wanted to know. He was glad he couldn't see her face, only her form huddled on the bed.

For a moment she didn't answer. Whether or not it was out of embarrassment because of the question he couldn't know. The wind and seas had risen. The motion was beginning to get uncomfortable.

"Not at first. He was too impatient. It was something he wanted to tell me. Something he said he had discovered while I was onstage, something he had been trying to think out for several years."

"I'm sorry."

"It's all right, Jack. Believe me."

"He was proud of you?"

"Yes, he was. He told me so. He told me that I'd risen to an artistic height. He predicted that I would be prima ballerina very soon. In this he was correct, and I was just giddy enough that night to believe him completely. There are two forces in all of civilization, he said. Two forces that distinguish civilization from chaos. The first is power, the second is art."

"You knew your art. Could he explain his power to you?" Horn asked a little more sharply than he had intended. Her story was beginning to solidify his disgust and hate for Jason.

"Don't do that."

"I think he is a murderer."

"So are you, Jack!"

"Not of innocent people."

"There are no innocents."

It was Jason talking, of course. Anna could never have originated such a thought. She was too kind, too gentle. He was beginning to be able to pick Jason out of her general conversation. His influence on her after all of these years was amazing. He'd been more than a lover to her during their eighteen months. Horn suspected he'd been her father too.

"Power and art," he prompted.

"You're making fun of me," she said.

"I wouldn't be here if I was, Anna."

He could hear her breathing, and he could smell her heat from across the cabin. Her presence glowed in the dark, filling the room.

"Art was bringing order out of chaos, he said. Whereas power was preventing chaos from happening in the first place. One was imaginative. The other was real. But without power there could be no peace in which art could take place. And without art, power was meaningless."

For a time Horn's thoughts went back to Odessa. In his mind's eye he could clearly see the GRU agent in the alley clawing for his weapon. He could see the look of abject terror in the man's eyes. He understood what the man must have been feeling at that moment. Yet now Horn was having trouble identifying his own emotions.

They were late arriving in Varna, Bulgaria's chief seaport and manufacturing center. The city had begun life in the sixth century under the name of Odessus, became known as Varna a few hundred years later, and was renamed Stalin in 1956 in honor of the Soviet premier. Khrushchev changed all that, returning the name Varna to the city.

The dawn was gray and dismal, and again Anna slept fitfully. She'd talked herself out. She'd told him what she knew about her Jason, the details, at least, that were important to her as a woman and as his lover. But Horn had felt a reluctance in her to speak openly about Jason, as if what she might say could still harm him. It was a barrier, he suspected, she would never open.

Their breakfast consisted of hard-boiled eggs, tea, bread, and even a small piece of salmon wrapped in wax paper.

At around ten in the morning, the rat-faced second officer who had guided them aboard showed up with a bottle of sweet Russian champagne and a pack of French cigarettes. His odor was worse than ever. His hands were filthy, his fingernails thick, chipped, and caked with grease. He had a furtive look, and Horn was expecting trouble.

"We will arrive in Istanbul before midnight, comrade. I will come for you when it is time to leave the ship." He tried to look over Horn's shoulder at Anna sleeping in the bed.

"Will there be any trouble?" Horn asked, blocking his view.

The second officer shook his head sadly. "Not aboard ship. Comrade Butenko has brought his girlfriend. He is busy."

Horn assumed Butenko was the political officer aboard. "I'll have the remainder of your money for you when we arrive."

Again the man tried to look over Horn's shoulder. "She is Anna Feodorovna, isn't she?" he said softly.

Horn's grip tightened on the edge of the door. "What are you talking about? She's an American."

The man smiled a little. From within his greasy coat he withdrew a Bolshoi program. Anna's photograph was on the front. He held it out. "Would you have her sign it for me? Please?"

Jason had gone to school at a place in Maryland that Anna thought might have started with the American letter *A*. Horn figured Annapolis. He was tall and somewhat husky. "Like you, Jack," she said. "Only narrower of hip." His eyes were blue, his hair dark but prematurely gray, and in those days he wore a small, neat mustache. He spoke terrible Russian, passable Italian, and very good French. He was knowledge-able about music, the ballet, and opera, and he understood a great deal about Russian history, art, and poetry. "Great is Holy Russia," he would cite the old proverb, "but the sun shines elsewhere too."

Anna had insisted that Horn clean up and lie down on the bed. He'd been exhausted, and in no mood to argue with her. "You will be no good to either of us if you don't get some rest."

They left Varna at around noon for the final nine hours or so to Istanbul and freedom. Anna spent most of the afternoon staring out the porthole at the big waves marching across the Black Sea. She only picked at her lunch, and afterward Horn lay down again. He was still very tired.

Horn woke up at around seven. The cabin was very dark. They had sailed out from beneath the rain clouds; he could see stars through the porthole.

"Don't turn on the light, Jack," Anna said. He could make out her figure in the chair.

"Are you all right?" he asked, sitting up.

"I'm frightened," she said. "We're very near Istanbul, I think, and I don't know what's going to happen to me."

"We're going to the United States. To Washington."

"Why?"

"To find Jason. You're going to help me find him."

"And then what, Jack? What will happen then?"

"I'm going to arrest him for murder, and for espionage against his country."

"And I shall always hate you for it. I never want you to forget that." She got up and crossed to the porthole. He could see that she was nude. In the starlight he could see her breasts, and her long dark hair flowing down her back nearly to her little boy's buttocks. Her legs were long and straight and well muscled.

He was confused. He found that he wanted her, and he felt guilty for it. He loved Christine. He'd always loved Christine. The children.

Anna turned toward him. "Will you make love to me now, Jack, even though I hate you for what you have done to me?"

"You don't have to do this . . ."

"There have been no others," she cried in anguish, though her voice was still small, breathless. "I'm not some whore to come to you like this. Is that what you think?"

"No . . ."

"Do you find me ugly?"

Horn felt a constriction in his chest. "No, Anna, I don't think you are ugly. You're very beautiful."

"Then what, Jack?" she pleaded, holding out her hands. "Is it my sickness? It's not catching."

"Oh, Christ," Horn said, looking away.

"Talk to me, please. What is it?"

The cabin was very close. Horn could practically feel the heat emanating from her. He did not want to feel pity for her, and yet he couldn't help himself. Poor little lost Anna who'd grown up to become a lonely, terribly unfulfilled woman, now for whom there was very little hope. Poor little lost Anna who had been brutally pulled from her secure existence by a monster who cared nothing for human life let alone the emotions of a young woman.

Love me, please. Horn remembered the words of Poor Butterfly. *We are people accustomed to little things, humble and quiet, to a tenderness which is gentle, and yet as wide as the sky, as deep as the rolling sea.*

"You have a wife," Anna said.

Horn nodded.

"And children?"

He turned back to her, but she had returned to the porthole where she was hugging herself and staring out at the sea.

"And children, Jack?" she asked again. "Do you and your wife have children?"

"Yes," he said. He pushed back the covers and got out of bed.

"Are they good children, Jack?"

"Don't do this."

"Do they have respect for you, for their mother, for their teachers?"

Horn went across to her and reached out for her shoulder, but then held back. How had his life come to this? How had he arrived at this juncture? He had no idea, and he did not know if he wanted to understand. But Christine had seen it coming. She had recognized the signs.

"Anna?" he said softly.

"I cannot have children, Jack. Not now. It is too late."

What could he have done differently? How should he have acted? But she was so terribly alone, and hopeless. She'd lost everything. Perhaps it was just pity. He hoped so.

He took her shoulder and gently turned her around. She looked up into his eyes, tears sliding down her cheeks, her lips trembling.

"I'm sorry," she said.

Horn brushed her tears away, then pushed a strand of hair back. In the starlight her face was luminescent, her eyes wide and dark with a life of their own. Here is a dancer. An artist. A performer. A woman for whom all of life was nothing but preparation for her performances. Perhaps Jason had given her something after all. She came into his arms, her breasts pressed against his chest, her lips soft and yielding. He could feel a shiver run through her entire body as she clung tightly to him.

When they parted her face was flushed, her nostrils flared.

"I'm sorry," she said again.

"No, Anna, not tonight. There is nothing to be sorry for." He lifted her gently and carried her back to the bed where he got undressed and lay down beside her. When he entered her she was ready, and a large sigh escaped her lips. She reached up and held him closely, her dancer's legs wrapped around his hips, her pelvis rising to meet his as if she wanted him to bury himself in her, as if she wanted to take in his entire body. He kissed her face and her ears and her neck and her breasts as they made love slowly and deliberately, savoring each moment as if it were their very last.

Anna cried out once, and afterward, when they were finished, she clung tightly to him for a very long time, and he could taste her tears again, warm and salty when he kissed her face, and he felt her body shuddering as she cried silently.

26

Staring out at the Asian side of the Bosphorus, Horn was brought back to his last night on Pamlico Sound. The future was vast and dark and empty. They'd passed beneath Istanbul's Galata bridge and he could believe he was in another, simpler time. In the morning he would drive back up to Georgetown and inform Monsignor Adams that he was resigning from the seminary. A barge was coming down the sound, and he could see its lights and hear its whistle echoing off the water. He could see the Cape Hatteras shoreline, see the lights, feel the decision he'd finally made wrenching his gut. "Is it a girl, Jack?" the monsignor would ask. How could he answer? "It happens to most of us at one time or another. But you are young. We understand." But the monsignor had already passed that hurdle, if he ever had, a century ago. Nor could he understand about the fighting in Vietnam. The excitement of contributing to his country's honor. "To the greater glory of God, Jack. Never forget who we all serve." But then his final admonition came, and it still hurt: "You will return to the Church, Jack. I pray to God it will not be too late for your soul, because the alternative is everlasting damnation in hell." In Vietnam, listening to the distant artillery and the not so distant rockets crashing in, listening to the screams of fear and agony, he thought a lot about the monsignor's hell. And he believed he'd already arrived. It was his guilt, then and now.

He stood at the porthole, Anna beside him, her arm against

345

his, though she wouldn't look up at him. She was ashamed. And frightened. She'd wanted Jason and she knew what she'd done to them both. They were steaming down the strait toward Hasköy up the Golden Horn where they would be docking. They passed the tower of Leander out in the strait where it turned south toward the Sea of Marmara. Across, in Old Town, was the Hagia Sophia, and Topkapi Palace, and a skyline of minarets and ancient buildings, a conglomeration called Eminönü. Up into the Golden Horn, the Halic, they passed beneath the Karakoy Bridge, dense with traffic, their whistle blowing, echoing across the city. He'd been here before. Six months of it in '78, on loan to the Agency's substation at the consulate on Mesrutiyet Street in New Town. He had gotten to know the city on both sides of the strait. It was a city for hiding out. A city for getting lost among its four and a half million inhabitants. He'd thought a lot about that on the way down, deciding at the very end that Jason would want them to run to some little rathole where no one would care if they lived or died. A perfect spot for assassination.

So where were the answers, Doxy? Now that they had come this far, where was the future? And more importantly, where were you? He'd lain awake in bed after he and Anna had made love, and he listened to her breathing as he thought about all that had passed. He could not bring himself to think about Christine, whom he had betrayed, so he had worried instead about his old friend. Please, dear God, please don't let Doxy be another Clay or Nobels. Don't let him be dead or dying somewhere, his blood leaking out, his heart stopping, another casualty of the Jason War as he'd come to think of it.

"Is this what the United States will be like, then, Jack?" Anna asked, her voice subdued.

"No. There's nothing this old there," Horn said. But wait until you see Washington, and New York, he thought. Wait until you meet the people, see the houses, the cars, the stores, the lights.

"Will they let us through customs when we dock?"

"I think so."

"But you don't know for sure?"

"No, I don't, Anna. But I have been in this country before. I think we will be able to buy our way through."

"Then it is true," Anna said. "What they say about the West. Money will buy anything. Anything at all. So, if you are poor, you do not have much of a chance, even at survival."

Horn looked down at her and figured he knew what she was worried about. If Jason was put in prison, she would have no one, no money, nowhere to go. She would die poor, forgotten in the West and vilified in Moscow. But it wouldn't happen that way. Not in America. Not for her.

"You'll be taken care of," Horn said.

"Yes?"

If we survive that long, Horn thought. "You won't have to worry about money, or a place to live, or for your medical expenses."

"This is going to be done for me?" she asked innocently, looking up finally into his eyes.

"Of course."

She shook her head sadly. "For a defector they will do this, but not for their own poor people. Does it make any sense to you, Jack?"

"No, it doesn't," he admitted. Not really. Though it wasn't as simple as all that, was it?

"But I'm getting ahead of myself, aren't I?" she said. "How silly of me, actually. We must first get off this wretched ship and into the city and onto an airplane or another ship. Just how will we get to America, Jack? Can you tell me that? And then they have to let us into the United States, and me with such a terrible passport, and finally there will be Jason whom you will try to arrest. But he won't want that, of course. He'll try to kill you, I think. That is if my uncle doesn't show up first. My uncle has been to America, you know. He has been to Washington and to the United Nations in New York. Years ago. But some things never change, don't you know that, Jack?" Her eyes had gotten wild. "Or maybe there will be a shoot-out like in your cowboy movies. Or maybe Jason will have forgotten me, or won't want to see me. Or maybe all of this has been an extraordinary lie. All of it, including you."

Ah, Jason, you bastard, what have you done? "I haven't lied to you, Anna."

"But you will lie to your wife," she snapped, lashing out. "Why not me?"

They were late. It was well past ten before they were actually docked. For the first hour or so there was a lot of activity up on deck. Customs and immigration officers coming and going, he suspected. The shipping line's representa-

tives from their office in the city. The political officers from
the Soviet consulate. The ship's papers would be gone over,
the crew's papers examined. All routine. Nothing out of the
ordinary unless they'd been followed from Odessa. Unless
someone aboard ship had turned them in.

They sat in the dark, ready to leave. Horn took out his gun
and played with the safety catch, but the noise made Anna
nervous, so he quit. The paper targets on the practice range
never bled like the real thing; it was something they didn't tell
you about at school. He'd seen enough blood in Vietnam to
last him a hundred lifetimes, but somehow that had been
more impersonal. Distant. Justified, in an odd sort of way.
Murder en masse was horrible but distant. One-on-one it
became terribly personal and very real. He was a spy, not an
assassin, he kept telling himself, but he could not drag his
thoughts away from the families of the men he had shot to
death. The wives, the children, the mothers. Shot down by an
American spy. Why doesn't Comrade Gorbachev do something about the American cowboys?

"What is happening, Jack?" Anna asked from the dark.

He looked to where he knew she was sitting on the bed, but
he could not see her in the darkness. "They'll come for us
when it is safe."

"Who will?"

"The second officer. The one you did the autograph for."

"I'm frightened."

Horn shifted the gun to his other hand. His mouth was dry.
The ship was very quiet now. Only a generator was running
somewhere below them. The silence after the main engines
had been shut down was ominous.

"He knows who I am," she said. "He might have told
someone."

"I don't think so. They'll still be wanting their money." A
day at a time, a step at a time, take it as it comes. He'd had
the advice; now he was living it.

"What if they don't, Jack?"

"Easy," he cautioned.

"They could come in here and kill us and take what they
wanted—"

A hatch clanged open at the end of the corridor. Horn
jumped up and put his ear to the door. He forgot which way
he'd left the Walther's safety catch. Feeling it with his thumb,
he also found he'd forgotten which way was on—up or down?

He heard someone coming down the corridor, the steps quick and sure. Horn stepped back. The footsteps stopped and there was a knock at the door.

"*Da*," Horn called out softly.

"It is time," the second officer said.

Holding the gun out of sight behind his right leg, Horn used his left hand to unlock the door, and he stepped back as he pulled it open. The light from the corridor was bright. The rat-faced little officer was silhouetted.

"Please hurry. There is only a few minutes before Comrade Butenko is finished with his conference. You must be off the ship by then. Hurry. Please."

Horn had already counted out the five thousand marks for their passage as well as the additional thousand he had promised Rat Face. He handed over the wrapped bundle. The man was very nervous. He hardly bothered to look at the money, stuffing it into his filthy jacket. He turned and looked down the corridor.

Horn slung his overnight bag over his left shoulder. Keeping his gun out of sight he stepped out into the corridor. Anna had grabbed her bag. She was right behind him.

"I will take you topside," Rat Face said nervously. "There will be two Turkish police on deck. Ignore them. Walk directly to the boarding ladder and go down to the dock. Do not look back. The gate will be open. There will be a taxi there waiting for you."

"What about the captain?"

"He is with Butenko in the wardroom. The curtains are closed. They will see nothing. Now, please, we must go."

Horn glanced at Anna. She nodded bravely, clutching at the strap of her plastic airline bag. He felt like a Jewish refugee all of a sudden, off the *Exodus*, escaping the Holocaust, trading it for a possible bullet in the back. He took her arm with his left hand, and as they followed Rat Face down the corridor, he stuffed the Walther in his coat pocket, but he kept his hand curled around the grip, his finger away from the trigger because he still wasn't sure about the safety.

They took the stairs up two levels. The ship smelled like a combination of diesel oil, cooked cabbage, unwashed bodies, and urine. Rat Face, Horn figured, hadn't taken a bath in at least a month, and possibly longer. His odors seemed to blend with the ship's. At the second level he motioned for them to hold up and keep silent while he scouted ahead. Anna was shivering, though it wasn't very cold and she still wore her rabbit fur hat, coat, and boots. Some men were below on the stairs; they could hear them coming up, talking, laughing. Horn turned and looked down, but he couldn't see anyone yet. His fingers tightened on the Walther's grip. A shoot-out here would be suicide. As long as they remained aboard the ship, they were still technically on Soviet territory and therefore subject to Soviet law. They'd never get off alive. But he wasn't going to be taken. Not like this.

Rat Face appeared moments later and Horn motioned frantically below. They listened. Rat Face heard the voices, and motioned for Horn and Anna to hurry. They emerged from the stairway, crossed a broad corridor, and ducked through a wide hatch to another set of stairs leading up. At the top Rat Face flattened against the bulkhead just inside the door.

"Just outside is the deck," he whispered. His face was flushed, and he was sweating heavily. His odor had gotten worse. It was nauseating. Anna shrank back.

"Thank you, my friend," Horn said.

Rat Face was staring at Anna. "I saw you in *Giselle*. I was younger then. I cried. Good luck."

Horn stepped up past him, but Anna stopped. She looked into the second officer's eyes, then reached out and kissed him gently on the lips. "Thank you," she said.

"Hurry."

At the top Horn eased the big hatch open a crack and looked outside. The forward portion of the deck was bathed in lights. One of the main cargo hatches had been opened and several men, two of them Turkish policemen, stood looking down into the hold.

Horn looked back. Again Anna nodded that she was ready. Rat Face had already started below. Horn took a deep breath, held it a moment, then let it out as he pushed open the door and stepped out into the cool night air. Anna came right behind him. He took her arm and together they walked carefully across to the opening in the rail where the boarding ladder angled down to the dock. Without looking back they started down. The quay was lit up like day. Two other ships were docked ahead of theirs, and teamsters with leather capes that fit over their heads were loading pallets for transfer aboard. A pair of Turkish soldiers, their rifles slung over their shoulders, stood a hundred feet away warming their hands over an open fire in a barrel, though it was quite warm compared to Moscow. Seventy-five yards along the line of warehouses to the south, the exit gate was lit by strong spotlights. Two Turkish police cars were parked just inside. They could see the taxi on the other side of the fence. At the bottom they hesitated only a moment, then started toward the gate. Horn took his hand out of his pocket so that it would be plainly visible. He was sweating. Halfway to the gate two Turkish officers stepped out of the guardhouse and watched them approach. They looked stern, their faces chiseled in granite under the harsh lights. A third police car pulled up behind the taxi, and a bulky man in plainclothes got out of the back and came through the gate. He said something to the two uniformed officers who glanced again down the dock, and then went inside. Anna wanted to hold back, but Horn forced her to go on. "Smile, Anna, and keep smiling," he said under his breath. He stretched a broad grin on his face. We are no threat, he was telling the cop. We are innocent, though tired, travelers. Guilty of nothing under Turkish law. With nothing to hide. But what was he doing here? Who sent him?

"Good evening, sir," Horn said politely in English as they reached the gate. "Do you wish to see our passports?"

"Yes, of course," the plainclothes cop replied in English, a faint smile on his thick lips.

Horn disengaged his arm from Anna's, pulled out both their passports, and handed them over. The cop opened Horn's first, looked at it for a few moments, thumbing through the back pages, looking up at Horn's features, then he opened Anna's. Horn stiffened. The uniformed cops were watching them from inside the guardhouse.

"Not a particularly good likeness, Miss Townsend," the cop said, looking up from her photo.

"She has lost weight recently," Horn explained.

Anna smiled uncertainly and nodded.

"And where have you two come from?"

"Odessa," Horn said evenly. There was no use lying.

"An unusual way in which to travel for two Americans, aboard a Soviet Black Sea steamer."

"It was not a good trip."

"No?"

"The weather—"

The cop looked again at the photograph of Gloria Townsend. He shook his head. "There will be an entry fee, of course."

There was no such fee in Turkey. He looked up. "You have not paid this as yet?"

"I have West German marks," Horn said, patting his breast pocket. He had taken the money out of the lining of his coat. "I would be happy to pay our fee now, if you would be so kind as to take care of the details for us."

"Naturally," the cop said, inclining his head. "For you, one thousand marks. Very reasonable."

Horn started to reach for his money.

"For the girl, the same."

Horn stopped. It would leave them dangerously low on money. They still had a long way to go. Of course he could use credit cards. By the time the transactions were traced, this business would be long finished. He pulled the money out and handed it over. The cop deftly looked through the bills, verifying the amount, then pocketed the money. He handed back their passports, touched the brim of his hat, and stepped aside. "Welcome to Istanbul. I hope your visit turns out to be a pleasant one."

"Istanbul is always a pleasant city," Horn said. "I have friends here. Many friends."

At midnight the streets of Istanbul were alive with people and traffic of all sizes, shapes, and descriptions. It was a spectacle and Anna couldn't get enough of it. "It's like Offenbach," she cried at one point. The relief from tension once they'd pulled away in the cab had been magical for her. She was a changed woman, more alive, more alert than in Moscow. She'd noticed Horn's concern about the money with the Turkish cop, and she asked him about it. "We have very little cash left," he said. "But it's all right."

"Yes, of course," Anna replied. She opened her purse and pulled out a thick bundle of French francs. She handed them to Horn. "I've been saving these for a very long time. In case one day I would go to Paris, to see Jason."

There had to be better than thirty thousand francs in the bundle, Horn figured. Around five thousand dollars. It was a lot of money. Her life savings.

"All right, Anna," he said. "All right."

She turned and watched out the window. The shops and the colors and the lights dazzled her. Moscow by comparison with almost anywhere else was a drab city. She was a country girl at heart, she told him at one point. She'd never even seen all of Moscow; most of her days were spent confined to the immediate environs of the Bolshoi Theater. "I'd always regretted that I wasn't allowed to travel, Jack," she said. "Just a little. But I never imagined it would be like this." She was dying, but she struck Horn as being so fresh and new.

"Every city isn't like this, Anna."

The notion couldn't have pleased her more. "Oh, I hope not, Jack. I sincerely hope not. I want them all to be different."

Twice on the way over to the Hilton in New Town, Horn looked over his shoulder out the rear window. Again he had the definite feeling that they were being followed, and he couldn't shake it. The driver noticed.

"Is there something amiss, effendi?" he asked.

"Someone is following us," Horn said.

The driver looked in the rearview mirror. "But that is terrible! I have seen nothing, effendi, I promise—"

"Pretend someone is following us. And for ten thousand liras above the meter, lose them." It was about fifteen extra dollars.

"Yes, effendi," the driver said enthusiastically. He dropped the cab into low gear, glanced in the rearview mirror one last time, and turned sharply down an exceedingly narrow and dark side avenue, the tires squealing as they accelerated down damp cobblestones, pedestrians and chickens and even a few goats scattering as he laid on the horn. Anna was thrown against Horn and she shrieked. It took him a moment before he realized she was laughing. Either she hadn't understood the English well enough to know what was happening, or she hadn't been paying attention. "What is it, Jack?" she cried. "He's a crazy man!"

"They're all like that."

They drove up through Yenishehir, then across Cumhuriyet, New Town's main boulevard, through the university, and back down around the Naval Museum and Dolma Bahçe Palace, lit in a dozen different-hued lights. They doubled back past the Kabatas Ferry across the Bosphorus, and fifteen minutes later cruised sedately by the Istanbul Opera, finally pulling up the circular drive onto the expansive grounds of the Hilton. Anna was clapping in delight, and the driver was winded and nervous, but clearly he too had enjoyed the ride.

"All right, effendi, all right," he said. "What the hell!"

"What the hell," Horn agreed. He reached forward and paid their effusive driver with some of Anna's French francs.

He wasn't quite sure of the exchange rate, but the driver seemed delighted. A doorman from the hotel came down and opened the door for them. A bellman was summoned for their overnight bags. Anna and Horn walked up into the lobby, the sound of water splashing along the walkway, and the noises of music and laughter drifting out to them from the casino.

"We're free, aren't we, Jack?" Anna said, suddenly serious. "We're actually here."

"We'll fly to Washington tomorrow."

She looked up into his eyes. "Maybe if we stayed here, it would not be so terrible after all," she said. "Maybe not."

They registered as Mr. and Mrs. Jack Hansen despite the difference in names in their passports. Turkey was still an Islamic nation, and even in the big Western hotels a certain fiction of propriety had to be maintained. Their room was very large and quite nice, on the tenth floor overlooking the city, the dark Bosphorus, and, beyond, the lights of Asia.

While Anna was taking a bath, Horn ordered up a snack tray of meats and cheeses, a bottle of wine, a couple of bottles of mineral water, and a pack of American cigarettes. He called the bellman and asked that someone be sent up for their laundry, and while he waited, he turned on the television. Only three channels worked. On one a folk dance company was performing, on another the news was being read in Turkish, a language with which he'd had only minimal luck, and on the third was an old episode of *Dallas*, surprisingly in English. He had begun to turn his mind to the problem of Istanbul. Now that they had gotten this far, Jason was not going to simply give up. Which meant they'd need help. He unlocked for room service, and a minute later the bellman arrived. Horn handed over his coat and slacks and shirt as well as Anna's skirt and blouse. "We'll need them first thing in the morning," he said. "Yes, of course, effendi." When they were gone, he poured a glass of wine and lit a cigarette. He stood in his shorts at the window, looking across the city. It was possible that Jason's people were here already. If the man had help in Moscow, which he almost certainly did, then by now he could have discovered that they'd run to Odessa. Even if the two GRU officers—how had they known his name?—had been only happenstance, every Soviet city of egress covered, their deaths would not be ignored. They'd know. Someone would figure it out and come here looking.

Anna's uncle, the KGB general, would be searching for her as well. And that man had a lot of power. The bathroom door opened behind him, and in the dark window glass he could see Anna's reflection. Her hair was up, she had put on one of the hotel's terry-cloth robes, and she looked tiny, frail, and not well.

He turned around. She was definitely very pale. "Are you all right, Anna?"

She remained in the doorway, one hand holding her robe closed at the neck, the other on the doorframe for support. She shook her head slightly. "No, I don't think so, Jack," she said weakly, and she started to sag.

Horn got to her just in time for her to collapse into his arms, her eyes fluttering, her complexion a deathly white, tiny beads of sweat forming along her upper lip. He picked her up and carried her to the bed, her breath hot on his cheek. He pulled back the covers and laid her down, then felt her forehead. She was warm.

"Jack?" she cried, trying to sit up. Her robe came open, and Horn was rocked back by what he saw. Angry red and purple bruises covered most of her tiny breasts, her sides, both hips, and several places on her legs. It looked as if she'd been in a terrible fight, or an automobile accident, or as if someone had methodically tortured her. What in God's name had happened to her? He had seen her body yesterday. There had been no bruises. And he'd been with her since then.

He got hold of himself and eased her back down on the bed. "It's all right, Anna. I'm here," he said, covering her with the blankets.

"My pills, in my bag. I need them, please."

Horn brought the two small vials to her with a glass of mineral water. She sat up enough to take a pill from each, though she had a little trouble swallowing. He took the glass from her and she lay back. He felt absolutely terrible for her.

"What is it?" he asked.

"My illness, Jack," she answered, smiling faintly. "Sometimes a weakness comes over me. I'll be better in the morning. I promise. I won't be a hindrance for you."

"What happened to your . . . the bruising . . ."

She smiled again. "Oh, that," she said. She was embarrassed. She turned away from him. "My skin is a little sensitive now. I'm not very pretty, am I."

"What happened, Anna? What did you do? Did you fall?"

She put a hand to her mouth. Tears began to leak out of her eyes. "No, Jack."

"What then? What happened?"

"We made love."

It struck him. Her illness. The leukemia. The low white counts, the anemia. "Oh, God," he said. "Oh, my God." He sank down beside her on the bed and reached out tentatively, not knowing now if he should touch her or not, or what he should do. He gently brushed her tears away, and she looked at him. "I'm sorry, Anna," he said. "If I'd only stopped to think . . ."

"It's not your fault," she said. "I seduced you, remember?"

"I should have known."

"No. You couldn't have." She reached up and touched his cheek, then pushed herself up so that she could kiss him. "It wouldn't have made the slightest bit of difference anyway, Jack, because I wanted you no matter what. And I still want you even though I know what you are trying to do to Jason, and even though I know that you are married. I'm just a little Moscow whore, and I think I love you."

She lay back and Horn replaced the covers. "Get some sleep now," he said.

"Okay, Jack," she said, her words slurred.

He watched her for a long time until he was certain she was asleep, then he took a shower and lay down beside her, the Walther on the nightstand next to him. He'd left the television playing, the sound off, and the last thing he saw was the beginning of a *M*A*S*H* rerun. The hotel had provided the programs for American tourists.

Their freshly laundered clothes arrived at around seven-thirty. And by eight, when Horn was ready to leave the hotel, Anna was still sleeping. He left a note for her on her nightstand, hung the Do Not Disturb sign on their door, and took the elevator down to the lobby. He retrieved their passports at the desk, and was directed across the lobby to the Hertz counter where he rented a two-year-old Peugeot, the best car they had available. He waited out front while they brought the car around. The morning was lovely and warm with only a few puffy clouds in a hazy blue sky. Two men dressed in tuxedos, their ties loose, stood talking at the entry to the garden that led back to the casino, the only one in Turkey. A lot of luggage was piled up on the sidewalk. As he waited, a dozen cabs arrived, loaded, and left. Some of the departing guests were German, a few of them Japanese, and a few others American. He heard them talking, and he suddenly realized that he missed home. He missed his own kind. The language, the food and drink, the sights and sounds and smells he'd grown up with. It seemed like such a terribly long time since he'd been back.

The Peugeot, which had been very expensive to rent, was in wretched condition. He didn't think there was a decent rental car in all of Turkey. He'd done this before.

Traffic downtown was very heavy, not so much with tourists, though there were always tourists in Istanbul, but with the normal twentieth-century workaday traffic along streets and alleys, some of which were a millennium old. He took his time, working his way up into the business district, away from the university. It was nearly nine by the time he found a parking spot off Istiklal Street and walked around the corner to the Central Telephone and Telegraph Office. He was reasonably sure that he had not been followed, though once he made his call, the game might very well be up. Still, he thought, he needed the help, so he would have to take the risk. And he had to know what had happened in Washington. He had to find out. One of the clerks assigned him a booth after he'd paid the minimum fee, and because of the hour—it was just two in the morning in Washington—his call went through almost immediately. The telephone rang once, twice, and on the third ring the sound seemed to diminish ever so slightly. A tap, or his imagination?

"Hello?" Doxy's wife answered.

"Hello, Donna. Sorry to be calling so late. Is Doxy handy and sober?"

There was a very long hesitation on the line. Something was definitely wrong.

"Who?" she asked.

It *was* Doxmeuller's wife. She recognized his voice. And something was very wrong. He heard all of it in the pause and in the single word.

"I need his help."

"He can't help you, Jack!" she cried desperately. "He's gone and never coming back—" The line went blank but not dead. They'd cut her off, but they were still working the trace, though it would be obvious the call had come in from overseas.

Horn hung up. Doxy had an ancient diesel-powered workboat docked on the Chesapeake south of Baltimore at a place called Gibson Island. He'd never told the Company about it. Horn was sure of that, because they'd talked about it. The boat was barely an hour and a half out of Washington. It was his go-to-hell spot. Always stocked with fuel, provisions, and plenty of drink, it was his answer to what he called the "credibility crisis." It was a spot, he said, that if ever all hell broke loose, he'd run to and never come back. His words exactly. "Never coming back once I pull the pin, Jack." And Donna had just told him that Doxy was never coming back. *Run, Jack, run!* His last words.

But Donna had not said that he was dead. She'd said *gone.* There was still hope. Doxy was on his boat. Waiting. Watching.

Back at the counter he paid in advance for a second overseas call, this one to McClean, Virginia. Again because of the lateness of the hour in the States, his call was put through almost immediately. Carlisle answered on the first ring, and Horn got the impression that the man was moving very fast, that he was in what the Agency wags called his "battle mode." He sounded as if he were surrounded by men and machines.

"Yes," he snapped impatiently. "Allan, is that you again, for God's sake?" The reception was very good. Horn thought he heard someone in the background talking. Carlisle was not alone. You never were during a crisis. "Get him on the other line, then," he told someone. "Hello?" he said again into the telephone.

"It's me," Horn said.

"Good Lord, Jack," Carlisle breathed. "Where are you?"

"I'm on my way in, Farley."

"Well, thank heaven for that," Carlisle said. Horn could hear the forced control in his voice. "But don't you think it would be wiser to stay put, and let us come pick you up? Less danger that way, a stationary pickup, you know the drill."

"Less danger for you, not me. Farley, I know who killed Boyko and Nobels and Edmund Clay and all of my madmen."

"We can discuss all of that once you're here—"

"Listen to me, Farley, because I'm not going to be on this line for very long. Jason's workname in '75 and '76 was Ted Wells. He was stationed at the Moscow embassy, yet his name doesn't show up on any of the station registers. But he was well enough placed that he was on speaking terms with Brezhnev himself, and he knew General Patrenko.''

The line was deathly still. Horn thought he might have lost the connection.

"Farley, are you there?''

"Jack, tell us where you are. We'll pick you up and everything will be fine.''

"Jason was Navy. And, Farley, the man had a bad habit of talking to his Russian girlfriend about submarines. Are you listening to me? I think he may have been indiscreet, and now what she knows is coming back to haunt him. He wants her stopped.''

"What are you babbling about, for christ's sake? What I want to know is why you shot one of our own people to death in some grubby little East Berlin tryst house. Was that an act of a patriot? You cannot imagine, Jack, you simply cannot imagine the fuss you have caused. The president himself is now involved. And God-only knows how long we'll be able to keep this away from the media. And if they get it, all of us will be booted out.''

"I have her with me, Farley. I'm bringing her in. She'll identify Jason. She'll tell the entire story. All of it. To *The New York Times* if need be.''

"You're a murderer, Jack,'' Carlisle said, his tone suddenly harsh. "The Russians want you, the East Germans want you, and we want you. Which will it be?''

"Think about it. All but one of my madmen are dead, and Jason is still able to operate in the Soviet Union. He has help over there.''

"If you are talking about a man named Yevgenni Sheshkin, he was shot to death last night. He and his wife. Is that who you're talking about? Early just telephoned. Every Soviet employee in the embassy has been pulled out. The ambassador's wife is serving lunch, for God's sake.''

Ah, Christ. Yevgenni was among the best. Had he known this would happen all along? Had he realized it the night Boyko showed up? Or hadn't it dawned on him until his old control officer arrived out of the blue?

"Let the girl go home, Jack, and then give yourself up. It'll be easier all the way around. On you, on us . . . and, Jack, easier on Christine and the children.''

Horn had a feeling of total disbelief, listening to what Carlisle was telling him. And then rage that such a monstrous bait could be suggested. "You son of a bitch. If you so much as go near my family, I swear to God, I'll kill you, Farley!"

"It's too late—" Carlisle started, but Horn crashed the telephone down and stepped out of the booth. He was shaking, his stomach tied in knots.

He looked across the hall. The clerk behind the long counter was watching him with an odd expression on her face. She was saying something into a telephone. A Turkish cop stood at the far end of the counter, but Horn didn't think the local police would have been brought in on this. Not yet. Carlisle would want to keep it clean for as long as possible. And so would the Russians if they had come this far already. And if Jason was working both sides of the fence, they'd be on their way. The American consulate was only a couple of blocks away. It was possible they'd have someone on the way right now. There had been time for a trace. He turned left and walked past the long row of enclosed booths and angled across the main hall toward the front doors. Carlisle and his whiz kids might have him pinpointed here in Istanbul, all right, but Istanbul was a very big city with all of Asia at its back door and all of Europe at its front. He could feel the clerk's eyes on him, and as he approached the end of the long marble counter the Turkish cop looked up. Don't do a thing, Horn thought. He could feel the weight and pressure of the gun in his belt at the small of his back. He passed the end of the counter and the cop turned back to the clerk he'd been speaking with. Carlisle and his gang were fast. That fast? The satellite link could have been open. He only had to get a block away from here, half a block, just around the corner, and he could lose himself in the crowd, then get back to his car. Istanbul was done for them, though they could probably hide in the city for the rest of their lives. But the airport and train stations would be closed to them unless they moved very fast. A gray Chevrolet sedan screeched to a halt at the curb as Horn stepped outside. He got the impression of three bulky men in business suits piling out of the car as he turned right, pushed his way around a Turkish family, and sprinted down the street.

"Horn!" one of the men shouted. "Jack Horn!"

Horn didn't look back. He pushed his way through another group of people, skidded around the corner, and raced head-long down Istiklal Street, morning traffic in full swing now, pedestrians everywhere. He crossed the main street just as the light changed against him, horns blaring, and careened down a very narrow side alley as the gray Chevy shot past the intersection. They'd spotted him, but there was no possibility of them getting turned around and back to him before he disappeared, and they knew it. But there had been only two of them in the car. The third was on foot.

He shoved open a steel gate and entered the courtyard of a small mosque enclosed by a tall brick fence. Ahead was the entryway, a line of shoes in front of the inner door. To the left and right the brick wall angled back to the building, narrow alcoves opening into what presumably were side passages into the mosque. The big American came around the corner moments later and pulled up short. Horn could just see him around the edge of the brick wall, through the tall iron gate. The man was puffing like a steam engine. He looked young. Horn decided he'd never seen the man before, but he was CIA. He had the look; earnest, they called it at the Farm. He advanced directly toward the gate. Horn stepped back further along the wall, out of sight. He opened his jacket and pulled out the Walther. His stomach was tight. He wanted no trouble, but he wasn't going to allow himself to be taken. Not yet. First Anna was going to identify Jason. She was going to have to tell someone else, a third person, everything she knew, everything Jason had told her, and everything she'd written in the letter. She'd have to be protected.

The agent was at the gate. Horn stepped a little further back into the alcove that ended not in a corridor but at a blank brick wall that faced the back of the mosque. This was a dead end. The gate opened and the agent stepped through. Horn moved back into the shadows and raised his gun, the safety off this time for sure. He couldn't see a thing now. He held his breath listening for footfalls along the path.

Someone said something in Turkish.

"Do you speak English?" the agent said. He sounded East Coast. Connecticut or Maine.

"Yes, of course, effendi."

"Did someone come in here? Just now?"

"No," the Turk said, his voice very soft. "No one has come through this gate for prayer this morning until you, effendi."

"Are you sure?"

"Yes, most sure, effendi."

The courtyard was silent for a beat, but then the gate closed with a crash. Horn remained where he was for the moment. It could have been a ruse.

"It is all right now, effendi," the Turk said softly from just outside the alcove entrance. "He is gone."

Horn carefully stepped around the corner. The courtyard was empty except for a very small old man dressed in flowing trousers, a tunic, a small vest, and a fez. Gold-rimmed glasses were perched delicately on the end of his nose.

"He is not a friend, I think, that man."

"No," Horn said. "But you are. I thank you."

"All who seek refuge here are welcome, effendi."

"Even the infidel?"

The old man smiled. "Weapons of destruction, however, are not."

Horn pocketed his gun. He went to the gate and looked out onto the street. The other one was gone. "Thank you again, my friend," Horn said, turning around. But the old man was gone as well. Walking away seconds later, however, Horn glanced over his shoulder before he turned the corner, and the Turk was watching him from the gate.

He approached the Peugeot with great care, keeping as much as possible to the narrower side streets so that his chances of escaping on foot would be greater should he be spotted again. They wouldn't give up, of course. By now they would be mobilizing the entire consulate to watch Yesilkoy Airport, the train stations, and the bus depots. He didn't think they'd have the personnel to watch all the hotels, though they might already have begun some spot-checking. He could not know if Jason had been aware that they had come to Istanbul, but he thought it was a safe bet the man knew by now. Jason's pipeline to the Agency—assuming he did not work for the Agency—was rock solid and apparently in real time: no waiting for next-morning briefings for him; he knew what was happening *when* it happened. It was the one aspect that Horn found difficult to grasp. Senator Wagner—if indeed he was Jason—was a powerful man, and he had a lot of friends in very high places. But it was hard to imagine him having such direct access to the Agency. The CIA had traditionally been very circumspect in its dealings with Congress. Yet stranger things had happened.

Horn's car was parked in front of a silversmith's. Several young street children were seated on the hood and trunk lid.

As Horn approached they clambered off the car and started toward him. They'd been waiting for the rich American who could afford to rent a car. Horn pulled out a handful of coins and tossed them down the sidewalk. The children scooped them up and took off. The old man in the shop laughed and nodded his approval. It was something for everyone. The boys had their money, the American had his car that the dark-faced gentlemen had been watching from across the street, and the old man had his pleasure.

Horn got behind the wheel and started the engine. Before he drove off he got the terrible feeling that he was being watched again, even now. That all of his efforts had been a waste, that everything he'd done had been in vain. His old network, the men he'd promised to look after were dead now. The destruction was complete, and there was nothing left for which to fight. Christine and the children were even in jeopardy now because of him. In the end, he'd seen Wallace Mahoney around the halls at Langley, and the man had looked battered, if not nearly destroyed. His entire family, except for the one son who had joined the Company, had been killed. Because of him, he seemed to say, or rather despite his best efforts to keep them isolated.

They had suffered. All God's children will suffer in their lives.

He turned at the corner, merging with the traffic on Istiklal, watching in the rearview mirror for the gray Chevrolet. They'd spotted him on foot, so they might not yet suspect that he had a car. Not unless they'd already been to the hotel. The Greek border was barely a hundred and twenty-five miles away, either north near Edirne, or south along the Gulf of Saros to Alexandroúpolis. From there they could drive to Thessaloníki where there was a good-sized airport.

If they could get out of Istanbul without being seen.

If the Greek authorities would accept Anna's passport.

But now Jason was expecting them.

The Hilton stood well back from Cumhuriyet Street on its own grounds, and because Horn was expecting trouble from behind, he very nearly missed Anna in the back seat of a dark blue Mercedes pulling away as he was pulling in. Her face was turned in profile to him. She was talking to a very substantial-looking man with thick dark hair and a long, flowing mustache. It was her uncle, General Patrenko; he was certain of it. There was no one else in the car with them except for their driver. The plates were Soviet diplomatic. He caught glimpses of them as they passed through the trees and then turned out onto the street.

As easy as that, they had come for Anna. All along they'd known where he'd taken her. They'd probably watched him from the very first day in Moscow. All of it, his madmen, the Company men he had worked for and with, and finally his tradecraft, or lack of it, meant absolutely nothing. Something rose inside of him: rage, indignation, fury, resentment. Not like this, he thought. It wasn't going to end so simply.

He slammed the Peugeot in gear as a doorman was coming over, peeled out around a taxi, nearly hitting one of its exiting passengers, and shot out into the busy street, the big Mercedes just turning at the light. The Russians also maintained a consulate in Istanbul. They could be going there, or to the ship, or, if they crossed over into Old Town, it could mean they were heading out to the airport. The general could have an airplane waiting for them. No matter what, there wasn't going to be much he could do about it. And he was sick at heart to think that Anna had gone willingly with her uncle. She'd known that he would show up sooner or later. But she had not known what she would do, what she would say to him, or how she would handle the situation. From what Horn had gathered, Patrenko had been as near a father to her as anyone. They were very close, and now he had come to Istanbul to reclaim his niece. Return her to Moscow where she belonged, to die in peace with her family gathered around her.

"No," Horn said aloud, turning the corner against the light, the Mercedes only half a block away now. "No, not like this. Not this way!"

27

Riding with her uncle through the Turkish countryside Anna had the sense that her life was finally at an end. The events of the past weeks had been nothing more than the final melodramatic strains of a Puccini opera in which the heroine takes entirely too long to succumb. It was now only a matter of the final curtain and the applause she would never hear. No more backstage gatherings, no more winter weekends at Dominic's Istra River dacha with Mother Anton clucking around like an old, ineffectual hen. No more warm summer nights or chill fall Sundays. Nothing. No Jason after all.

Nearly two hours earlier they had crossed the Halic on the Ataturk Bridge, thick with slow-moving traffic, then they had passed through the western portals of the old walled city on Milet Street leading to the main highway to Edirne on the border. The countryside was surprisingly hilly but well cultivated with sugar beet farms, fallow now at this time of year, brown furrows stretching like narrow ribbons up and down the undulating land. The weather was much colder away from the sea. Their driver had opened his window, and Anna was a little chilly.

"How do you feel, chou-chou?" her uncle asked.

She had been staring out the window. She looked up dully. "May I have a cigarette?"

He clucked sadly, but he took out a cigarette and lit it for her. "Dr. Mazayeva is worried about you. She wondered if you had been taking your medicine."

''You knew?''

He nodded.

''How long?''

He watched her smoke for a moment before he replied. This was hard for him; she could see it in his eyes. ''From the beginning.''

''You had me followed? Those two?''

''For your own good, chou-chou. But the doctor telephoned me first. She was concerned that you had not visited with the theater doctor. That you were not getting the very best care in the Soviet Union. She didn't know what to do, so I do not want you blaming her. She is a very good woman. She wanted to recommend a specialist for you.''

''Why didn't she?''

''It would not have helped, from what I am told. She admitted it.'' Her uncle's eyes glistened. ''Your Auntie Raya has guessed, but no one else knows.''

''And now?''

''We are going home. In less than two months there will be a party for you. I told you about it, and I promised a surprise.''

The cigarette was making her a little light-headed. She hadn't had breakfast, and she was hungry. Uncle Stepan had brought along a hamper with food and wine, but her stomach was unsettled. She didn't think she could eat. She was feeling a little irascible. ''We're going to *drive* to Moscow?''

He ignored her uncharacteristic sarcasm. ''To Sofia. There is an airplane waiting for us. We'll be there before dark. I thought it best to leave Turkey.''

''Are you afraid that Jack will follow us?''

''He might. But I do not think he would be so foolish as to try to get across the Bulgarian frontier.''

''Do you hate him?''

''No, chou-chou, I do not hate your Jack Horn.''

She hadn't known his real surname. It was odd hearing it. She was goading her uncle, and she didn't really know why, because she loved him and none of this was his fault. He was just Uncle Stepan. But she couldn't help herself.

''He is a spy, you know,'' she said.

''Yes.''

''I made love with him.''

Her uncle seemed to shrink a little. She could see his age. ''Ah, chou-chou, I am sorry. Truly. There have been certain aspects of your life that have been difficult. But you are different. Very special. At your upcoming party, Comrade Gorbachev himself will present you with a special Medal of Honor. It is a new thing, chou-chou, and you will be the very first in all of the Soviet Union to receive it."

Medals meant nothing to her. She was surprised and saddened that her uncle had told her. What did he expect? But in her heart of hearts she'd known their reunion would be like this. Very difficult for both of them. But she couldn't give up. She had to know everything now. She figured, finally, that it was her right.

"Did you know him, Uncle?"

"Who?"

"My Jason."

"Why are you doing this to yourself?"

"I must know!" Anna snapped.

Her uncle's lips compressed. He nodded his big Georgian head. "Yes, I knew him."

"It was you who arranged our introduction. Did you know that we were lovers?"

Again her uncle paused before he nodded. "Yes, I knew that too."

"Auntie Raya?"

"No, no one else."

"And you still know him?"

"Yes."

"Then tell me his name, Uncle. I have a right to know."

"I cannot."

"Why?"

"I cannot. And it would do you no good, believe me in this, chou-chou."

She looked into her uncle's eyes. "I don't, Uncle. Not any longer."

It hurt him; she could see that, too. And for the very first time in her life she could see that he was indeed a KGB general. She was growing up, she supposed. Her naïveté finally washing away beneath the torrent of lies and half-truths she had been told.

"It was you who had the courier, Boyko, murdered."

He sighed.

"You took my letter, you have it, you've read it."

"Don't do this to yourself."

"Answer me!" Anna demanded.

"No, child, I did not take your letter. I have not read it. But listen to me—your Jason is not the man you think he is. He is a bad man. A very evil man."

"Whom Jack wishes to destroy."

"They will destroy each other."

"But without me he will fail."

"Undoubtedly—"

"Comrade General," their driver interrupted softly. He was glancing in the rearview mirror.

"*Da?*"

"We are being followed. It is the same car, I think, since Istanbul. It was at the hotel. We lost him for a time, but now he is there."

General Patrenko turned and looked out the rear window.

"The Peugeot, Comrade General. There is only the one man, but he is too far back for me to tell who it is. I suspect it is the American."

"Jack?" Anna said, looking out the back. "Jack?" She started to wave, but her uncle grabbed her arms and gently held her back.

"Listen to me, chou-chou," he ordered sharply. "I do not wish to see your Jack Horn hurt."

"Please stop the car, Uncle."

"Do you hear me, child? I do not want to see him killed. He has a wife and two children who themselves are in danger at this very moment. Think what his death would mean to them. Think!"

"God, let me go!" Anna wailed.

"You must not!"

"Yes!" she shrieked. "Yes! *Yes!*"

Her uncle shook her once, like a little rag doll. "Anna, listen to me! Listen now!"

"Shall I lose him, Comrade General?" the driver asked. "He could not keep up with us."

"No," the general snapped. "We will stop, Anna, and you will talk to him. Tell him that you must return home where you belong. Make him understand that it is over, that he must return to his family. It is the only way that you can save his life today. Otherwise I will have him killed."

"No."

"It is the only way, chou-chou. Believe me. It is for the best. Believe me."

And it was over. Truly, she thought, there was no point in

jeopardizing any more lives. Her would-be defection had already caused so much destruction that she knew she would burn for eternity in hell. Religion in the Bolshoi was nearly as strong as the dance. None of them had much else.

"Anna?"

"Yes, Uncle," she said, subdued. "I will tell him."

"You will have to convince him. No easy task, I think."

"I'll do it."

The big Mercedes had pulled over to the side of the road. Horn had stopped about thirty yards back. He had transferred his gun from his belt to his jacket pocket. They were about twenty miles from the border with Bulgaria here, and even nearer the Greek border. He could see Anna talking with her uncle in the back seat. Their driver had gotten out of the car. He stood near the right rear fender looking back. Horn got slowly out of his car, his hands in plain sight as he walked a few feet forward. The general's driver straightened up, his hand reaching inside his coat but then stopping there. A car passed on the highway. Horn stopped.

Anna looked out the rear window at him, and a moment later the back door opened and she got out. She had his black overnight bag from the hotel. Her uncle evidently said something to her from inside the car because she looked in, and shook her head.

"Anna?" Horn called.

She turned. "My uncle says for you to throw away your gun."

"I can't do that, Anna," he called back.

She said something else to her uncle. "Please, Jack, do as he says." He could hear that she was distraught. Her voice was on the edge of cracking.

"I'm not going to leave without you."

Again she and her uncle exchanged a few words. She nodded at length, glanced at the driver on the opposite side of the car, then started toward Horn. Behind her the general got ponderously out of the car. The countryside was empty except for an old truck that moved along a road at the top of a distant hill, dust rising behind it. There hadn't been much traffic on the highway this far out of Istanbul, for which Horn was grateful. He didn't want the complication of innocent bystanders, or worse yet, the Turkish police or military.

"I brought your things," Anna said, stopping about ten feet from him. She held out his bag.

"What about yours?"

"It's in the car. I'm returning to Moscow with my uncle."

"What about us, Anna? What about Jason?"

"It's too late. And it's no use. It was Jason's people who killed Boyko and took my letter."

"Maybe it was a mistake. Let's go to him. Tell him—"

"My uncle says he is an evil man."

"Your uncle knows Jason?"

"Yes."

"He's known him all along?"

"Yes, Jack. So you can see that it's no use for me."

"Who is he, Anna? His name?"

"I don't know. My uncle refuses to tell me."

It came to Horn that General Patrenko was Jason's Russian connection. He had been from the very beginning. And the general had probably introduced his niece to the man. Why? Unless she'd merely been an uncle's pride. Look at my lovely niece, what a wonderful dancer she is. Or had she been a bribe, a honey trap, an enticement? Looking at Anna now he didn't think she'd made that connection yet. Nor would she ever make it on her own. She was too innocent. He was her dear Uncle Stepan. A man who had been like a father to her. He couldn't possibly have done anything to harm her.

Horn moved to reach for his bag, but Anna stepped back a little, skittishly. The general's driver pulled out his gun.

"Wait, Anna," Horn said softly.

Her eyes were wide.

Horn looked beyond her to her uncle and his driver. They were tense. The situation was about to explode. "I'm going to take you with me," he said to Anna softly so that only she could hear him.

"I can't, Jack."

"Do you want to return to Moscow? Is that what you really want?"

She started to shake her head but then stopped. "I don't know . . ."

Horn came closer, reached out for his bag, then grabbed Anna's arm, pulling her toward him. The driver brought up his gun. The fool was going to shoot!

"No!" General Patrenko shouted.

The driver held up.

"I'm taking her with me, General," Horn called out.

"To where, Mr. Horn?" General Patrenko asked. His left

hand was out, holding the driver back. "Back to Istanbul where your own people are at this moment searching for you with orders to shoot to kill? Or perhaps to the Greek border. It is only thirty or forty kilometers away. But of course we would not let you cross. Even for an American, kidnapping is illegal."

"We're going to the United States. Anna will identify Jason."

"To what end, Mr. Horn? No one cares that an American slept with a Russian ballet star. It has been twelve years. The world is a more sophisticated place these days. Besides, you are yourself wanted for murder. Who would believe you?"

"Jason is an agent of the Soviet government. Your agent, General. And when your own niece defects, and then your star agent falls, your career will be over."

"I can't, Jack," Anna said, trying to pull away from him.

"You must, Anna! Think of the people who have already been killed. It won't stop here, dammit!"

"But he is my uncle!"

"He and Jason are both murderers."

"No!" Anna screamed. She pulled away from Horn and stumbled backward.

The general's driver raised his pistol again. This time he fired a shot that plucked at Anna's coat, pulling her off-balance.

"You fool!" General Patrenko bellowed, whirling around against the driver, knocking the man's gun aside so that the second shot went high.

Horn rolled right, away from Anna so that she wouldn't be so near the line of fire. He dropped his overnight bag and yanked the Walther from his coat pocket. This time, by instinct, he knew which way the safety catch had to go. He fired three times in rapid succession, the first slamming into the Mercedes's trunk lid, the second catching the driver in the right kneecap, and the third hitting the man high in the chest, driving him backward into the ditch beside the road.

Anna was down on her knees, shouting incoherently as she tried to get up. The general was turning as if in slow motion toward Horn. He had the driver's gun in his right hand.

"Don't do it, General!" Horn shouted desperately.

"Fool!" the general roared. He fired prematurely in his haste, the bullet ricocheting off the gravel a few feet from Anna.

Horn crouched in the shooter's stance, both hands on the

pistol, and he fired one shot, hitting the general in the middle of his chest, causing him to stumble backward against the Mercedes's trunk lid and then sink to one knee. He lowered his head. It was too heavy a burden to hold up.

"Uncle!" Anna screamed, racing toward the car.

The general looked up and tried to stand, but he settled backward, sitting down hard on the gravel, his head bouncing off the Mercedes's bumper, the gun slipping out of his hand.

Horn looked down the road to make sure no traffic was coming, then hurried to where Anna was on her knees next to her uncle. She was crying and screaming and babbling out of control. Her uncle just looked at her, his eyes very wide, very dark, a small trickle of blood leaking from his mouth. He was having some difficulty breathing. Horn started to open his coat and loosen his tie. Anna shoved him aside. "Leave him alone! Don't touch him!"

"He needs air. Let me help him."

"Get away!" she screeched. "Get away, you!"

Horn stepped back a little. He looked down at the general. "I'm sorry. I didn't want this."

"Fool . . ." General Patrenko said, choking on the word as a great rush of blood gushed from his mouth. He suddenly stiffened, his back arching, and then his body went slack and he fell over, dead.

Anna raised her hands as if in supplication to some god for divine intercession, and a high-pitched keening came from her lips. "No, Uncle!" she cried. "No!"

Horn walked a few feet away and tossed his gun into the ditch. He looked back at Anna. He didn't know how this was going to turn out. But she was still the key. Without her, Jason would have won.

They crossed the Greek frontier a few minutes after noon with absolutely no trouble. The Turkish border guards barely glanced in the back seat at Anna's sleeping form, nor were the Greek border patrol much disposed to waking her, though they did examine their passports and their overnight bags quite carefully, and they even looked in the trunk and under the hood. They made the long run south along the Meric River, Turkey just across the stream, through Souflion and Férai, passing through the ancient Thracian city of Alexandroúpolis on the Aegean Sea at around one-thirty in the afternoon, and then on the Greek E5 south through Komotini,

Kavala and finally Thessaloníki itself, which was a city of nearly half a million with a small but modern airport. From there they parked the car along a side street downtown, took the shuttle bus out to the airport, and caught the six o'clock commuter flight to Athens that got them to Hellinikon Airport in time to make the transatlantic flight via Olympic to Montreal.

Through it all Anna moved as if she were sleepwalking, which in a way she was. She answered questions put to her, providing they were simple and were posed in French or Russian. And she allowed Horn to move her along much as a small child who has traveled for three days and nights would, allowing its parents, or anyone else for that matter, to guide it wherever they would, trusting in some higher, sentient authority to take charge momentarily. One by one, in his mind's eye, Horn watched each man he had shot down fall back, their blood pouring out of their bodies, their eyes growing dull. One by one he heard the final admonitions of the others. Nobels, Sheshkin, Doxy's warning, Boyko's supposed last words. He was afraid now for Christine and the children, but there wasn't a thing he could do for them that he hadn't already done. There seemed to be death all around him. In any direction he turned, blood had been spilled. He didn't think it was finished. Not yet.

He thought too about Jason, and he wondered how the man was going to react when he learned of the death of his Russian control officer. They had presumably worked together for at least a dozen years. It was a long time for two men in this business to be associated. They'd have formed a very strong alliance. A symbiosis, he'd heard it called. The relationship between a control officer and his madman was something akin to a close marriage. There was no telling how Jason would react.

And finally there was Anna. Again she had dropped off to sleep in the window seat beside him. In profile her features were delicate and finely formed. She looked like a porcelain doll in repose: innocent, sweet, and ageless. Jason would be moved, he decided, when he saw her. How could anyone help but be moved by her tragic sweetness?

28

They arrived in Montreal sometime after ten in the evening, local time, and had no trouble clearing customs. It was nearly as cold as Moscow, and after Greece the weather took their breath away. Horn rented a car under his Hansen workname, which were the only papers he had left, and it was nearly midnight before they got going. Montreal and the car were his insurance policy. He was almost certain that his photograph had been posted with Customs and Immigration in New York and Washington where they would have been expected to enter the country. He was very tired. Anna had taken her pills and had gotten some rest on the flight, but she looked bad again. Wan, drawn, weak. The border with New York was barely forty miles from the Montreal International Airport. The big customs crossing post, all stainless steel and glass and yellow brick, lit as bright as day under huge sodium vapor lamps, wasn't busy at this late hour. A couple of semis were parked off to one side, and a Greyhound bus was in the far right lane, leaving two others with green lights. Anna pretended to sleep again, and as before the Canadian and American border officers were considerate of her. "She's had an extremely trying trip," Horn explained. "She is ill. It's cancer. Her mother is expecting us." He shook his head, and sighed. "It's very sad. Her mother lives in Boston, so we have a long way yet to travel."

"Welcome home, Mr. Hansen," the young American officer said, handing back Horn's driver's license and Anna's passport. "You have nothing to declare, sir?"

"Not a thing."

"Boston has the best hospitals. Maybe she'll get lucky."

"We can only hope."

Driving away from the customs post, Horn watched in his rearview mirror until the officer went back into the building. There was no other traffic behind them. Now there was nothing but distance between them and Jason. Distance and conception, because he still could not fathom what role Anna was supposed to have played between her uncle, the agent runner, and her lover, Jason the spy.

"So this is America," Anna said. They were traveling on Interstate 87. There was nothing to be seen except for some lights in the distance, the occasional exit ramp, and very sparse traffic. The sky was clear, the stars brilliant.

"I'm sorry, Anna."

"For what, Jack? America?" she asked, looking into his eyes. She'd changed. There was no innocence there any longer, only a dull acceptance of whatever might come. It was the Russian fatalism. They'd accumulated a thousand years of oppression. They finally knew how to take it.

"For your uncle."

"He would have killed you. So it was either you or him."

"He and Jason were spies together."

"I know," Anna said, a brittle edge to her voice. "The only two men in my life that I truly loved turned out to be spies." She looked at him in the light from the dash. "And now here I am with you. What is it with me, do you think?"

They had bacon and eggs and fried potatoes at an all-night truck stop outside of Glens Falls. He had changed enough money at the airport to get them to Washington.

Horn was beginning to worry that Jason would have changed so much that Anna wouldn't recognize him. Without Doxy's help, they'd be lost.

"It's his eyes," she assured him. "They never change. I'll know him. He told me that plans and hopes for the future were what separated people from animals. He had such wonderful plans, you know. Someday, he said, his voice would be decisive for insuring world peace. He wasn't bragging, though. It wasn't like that with him."

"Did he want to be president?" Horn was thinking about Senator Wagner.

"Do you know why we Russians love our country so fanatically?"

"No."

"Because everything we need is provided for us. Hospitals, education, apartments, food, work. She is our *rodina*, our motherland. And you can't hate your mother. Not if you're normal, Jack."

"Did Jason understand this?"

Anna nodded. "He understood the *kollektiv*. He understood that we must all work together in order to accomplish anything worthwhile. The prima ballerina onstage cannot be there without the orchestra, the stagehands, the scenery painters, the costume designers and seamstresses, the director and the coaches, and the corps."

"But the audience applauds the ballerina," Horn said carefully. She was on the verge of breaking down. He could feel it coming from her like heat from a radiator.

"Oh, no, Jack. In Russia the audience knows what must have happened in order for her to be up there. They know and appreciate it."

"Yes?"

"Jason didn't have to be president, you see. He had other plans." She burst out crying. For her uncle, Horn thought.

An hour or so before dawn Horn simply could go no farther. They stopped at a Holiday Inn just outside Albany. Anna watched television while he slept for a few hours.

He got up at noon. Anna had fallen asleep on the other bed. The television was still playing, the sound low. The news was just coming on, so he turned it up a little. He looked out the window. The day was bright and very clear. They were just below the interstate. He watched the traffic for a minute. He felt disconnected; he felt a sense of isolation, of unreality now that he was home. Christine and the children weren't very far away now. They'd be up, thinking about him, wondering, worrying where he was. All Anna's talk about love of country and loyalty had somehow depressed him. It still hung over from his sleep. He felt as if he were on a downward spiral.

"Is it a nice day?" Anna asked.

Horn let the curtain fall back and turned to her. She was sitting up, her hair down around her shoulders. She looked much better than she had in the night. Her color was better, but her eyes were still vacant. When her uncle's death finally hit her, he figured she would collapse. He felt sorry for her. She had nothing now, not even a country.

"The sun is shining. We'll be outside Washington by dark."

"And then what will become of me?"

"We'll see a friend of mine. He will help us."

"Yes, but then what, Jack? Once we're there, with your friend, and I tell him about Jason. Then what?"

"Then Jason will be arrested, there will be a trial, and you will be free."

She looked at the television, not wanting to face him for the moment. "Free to do what?"

"Anything you want."

"No," she replied matter-of-factly. "Even I am no longer that naïve. There is no Cinderella, really. It is simply Prokofiev."

Horn didn't know what she meant.

"I'm not free, for instance, to go home. I'm not free to have dinner with my uncle. I'm not free now to dance. I'm only free to die, you see, and I had that in Moscow without defecting."

Senator Wagner was on the television. He was speaking from a podium that bristled with microphones. He was handsome, somewhat reminiscent, to Horn, of the Kennedys, with a rugged East Coast outdoors color and demeanor. One of the chosen few by looks and attitude. He'd come from a long line of politicians, but there was money in the family too; Oregon lumber and fishing, perhaps. He had stage presence, charisma, even over the tube.

"There," Horn said softly. He went to the television and turned up the sound. Wagner was saying something about the French denial of their airspace for overflights of U.S. fighters from bases in England on their way out to the Middle East. "There," Horn said again. He was waiting for the glint of recognition in Anna's eyes.

"What?" she asked.

"It's him."

"Who?"

"Senator Wagner. Jason. Don't you recognize him?"

She looked at the television, and then back up at Horn. She shook her head. "I am sorry, Jack, but that man is not Jason. Not him. Jason's voice was much deeper, his eyes were different, his hair, his head. . . . That man is not my Jason."

Horn turned up the sound even louder, even though he realized it was a stupid thing to do, and he went to Anna's side. "Look," he insisted. "Are you certain, Anna? It's been twelve years. Are you absolutely sure?"

"It's not him, Jack." She glanced at the television. "I'm sure."

"Couldn't you be mistaken?"

"No."

Then who was Jason? Horn sank back. Where was Jason? What was Jason?

He drove very fast but not recklessly, passing all the slower cars, keeping up with the big trucks equipped with CB rigs warning them of police radars ahead. He'd thought about flying from Albany, but decided that in his state it would have been too risky. He needed the time to calm down, to think it out, and yet time at the very end was his mortal enemy. In the sun the snow on the fields was a brilliant white, the cities they passed alive and bustling in midwinter. But he was of no mind for that, or for the dense traffic through Hackensack and Newark and Elizabeth, or for the more pastoral scenes south again down the New Jersey Turnpike. To be transported instantly through time and space. To be somehow granted a moment of absolute knowledge, and therefore understanding, was a gift he'd fervently and earnestly prayed for. He'd been here before. He knew these roads. He'd driven up from Washington with Christine and the children to her father's house on Long Island, had driven up to New York City; once they'd driven all the way up to Maine just after Marc had been born. It was summer and they were excited and in love and happy. But this time was different. This time he felt such a terrible sense of urgency that he could not take enjoyment even from the simplest things, even memories. He could have been utterly alone in a foreign land for all anything mattered to him now. He seemed to drift through the toll booths. He remembered once when he and Doxy had driven up to Canada for their "First Annual Wilderness Fishing Expedition" . . . and their last. It had rained for the entire week. They'd gotten lost. Near the end they'd dumped their canoe and most of their provisions in the lake, and they'd been reduced to two bottles of Jack Daniel's which they drank that very cold night in lieu of a campfire because all of their matches were wet. It became their official drink after that night. Though they'd never gone back, they'd remembered the experience with a certain masculine fondness. Christine and Donna thought they were nuts, and rightly so. They'd rented a sailboat the following year in the Virgin Islands, the four of them, and hired a charter captain after the very first day. Their very best time, though, had been the weekend at Gettysburg. Doxy had cried when he walked over the battlefield, and afterward he lectured them about the fact that America's best minds went into industry and science, while the worst went into politics. "Those who can't do, either teach or lead," he said. So where are you now, Doxy, when I need you? Snug in your boat, safe from the winter winds, the heater cranked up, the Jack Daniel's out? Are you waiting for us to show up, Doxy? Please, dear God, be there, Doxy. Please.

Anna had been respectful of his silence, his fear, and his urgency. She had her own terrors to deal with. For the most part she stared out at the heavy traffic and construction that seemed to be everywhere. She dozed a little, off and on. She seemed to need a lot of sleep, not only because of her physical condition but because of her mental state. Overloaded with the terrible things that had happened to her, she wanted to drift off. Horn couldn't blame her.

They passed through Wilmington at around five, and in the lowering sun raced the final sixty miles down to Baltimore, their side of the interstate mostly empty, the bulk of the homeward-bound traffic streaming north out of the city. They encountered a traffic jam just before the harbor tunnel, however, that delayed them nearly forty minutes, so that it wasn't until well after seven by the time they'd passed through Glen Burnie, Green Haven, Armiger, and Jacobsville, the road changing from the heavily traveled freeway to State Highway 177, a narrow, two-lane blacktop that led the last six or eight miles in the darkness out onto Gibson Island. He remembered the old brown shack on the hill before the tiny village, the Narragansett Beer sign below, the rutted dirt road just after the rock cairn that led down into the tiny marina protected from the Chesapeake Bay winds on all four sides except for a very narrow opening. The few trees here were bare, and out on the bay a stiff wind whipped up the whitecaps. Nothing moved in the fishing village below, though the beer sign was lit in the tavern window. The marina was filled mostly with independent fishing vessels and other workboats, along with a couple of battered sailboats. A forty-footer, gray-primered hull, black sheer stripe, big pilothouse forward, and a low doghouse leading aft was how Doxy had described his retreat. The boat was steel, its thick lines old and barnacle-encrusted where they dipped into the water at high tide, the gray primer chipped and the hull rusting. Closer, he could see that all the windows aft were curtained. The boat seemed dark, neglected, long deserted, as if no one had been there in years.

Horn pulled up next to an old pickup truck parked in front of what apparently was the marina office housed in an unpainted brown shed. He shut off the engine and rolled down his window. The air was cold and smelled of tidal flats, but there was almost no wind. A sea gull or some other bird cried out off toward the bay, but there were no other sounds.

"What is this place, Jack?" Anna asked uncertainly. "Are we taking a boat now?"

"My friend may be here," Horn said. There was something about Doxy's boat that wasn't sitting right with him. Something wrong. Something out of place. Now he wished he had the gun.

"This friend will help us?"

"I hope so," Horn replied. He opened the car door. "Stay here," he said, and he got out.

"Wait! Don't leave me here like this, Jack!" Anna cried in alarm.

"I'll just be a minute. But I want you to stay in the car until I call for you. Can you do that for me?"

She didn't hate him for killing her uncle. It was incredible, but it would come later, he thought. For now she was still in shock, and very frightened. He was her only link with survival, with any kind of sanity. She needed him. She nodded, finally. "Okay, Jack."

He went around the pickup truck. The plates were Maryland. As he passed the driver's side he looked inside. The keys dangled in the ignition. He stopped. "Hello?" he called. But there was no answer. Only the silence, and in the far distance, perhaps, another sea gull. He looked back. Anna had rolled down her window and was watching him, her eyes enormous. He motioned for her to stay where she was and he

approached the brown shed. The latch gave way easily and he
shoved the door open. The interior of the office was in
semidarkness, but there was enough light for him to see that
no one was there. There were lines and blocks and odd bits of
netting and cork floats in jumbles everywhere. In the corner a
small desk was piled high with papers and clipboards and
charts and tidal prediction pamphlets, and half-empty coffee
cups and a large ashtray overflowing with cigarette butts. In
the corner a barrel stove was barely warm. A telephone hung
on the wall above the desk, but the cord had been ripped out
of the wall. Horn stared at it for a long time. There had been
no outward struggle in here, yet the fire had been allowed to
die down, and the telephone had been rendered useless. He
turned and looked out the door across the old dock at Doxy's
boat, and he suddenly realized what had bothered him. The
smoke head for the cabin heater was clearly visible aft on the
pilothouse roof. It was very cold outside, yet no smoke was
coming from the little capped chimney. If Doxy was in
residence, he had let his fire go out, just as someone had let
the fire in the marina office die down.

"Oh, Doxy," he said to himself as he walked past the
pickup truck and out to the dock, willing his legs to work. He
climbed over the rail of Doxy's boat amidships, went aft to
the cabin door, hesitated for just a moment, then tried the
lock. It was free. He took a deep breath, let it out slowly,
then opened the door and looked inside.

Vincent Doxmeuller, his oldest and best friend, his confi-
dant, his alter ego at times, especially when it came to his
faith, his mentor since day one in the Agency, lay spread-
eagled on the floor of the wrecked cabin, his face destroyed,
some of his brains lying splattered on the dark wood. Horn
looked away, bile rising sharply at the back of his throat, his
stomach heaving, his chest constricted. Whoever had killed
Doxmeuller had thoroughly searched the boat. There was
nothing left intact in the saloon, including the galley stove
and cabinets. Boxes of food had been opened, cereal and
crackers and macaroni spread everywhere. Jars of mayon-
naise, ketchup, and mustard had been dumped in the sink.
Even a head of lettuce had been cut open, as had several
apples and oranges.

Looking back again, Horn forced himself to try to piece out
what had happened here. Doxmeuller's hands were tied over
his head. His chest and feet were bare. He could see cigarette

burns around Doxy's nipples, in his armpits, and on the soles of his feet. They had tortured him, and in the end they had shot his lower jaw away at close range—Horn could clearly see the powder burns on Doxy's marble-white skin—and finally they had shoved the barrel of the gun into his left eye and blew away his temple and part of the back of his head. The savagery of the assassination was Russian. KGB *mokrie dela* squads typically destroyed the face of their victim. It was meant as a clear-cut warning to others. *The man's history will be expunged, beginning with his face.*

Horn remained standing at the open cabin door for a long time, unable to step inside and yet unable to back away. Doxy had been his last link. His only hope. Jason had won. But, oh, the destruction. The deaths. The heartaches, the pain, and misery. Had it been worth it to know that Jason's value as a spy, at least, was at an end? *As goes the runner, so goes the agent.* General Patrenko was dead, as were so many others. Who would Jason trust now? Who could he trust?

I believe in God, the Father Almighty, Creator of heaven and earth/and in Jesus Christ, His only son our Lord/Who was conceived by the Holy Ghost/Born of the Virgin Mary/ Suffered under Pontius Pilate/Was crucified, died, and was buried/He descended into hell./The third day he arose again from the dead,/He ascended into heaven/Sitteth at the right hand of God, the Father Almighty/From thence he shall come to judge the living and the dead. . . .

It was the profession of faith. All God's children were asked this one simple act of kindness and understanding. But Doxy had believed only in mankind. His favorite quote was from Bertrand Russell: "For years it was said that God could move mountains, and *much* of the world believed it. Today it is said that atomic bombs can move mountains and *all* the world believes that!" He had probably told them nothing, though; otherwise they wouldn't have torn apart the boat. Looking for what? Notes? Had they believed Doxy kept notes?

So what do you believe in these days, Jack? Horn asked himself. God or mankind? At this moment, looking at the destroyed remains of his friend, he couldn't honestly answer. Both God and mankind had in the end deserted him. What was left other than the dark slide into the abyss of absolute cynicism?

The single light at the end of the dock went off, and he heard Anna cry out, "Jason. My God, it's you!"

He closed the cabin door and stepped softly around to the side, keeping in the darker shadows now. At first he couldn't see much of anything. No other car had come down the hill. But then he spotted Anna between the pickup truck and their car. She was looking toward the marina office. Then he could see that someone stood in the darkness, but he could not make out who it was. He could only see a form in the night. He stopped.

"It's been so terribly long," Anna said plaintively.

"I know," Jason answered. "They say your uncle is dead."

Horn could scarcely believe his ears. He knew the voice! And now he recognized the figure. All the anomalies, all the questions fell into place knowing who Jason was. For a split instant he could see everything with a clarity that was nearly preternatural. He saw an event in Czechoslovakia, a week of terror in Poland. He saw the faces of all his Moscow madmen as they had looked in life, and he could imagine their death masks. He saw now how Edmund Clay fit, and he could see a dozen other Company failures in as many years past. What terrible fools they'd all been. What arrogance. What conceit.

"I missed you," Anna was saying. "I wrote you a letter, but it got lost."

"I am sorry, little Anna, truly I am, but there was never a day that went by that I didn't think about you. Think about our days together in Moscow. Think about how it could have been had our lives been simpler, had you not been the niece of an ambitious man and I . . . I not what I was."

"Can't it work yet? I've so little time."

"Time is relative. Hadn't you guessed by now? A few years does not balance well with all of eternity."

"Only a few months, my dearest," Anna pleaded. She still did not understand. Not completely. She still had not totally lost her naïveté.

"You can't know how sorry I am, Anna."

"I've come all this way. I've given up so much. I wasn't asking for so much . . ."

"Don't do this to yourself, Anna. Remember we used to talk about dignity? It was so critical to your dancing. Do you remember that?"

"Yes," Anna said in a very small voice.

"Jack Horn," Jason called. "Come down here if you please."

For all these years, rising through the ranks in the Company, Jason had lied to them all. His was the blessed career, the charmed life. He was the penultimate driving force in the Agency: the voice on the telephone, the signature on the orders, the stern presence across the big desk on the seventh floor who was looked upon with the utmost respect by everyone. Presidential appointments came and went with the vagaries of the political scene. "The job of director of the Central Intelligence Agency is nothing more than a plum," Doxy had said. "Democrat this year to appease the majority leader, but Republican in the next administration for no other reason than the folks in California and the power in New York State thought they had the solution." But to the career bureaucrat, the one force that provided a necessary continuity to the Agency, to that force had to go trust and respect.

Horn climbed off the boat, walked down the dock, and went to where Anna stood, her hands folded together as if in prayer, raised to her mouth to stifle a cry.

"Good evening, sir," Horn said.

"Hello, Jack," Admiral Alvis Winslow Taylor, deputy director of Central Intelligence, said. He was a tall man, his hair thick and dark except for streaks of gray at the temples. His eyes, or so the Agency wags were fond of saying, could bore holes in a recalcitrant subordinate at a hundred yards. Lasers. He was a man who never had, nor ever could, brook any nonsense. "We have a job to do, gentlemen," he was fond of saying. "So let's get on with it." Of all the people to have betrayed, he was the most damaging, the most difficult to understand, the hardest to accept. He wore a dark overcoat, his head bare, a MAC 10 subcompact submachine gun in his right hand.

"Why Doxy?" Horn asked.

"I didn't kill him, Jack. I found him like that this afternoon."

"The Russians?"

"I would expect so. They had their ax to grind. Stepan Patrenko was trying to plug the gaps."

"Your control officer all these years."

Taylor laughed. "You still don't see, do you."

"You're a double. A mole—"

"Oh, don't use such spy novel names, Horn. I'm a realist. I suspected you were too. Stepan and I had an arrangement.

We worked together. We had from the beginning. We helped each other.''

Horn thought about Taylor's meteoric rise to power within the Agency. His was said to be a rare insight into what made the Russians tick. Of course all this time he had had an inside track.

''Why?''

''Don't be a fool. This is a difficult world in which we live, Jack. You know that as a field agent. You see what's happening out there. The Soviet Union is not our enemy.''

''Who, then?''

''The developing powers, of course. The real seat of international unrest and terrorism. Israel with her nuclear capabilities. Pakistan with the bomb. India with ICBMs. Makes you shudder, doesn't it? France with her unstable government. China, in the end, because of the sheer pressure of population. First we loved them, and then under Mao we learned to hate them. After Nixon we loved them again. Keeps them off-balance. They are the real scourge. You know that, Jack.''

''But it wasn't for all that, was it, Admiral. It was just for power.''

''Power?''

''Your own. General Patrenko's.''

Taylor stepped forward. He looked a little wild, unfocused.

''Jason?'' Anna said. ''Did you love me?''

Taylor said nothing. He had eyes at that moment only for Horn, the real threat.

''Answer her, Admiral, if you can. Did you love her, or did you lie to her, too?''

''I loved you, Anna,'' he said softly.

''You didn't object when her uncle introduced you, did you,'' Horn said. ''Even though you knew what was going on.''

Anna turned to look up at Horn. ''What are you saying, Jack?''

''Tell her, Admiral.''

''It's true, Anna, that your uncle used you. I had too much on him in those days. I'd been using him for a couple of years by then. I was already deputy director of Operations, and he was only a major. But a rising star, because of my help.''

It was beginning to make even more sense to Horn now. The general's rapid rise to power, and the admiral's similar rise in the States. They'd used each other. Helped each other. For power.

"I was never actually stationed in Moscow, you know. I was just visiting. Rubbing it into him. He hated it. He wanted to cut me down to size. Silly, really."

"You worked with Tom Wagner."

"That's right."

"It's why your names never showed up in the Embassy directories."

"Yes."

Anna was on the verge of collapse. All those years she had loved her uncle, and had loved this man, yet both of them had used her. Horn didn't think she understood the full significance of it yet, but she was learning. And more than her cancer, the knowledge had the capacity to destroy her if she let it. It was the final cruelty for her.

"But I loved you, Anna. At the end I truly loved you, and your uncle used that as I knew he would. He used it for all of these years."

"Why?" she asked softly.

"For power," Horn said.

"No!" Taylor barked. "You still don't understand. You don't know what Kennedy did to us. How close we came to nuclear war. My God, man, don't you realize what that means? The end of all life as we know it."

"That was your mission, Admiral? Preventing war?"

"Yes, you stupid bastard, yes."

"Sacrifice the few to save the whole?"

"It was necessary . . ."

"Why didn't you run for president, then? With all due respect, sir, you could have made it. You would have been able to do more good."

Taylor was shaking his head. His eyes were becoming wild. "You don't understand. None of you do."

"Jason?" Anna said, raising her hand to him. She would never understand.

"I loved you, Anna," Taylor said in anguish. "It was your uncle who blocked your foreign travel."

"Why?" she asked.

"Had you been allowed to come to the United States I would have grabbed you, and he knew it."

"Then the advantage would have been yours," Horn said

harshly. "All those years, knowing she was in Moscow safely out of your reach must have galled you."

"And now it's too late, Jason?" Anna asked.

"Yes . . . no," Taylor cried, stepping back.

"You were interested in the game, Admiral. As deputy director you had the autonomy you could never have had as president."

"Shut up!" Taylor screamed.

"How many men did you send to their deaths by your little games? Yours and General Patrenko's?"

"You can't know!" Taylor shouted. He raised the MAC 10.

Horn shoved Anna aside as Taylor fired, the burst smashing into the side of their car. A powerful spotlight came from the little cove behind the docked boats, illuminating the boatyard suddenly as if it were day. Taylor stumbled backward.

"Throw down your gun," Farley Carlisle's amplified voice boomed over the marina.

Horn had stepped back against the pickup truck. Taylor fired a short burst, one bullet catching Horn in the left arm. Then he turned and raced around the back of the marina office. Someone shouted something from above, on the hill, and the lights of a half-dozen automobiles showed up over the crest. Anna screamed something as she jumped up and raced after Taylor.

"Anna!" Horn shouted. His arm was numb. It hung useless at his side. There was a lot of shouting and running behind him. The cars were coming down the hill. The spotlight from the boat was flashing around. A big diesel engine was roaring, and in the distance he could hear at least two choppers coming in.

Horn shoved himself away from the pickup truck, and mindless of what was happening around him, he raced around the side of the marina office and nearly fell headlong into a shallow drainage ditch in back. Tall grass, brown and stiff in the cold winter winds, led down a gentle slope to a half-frozen marsh. The spotlight on the other side of the shed threw weird shadows across the slope. Anna and Taylor had stopped about ten yards away. Taylor held the MAC 10's barrel to his temple. Anna held out her hands.

"No, Jason," she said calmly. "Not this way. Not like this, darling."

"Admiral," Horn shouted. "We'll work it out. I promise you."

Taylor stepped back.

"Oh, God, Jason! I love you!" Anna shouted. She stepped closer to him.

Horn jumped across the ditch. The first helicopter was nearly overhead. "Listen to me—"

Taylor fired, the burst taking off half of his head, his arms flying out, his body twisting and falling, forever it seemed, down into the deep, deep, brown grass, the shots echoing and re-echoing off the water, the spotlight flashing, the helicopter swooping past with a powerful roar, cars coming, men running and shouting, and over it all Anna screaming the only name she'd ever known him by, over and over and over again: "Jason! Jason! Jason!"

EPILOGUE

Much of it Horn told his wife Christine. But not all. He was bound by Agency covenant, of course, and for some of the other . . . well, there was no need to add to the hurt. And besides, it all seemed to have happened such a terribly long time in the past.

Summer came early that year. By April Washington was abloom and even New York's Central Park had begun to turn green. At the end of the month PBS agreed to televise a Lincoln Center three-hour special, underwritten by the Ford Foundation and co-hosted by Mikhail Baryshnikov and Beverly Sills: "A Tribute to Anna Feodorovna." It was a black-tie affair, naturally, with tickets at five hundred dollars a seat, the proceeds to go to Anna's medical fund. She was in remission, her doctors at Sloan-Kettering had assured them. They wanted her condition to remain so. A very expensive process in this day and age. Horn had seen a lot of her during the initial debriefings which were, for the most part, carried out in reasonably good taste by Farley Carlisle and his bunch from Operations, with a few experts thrown in from the DDI's bailiwick. "A nigger in the woodpile," was how Carlisle had very indelicately described Taylor. "We knew, or certainly we guessed, that someone with the Company at high levels—mind you, we never suspected just how high the light would shine—had been handing us over to the Russians on a silver platter." Moscow Station had been in a shambles for years. One by one the old networks had been going by the

389

wayside, the stringers either losing interest because of indirection, or simply dying off as in the case of Horn's old madmen. The business with Anna's letter and the courier Boyko, as far as Carlisle could figure it, had probably been engineered by General Patrenko, Anna's uncle, who had again wanted to shake Taylor out of his complacency. He wanted to make Taylor understand just who was the boss, or at least an equal partner, in their relationship. Taylor's people, a group he had cultivated from the French underworld during his sojourn with the Paris Station years before, had killed Boyko, though, and snatched the letter. From that point on it had been a cat and mouse game of provocation on General Patrenko's part, and containment on Taylor's.

Christine, who had been told only bits and pieces, gave voice to the one ghastly aspect of the business that no one else had had the courage to bring up. If General Patrenko had introduced his niece to his star pupil, and had engineered Anna's letter-writing campaign twelve years later, knowing that someone such as Horn would come out to investigate, then how did the general insure that Anna would indeed write such a letter?

"Was it possible, Jack, that he gave her something that caused her cancer? His own niece?"

Horn had said nothing to Carlisle about it, but he asked Anna's chief doctor if it had been determined exactly how and when she had contracted the disease. The when was relatively simple. The how was impossible at this stage of medical science to determine. "She has a form of leukemia that we're learning how to treat. No guarantees, but at this point we're looking at two years for her. Afterward . . . ?"

The story was disseminated that Anna had traveled to Montreal to visit, when she decided, with the help of an unnamed American friend, to defect to the United States. "For my artistic freedom," she told the press. *Pravda, Izvestia*, and TASS were silent about her, of course. She had become a nonperson.

Throughout the vast Metropolitan Opera House at Lincoln Center, a hush had gradually begun to settle over the sold-out crowd as it neared the eight o'clock curtain. Horn would never forget Anna. Not as he had first seen her in the photographs in Moscow. Not as he had first confronted her face-to-face at her apartment when he had pretended to come as an emissary of Jason's. Certainly not during their flight West when they had made love in the darkness, tenderly, gently, he thought. Nor would he forget seeing her terribly battered, bruised body the next morning. That was a picture indelibly etched in his brain. He would never forget her wail of anguish as she watched her uncle die, or the horror in her eyes, in her entire body, when her Jason had committed his ugly suicide in front of her, the ultimate rejection of anyone's love.

Christine gave his arm a squeeze. He looked over at her. "A penny," she said, gazing into his eyes.

How much did she know? How much had she guessed? His homecoming had been awkward, in part because of the crimes of which he had been accused—which she didn't believe for one minute, but that were there nevertheless—and in part because of something she had seen in his eyes. He had changed. Oh, yes, he had definitely been changed by his association with poor little Anna, and with all the killing. But in the end the guilt he carried with him, and which he would carry for the remainder of his life, wasn't so much his denial of faith or the killings, or the lies and deceit, but his guilt that for a time he had given his body as well as his soul to another woman. A woman in need perhaps, a woman terribly alone and in desperate need of succor, but another woman for all of it. He had been unfaithful not only to his God, but to Christine and their life.

He forced a smile. "Would you believe that I love you?" He meant it. Truly and to the depths of his heart.

She nodded.

"Then forget the penny, Chris. Just hold onto the fact that you are loved. It's all we really ever have, you know."

"Are you back, now? This time for real, Jack?"

"I'm back," he said.

The lights dimmed and the music began. It was a magical evening.

Bestselling Thrillers — action-packed for a great read

__ $4.50 0-425-10477-X **CAPER**
Lawrence Sanders

__ $3.95 0-515-09475-7 **SINISTER FORCES**
Patrick Anderson

__ $4.95 0-425-10107-X **RED STORM RISING**
Tom Clancy

__ $4.50 0-425-09138-4 **19 PURCHASE STREET**
Gerald A. Browne

__ $4.95 0-425-08383-7 **THE HUNT FOR RED OCTOBER**
Tom Clancy

__ $3.95 0-441-77812-7 **THE SPECIALIST** Gayle Rivers

__ $3.95 0-441-58321-0 **NOCTURNE FOR THE GENERAL**
John Trenhaile

__ $3.95 0-425-09582-7 **THE LAST TRUMP**
John Gardner

__ $3.95 0-441-36934-0 **SILENT HUNTER**
Charles D. Taylor

__ $4.50 0-425-09884-2 **STONE 588** Gerald A. Browne

__ $3.95 0-425-10625-X **MOSCOW CROSSING**
Sean Flannery

__ $3.95 0-515-09178-2 **SKYFALL** Thomas H. Block
